An Education in Ruin

also by ALEXIS BASS

Love and Other Theories

What's Broken Between Us

Happily and Madly

ALEXIS BASS

An Education in Ruin

TOR TEEN

a tom doherty associates book

new york

AN EDUCATION IN RUIN

Copyright © 2020 by Alexis Bass

A Tor Teen Book
Published by Tom Doherty Associates
120 Broadway
New York, NY 10271

www.tor-forge.com

Tor® is a registered trademark of Macmillan Publishing Group, LLC.

The Library of Congress Cataloging-in-Publication Data is available upon request.

ISBN 978-1-250-19595-1 (hardcover)
ISBN 978-1-250-19594-4 (ebook)

Our books may be purchased in bulk for promotional, educational, or business use. Please contact your local bookseller or the Macmillan Corporate and Premium Sales Department at 1-800-221-7945, extension 5442, or by email at MacmillanSpecialMarkets@macmillan.com.

First Edition: 2020

Printed in the United States of America

0 9 8 7 6 5 4 3 2 1

For my mother, who only invests in lovely things

An Education in Ruin

AUGUST

One

I find him in the study hall entrance of the library, right where he's supposed to be. He's past the rows of long oak tables topped with dark metal lamps, leaning against a wooden column. Above us is a towering ceiling ignited by the outside light through stained-glass windows. My loafers shuffle against the floorboards as I approach him, passing a collection of students perched with their heads bowed over books, already at it even though classes don't start for two days. It's as beautiful as a cathedral, and this is how the students at the Rutherford Institute worship.

His eyes scan the room, taking their time before they land on me as I make the journey to get to him. I can tell by the way his gaze flickers away before it returns to me, that I'm not what he was imagining.

He looks exactly as he did in the photos. Tall, with a cascade of brown curls that seem chaotic in the way they lie against his head, but also purposeful in the way they stay out of his eyes. His maroon blazer is perfectly tailored to fit his narrow shoulders and lengthy figure, and he's wearing a gray striped tie, even though a tie technically isn't required since this isn't an official school day.

"Collins Pruitt?" he says as I approach, keeping his voice low.

I nod. "You must be Jasper."

I notice a small red welt on his upper lip, like he must've nicked himself shaving, and I smile because there it is, a glaring imperfection. He's a fourth year and a Rutherford Institute legacy, with three lacrosse championships under his belt, breaking the school's twenty-year dry spell. He was accepted early to Dartmouth after being lauded into academic stardom last year when he won the national academic decathlon, setting some kind of record for the most right answers and the quickest time answering the final round. He spent last summer interning at Robames Inc., a world-popular company, because their founder is a twenty-year-old Yale dropout and a Rutherford graduate herself. Jasper was the only high school intern they've taken on in the two years since they've been in existence. All this to say—he's an academic savant and a lacrosse god, but this cut on his face is proof of his humanity. He's like everyone else. I don't need to be so nervous.

"This way." He leads me past the archway and down a corridor lined with glass-paneled doors. He rotates the brass knob of the third door on the right and holds it open for me as I walk into the private study room he must've reserved for today. After he turns on the light, closes the door behind him, and we each take a seat across from the other at the table, he sets his books down so their spines are facing me, and I wonder if that's on purpose, to make sure I can see that he's studying molecular chemistry and theoretical physics and moral philosophy.

"According to your entrance exam, you had trouble with limits and derivatives," he says, barely looking at me. He makes no time for pleasantries; he's all business, so very serious, and while I figured he would be like this, I'm still surprised by his intensity. "I thought today we would focus on limits, since they'll be covered in the first few lessons of your calculus class, and that way you won't have to play catch-up from the start. Okay?"

"Okay."

I scramble to pull a notebook and pencil out of my bag, as Jasper flips the textbook open and starts writing down equations in his own notebook, explaining each step and pointing to the correlating lesson in the book as he continues.

"Can you—hold on—slow down?"

"Slow down?" he asks as though he doesn't understand this combination of words.

"Yeah," I say. "Yes," I amend, remembering it's more proper than *Yeah*. "Can you go back—go back to this part?" I turn to the previous page.

"Sure. If that's what you need." There's judgment in his voice.

I'm not sure why he's being so uptight—borderline rude—when the whole point of this overview is to prepare me for my first year at Rutherford, coming in as a third year in a subject where I placed weak on the entrance exam.

He flips to a fresh page of notebook paper and starts to rework the equations he already did, talking deliberately slower this time.

"Wait—" I cut in, blocking his pencil with mine to get him to stop writing. He takes a deep, measured breath. "Sorry." I tap my pencil at the part of the equation I don't understand. "What's the reason for this?"

"It's the same thing I did in the first equation. You see?"

I don't. But there is a time to argue and a time to observe, and this is the time for the latter. I keep my mouth shut the rest of the session.

When the hour is up, I thank him. "I understand now," I say. "I feel ready."

He nods as he repacks his things. "If you're going to succeed here, you have to keep at a certain pace. And honestly, this is very basic stuff. You got into this school; you should have no trouble with it."

Jasper appears to not really have an opinion about my progress, if he feels any was made. He doesn't look smug or relieved. Just bored. I might not have had all my precalculus questions answered, but I did learn something today. Jasper doesn't care about being a hero, rescuing a girl from academic mediocrity. He has no patience for it. It doesn't give him a deep sense of self-satisfaction. And he definitely has no soft spot for the underdog. I venture the underdog quite annoys him, actually.

He doesn't wait for me when we leave the library, and I don't attempt to keep up with him, which would not be an easy feat given his legs are at least four inches longer than mine. I reach the main level and fall in line with the swarm of students on their way to the courtyard since we're all on nearly the same schedule today.

I watch from a window before I head outside with the rest of them, letting it sink in: the reality of what I've gotten myself into by coming here.

The students flood the courtyard from one side, the parents from the other, floating over the grass and stone squares laid out in a diamond pattern, weaving through the statues and thick green hedges trimmed to look like domes, until they merge in the middle, spotting their families, comingling with friends. We've had separate orientations this morning. While the orientation for students was shorter to allow time to get unpacked and settled in our dorm rooms, plus free time for things like peer tutoring and academic overviews for those of us who didn't do as well as expected on our entrance exams, the parents' orientation was all day and consisted of a tour of the grounds and teacher meet and greets. I'd guess theirs was about reassurance—*We're the Rutherford Institute and worth the money.* Ours was about all the reasons we should be proud of ourselves for being the chosen few to attend, with a pep talk that hinged on fear: if we don't have what it takes and can't follow the rules, they won't hesitate to kick us out, and there are even more ready to take our places. According to them, we are both extremely replaceable because they don't have time for nonsense, and yet also exceptional and rare to be accepted in the first place.

My father appears in the crowd, walking slowly with his hands in his pockets. His hair is combed back since he didn't have time to get it cut at the only barber he trusts with his head in Manhattan. He's insecure about the length; I can tell by the way he keeps running a hand over his left side. He told me on the drive from the airport that if I didn't like it here, I was allowed to leave, that he wouldn't care. But it's apparent as I watch him meander through the courtyard, nodding and smiling at the other parents, that he is unequivocally impressed by this place. He's good at hiding how he really feels and his true intentions in any given situation, a great business tactic for his successful career as an investor and a good life hack, but by now I can see through all his tells. His eyes linger on no one for too long, until he notices me finally emerging from the doors. Then they light up and he smiles, as if it were only me he was looking for all along and not them. As I walk to reach him, I spot the four of them to the left, so he must've clocked their location merely seconds ago, too.

He greets me with a hug, then offers me his arm.

"Well, this place seems nice, if you're into rose gardens and historic architecture," he jokes. He's a good dad. Truly, the very best. Even living a thousand miles away, the man doesn't miss a birthday, a holiday, a recital, a playoff game. Every year he takes the entire month of July off to spend time with me at the vacation spot of my choosing. Last year it was Cape Town. This year we went to Barcelona.

My father and I ignore the family to the left until, by way of the shuffling crowd, we've moved too close to deny them any longer.

"Jake!" Garret Mahoney says, seemingly surprised to find my father here. "This must be your pride and joy, Collins!" He extends his hand, and I shake it. Hidden inside his palm is a peppermint, which he passes to me when our hands meet. He winks at me, and I give him a bashful smile. Garret Mahoney has a wide grin that reaches his forehead and a sunglasses tan around his eyes—probably from the Mahoneys' annual vacation to St. Barths. He has this clumsy genuine quality about him like maybe he really didn't know that my dad had enrolled me at the Rutherford Institute or that the Mahoneys' endorsement had anything to do with it. Of course, it wasn't his endorsement that got me here. It was *her* endorsement.

Marylyn Mahoney is wearing what I can now see is a grown-lady version of the Rutherford Institute uniform. Her slacks are the exact Rutherford heather gray, and her crisp white button-up is paired with a maroon sweater, a gray silk scarf, and a pin with four black pearls to signify the four years she spent here. A Rutherford Institute legacy. She has dark hair like her sons. When Mrs. Mahoney introduces them, Jasper gives me a tight smile and mumbles, "Nice to see you." My father and Mr. and Mrs. Mahoney don't pick up on the insinuation that we might have already met, but Jasper's younger brother, Theodore, glances back and forth between Jasper and me, and I think I spy the slightest smirk on his face.

"I'm Theo," he says, revising to the name he prefers to be called versus what his mother introduced him as, nodding at me, still with that subtle grin. Theo is a third year like me. His hair is a shade lighter than Jasper's and shorter, with tighter curls. His eyes are green. His whole demeanor is altogether friendlier. He's probably easier to get to know and easier to impress, but he shares my sexual preference for men, so it's next to impossible for him to desire me the way I need one of the Mahoney brothers to desire me in order for this to work. There's more power in love and in want, is what I was told—what I was promised. And besides, Theo has a different weakness—an already-open wound. Not one I'll have to create myself.

Mrs. Mahoney is rattling on about Jasper's early acceptance into Dartmouth—*just like his father*—and telling us that Theo's a Princeton hopeful—*just like she was*. Jasper keeps that polite smile on his face that isn't exactly friendly but does make him appear more pleasant. Theo has stopped listening and is waving at someone across the courtyard. A girl with long auburn hair waves back. I recognize her; I met her earlier while I was moving into the girls' dormitory. She's a third year named Anastasia Bowditch. But as she prances over to him with her family trailing behind her, she doesn't acknowledge me. She reaches Theo and grabs his arm, and he gladly lets her steer him toward her family. Anastasia's very young sister jumps into his arms. And so the Mahoneys are forced by social graces to migrate toward the Bowditches, effectively leaving my father and me on our own. Mrs. Mahoney glances back once more to smile, and to anyone watching, it would appear she's simply ensuring the abrupt exit wasn't rude, the way her husband gives us one final wave, saying, "We'll have to catch up later this year when I return from Munich."

Jasper doesn't look back at all. Theo does, wearing a peculiar expression, as though maybe he can feel it coming already, the curse of what's about to happen to them.

Two

"This is what you really want?" my father asks as we sit on the brick patio of Bello Italiano having dinner. We're beyond the wrought iron gate and brick walls of the Rutherford Institute, in the Cashmere, California hot spot of Guthridge Square, where an assortment of shops and restaurants surround a courtyard and a fountain.

The Mahoneys are eating at the burger place across the square, next to the gift shop. My father and I pretend we haven't noticed.

"Of course," I say. It's not the first time he's asked me this.

He's always suspicious of my answer, as if his instincts are telling him that something is off. His instincts are usually not wrong. But he also has no reason to assume I would lie to him about something so big.

We used to tell each other everything—or most things anyway. Now he sits there eating carbonara and sipping red wine, pretending he isn't about to ruin our lives because of the woman wearing a black pearl pin across the square.

I pretend I'm at Rutherford for the higher learning, for the prestige, for the opportunity.

He pretends he doesn't still have his doubts about leaving me here.

Convincing him wasn't easy. He didn't understand what was

so wrong with the private school I was currently attending. He didn't understand why I wouldn't want to live at home with Mimi—which is what I said instead of *Mommy* when I was learning to speak and so it stuck—or why I'd want to leave my lifelong friends, Cadence and Meghan.

I'd prepared a whole argument about needing to be challenged, about wanting independence, about all the additional opportunities attending a school like Rutherford would provide for my future, and I'd done it in a way that he would understand. My father made his fortune at twenty-five by investing his entire meager savings into a company that manufactured a contraption that made underwater communication seamless. His best friend from Penn State had invented it. His friend got the patent but didn't have the funds to make his invention until my father stepped in. This turned out not only to be a very, very profitable business venture but also allowed my dad to uncover his true passion and hidden talent, which was that he was good at analyzing potential business ideas and savvy at investing in and building great rewards off said potential. So I spoke his language and broke things down into a cost-benefit analysis, an approach I knew he'd have a very hard time arguing with. And I was right.

After a few months of my insistence, he finally caved. "I happen to know someone who would be able to put in a good word for you and help you get in even as a third year," he'd told me— something I already knew and was counting on.

"Have you called your Mimi and Rosie yet?" he says. "I'm sure Rosie would love to hear *all* about it." He takes a long sip of wine.

Probably the hardest part about letting me come here was that it had been Rosie's idea.

"Rosie and Mimi are probably somewhere over the Atlantic right now."

"That's true." He smiles. He likes picturing Mimi on an adventure. "Leave them a message anyway."

Rosie is my aunt Rose, who only lets me—and no one else—call her Rosie. My father and Mimi only ever use Rosie when in reference to me. My dad has many reasons to be wary of her, and in this case, he's right to be.

"I'll try them before bed." Another lie. But my father doesn't know that I'm not speaking to Mimi. Coming here was about getting space from her, and as she jets off with her sister, she's getting space from me, too. But I don't feel entirely guilty about not telling him this. He's the one who started keeping secrets first.

We leave the restaurant, and the sky turns fuzzy as the night creeps in. The other families are slowly disappearing from the square too. The Mahoneys were gone over an hour ago. We reach the curb where a car service is waiting to take me back to Rutherford, and my dad looks devastated.

"Are you sure this is what you want?" He's stalling; he doesn't want to say goodbye yet. "I hate leaving you here, all by yourself. Practically on your own."

"I'm not all by myself or on my own. Not in the way you were." Secretly, his worst fear is that I should ever feel unloved or neglected, the way he felt growing up with parents who instilled in him a great work ethic but only by example. He told me once that he still felt to this day like he never truly knew his parents. Mimi and Rosie had the opposite problem. Parents they couldn't wait to escape—parents who were alcoholics in that functioning way that kept food on the table but turned every day into a juggle of their mood swings complete with hiding behind locked doors and walking on eggshells. They did escape them eventually, when cancer took their mother and a car accident took their father.

My dad nods and rubs his eyes. I hope he believes me. I hope he doesn't worry the entire time I'm here.

"I'm going to miss you," he says. I feel a tightening in my chest as I give him a hug and we say our final goodbye, knowing this really will be the last I'll see of him until the winter holidays.

"Don't go easy on them, kid," he says as we break away. Something he says to me every time I'm about to do something new.

I answer the way I always do, with a promise. "Never."

"Wait," he says when I'm about to get in the car. "You've never listened to Rosie before." True. "Why now? For this place? You don't have to believe what she says about adventure, you know. All that traveling she does—she's searching for something, but she's also running. It's not any way to live."

"I know that," I tell him. "That's not why I wanted to come here. I just wanted something new. Something great."

He nods, and I make a silent wish that when I finally get in the car and drive away from him, I've quieted some of his fears. Even if I can already feel that heavy sadness of how much I'm going to miss him.

The truth is, I never believed anything Rosie said about adventure and what it means to make the most of your life. But then I learned that Rosie was the only one in my family telling the truth. And that makes me look back on everything she said and consider what's actually possible.

Three

When I return to Rutherford that evening, first and second years are gathered in the west wing, and third and fourth years are in the east, in a common room that's full of tuft sofas made of brown leather, a few foosball and pool tables, and a couple of high-top tables where people are playing cards.

Jasper is easy to spot. He's sitting on the thick arm of one of the sofas reading a book. He has to bend slightly so light will hit the pages. The room is only lit up by lamps in a way that casts many shadows and gives the east wing common room the feel of a 1940s smoke room. Despite how antisocial he's being, Jasper's still surrounded by a group of guys. They laugh and talk around him like they don't notice he's ignoring them in favor of fiction. Or maybe they're just used to it.

Theo is at one of the tables playing cards. Anastasia is with him. They look like they might be having the most fun out of everyone, the way they're laughing. And people flock to them like magnets, like their happiness and good time is contagious.

I turn back to Jasper. How is a person supposed to get his attention when this is how he chooses to spend his time in an atmosphere intended for socializing? I watch as a girl wearing a bright purple sundress tries. She taps him on the shoulder. He hesitates to look up from his book, but when he does, he smiles at her in a way that makes him seem like someone who at least has the capacity to be warm. She says something, and he lets the book dangle by his knee like he's forgotten about it. Something makes him laugh. Something makes her touch her hand to her cheek. Next, she puts a hand on his shoulder, and he proceeds to talk as though he hasn't noticed. It embarrasses her a little, his lack of reaction, and she casually removes it. It's hard to see the imperfections in Jasper now that he isn't reading in the middle of a staff-orchestrated party. It's easy to see why the girl in the purple is turning pink and why she keeps shifting from one foot to the other. He looks very handsome like this, with a smile that is more charming than I'd thought it would be, and a cool demeanor like nothing on earth could faze him.

I can't quite imagine what he'd be like in love with someone—realistically—and yet, it's effortless to fantasize about it. The girl leaves him, and though he watches her walk away wearing an expression I would definitely want someone who's watching me walk away to be wearing, he's back to his book the moment she's out of view. *I should go up to him,* I think. *He was happy to talk to that other girl, and he'll be fine to talk to you,* I try to tell myself. But my feet stay grounded. He's too attractive in this light, the shadows over his face. The way he's focused on that book—the memory of the way he was fixated on the girl while she was leaving him. I stare at him, but I can't think of him this way. I have to remember the boy who cut himself shaving and who was impatient during my overview. I have to remember what Rosie told me before I came here and the reason I know I can believe her.

It was a year ago the first time she told me that I had the ability to make anyone fall in love with me. Rosie has always been a whirlwind, showing up at Mimi's without calling whenever she's run out of money or is in between traveling bouts. She stayed with us pretty regularly the entire year before I left for Rutherford.

Mimi was listening from the open kitchen window where she was pinching rosemary over the sink. Rosie and I were out on the patio watching the sunset.

"Is this some sort of Olsen woman power that I've never been told about?" Mimi joked when she heard what Rosie was telling me.

Rosie waved her hand, brushing away Mimi's comment. "This is something that's true for everyone," she said. She pivoted in her chair to face the open window and speak directly to Mimi. "You've chosen to live a solitary life, Michelle. You could've had men lining up for you if you'd wanted."

"Well, darn." Mimi put on a loud, sarcastic voice anytime she responded to Rosie's Unsolicited Advice, as she called it sometimes. Other times she called it *trivial nonsense*.

"It's probably too late for you now. It's strongest when you're young." And I knew that with that comment, Rosie was talking about me.

"Then you've probably lost the power altogether," Mimi called. Any chance to remind Rosie that she was the older sister, Mimi took it.

"If you hone the power and never stop using it, you can keep it for longer," Rosie said.

Mimi walked away from the window, shaking her head.

Rosie and I sat in silence for a bit, staring out at the pastures as the sun went down, creating a shadow across the barn. When I was born, Mimi was living in a small apartment in Madison, and my father was living in a penthouse in Manhattan, where he still lives. He bought Mimi her dream house, a ranch-style home outside of town on twelve acres with a barn and a pond, before my first birthday. I used to think it was what they thought was best for me, growing up in the suburbs, lots of land for roaming, and that's why she didn't move to the city, to his mansion in the sky. But that wasn't the case.

"Don't you want to know how to do it?" Rosie asked me. She pushed her foot against my chair, making it spin toward her.

I'd recently turned sixteen. It felt the exact right age to learn about how to make someone fall in love with you. And I did have a boy in mind.

"It doesn't seem possible," I said.

"Ever the skeptic." The same thing she'd said when I was nine and told her I'd never believed in Santa.

"Well, what if they don't think you're pretty? What if you aren't their type?" Lucius Castle had never stared at me the way I'd seen him stare at the other girls—like Carly Gomez.

"You think you have a type—you're wrong about that, believe me."

I understood that she had a point, even if I liked to love with my eyes first.

"So how do you do it?" I asked. The sky was turning a bright pink with the setting sun. We could see it for miles from the vast, flat terrain of the property.

Rosie smiled. She had this wide grin that made her squint. She looked so beautiful in that moment. Excited and full of hope. "I'll tell you exactly how."

The sliding door creaked open and shut as Mimi came outside. She refilled Rosie's glass of white wine. "This ought to be good," she said.

"You find a way to bring out their best qualities."

Mimi and I waited for the rest.

"*That's it?*" Mimi said it before I could.

"It's not as simple as you think. The trick is you have to be able to find the good in them." She side-eyed her sister as she took a sip of wine. "That's something you've never been skilled at."

Mimi put up her hand, dismissing the comment as nothing. But her face turned stiff, and her eyes got sad. She drank wine to cover it and got up, pretending she had to check on the vegetables steaming in the kitchen.

"You could do it easily, Collins," Rosie said to me. She waited until I'd taken my eyes off Mimi and was focused on her before she continued. "You get that, right?"

I answered her honestly. "Not really."

"You should know that about yourself at the very least," she said. "It's *in* you, and no one can take that away."

Tonight, in the east wing common room, I wonder what's good about Jasper Mahoney. He's dedicated and very intelligent. He's handsome, athletic. That's not going to be enough, though. Those are surface-level qualities only. Anyone could meet Jasper and see these things about him. Throughout the night, he takes breaks from his book to chat. But he is also the first one out of his group of friends to leave. He does it so quickly, without saying goodbyes, that I nearly miss it.

Theo and Anastasia stick together all night, migrating effortlessly around the room. Everyone seems to have something to say to them, including the group I've sat with, casually joining in on a foosball rotation. But they don't stay long, wherever they go.

There's a moment when I think they've left the party, when I can't spot them anywhere in the room, but then a half an hour later, there they are. They seem like the type of people who would know places at this school where you can disappear, hide. Because from what I've learned about Theo, keeping private things hidden is something he's very familiar with.

Four

The truth about Rutherford, now that I've been here a couple of weeks and am starting to catch on, is that it does feel *worth the money*. Life at Rutherford is very structured, very demanding. But it's also like this: every day, I wake up and shower on clean white tiles, under a rainfall showerhead, the hot steam smelling like a field of lavender. I take courses like number theory, comparative religions, economics and post–Cold War Europe, and writing for contemporary media from some of the most prestigious teachers the world has to offer, in perfectly preserved, century-old brick-and-stained-glass buildings. I practice field hockey in state-of-the-art athletic facilities, eat a dinner prepared by a world-renowned chef, study in an ergonomic chair at my desk with a view of the deep forest, the roaring ocean, and a beach littered with driftwood. "Where the ocean meets the forest," is how the small, isolated town of Cashmere, California, is described on the Rutherford Institute's website. It's as beautiful as was promised, I'll give them that. And every night, I fall asleep on a mattress that feels like a cloud.

It does get to you eventually, the way everything here is exquisite and distinguished, and just for us. It somehow creeps in, that subtle thought: *I deserve this.*

This is the thing about Rutherford that the website doesn't tell you: being here really is like having pretention pumped into your veins. It becomes very hard not to believe your own hype.

But I still hear Rosie's voice in my head—*You can't lose focus. What I'm asking you to do isn't easy, but you know why you have to do it, and it's up to you to take these risks—and I get that they are huge risks, but that just means the reward will be great. It will be exactly what we want it to be.* Maybe I shouldn't have believed her. Throughout her life, Rosie had earned and lost a lot of money. She was a gambler, not at casinos but in what my dad would call *putting all her eggs in one basket*—spending all the money she'd earned working the VIP section at a nightclub in Tokyo on an initial public offering that sounded like a good idea but turned out to be a dud, or taking the money she'd gotten from selling her Parisian apartment into flipping houses in Sacramento with a guy she met in Sydney who claimed he knew what he was doing, only to lose it all to bad construction management and a failing market. Those get-rich-quick schemes were what she was searching for; they seemed to be the only investments she trusted. It was always all or nothing in terms of Rosie having money or a place to live. Mimi said it was irresponsible, but Rosie simply called it *living*. To her credit, a few of her gambles had worked out. Rosie's lived in some of the most beautiful places in the world. Paris, Medellín, San Sebastián, Kyoto. To me, it did say something that she'd been in such high-risk scenarios, where she didn't always reap big rewards, and yet she never hesitated to take the next big risk.

By now, I mostly know where to find Jasper at any given point in the day. He's serious while school is in session, stopping only occasionally in between classes to chat with his friends. After school, he meets with his teachers during their open hours, then heads straight to the library even though he only has fifteen minutes before he'll need to be at the soccer fields.

While he's at practice, I take water breaks from running drills for field hockey and watch him through the chain-link fence. He's intense, playing like there is a scout observing, hanging his head and cursing to himself whenever he makes a mistake as if he could still be cut from the team, even though soccer isn't even his main sport, just what he plays because it's not lacrosse season.

At dinner, he joins his friends at the long table at the far end of the cafeteria. He stays only the ten minutes that it takes him to eat his entrée before he leaves, rushing out the side doors, barely saying goodbye and not looking back.

Theo is a different story. He's impossible to track. He changes his route to class, the group he eats dinner with, even the times he arrives and leaves from water polo practice, always veering early or late. The only constant in his everyday ongoings is his best friend, Anastasia, who is never far from him.

At dinner that night, Theo and Anastasia are nowhere to be found. Jasper is doing his usual: eating quickly and readying his things to leave.

"Where do you think he's going?" I ask Elena, nodding in Jasper's direction. Elena Garcia is my roommate. She's from Ann Arbor and is pleasant in a way that's made the transition from only child to sharing a room quite seamless. So far, my lone complaint is that each morning I'm startled awake by her alarm blasting "Walking on Sunshine." Elena will then proceed to bat at it absentmindedly until she manages to hit the snooze button.

I've been eating with Elena and her friends since classes began, and they've graciously accepted me and didn't even question why I was tagging along or accuse me of not having appropriate roommate boundaries. Elena is the only person who knows I have a specific interest in Jasper, though she thinks it's only a crush.

"Where *who's* going?" Ruthie asks. Ruthie is Elena's best friend.

"Jasper Mahoney," I say, deciding it's okay to tell them, my closest, if also my newest, friends. Maybe they'll surprise me by having the answer.

"*Oh,*" Ruthie says.

"That's who you like?" Elena's friend Matt moves his eyebrows up and down.

"I find him . . ." *Careful, careful.* "Mysterious."

"Jasper's not mysterious," Elena says. "He's aloof."

"Aloof isn't so bad, is it?"

They all laugh—all six of them at the table. I'm not sure that's the reaction I'd expected, but that's part of the fun being here. Nothing is quite what I'd anticipated.

I generally like being with Elena and her friends. But they aren't going to help me much. None of them play sports with Jasper; none of them have classes with him. None of them really know him or care to. And even as Theo seems to be friends with everyone, he doesn't spend much time with them. None of his extracurriculars line up with theirs either. They are heavy into theater, and Theo's life is already a stage.

We hear an eruption of laughter across the cafeteria. I know before I turn my head to look that Theo is the cause of such commotion. Theo has what Mimi would call *the gift of charm*, that ability to make people feel like they're standing in the sun whenever they're around you. The students flock to him, they really do. I haven't quite gotten to experience him firsthand—yet—but it's the kind of thing you can observe from afar. And he's nondiscriminatory with this charisma, spreading it everywhere and to anyone. No one seems to mind sharing either, even if it's crystal clear that Anastasia Bowditch is indeed his favorite.

"Should we start?" Ruthie says, glancing at her watch. "Are you ready?" For this question, they all turn to look at me.

"I'm ready." Hopefully, this is the truth.

Elena and her friends like to play games at dinner. Sometimes card games, sometimes word games. Today, they want to play the game of bouncing quarters off the table and into a cup. Like all their games, the fun isn't in the playing; it's in the betting, and today, whoever loses has to drink from one of the truly disgusting concoctions that Matt mixed up during lunch. Things like French onion soup with chocolate milk and iced tea, or blue cheese dressing combined with fish sauce and mayonnaise.

I know. It sounds really juvenile and ridiculous, but after studying things like computer science and cryptography and organic chemistry for the past eight hours, this is a good way to unwind.

As the game picks up, I laugh so hard my eyes leak tears. They're all laughing, too.

"What in the world is going on over here?" I feel someone touch my shoulder and turn to see Theo standing over us, one hand on my shoulder, one hand on Matt's. We both slide over so he can join us at the table—welcoming him gladly into our already blissful conversation.

He edges a knee into the empty space instead of sitting down—an uncommitted way to join in. We tell him about the game, and he laughs, starts shaking the mystery cups like this will tell him something. He knows better than to smell them.

Across the room, where Jasper usually sits, I see a flash of him—messy curls, lean shoulders hunched under a maroon jacket. He's back? His friends greet him, but he doesn't stay long; it would seem he'd forgotten a book and had to return for it. As quickly as he was here, he's leaving again. But to where?

"Are you staring at my brother?" Theo's voice has a teasing tone and isn't at all mean. But my face gets hot. If he's noticed this slight glance, has he noticed all the other millions of times I've stared at Jasper since the start of the school year? At Theo's comment, the entire table turns toward the direction I was looking to watch Jasper escape out the west exit.

"How mysterious, eh?" Matt laughs. He elbows me playfully.

"My brother? Mysterious?" Theo directs all his attention to me, and I must say, I do feel like the sun is beating down directly on me. Theo's being as friendly as ever. But my face still reacts with intense heat and probably the accompanying redness.

I will my expression to relax into a smile. *Play it cool.* "Maybe you can clear up some of the mystery?"

Theo smiles and leans toward me. "I'd be happy to."

This is a natural progression, I decide. This line about finding Jasper mysterious, it could be planting a seed. Adding to my story, so that in a few months, when Jasper is hopelessly in love with me, all of them will recall this conversation and think, *Aha, I know exactly how this started for her.* I can roll with this—*yes.* It's better this way.

"What do you want to know about him? Go ahead, try me."

"It seems like all he does is study." This is also a guess as to what he's doing when he leaves dinner early every day.

Theo laughs. "That's all we all do."

This is inarguable—even though it's barely been two weeks, I am sometimes having to skip dinner myself, in need of extra time to do homework and finish reading assignments before the eleven o'clock bed checks, when lights must be out, no exceptions.

"But I never see him having any fun—I don't know. That's the impression I've had of him since he led my calculus overview at the start of the year."

"Honestly?" Theo says. "Your initial impression of him being not very fun, uptight, and school-obsessed, with no work-life balance, is completely right. He's not mysterious, he's boring. And I'm allowed to say that because I'm family. So it comes from a place of love."

"But where does he go every day during dinner?"

"Probably anywhere there isn't a crowd and no one will annoy him."

I don't know what to say to this. It seems like a not-so-subtle warning from Theo to stay away. Or a hint: *Don't bother.*

I can sense in the way Theo leans back that he's about to leave us. Matt must feel it, too, because he peppers Theo with questions and tries to convince him to play one round of the game with us. But I'm ready for Theo to move on, shine his spotlight somewhere else.

As he walks away and rejoins Anastasia, he says something that makes both her and the other third year constantly at her side, Ariel Maddox, turn back our way. They're looking at me. Theo's face reads exuberant, like he could've said anything, mean or nice or nonchalant. Ariel's expression is dry, nothing revealed. But Anastasia looks at me with wide, curious eyes. Like something Theo said must've intrigued her.

Five

Another day of Jasper passing me in the hallways without a second glance, always in a hurry and walking too quickly for anyone to catch up to him, but I don't feel bad that I've made no progress in getting Jasper to notice me. Not yet. I have a new plan. Love can't be rushed, and it can wait. Because while love is something you can hold against someone, laws broken and nondisclosure agreements tied to millions of dollars are more straightforward in terms of what can be used for entrapment. Therefore, I decide to turn my attention toward Theo. And the key to Theo is Anastasia Bowditch.

Elena and her friends regard Anastasia as the school gossip— *hair so big it's full of secrets* jokes abound. And while I never doubted that Anastasia doesn't know all the skeletons in Theo's closet, this reputation of hers makes it seem like it'd be a guarantee that if I'm close enough to her, she'll tell me whatever I want to know about him.

Anastasia strolls a few feet in front of me in the hallway with Ariel Maddox. If Theo is Anastasia's number one, Ariel is her number two. Ariel hardly ever smiles, from what I've seen. She has a constant poker face. It doesn't make her seem unfriendly, though. I think this is probably a quality Theo and Anastasia like about her—what makes her a good ally and fellow gatekeeper to all the secrets Anastasia knows, Theo's transgressions included.

To make myself valuable to people like them, I need to have something they want. And if they trade in information, then that's what I'll use to barter my way closer to them. Even if the information I give them isn't good or even true.

"Hey," I say, approaching Anastasia and Ariel. They slow their pace and stop their conversation, but neither of them say *hey* back. They stare at me, waiting. Like they know I'm about to present something to them and are waiting to see if it's worthy of their time.

"I heard something weird, and I didn't know if it was true . . ." Bored. They look so bored. "And it's about Theo, so I thought—"

"What did you hear?" Anastasia stops in her tracks. Ariel walks to the other side of me, so I'll be forced to stop, too.

Their wide eyes blink impatiently at me. Their lips purse into judgmental pouts. I'm almost tempted to tell them the truth. *I know what Theo was involved in two summers ago.* But it's too early to play that card. It would make me seem suspicious to them—a possible threat.

"I heard that Theo was on steroids."

They stare at me, their expressions unchanging until they both start to laugh. Even Ariel has broken her poised glare to chuckle in my face, at my expense.

"Theo has muscles, but not *steroid muscles*," Anastasia says.

"I mean, people don't just use steroids to build muscle mass," I say. "They can be performance enhancers, too—"

"If that were true, Theo wouldn't be second-string on the water polo team." Anastasia laughs so hard she has to wipe a tear from her left eye.

This isn't the reaction I was expecting.

"But aren't you concerned that this rumor is going around? Couldn't it jeopardize Theo's chances at getting into college or—"

This, if you can believe it, makes them laugh even harder. It's mortifying. I thought they would want to know who'd started this rumor. I thought they'd thank me for telling them before it got out of hand.

Instead, Ariel shakes her head at me. "Get a better source," she says.

They're still laughing as they walk away.

Okay, fine, so that backfired. It was a lie and a faux rumor, and the two of them could smell it from a mile away.

I round the corner and collide with someone, both of our books falling to the ground. This time, it's the gods who are laughing, because the person I rammed into is Jasper.

"What are you doing here?" I actually say out loud. *Shoot.*

He scowls at me. But really, he has organic chemistry this period, and that's in the other direction—except I look up and see the lab right in from of us. Oh no; it's me who was going the wrong way, distracted and caught off guard by Anastasia and Ariel's reaction. And now he's seen me like this—flustered and clumsy.

"Are you lost, Collins?" he says.

"No." It comes out too defensive, and Jasper leans away from me. "I was just—I thought—" Nope, no excuses are coming to mind. No recovering from this.

"Hey, I get it," he says, his voice friendlier than I've ever heard it. He reaches down to pick up our spilled books. "It's been a long week."

"Yeah," I say. "Yes. This week—it just . . . keeps going."

He hands me my textbooks, and my face flashes hot. He smiles, and he seems warm and nice. Maybe I've caught him at a peaceful moment, right before O-Chem lab; the calm before the academic storm when he'll turn intense and boring, as Theo says, or serious and rigid and impatient, the way I'm used to him.

And as I walk away, I wonder if he's watching me the way he did the girl in the purple dress the first night at Rutherford. I don't keep my cool; I glance back. He's not there anymore.

Six

Anastasia's in my post–Cold War Europe history class. For this hour, we're allowed to sit anywhere. Usually, she sits next to Ruby Rivera, but today, I arrive at class before Ruby and take Ruby's seat. Ruby only blinks at me when she walks in and notices. But Ruby is like everyone here and has more important things—like college applications and academic mediocrity—to worry about than where she sits in class.

"Hey, Anastasia?" I tap her shoulder when there's five minutes left in class and we're let loose to start the assignment.

Here's what I've learned about Anastasia Bowditch since making her my main focus. She absolutely does not like to be called *Ana* and will not respond to it. She frequently gets reprimanded for wearing four rings instead of the Rutherford-approved two. She's from Seattle, so she often sees Theo even when they aren't at Rutherford, since his family's home is across Lake Washington in Bellevue. She's a vegetarian who likes steak seasoning on her steamed broccoli—observed on more than one occasion during dinner. She's on the swim team and, like many other students here, has a private coach who trains her when she's not at Rutherford. She used to go out with a third year named Zayn Patel but has been single since mid-July.

The most important thing I learned?

Anastasia turns toward me, her eyebrows raised, her expression a question mark. "Yes?" she finally says when a second has passed and I still haven't spoken. Her tone is neither friendly nor annoyed.

"Does anyone ever call you *the Red Scare*? You know, because of your hair." The most important thing I learned about Anastasia Bowditch is that more than gossip, she loves a good compliment. It is, however, unfortunate that *scare* and *hair* happen to rhyme.

Anastasia squints at me, and her lips part. I honestly don't know what to expect from her at all now because really how would anyone respond to a person they don't know giving them a nickname about the spread of communism based on their hair color? I thought it would translate, be something she'd find amusing and complimentary, and maybe I'd get points for using a term from this very class, but I was oh so wrong.

"Um. No," she says. She glances down at the luscious red curls cascading around her. Then she laughs.

Curious. I can't decide if this is the demeaning kind of laughter like when I told her the faux rumor about Theo or if this is genuine.

"But people *should* call me that," she says. She smiles. *Thank goodness, thank goodness, thank goodness.* "That's funny. I'm going to tell Theo."

She turns back to her reading, but I understand the accolade that is *telling Theo,* because most everyone here would want his approval and to be given credit for saying something deemed clever by Anastasia.

After class, I try again, going for that combination of flattering and funny that Anastasia seems to respond to.

"Where did you get that ring?" I signal to her right hand, the coil of silver around her pointer finger. "That's the kind of thing you wear when you want to spread your regime."

She sighs and stares at the piece of jewelry; she doesn't laugh, like maybe she didn't get the regime joke.

"Thanks," she says. "This guy Douglas gave it to me. I like the way it looks, but I don't like that it reminds me of him."

"Oh no, why? What happened with him?"

We walk down the hall, and she regales me with the tale of Douglas Begley, the son of her parents' friends who used to try to get her to make out with him in the bathroom during dinner parties.

"I only sort of liked him," she explains, very nonchalantly.

We pass through the B wing hall, lined with windows, giving way to a view of the courtyard, and Theo falls into step with us.

"Mr. Guthrie is trying to kill us with boredom, I swear," he says. He nods at me. "Hi, Collins."

"That's right—Collins," Anastasia says. "I could've sworn I knew your name, but then couldn't remember it to save my life. Don't you hate that?"

"You're so rude," Theo says to her, laughing.

I find myself nodding in agreement with her assessment of forgetfulness even though I also agree with Theo, the rude part being that she didn't *have* to tell me I was forgettable to her.

"What?" Anastasia says. "She's new, and my brain can only retain so much at once. I couldn't remember her name; so sue me."

"*So sue me*? I love when you start using catchphrases that were popular before you were born that you clearly picked up being trapped in Saint-Tropez with your mother for three weeks," Theo says.

"I do remember that Collins is from the Midwest and that she had to do her overview with Jasper." Talking like I'm not even standing right here, until suddenly she turns to me. "How was that, by the way?"

My face gets warm. Of course, Theo must've told her about

how I was staring at Jasper in the cafeteria; how I'd called him *mysterious.*

"It was . . . efficient."

"I'll bet it was," she says. Theo elbows her, and any chance he had of being discreet about it is ruined because Anastasia replies with a loud, *"Ouch."*

"That reminds me," she says, wiggling away from Theo. "Are you going to the Labor Day dinner event?"

"Is that not mandatory?" I say.

"Oh yeah, it is for sure if you're staying here for Labor Day. Sometimes people don't stay. Especially first years or, like, if you're new and homesick."

I take this as a bit of an insult, that she's implying I can't even handle a few weeks at Rutherford before hightailing it home. But as the two of them stare at me as we walk, waiting for my answer, I think that maybe this is a test. They're waiting to see how strong I am.

"I'll be here," I say.

I don't know if Anastasia's heard me because suddenly she exclaims, "So don't look now, but Teagan Quinn is desperately hitting on Matt Reiner, over there by his locker. You have to look—but don't be obvious."

Matt Reiner is Elena's friend, the mastermind behind their cafeteria dinner games. I glance as he leans against the wall, chatting with a girl wearing a long braid and a skirt rolled shorter than the Rutherford dress code allows.

"She's talking to him," Theo says. "How scandalous."

"Oh, *come on,*" Anastasia says. "That was flirting! You saw it, right, Collins?"

I absolutely did not see it—but I don't want to stage a disagreement with Anastasia yet.

"I thought Matt Reiner was dating Constance Gilbert." As soon as the words escape my lips, I wonder if this is a secret, something only those at Elena's table are privy to, and I've blown it.

"Is that true?" Theo says. "Or did you get your information from the same person who allegedly told you I was taking steroids?"

I don't know what to say—whether it's better to apologize or act naïve. Luckily, Anastasia is not about to be thrown off topic. "They *are* still dating," she says, seemingly impressed that I, too, knew about Matt and Constance. "Teagan wants to break them up."

"That's not very nice." I'm so relieved to have good information and that Anastasia is making light of the whole steroids thing. So completely relieved.

"Well, Teagan Quinn is the definition of not very nice." Anastasia launches into a story about their first year at Rutherford when Teagan tried to steal Anastasia's then boyfriend, Jacques Delon. "She even tried to steal Theo's boyfriend once. At the class trip to Stanford—remember?"

"It didn't work. Surprise, surprise," Theo says.

"What was his name again?" Anastasia says.

"Ross Vendermine," Theo says. "He stopped coming here after his first year."

"That's right. Didn't his father's company defraud the government or something?" Anastasia says.

"I have no idea," Theo says.

Something about the name *Vendermine* sounds familiar. *Oh yes.* "Did his parents own Vendermine Management?"

"You know it?" Anastasia's eyes widen, and she steps closer to me. I was right after all. Flattery initially got Anastasia's attention, but having useless information and gossip is what's hooking her. "Do you know what happened?"

Sort of. "Yeah. Something about asbestos? It was damaging enough that the whole company went under." *I think.*

"How do you know about that?" Theo says. "Don't tell me you dated Ross, too?"

I laugh and shake my head. Sometimes my dad's friends and business associates talked shop at the penthouse when I was there. They liked me to join in sometimes, even though I had nothing to add. They thought they were teaching me a thing or two about business and life. Mostly, they were bragging, and my dad always laughed about it after they left; how they liked talking about others' failings as an excuse to tote their own successes.

Anastasia's mouth drops open. "That's what it was—I remember now." She rewrites the headline. "His parents' company was, like, killing people with asbestos, basically."

"It was a really big deal." *One would assume.*

She's nodding. All friendships have a currency, and this is hers. Rumors and gossip, anything even borderline shocking—or anything ordinary that can be spun into something outrageous. Extra points if you can give her that thrill of being the first to know something.

"Hey, Collins, tell Theo my new nickname," she says. She turns to Theo. "It's totally funny."

"The Red Scare."

"Isn't it perfect?" Anastasia says. "I'm like a regime."

"That's the regime you want your nickname associated with? Really?" He laughs.

She flips her hair so the strands hit him in the face. "Whatever. Eat my shorts."

"I don't even want to know what that means or why your mother was saying that over the summer," Theo says.

Theo and Anastasia eventually go right where I go left, but before we part ways, I tell them I'll see them later.

At dinner, I walk up to the table where Anastasia sits with Theo and Ariel, and while Ariel sizes me up, Anastasia slides over, starts talking at me a million miles a minute, telling me that she's changed her mind about being called *the Red Scare*. And just like that, I'm eating dinner across from Theo Mahoney and only a table away from where Jasper gathers with his friends before he disappears for the evening.

Seven Months Later

There are some things that are too complicated to understand unless you know the whole of it. The entirety. What came before and what comes after. The broken-down parts, each piece making both the foundation and the destruction. A moment-by-moment recount until the abhorrent conclusion.

I can read my father's face right now—sad and broken, but hopeful, even if slightly weathered. He's thinking that what's been done can never be undone. He's wondering how he'll explain it to himself. He's running through all the possible ways this backfired on him so badly, counting the ways everything's already been ruined.

He comes to the right conclusion, though.

After we cut over toward the other side of Cashmere, and start moving straight on toward the water, he wipes his hand over his face, taking extra care in rubbing his eyes. He rotates his shoulders. He looks out the window at the tall trees sliding past him under the sky full the of clouds. He clears his throat. And then he turns to me.

"What do you want to talk about, Collins?" he says.

I lean back, resting my head against the seat, finally relaxed.

Some things are very simple.

SEPTEMBER

Seven

"Slow down, Collins, jeez," Anastasia calls to me as we walk the forest trail that leads to the beach down below.

"Keep up," I say again for the millionth time. They don't listen to me and make no effort to match my pace.

"Would you relax? We have plenty of time before the tide comes in," Ariel says. Ariel's personality is best described as *wry*. She has a low tolerance for, well, anything in large doses, really—too much laughter, too much emotion, too much nostalgia. She's a third year from Hanalei. She's on the swim team with Anastasia, which is how they became *fast friends*, as Theo calls them. I wonder how he describes my new but consistent friendship with Anastasia. Fast, *sure*. Calculated, *definitely*.

"Collins is so excited." Theo laughs. "It's like she's never seen the ocean before." They do this often, talk about me, not to me, when they're right in front of me. They do it to each other, too, like it's a way for them to do what Anastasia loves best—discussing people behind their backs—except out in the open, face-to-face, and under the safe umbrella of friendship.

"Excuse me, I'm not like the three of you. I've never lived on the West Coast before. I almost never get to see the Pacific Ocean." The last time was when I went to Oahu with my dad. I was thirteen.

"It's only the ocean," Ariel says. Rich, coming from her.

The four of us trudge over the hard dirt path that cuts through the forest. It's early enough that it's still cool outside, especially under the shade of the towering pine and redwood trees surrounding us.

We're not allowed to go to the beach by ourselves, and when we do get the opportunity to go, there's a time limit. Once the tide comes up, the beach disappears almost entirely. The water creeps up all the way to the tree line, where the forest starts. We work hard during the week, between our classes and homework and required readings and clubs and sports; even the weekends are full. Today is a real live holiday—Labor Day—and the opportunity to see the beach excited me as much as sleeping until noon excited Elena.

Anastasia, Ariel, Theo, and I finally reach the part of the trail that turns steep, steering us down to the beach, but there are students in front of us who are taking their sweet time, and there's not enough room on the path to pass them.

"You're like that driver who goes way over the speed limit and weaves lanes to pass everyone and then gets stuck at the red light with everyone else, anyway," Ariel tells me.

We emerge onto the beach and are hit immediately with a gust of wind and a chilly mist. I look out at the waves in the distance, the way the water is both dark and clear. This close, the waves are loud.

"Worth all the stress?" Theo asks. He laughs when I nod.

"Let's sit over there," Ariel says, pointing to the side of the beach opposite from where the chaperones have set up their canopy.

I scan the shore until I find him standing with his feet in the water. He's wearing a backward hat and swim trunks, and he's tossing a football with the two friends I've noticed him with the most. Stewart Laing and Daiki Nakamura. They're both fourth years who play lacrosse with Jasper. Stewart is stocky with thick hair so blond it's nearly white. Daiki is tall and lean like Jasper. He has dark hair and brown eyes and, to be blunt, he might be the most attractive person I've ever seen. I know from hearing others talk, because Daiki is definitely the kind of beautiful boy that everyone talks about, that he is not only *super sweet* but also has a very, very serious girlfriend back home in San Jose, who he somehow manages to see at least once a month. Daiki is forget-your-own-name-good-looking, and I'm grateful that Jasper Mahoney is not Daiki Nakamura; otherwise, this ploy would be entirely out of my control.

"Hello? Over here, Collins." Anastasia calls to me from a few feet away, in the direction the three of them have started walking.

Oops. I jog to catch up.

"Get ahold of yourself," Theo says under his breath, wearing a teasing smile as he falls into step with me.

The four of us spread out our beach towels on the sand. We're positioned a few feet from where the tide is reaching. Theo and Anastasia are in the middle, Ariel and I flank them on either side. We shed our clothes so we're in our bathing suits, and we lather ourselves in sunscreen. The sun is still playing peekaboo with us from behind a stubborn cloud.

"What if it rains?" Anastasia says. This is something she tends to do, point out a worst-case scenario.

"It's not going to rain," Ariel says, rolling her eyes.

Theo laughs and says, "So what if it does?" I've heard him say this to Anastasia on more than one occasion, and I think this is a testament to how deeply he understands her—he knows that she needs to hear a response akin to "So what? It will be okay," instead of being told how unlikely it is that her worry will come to fruition.

I scoot to the edge of my towel, sitting with my knees bent and my feet in the sand.

"Joyce's suit is so tacky," Anastasia says.

"Her style as usual. She's always a walking designer label," Ariel says.

"And here you both noticed her, so everything's going according to her plan." Theo picks up a handful of sand and lets it run through his fingers. "Hey, Anastasia, remember your suit two years ago at that Fourth of July party in Martha's Vineyard?"

The three of them start laughing.

"Untangle me, untangle me!" Ariel flails as she mimics Anastasia in this particular memory.

Anastasia says, "Shut up! It was not that funny!" But she is laughing, too.

Theo leans my way. "So her suit looked like bondage—something ridiculous her mother bought her in Saint-Tropez." He launches into the rest of the tale about how Anastasia got stuck in her swimming suit, and somehow this segues into a chronicle of the best parties they've ever attended at Martha's Vineyard. I think part of the reason they don't mind me hanging out with them is that when they reminisce, they get an excuse to tell their stories to someone who's never heard them before. It makes me miss Cadence and Meghan from back home, and I wish I had a reason to talk about them. When I told them I was enrolling at Rutherford, they couldn't understand why I'd want to go, and I didn't know how to explain it to them, not when there was so much I'd have to omit. It made a distance between us even before I left, like they could tell I was keeping something from them, a part of me closed off.

"Heads up!" someone calls, and a football flies at us. Theo reaches out his arm and catches it.

"Nice one, Theo. You're making us look bad." The owner of the ball is Sebastian Guerrero. Aside from being a known playboy, Sebastian also has a reputation for being shameless.

"What do you want, Sebastian?" Theo asks, making no attempt to hand the ball back.

Sebastian laughs. "Just enjoying a day on the beach. If only that cloud would move."

"You could've walked up to us like a normal person if you wanted to talk to us. You didn't need to endanger our safety as an excuse," Ariel says. Anastasia nods.

"I like to make an entrance," Sebastian says.

"Nice tan lines," Ariel says.

He looks himself up and down. His eyes stop on the dark lines around the front of his legs, where the skin is noticeably lighter. A shin guard tan. "What can I say? This is the price of playing soccer in São Paulo for the last half of the summer."

"I love it there so much," Anastasia says.

"Have you been?" Sebastian first looks at Ariel, who shakes her head, then at Theo—same response. He stops on me next. "Hey, you're new—Collins Pruitt, right?"

This is the first time Sebastian's spoken to me since I arrived, but I've heard about how he's enchanting—hypnotizing, even. And it's not only because he's what my friends from back home would refer to as a *stone-cold fox*. It's that when he looks at you, he really looks at you.

"That's me," I say. He smiles.

"So how do you like it here so far, Collins Pruitt?" He's got his eyes locked on me as though I'm the most entrancing girl on the planet.

"Are you going to keep calling her by her full name like that?" Ariel says.

His eyes still don't waver from mine. "Maybe. Depending on if Collins Pruitt likes it or not."

Blast my mouth, my smile is so big. Ariel and Anastasia are probably immune to this kind of blatant flirting, and they probably know exactly how to hold themselves together when others are there to witness it. But I do not have that kind of control. It's so *flattering*, not only that someone I find handsome would want to flirt with me in the first place but that he is doing it so openly, so publicly.

"What's your impression of Rutherford?" he says again, lowering his voice as though that makes the conversation qualify as being only between us.

I shrug. This seems like a better move than actually speaking.

"Some things will have to remain a mystery, I guess. For now. You're not off the hook yet, Collins Pruitt."

Theo tosses the ball at him to dismiss him. Sebastian takes the hint. He smiles and waves at us as he takes a few steps backward, watching us—watching me—before he turns and starts running toward the group he was playing catch with. He never makes it, though; Joyce intercepts him.

"Well, don't they look chummy," Anastasia says, nodding toward Sebastian and Joyce. Joyce, for whatever reason, is on her hit list this morning.

"Must be that killer bathing suit." Theo puts his hands up in surrender, already anticipating how this comment is going to annoy Anastasia.

"Did you hear her father was caught with a prostitute over the summer?" Anastasia says. "Her mother is divorcing him. Ruby told me, but it was, like, in the regular news, too. Her father's East Coast–famous."

"What happens to his company if this is what's in the news, I wonder," Theo says.

"He's ruined for life," Anastasia says.

"He'll probably have to appoint someone else as CEO, take a back seat for a while," I say.

"That's what your dad would do?" Theo asks. "For the companies he manages?"

I nod.

"Whatever," Anastasia says, "Joyce's mom is going to take him for all he's worth to keep that designer swimwear lifestyle. Joyce is out there laughing and flirting like nothing is wrong."

"Lay off her for a while, will you?" Theo says.

We watch as Sebastian and Joyce splash each other in the surf.

"Sebastian likes shiny objects, but he bores quickly," Anastasia says.

"He *is* a shiny object," Theo says. "You'd never go back for seconds?"

"Don't you mean *fourths*?" Anastasia says.

It takes me a moment to realize Anastasia and Theo are talking to Ariel, because Ariel doesn't answer right away. Like she's considering this.

Finally, she says, "I have zero interest in dating him ever again."

"You dated him three times?" I ask. "Like you were his girlfriend on three different occasions?"

"Why do you sound surprised?" Ariel says.

"I thought everyone was too busy studying to date," I say.

The three of them laugh.

"We date how anyone dates. I sneak around at Rutherford as much as I do at home," Ariel says.

"Ariel went out with Sebastian once when we were first years, once when we were second years, and the last time was over the summer," Anastasia explains to me.

"Why don't I remember the third time?" Theo says.

Anastasia puts her hand over his—they do this sometimes, like, by way of their hands touching, they are transferring knowledge.

53

"You were having your own romance with Roman at the same time. You were *muy ocupado*."

"Ah, Roman." Theo sighs. "Sad to leave that one."

"But long distance isn't really your style, and you're almost never in Spain." Anastasia and Theo nod at each other.

"She's not his type," Ariel says, still watching Sebastian and Joyce.

We all stare as he takes Joyce's hand and pulls her, Fendi swimsuit and all, farther out into the water, until they are in up to their belly buttons. Sebastian's hands are hidden under the water, but unmistakably, they are resting on Joyce's hips. Mr. Locke blows his whistle and signals for them to come back to shore, and I'm not sure if it's because of the placement of Sebastian's hands or because they went too far out in the water, something we've been warned not to do.

For the next hour, we're surrounded by people stopping by our towels to talk. Because of Theo, we're a social sun, everyone in his orbit. Anastasia loves it, Ariel tolerates it. The collection of people who come over to see Theo doesn't include his brother, so after a while, I'm annoyed by it. I secretly wish that Sebastian would make another visit. But he seems otherwise engaged with Joyce.

Jasper and his friends take a few breaks, but they mostly spend the day throwing around that football.

I watch as Stewart instructs Jasper and Daiki on where to run, and backs up as they take off, falling down in the sand as he throws the ball and Jasper and Daiki both race down the beach. Jasper is able to launch himself higher in the air and is the one to catch it. He holds the ball up, victorious.

"He's going to be sorry," Theo says. He was watching, too. "He hurt his ankle two years ago and his coach is always on him about not reinjuring it."

When Jasper stands up, he hops twice on his right foot, like he might've landed wrong on the other foot. He shakes it off and walks normally again, but Theo still says, "He needs to tape that if he's going to play in the game next week," and gets up to check on him.

"What a good brother," Anastasia says.

Stewart and Daiki walk toward him also. But when Stewart sees Theo, his eyes tick over to where Theo was running from. His gaze lands on Anastasia and, as I've witnessed a few times during dinner and in the hallways, it lingers.

"Does Stewart Laing always stare at you like that?" I say.

Their heads snap in Stewart's direction.

"Probably," Anastasia says.

"Seems right," Ariel adds.

"Have you ever gone out with him?"

"Not yet." Anastasia laughs. She shrugs. "He's cute and nice. But Theo isn't really a fan."

"I thought Theo liked everyone."

"He does," Ariel says. "He doesn't like him well enough for Anastasia to date him. Which makes me think Anastasia should absolutely date him."

Interesting. If Anastasia dated Stewart, it would give me an excuse to interact with Jasper.

"If you're into him, nothing should stop you," I say, adding, "He's really handsome."

"Stewart is pretty hot," Anastasia muses. *It's working. Behold the power of suggestion.* "His parents have three houses in Europe and two yachts," she adds—revealing maybe the real reason his odds are tipping in her favor. "He speaks several languages and sometimes it will randomly come out during conversation."

"Wow, impressive," I say—because I will encourage this however I can.

We look over at them, where Theo is down on the ground, inspecting Jasper's foot as Jasper seems to be shaking his head, telling him not to worry.

"Maybe we should see if he's okay."

"Oh, you'd like that, wouldn't you?" Anastasia smiles at me.

"You did your overview with Jasper, right?" Ariel says.

"Yes." The two of them exchange a glance. "What?" I say. It's peculiar how much it gets brought up—it was only an overview.

"We're not supposed to tell," Ariel says.

"Oh, come on," Anastasia says. "We can tell Collins. Besides, she should know. At least half of it."

"Theo's going to kill you."

"Tell me what?"

"The last time Jasper was in an overview, he hooked up," Ariel says quickly—like she's trying to beat Anastasia to it.

"Oh. Okay." I think of how cold he was with me during our overview; how completely uninterested he was in making our interaction anything more than transactional.

"I thought only fourth years could lead overviews." But maybe they make exceptions for Jasper and his advanced brain.

"That's why it's a secret," Anastasia says. "The girl he hooked up with was a fourth year, and he was a second year. And wait until you hear—"

"Are you serious, Anastasia?" Ariel cuts her off, shaking her head. She turns to me. "We were only curious if in your overview the student had become the master—or whatever that saying is."

This makes Anastasia and me burst out laughing.

Really, I don't know what to make of this information. Is the lesson here that Jasper prefers older girls or girls he deems to be smarter than he is?

Across the beach, Stewart and Daiki help Jasper up, and he walks beside Theo over to the chaperones' tent.

"We could ask Stewart how Jasper's doing," I say again, bringing the attention back to Anastasia, where she is most comfortable with it being anyway. Jasper seems fine, but Ariel must have the same idea as I do. She says, "Yeah, come on."

We stand and walk slowly, weaving to disguise the direct beeline we're making toward Stewart. But soon we're close enough that Stewart gets we're about to come up to him. He is not smooth about it. He grins. He elbows Daiki. He even steps to the side of Daiki, making room for us. Daiki smiles, and I forget what we're doing here in the first place. I forget my name and the color of the sky and what chocolate tastes like.

The five of us stand in a semicircle.

"He's going to be able to play in the game next week?" Anastasia asks, nodding toward Jasper.

"Looks like it," Stewart says. He runs his hand over his thick blond hair.

Nearby, I watch Jasper returning to a row of towels, where the three of them must've laid down their stuff when they arrived. He's walking normally, but holding a roll of medical tape. Theo's been sucked away by a group playing cornhole with inflatable boards. Daiki motions to Jasper, sitting on his towel wrapping his foot, and we casually walk over to him.

Theo's still holding court at the cornhole game, too busy to notice when we sit down with the boys.

Jasper's almost as quiet as I am as everyone continues to chat.

I'm learning that Jasper doesn't do anything for the sake of being polite, and that includes small talk. He doesn't laugh unless he really finds something funny, even if that means he stares blankly as everyone chuckles. He doesn't ask questions unless he truly doesn't understand something. Like, "Why are the swim meets so early?" And, "Why didn't you like having Mr. Hunan as your bio teacher?" He doesn't make much eye contact with anyone, but it doesn't seem like he intentionally wants to avoid us or that he's irritated or uncomfortable that we've joined them. Mostly, he seems like his mind is elsewhere.

It's not clear when Theo's noticed we're sitting with Stewart, Daiki, and Jasper, but I guess he lets his opinion about the obvious flirtation between Stewart and Anastasia be known in other ways. For one, he doesn't stop to see us despite walking past several times. And when he does approach us, it's to bring the towels and bags we've abandoned on the other side of the beach. He drops them at Anastasia's feet.

"It's almost time to leave," he says.

Anastasia starts to protest, but the chaperones begin blowing their whistles, motioning for us to leave.

Stewart offers to carry Anastasia's towel since it doesn't fit in her bag.

"I've got it," Theo says, casually grabbing her towel and throwing it over his shoulders.

Everyone from the beach slogs along the trail together to get back to Rutherford's campus, keeping a tiresome pace thanks to the large group and the bottlenecking that occurs at the narrow and steep parts in the trail.

Theo surprises me. He's done with the subtle hints that he might be irritated Anastasia joined Stewart at the beach. He's downright cheerful. He teases Anastasia like nothing is wrong. He jokes with Stewart the way he jokes with everyone else. Theo the chameleon, blending in however will make him the most popular, whatever pleases the crowd. No matter how he's really feeling.

Eight

That night, we emerge from the bathroom, our high heels tapping against the hardwood, the usual scent of lavender replaced with the smell of perfume. Burberry Brit and Marc Jacobs Daisy and Kate Spade Walk on Air and Chanel Chance. Our collarbones are showing, our shoulders are bare. Our hair is curled. Our fingers hold sparkly rings. Thin bracelets slide down our wrists. Our ears are decorated in pearls or diamonds or gold hoops. Our eyelashes are faux, our nails are painted, our lips are stained and glossed. Our dresses still hit at our knees—this is the one unbreakable dress code rule, it would seem—but they are not made of wool or cotton. We are covered in marbled velvet, Paris chiffon, silk georgette, French crêpe light, duchess satin.

We crowd the courtyard, merging with the boys as they walk up from their dormitory. They are suited in dark jackets and colorful ties, and their hair is styled instead of just combed. They smell like sandalwood and black pepper and sweet myrrh. Their shoes are polished.

Rosie said that falling in love has little to do with looks. But this certainly can't hurt.

Elena and I laugh about our high heels sinking into the grass on the walk to campus, and upon meeting up with her other friends, we make wagers on what kind of chicken they'll be serving tonight, between rosemary or lemon and pepper or piccata, and on how many times tonight's guest speaker will refer to her tenure at Rutherford or casually drop the current net worth of her business. The losers have to wear their shirts inside out on Tuesday and see how long it takes before someone on faculty makes them change.

I spot Anastasia and Ariel a statue away. They're easy to find because Theo is easy to find. The crowd pulses off him. I break away from Elena and her friends even though they had me laughing so hard I had to touch up my eye makeup.

"Stunning," Theo says when I approach. He kisses my hand like I'm royalty.

"You look handsome, as always," I say.

"I'm starving," whines Anastasia. She looks around as though she's hoping to see the cafeteria doors opening to welcome us in. But I know what she's really doing. She's looking for Stewart.

Anastasia has her hip popped slightly, and she is suddenly less fidgety, which can only mean one thing. I scan the crowd until I see them making their way through the courtyard. Stewart and Jasper and Daiki.

Our timing is off, though, because the very moment Stewart notices Anastasia and waves, the cafeteria doors open, and the faculty signals for us to move inside, where we will be seated according to class year for dinner.

The cafeteria is dimly lit this evening. More chairs have been brought in, and the tables are covered in maroon tablecloths and centerpieces with large white flowers. After a brief speech by the headmaster welcoming us to the evening's program, dinner is served. A lovely chicken piccata.

I try to find Elena and her friends to see their reactions and finally am able to follow the sound of hushed excitement and moans of disappointment coming from a few tables away. I watch as those who chose chicken piccata high-five each other. None of them are looking around the room for me to see my reaction.

When dinner is over, we're ushered back to the courtyard for the ice-cream social portion of the evening. Twinkly lights have been set up even though the sky is barely dimming, and a string quartet plays quietly in the corner. Stewart and Anastasia find each other like magnets. She wanders off to refill her punch and grab a macaroon, and the next thing you know, she's bumped into Stewart, Jasper, and Daiki and is enthralled in what I can only assume is some serious flirting from the looks of it. Lots of tossing her hair and smiling, her eyes zoned in on Stewart as if she might be immune to Daiki's general hotness, which is in full effect tonight, believe me.

Ariel and I exchange a look and walk over to them. Theo sees that it's either join us or entertain the water polo second years, who are calling to him with questions about a goal he scored at last week's match, and he tags along, too. His first order of business is to mess up his brother's hair, loosening Jasper's curls from where they were combed away from his face and letting them tumble forward. It only improves his appearance, in my opinion.

"Trying a new look?" Theo says, shaking his head. Jasper makes a quick attempt to push his hair back to how it was, but when it's clear it's going to be useless, he gives up. He pops his jaw in annoyance.

"Remember what happened at the Labor Day event last year?" Stewart says. This makes everyone smile, even Jasper.

Theo starts to tell me the story. "Dr. Gibson fell asleep while they were introducing him, and when they tried to wake him, he said—"

Stewart cuts him off to give an impression of Dr. Gibson using a croaked, grouchy voice. *"Leave me be, Gertrude!"*

We laugh.

"Who's Dr. Gibson?"

"Only one of the engineers whose contributions to NASA allowed for modern space travel," Jasper says with a hint of amusement, like he can't believe I didn't know this.

It was the wrong question. *Shoot.* I should've pretended like I knew and looked it up later.

The quartet stops playing, and Mrs. Flory announces that it's time for the program to start.

"Please make your way to the auditorium for 'An Evening with a Brilliant Mind,' featuring one of our very own, a recent Rutherford graduate, Rob James."

A wave of students plows down the path to the auditorium. I'm certain there wasn't this kind of rush and excitement for Dr. Gibson. Rob James is a different story. Possibly the most exciting thing to happen to Rutherford alumni since one of their pole-vaulters competed in the Olympics and took the silver medal.

"I wonder if she'll be wearing those gold shoes," Anastasia says as we curve past the west campus tower.

"She always wears them," Ariel says. A well-known fact. For public appearances, Rob James is always in a white suit with gold jewelry and gold pumps.

Rob James graduated from Rutherford only three years ago. Her name is actually Roberta Jane Witherby, but for as long as she's been making waves in the business world and headlines in the regular world, she's been going by Rob James.

"I hear she takes a shot of wheatgrass before every speech, and sometimes you can see it in her teeth," Ariel says.

"How close to her do you think you're going to be? Not close enough to see wheatgrass clinging to her teeth." Theo shakes his head.

The big deal about Rob James isn't that she changed her name or that she graduated valedictorian from Rutherford. Rob is only twenty, and she's already invented a device that's supposed to revolutionize how people take intravenous medicine. It's an implant that can alter the rate at which your body absorbs the medicine by detecting your temperature and DNA coding and distributing the medicine accordingly—essentially tailoring the intake to a person-by-person basis, since medicine reacts differently depending on a person's DNA and therefore needs to be administered differently. Her company is called Robames Inc. It earned a substantial backing from investors—my father included—during its R&D stages, but after taking the products to the market, is currently worth over $5 billion. That's *billion* with a *B*.

"I heard from the girls who graduated with her that she used to wash her hair with rose water because she wanted to smell like roses," Anastasia says. Stewart nods like this is something that actually interests him very much.

"I thought she smelled like the tears of Bruce Flannery and Elouise Jerkins." Theo leans toward me. "Those were the people she beat for valedictorian."

"I imagine now she smells exclusively of money," says Ariel.

"Money and arrogance," Jasper adds. An interesting comment considering he interned at Robames over the summer.

I'm the only one of Anastasia's friends who hasn't said something about Rob James. I have to remind her of why I'm here, why she likes having me around.

"I hear her company might be in trouble," I say.

"No bueno. What kind of trouble?" Stewart says.

"Did your dad tell you this?" Anastasia is enthralled. "He's a Robames investor, isn't he?"

"So are our parents," says Theo.

"And mine," Stewart says. "My grandparents, too."

"Literally everyone and their mom," Ariel says.

"She hit Rutherford alumni up for money hard, and she knocked it out of the park," Anastasia says. "But why do you think her company is in trouble, Collins?"

Here we go. "There's an investigation. Company documents were subpoenaed."

"An investigation for what?" Ariel asks.

"I don't know. I only remember my dad saying certain documents had to be turned over."

"Doesn't this kind of thing happen all the time to new, innovative companies?" Stewart says.

"That sounds like something your parents must be telling themselves so they can sleep at night," Ariel says.

The problem is Stewart's right. When my dad was bemoaning about the subpoenas, he did so with a sigh and a roll of his eyes. Business as usual; nothing strange about this hiccup, a typical annoyance. But it makes my story much less juicy, much less valuable to Anastasia.

"Maybe," is how I respond.

The path widens and steepens as we approach the auditorium. A girl a few feet ahead of us trips. We take note and slow down. Walking in heels at this gradation over a path made bumpy by overgrown roots is no joke. Theo loops his arm around Anastasia at the same time that Stewart extends his arm to offer her assistance. Ariel takes it, so his gesture doesn't get rejected completely. Daiki, a damn hero, notices a girl a few feet ahead of us struggling and helps her down the path. Jasper and I look at each other at the same time. Since he's closest to me, he offers me his arm; being polite, I suppose.

Jasper clears his throat in a way that startles me. I notice his forehead is sort of damp. His eyes jump nervously from the ground to his friends to directly in front of him. Jasper doesn't like a damsel in academic distress, but maybe he likes one in high-heel distress wearing a strapless dress and smelling like amber and vanilla. Maybe he knows I like him, that I've been staring at him and publicly calling him *mysterious,* and that's what's making him nervous. *This* is why Stewart and Anastasia need to continue their courtship and provide us with an excuse to be around each other. Look at the possibilities already.

Ariel says, "I hate heels. Sure, they're pretty, but they're completely useless unless you need to stab someone in the eye."

"Damn," Stewart says, chuckling. He's not used to Ariel's comments the way Theo and Anastasia are, who nodded along as she spoke.

"I'm definitely finding her if the apocalypse strikes," Daiki says to Jasper and me.

"Same, too," I reply. In the split-second decision on whether to say *same* or *me, too,* this is what my brain came up with thanks to Daiki and his jaw-dropping face. He's a gentleman, so he pretends he didn't hear me, but Jasper raises his eyebrow at me as we join the crowd getting swallowed by the auditorium for this evening's program.

Nine

We file into the auditorium. It's the most modern building on campus aside from the athletic facilities, which get updated practically every year. The rows are stacked, and the seats are a deep red to match the traditional curtains.

I end up sitting next to Jasper and Ariel. Stewart and Anastasia are beside each other with Theo on Anastasia's other side and Daiki beside him.

As I watch the rest of the student body enter, I spot Sebastian, who is walking down the aisle to his seat with his hand resting lightly on Joyce's back.

I hear Ariel sigh beside me and wonder if she was watching him, too. I don't ask her.

The lights flash, signaling us to be quiet. The Rutherford event coordinator, Mrs. Brevard, walks across the stage. She introduces Rob James to the crowd, giving a nod to her amazing grades, her inventive thinking, the dedication she put into seeing through the development of her idea, and, because this is Rutherford, after all, a place where money matters, she talks about the net worth of Robames. A real achievement, she says.

"We'll see, though," Anastasia whispers to me, and I'm pleased that she seems to be up and running with this bit of gossip I've provided. Even if it's not that juicy at all.

We clap enthusiastically as the auditorium gets dark and a single spotlight appears. When Rob James steps into the light, the room erupts. A much bigger hit than last year, I suspect. Everyone stands except for Jasper, who seems to have the attitude that this whole ordeal is a waste of his time. Theo yanks him up by the elbow, and in the end, he is clapping along with everyone else as Rob James takes her time waving and walking to the center of the stage.

She is in her usual white and gold, but her hair, usually swept up in a loose ponytail for her appearances, is down and slightly wavy. It's the way her hair was in her Rutherford senior photo, something splashed around the media, and also included in tonight's program. I wonder if this is for us, her hairstyle tailored for her specific audience as much as her speech.

"How's it going out there, Rutherford?" she asks. Her microphone is hands-free, so she's able to wave and point to the crowd with both her hands. She waits as we clap again. "I have to tell you, it's so strange being back here. I'd always dreamed I'd get to return like this—with knowledge and wisdom and experience to share."

Next to me, Jasper scoffs. "She's been out for barely three years. So much knowledge and experience, I'm sure."

"Shut up," Theo whispers.

"The ability to innovate is within everyone. All of us can do it. We only need to harness the energy; find the bravery to believe in ourselves and the strength and perseverance to let others believe in us, too."

She launches into the story of how the idea for the Roba-Fix came to her the first week of college, during a walk through the Yale campus in the middle of the night when she was taking a study break and getting fresh air. She tells us she knew she had something special and, despite not getting any support or encouragement from her peers and being told by many of her professors that she was too young and that she was wasting her time, she worked hard to develop a conceptual model and business plan.

"You can't count on anyone to believe in you except *you*," she says. "And *you* is all you need."

Jasper gives another sigh for the ages.

When Rob James is done with her speech, she gets a standing ovation. She announces, "Everyone will be getting an early copy of my book, *The Inventor Inside You,* out next week," and gets even more cheers.

The lobby and the front patio outside the auditorium have been transformed for another social hour. The entire area is decorated in gold and white—white linens over the cocktail tables, gold vases with white roses as centerpieces, white and gold balloons hanging off the railings. We're served sparkling cider in champagne saucers and sugar cookies and cupcakes with white frosting and gold sprinkles.

We're all excited about being gifted her book and even more excited when we're told she'll be mingling at the social hour and will be happy to sign our copies. Jasper positions us at the table in the lobby that's farthest away from everyone, practically around the corner from the event. No one argues about being this far off from the action, so to speak, but when we see Rob James has started making the rounds, no one wants to risk missing the chance to get her autograph, and all of us abandon Jasper and our cider and cookies at the no-man's-land table to approach her.

It's true, she does smell like roses. She uses a gold Sharpie to write *You are limitless* into our books as she signs her name with a loopy signature. Rob James takes the time to make sure she spells our names right and looks directly into our eyes when we tell her we liked her speech. Up close, I can see how much foundation she has on and the few flakes from her mascara that have fallen onto her cheeks. Evidence of her humanness. It makes me like her even more.

There's a buzzing in the air reflective of how thrilled everyone is that she's here. They're inspired, too. I know I am. Even if I don't have any big ideas like she does—yet. Her speech was about determination and believing in yourself and working hard. I get the hype. Her brilliant invention aside, I understand why so many people were ready to put money behind her, backing what she's doing now with the Roba-Fix and all the things she's sure to accomplish in the future. I see exactly what made my dad choose her as a good risk, what made him refer to Robames as a "sound decision," even when it was in its earliest stages.

As the evening winds down, Anastasia, Ariel, Theo, Stewart, Daiki, and I make our way back to our corner table where we left Jasper and our food. Jasper's not at the table. He's a few feet away, near the curve in the auditorium wall, talking reluctantly with Mr. Reis. Rob James approaches them from the opposite side, as though she must've stepped out for a moment and returned using a less public door. Mrs. Juniper also walks over to them; she greets Rob James, then pulls Mr. Reis to the side to tell him something. For those few seconds, it's only Rob James and Jasper. She leans forward. She speaks quickly. Her eyes are wide and alive. He nods as she talks, hardly looking at her at first. But soon his eyes are locked on hers. She places a hand on his shoulder, and he jerks away from her in such a sudden movement that her bodyguard takes a few steps toward them. Mr. Reis and Mrs. Juniper are in a tizzy, for having not witnessed what's happened but being completely aware that *something* has. Jasper walks away, right toward us, his back to the scene as if that will make him invisible and he'll get out of any consequences that might come down on someone for being so rude and abrasive toward a guest speaker.

"What the hell?" Theo says to him, grabbing him by the arm and steering him in closer to us, like our group can shield him, too. "You need to be careful," Theo tells him quietly.

Jasper is shaking his head when Mr. Reis approaches. "Jasper, can I see you for a moment?"

We watch as Mr. Reis steers Jasper away and chastises him. Rob James steps toward them shaking her head, smiling that smile of hers. Soon enough, they are all smiling; Jasper's smile is very clearly coerced.

Theo breathes out in relief. Stewart and Daiki exchange a look. Jasper is dismissed and returns to us with his head down, his hands in his pockets.

"That's the kind of asinine behavior that could get you expelled," Theo says.

Jasper shakes his head. "I won't be kicked out of Rutherford."

The music cuts out, and Mrs. Juniper announces that it's time for us to return to our dorms.

On our way back, when we reach the hill, I take Jasper's arm. He wasn't expecting it, but he doesn't pull away; he shifts so that I can get a better grip. Stewart notices us and this time manages to give Anastasia his arm before Theo. Daiki is at it again being the hero, a new girl on his arm for support up the hill. Ariel jumps ungracefully on Theo's back, and he carries her through the crowd for a few seconds, as long as he can manage before one of the facility tells them to knock it off. I slow my pace, and Jasper matches it. Soon enough the others are ahead of us.

"What happened back there? With you and Rob James?" I keep my voice low.

Jasper is quiet for so long I don't think he's going to answer. For a second, I wonder if it was too bold for me to ask about that and if, instead of letting me discover more about him, it'll push him even further away from me.

"Anastasia didn't tell you?" he says, his voice lighter than expected.

"Tell me what?"

"Theo might be the eyes and the ears of Rutherford, but Anastasia is the mouth."

He looks over my expression like he's trying to see if I'm being honest about not knowing. His skepticism is intriguing. But then it clicks in my mind, all at once.

"It's Rob, isn't it?" I blurt out. The way she touched him as she approached him, the way her lips moved so fast like she had a lot to say, the way her eyes got big and round; the way he was comfortable enough to jerk away from her. "She's the girl you had your overview with."

"So Anastasia did tell you."

"Just about the hookup during your overview, not about who it was with. Things didn't seem . . . *pleasant* between the two of you." *They seemed complicated.* "It seems like you hate her."

"Would you believe it's nothing but a good old-fashioned problem with authority?"

"Sure." But I shake my head. This makes him smile a little. "It didn't end well?" *Or did you react like that because you still like her?* Rosie never told me what to do if the boy in question was unwilling and unable to fall in love with you because he was already in love with someone else.

He takes his time. "Not really."

I have a lot of questions. But I can feel him closing off, sealing himself up. He rubs his eyes like the evening has exhausted him.

Rob James is the exact kind of person I'd think would be kryptonite to Jasper.

"I won't say anything," I tell him. Still trying to keep some semblance of trust between us.

"Thanks," he says. I'm not sure he believes me.

This is the first true secret I've learned at Rutherford. Something real and hidden about Jasper Mahoney. There's a bit of a scandal here. But the reveal of a young founder and CEO who hired her intern because she'd been secretly hooking up with him probably wouldn't result in any repercussions for Jasper. Or any shame. He might even be lauded a hero, while she would be seen as unfair. And these are only rumors, without proof. Would Mrs. Mahoney care about protecting this? I don't think so. It's not enough. It's not like Theo's secret, that's ripe for unraveling. Something that's already been covered up.

When I've got a grip on both of them—on Theo's past, which can be used as a threat, and on Jasper's heart, an asset when I have the power to break it—they will be vulnerable for different reasons.

And there'll be only one person who can save them.

Ten

"I know about Jasper and Rob James," I announce to Anastasia and Ariel a few days later as we're making our way back to the girls' dormitory, when we're far enough removed from others that the two of them might speak more freely about this topic.

"He told you?" Anastasia is floored.

"I figured it out. He made it pretty obvious with the way he was acting toward her after her speech. So I asked him, and he confirmed."

The reason I'm bringing this up now with them, instead of right after he confessed after the event, is because after much contemplation, I've decided that the best way to get information from Anastasia is to be direct, and I have a few pressing, unanswered questions about Rob and Jasper.

"Crazy, right? But Theo will kill you if you say anything. It's not a good look for Rob. Or for Jasper—not even with those curls and that bone structure," Anastasia says. "It's like nepotism or . . . what's the word?"

"Favoritism," says Ariel.

"Whatever it's called, it's got to be completely illegal," Anastasia says. "Everyone thinks he got the internship for being smart and winning that quiz competition." Ariel opens her mouth like she's going to correct *quiz competition* and tell her it's actually called a *decathlon,* then decides it's not worth the energy. "But I think it's really because they wanted to be together, and there was no other excuse for him to spend the summer in Connecticut than if he had a job at Robames headquarters."

"Were they, like, a couple?"

"They were off and on, never public about it. Maybe it was just about hooking up, maybe it was more," Anastasia says. "If Theo knew, he wasn't very forthcoming about it. He's naturally protective of Jasper. It's so sweet and so annoying."

"Does Stewart ever talk about it?" I ask.

We haven't started eating dinner with Stewart like I'd hoped we'd start doing. But I caught Anastasia texting with him after field hockey, and after class today, we ran into him and Jasper in the halls and talked to them for at least two seconds before the bell rang. It's slow progress, but I guess it's still progress.

"I don't talk to Stewart about it! Seriously, Collins, it's supposed to be a secret. Now that you know, you can't go around telling people."

"Do you think he still likes her? Why was he so rude to her at the event?"

"Oh, he *hates* her now, for sure," Anastasia says. "According to Theo, Jasper even came home early from the internship. Whatever happened while he was there was the final knife in whatever they had going on for the past couple of years." She smiles and pats my shoulder. "Your crush on Jasper is so cute. I dig it. Even if I don't understand why you'd want to bother with boring, intense Jasper."

"Thanks." Seems like the appropriate response. I also think she's placating me. Like when Theo told me Jasper hated people and it sounded like a warning. My crush is *cute* because they don't think I have a chance with him. They don't think Jasper would want me when his type is superhuman Rob James.

The thing they don't know about me is this: I like proving people wrong.

There's no denying that Rosie's tricks work, and Jasper is not going to be the exception. I'd wanted her techniques to work on Lucius Castle. I'd wanted to make him fall in love with me. He was in my grade at St. Paul's, and no matter how much I complimented his car or told him I found the songs his band played at a coffee shop downtown every Wednesday night to be brilliant—and even recognized that the song called "Little Rainy Day" was about the afternoon he forgot to put the top on his convertible and it rained he didn't feel the same way I did. Not even a little bit. He took Carly Gomez to prom, and I got the *I like you so much as a friend* spiel.

Instead, my friend Pauly Mason fell in love with me. I mean, he never used the *L* word, and he was right not to since his feelings for me were entirely unrequited. I'd known Pauly since we were five and Mimi sold her goats' milk to his mother, who owned an organic restaurant. Pauly was older by a year and good-looking, I guess. He was responsible and funny and kind. Pauly, like so many of us, felt lost. Lost for Pauly meant not knowing if he should live with his mom or his dad when he was old enough to have a say in his own custody and, most recently, being unsure if he wanted to leave the state for college and go to Ohio, where he'd received a scholarship, or stay close to be near his much younger half sisters. I could see it plain as day how Pauly would land on his feet whatever he decided. If he left, he wouldn't disappear from his sisters' lives; he'd call and video chat, and he could send birthday presents. If he stayed, he'd make the most of wherever he went. Either way, he was going to be great, and never lonely. He was easy to talk to and fun to be around, and he'd make friends fast.

Right after he graduated, he tried to kiss me. He was polite about it, taking a moment to place a hand on my shoulder, leaning in slowly, saying, "Collins, this is why I like you." In that instance, he was referring to some joke I'd made about the drones that swarmed the stadium to take panoramic views of his commencement ceremony. But I knew what had really happened. It was not the joke or my sparkling personality or the way I looked. He'd fallen in love with how I saw him. As someone thoughtful and good, who would be happy and successful and fulfilled no matter what future he chose. It was exactly like Rosie had said. I quieted his worst fears about himself because I believed in him. I looked at him in that moment before he went in for a kiss, his soft expression, the way he leaned toward me, and knew I could've taken anything from him that I wanted. Twenty dollars or a date to prom or the next five years.

Eleven

"Collins, follow my lead," Theo says to me in a low voice one evening in the upperclassman common room where I'd been sitting
next to Anastasia and Ariel, waiting to see what kind of excuse
Stewart would come up with to migrate over to Anastasia, something he does often. Waiting to see if Jasper would appear at all.

"What—?"

"You can ask questions later," Ariel says.

Anastasia gives me a large smile until Theo and Ariel glare at
her and she purses her lips to cover it.

"The correct response to anything I say from here on out is a
simple nod," Theo says.

I give him what he wants, and instead of looking relieved, he
sighs.

"Follow me," he says. "But don't *act* like you're following me."

I keep quiet the many, many questions I have about this; I nod.

Theo gets up. I do the same. Theo rounds the front of the couch
to leave, and I round the back. He crosses the rows of couches to
exit out the side door, so I cut through the clusters of tables.

Once we're out in the dim hallway, Theo walks toward the
bathrooms. I do the same. But before he reaches the restrooms,
he makes a sharp turn. When I walk past, he's unlocking the door
and holding it open for me. It's labeled *Storage*. As I enter the dark

room, Theo turns on a dull light that fills the room with shadows, but it allows us to at least see a few feet in front of us. He walks past four tall shelves until we reach the far corner. From there, he pulls a cardboard box from the highest shelf.

"Did you bring the earrings? Like Anastasia told you to?"

"Yes, but—"

Theo gestures for them impatiently as I reach into the pocket of my sweatshirt and pull out the two diamond studs my father bought me for my thirteenth birthday.

"I thought she wanted to borrow them."

"Oh no," he says. "She doesn't want to borrow them. She wants to win them."

"Win them?" I hold them away from him. "Will you tell me what's going on?"

"It's better if you dive in headfirst. It'll sound like a bad idea, but really, it's not. You have to allow yourself to get addicted."

"Theo—what? Can't you just tell me what's going on?"

"That's not how it's usually done. You go in blindly or not at all." He reaches into his own pocket and pulls out a gold watch. He tosses it in. "Trust me?"

I peer into the box. There are a few other watches. A few impressive rings and pendant necklaces. A yellow bottle of prescription drugs and a Dior wallet. A pair of Gucci sunglasses. A roll of foreign cash. A bag of weed.

"Fine." I set the velvet satchel containing my earrings into the box next to the sunglasses.

Theo smiles. "You won't be sorry. Or maybe you will be."

We hear the ticking of the door opening. A cascade of light comes into the room from the hallway.

"Get down!" Theo whispers, and we huddle to the floor.

The door shuts, and we listen as footsteps meander to the exact spot in the corner where Theo and I are hiding.

"Damn it, Sebastian," Theo says, standing up. I follow his lead and rise also. "This was *our* time slot." He motions to both of us. "You weren't supposed to leave yet."

"So I lost track of time." He shrugs. His hands are in his pockets like he isn't fazed at all. He looks me up and down in that way that I find insatiably flattering. "Hey, Collins Pruitt. You're playing, too?"

"Yeah," I say.

"We have to get out of here," Theo says.

"Jetting already?" Sebastian says.

"Per his sparkling reputation, if anyone from faculty notices Sebastian is gone, they immediately suspect something is wrong and go on a hunt," Theo explains to me, talking about Sebastian right in front of him.

"At this point, I'm pretty good at sneaking around," Sebastian says. "You don't have to worry."

This reassurance only makes Theo panic more. "We have to *go*."

"If you insist," Sebastian says. "Hate to see you go, but love to watch you leave." He looks at me as he says this. I don't know if it's the way the lighting in here cuts shadows across his jaw or if the smell of cleaning supplies is getting to me, but Sebastian is dreamy as ever. He's flirting. With *me*. Even in this high-stress situation while Theo is glowering at him.

Theo grabs my hand and spins me around.

"Pull yourself together," he mutters.

We hear the door again. This time, it's the clicking of the knob trying to turn against a locked door.

"Shit," Theo whispers.

"Don't worry, Collins Pruitt. The locks have been changed, and faculty can't get in here."

"And if faculty realizes the locks have been changed on them, then what?" Theo snaps.

"Oh, right," Sebastian sighs.

"This is your fault," Theo barks at him. "You have to sacrifice yourself."

"Fine," Sebastian says. He doesn't move as the door handle jiggles again.

"What are you waiting for?" Theo nudges him toward the exit.

"They aren't going to believe I'm in here alone."

"*Shit.*"

"And given my track record, they aren't going to believe I'm in here with you."

Theo sighs again. They're both looking at me.

"What's going on?" I protest.

"That's perfect," Theo says, turning to Sebastian. "She has no information to spill." *If he only knew.* He looks to me and grips my hand in his. "Listen to me, Collins—you're new here, and your father is *the* Jacob Pruitt; you're going to be fine. But if you say anything about what we did in here just now, you will spend the rest of your time at Rutherford regretting it. Got it?" He doesn't wait for me to answer. The doorknob has started to rattle again. "*GO.*" Theo pushes us in the direction of the door and rushes around the corner. Sebastian turns off the light as he opens the door.

Dr. Libby is standing on the other side with his hands on his hips.

"Mr. Guerrero, what a surprise." He sighs. "Miss Pruitt." He looks at me with disappointed eyes. "Come with me."

We follow him down the hallway. While we're walking, I glance at Sebastian. He winks at me.

Dr. Libby escorts us into his office, and we sit in the brown leather chairs across from his desk.

"Would either of you like to tell me what you were doing in the storage closet?" he says.

"Nothing," Sebastian says. "These days, I get away with *nothing*—you know this, Dr. Libby."

Dr. Libby squints at him. His glasses slide down his long nose. After a moment, he takes the time to push them up.

"Miss Pruitt?" he says.

"It was nothing," I blurt out. My hands are shaking, so I fold them in my lap.

"No funny business?" he says.

"None," I say. My face gets hot imagining what he's assuming. The things he thinks Sebastian and I might've been doing in that dark, isolated room.

"We're very, very sorry," Sebastian says. He gestures with exaggerated movements with his right hand as he talks. "It won't happen again. It was a momentary lapse in judgment, and you found us before anything started to get *funny*. I don't want you to overreact here. And I certainly don't want any stigma or unfair consequences to fall on Collins Pruitt her first year at our wonderful, exceptional school." He does an overexaggerated chin scratch, when I notice the large gold ring on his pointer finger. The reason for his hand motions. Something he wanted Dr. Libby to see. "You know what I'm saying, Dr. Libby?" he taps his finger against his lips, the light glinting off the ring.

Dr. Libby glances downward in a way that makes me think he wants to smile but doesn't want us to see.

"Far be it from me to mess with tradition," he says. He clears his throat. "So in keeping with the Rutherford tradition of reprimanding students for breaking the rules, the two of you are not permitted to attend the next five social nights."

I gasp, and I know I should be thankful that this is all that's happening to us, but this sound comes from my genuine feelings because the truth is, I love those nights in the upperclassman common room, with no one ever pretending they're lame, being rounded up with caffeine-free sodas and healthy snacks, expected to play games and have deep discussions on couches, with no television and low background music we didn't have control over. There's something earned about them that makes them delicious. Rutherford's schedule is no joke. Every second of our time is accounted for from the second we wake up to the moment bed checks are completed. Our days are full of classes and office hours and study sessions and club meetings and sports. And I love every second of it. Even the hardness of it, how the field hockey adrenaline rush I get is intense and all that time in the classroom and studying, the constant stream of information that is both tiresome and exhilarating. Not to mention it provides the potential for interacting with Jasper.

"I'm sorry, Miss Pruitt, but those are the consequences," Dr. Libby says.

"I understand."

He walks behind us as we leave his office. He waits by the doorway of the upperclassman common room as we gather our things. Theo, Anastasia, and Ariel are sitting at a large round table playing cards with Stewart and Daiki and a few others. Jasper is seated there, too, and though he's hanging back with his legs outstretched reading a book, I do notice cards in his hand. He looks up when he sees me, and I watch his eyes tick back and forth between me and Sebastian. The whole room starts to take notice; subtle stares at Sebastian and me, knowing glances exchanged between people after they clock that we're both being escorted away by Dr. Libby. I can feel all their eyes on me, actually. When I look to Sebastian to see if he notices it, too, he gives me a small smile, a light shrug. And then he lets his eyes linger on me as he picks up his jacket hanging off an arm of the couch.

I'm aware of the rest of their stares as I pull on my coat and grab my purse. Unwanted attention—or maybe I do want it. Maybe, in fact, I kind of like it. Are they jealous? Do they think I'm naïve for being caught with him? Or is this the kind of admiration that's contagious? People noticed the way he looked at me and think there's something to see. He's captivated with me, so I must be captivating.

Jasper looks up from his book one more time. Right at me. He doesn't seem irritated. Just curious. Like the rest of them.

Sebastian wasn't part of the plan to get to Jasper. But maybe he could be.

I've gathered my things and wait for Sebastian by the door next to Dr. Libby so he can escort us back to the dormitories. I watch as Sebastian moves past Joyce, who is also at the table with Theo and Anastasia. He pats her on the shoulder, and her hand comes down over his, giving his a tight squeeze. They stare at each other for a second; something unsaid between them. It's brief, but still obvious and unguarded.

"Mr. Guerrero, please hustle," Dr. Libby calls from the doorway.

It sort of bothers me that he did that—and it humiliates me at the same time, because everyone saw the *look* between him and Joyce, too—that special gesture just for her. Was he reassuring her that whatever happened between us that we're getting in trouble for was nothing? Like he can be brazen and flirt with me and still only care what she thinks.

But then when we reach the place in the path where he's to go right and I'm to go left, he raises his hand and waves obnoxiously.

"Good night, Collins Pruitt. Sleep tight. Don't let the bedbugs bite. Dream a little dream of me."

"That's enough, Sebastian," Dr. Libby says.

Sebastian waves once more. A big, overstated gesture. This

time, I get it. The ring on his hand is gone. He winks at me, and I smile so he'll know I saw it. Even if I don't know what it means. Looking back now, I think Joyce must've been the one to take it from him—to steal it away to be placed in that box for whatever game I've unknowingly entered into.

Twelve

Theo, Anastasia, and Ariel don't talk to me about what happened in the storage room. I know better than to bring it up.

I don't hear about the *game* or my earrings again until several days later, when I'm studying next to Anastasia in the third-year girls' lounge, and she passes me a piece of paper that says, *Meet me in the bathroom at 1:00 a.m.* She and Ariel stare at me like they're waiting for something. I take my pen and write, *OK*.

They look at each other. Anastasia writes, *Wear shoes and bring a coat and take out your retainer.* They wait again, and again, I write, *OK*. Then Ariel grabs the paper and rips it up into very small pieces.

That night, I set my phone alarm to vibrate and nestle it under my pillow as I lie in bed. I'm sure I'll be too anxious to sleep, but between the drills at field hockey practice and studying, it's the same as it is every day, and I'm unconscious the second my head hits my pillow.

At five minutes to 1:00 a.m., I'm jolted awake by the tremors of my alarm. I slide out of bed and put on my boots; I grab my jacket. I walk quietly down the hall and into the bathroom at the end of the corridor. Anastasia and Ariel are waiting for me, long sweaters and puffy coats covering their pajamas.

"Are you ready, Collins?" Anastasia says, smiling at me.

"Ready for what?"

Ariel says, "Just nod."

"Let's go," Anastasia says.

We take the stairs, our shoes padding the cool tiles. As we reach the main level, where the dorm faculty stays, I whisper, "Won't they hear us?"

"It's fine," Anastasia says, her voice low and quiet. "This is Thursday night when the faculty all go to Mrs. Wiggins's house to watch *Love Match at Paradise Hotel*. They all go and have too much wine and will sleep through anything."

I'm not entirely confident in this theory, but I follow them past the rooms of sleeping faculty, through a door at the end of the hallway near an emergency exit that's unmarked. It creaks as we open and close it when we step through. We all use the flashlights on our phones to descend a narrow staircase with no railing. I notice as we reach the bottom of the stairs that I don't have any service. We turn down a hallway that is first as tapered as the staircase, but as we walk, it gets wider and wider. The floors are paved, and the walls are tiled like a subway with matte-gray tiles. The grout is stark white—either perfectly preserved or this underground tunnel has been remodeled. I think of Sebastian flashing the gold ring in Dr. Libby's office, the emphasis Dr. Libby placed on tradition when he gave us our punishment, and wonder if we're getting away with anything at all. Or if these Rutherford secrets are somehow respected and anticipated by those who run things here.

The corridor continues to widen until we reach a circular area. We can hear others approaching on the opposite side—voices and scuffling. Boys coming from the other end. It's Theo and Sebastian with Stewart and a fourth year named Randal Law, who plays water polo with Theo. Stewart holds the light streaming from his phone flashlight as Theo opens a metal compartment in the wall. He pulls on a lever, and the circular area connecting the tunnels between the boys' and girls' dormitories lights up. Above us is a chandelier. A fancy one with a metal circle holding candles with light bulbs for wicks.

"Pretty wild, right, Collins Pruitt?" Sebastian is wearing red plaid pajamas under a bright yellow ski jacket and a lively smile.

"Where are we?" I say.

"The room that connects the tunnels," Stewart says. Unhelpfully.

"We don't know what these were used for," Sebastian says. "Maybe originally they were meant for shelter from war or something. Or secret society meetings. Or for middle-of-the-night sneak-outs between the two dormitories." His eyes linger too hard and too long on me when he says this, as his lips turn up into a lopsided smile.

I glance away when I notice Stewart and Anastasia talking. He tugs on the strings of her jacket, and she pets the velvet along the collar of his robe. We've been interacting more and more with Jasper's table during dinner. Flirtations are rising between Stewart and Anastasia. Jasper still leaves early. Now I've gathered he goes to either the lacrosse gym or a private room he's reserved for himself in the library or back to his room to study.

Jasper and Daiki appear next. Both are in plain sweats and black winter coats. When we capture the attention of the lacrosse table, I spend a lot of dinner trying to remember my own name around Daiki while daydreaming about being his girlfriend and getting to kiss him after every game and go on vacation every winter to visit his grandparents in Japan the way I've come to understand his current girlfriend does.

The next to arrive come from the girls' dormitory—Joyce and a fourth year named Kiara Laurence. Theo, Anastasia, and Ariel exchange glances, and I've gotten to know them well enough now to understand this look is judgment for Joyce's label-covered slippers and jacket.

"Who has it?" Joyce says.

Jasper slips off his backpack and reveals the contents of the box.

"Collins should get her earrings back since she didn't get to play," he says. A quick side-eye to Sebastian, who smirks.

"We were the sacrifices to keep the secret," Sebastian says. "Rules apply to her, too, even if she doesn't know what they are."

"He's right," says Theo. He meets my eye. "Don't worry."

But Jasper sighs, and I do—I do worry.

Jasper hands Sebastian two red dice.

He refuses them, putting his hands up. "Ladies first. Come on, Jasper."

Jasper crosses the circle to get to me. I hold out my hand, and he sets the dice in my palm.

"I just—roll them?" I feel embarrassed asking this because honestly, what else does one do with dice? But Jasper nods like this is a perfectly reasonable question.

He steps next to me so the ground in front of me is clear. I rattle the dice in my hand and then kneel and let the dice fall. Everyone bends forward to see how they land.

"Two sixes," Stewart announces.

The room is filled with a mixture of sighs and gasps. I can't tell if this a good thing.

"Tough break," Anastasia says.

"Pas bien," Stewart says.

"I'll take her results, and she can have mine," Sebastian says.

"That's fair," Theo says. "Since it was your fault she didn't get to play the normal way."

"Are double sixes bad?" I say.

"The worst," Ariel says.

Anastasia explains, "We work off a point system, ranking the winner as one. You got twelve."

"That's last place," Joyce adds.

"Yeah, she gets it, Joyce," Ariel says.

"She's not in last place; I am." Sebastian retrieves the dice from the ground. He squats down and rolls them. "She got . . ." He examines the dice. "Five." He looks up at me and smiles. "Congratulations, Collins Pruitt."

"All right, then." Stewart types into his phone. "The result are in. Sebastian . . ." He nods toward Jasper's bag. Sebastian reaches in and pulls out the prescription bottle.

"That's what the loser gets every time," Anastasia tells me.

"What is it?"

"It's full of oxy and cocaine."

"*What?*"

"The loser has to take it. It's a risk. Having illegal drugs on you at this school. Much riskier than actually taking the drugs."

"I don't know about that." But my palms are sweaty at the thought of having to hide something that would definitely result in expulsion.

"And the winner is," Stewart announces, "Theo."

Everyone sighs.

"He always wins," Anastasia says.

Theo reaches into the bag and pulls out a watch, different from the one he'd put in but still big and shiny.

We go down the line, everyone taking something from the bag. I end up choosing the Dior wallet. I'm not sure what the fun is in this exchange. We all have wealthy parents. We have nice wallets and jewelry. Surely, Anastasia's parents could buy the diamond earrings she wanted of mine—which she didn't get because Joyce beat her to them. It's a weird reward for this crowd.

"What'll the next game be?" Stewart asks Theo.

"Winner's choice," Anastasia tells me.

"Spades," Theo says. "We'll break off into groups."

Stewart and Daiki high-five this decision. I smile to myself. Thanks to my dad, I'm excellent at Spades.

"For next month," Stewart starts. Everyone takes out their phones. He assigns the staggering times for everyone to go to the storage room to drop off their stuff and which social next month the game will take place. The meeting to exchange gifts happens at the same time—the third Thursday of the month when the teachers get together for drinks and to watch their guilty pleasure show. We mark these times and dates in our calendars, and Anastasia instructs me to label the events with an *X*.

As we walk back to the girls' dorm, Anastasia takes my arm and gives me what she calls *the lowdown*.

"The game is a tradition," she says. "Jasper and Theo's mother used to play it, and she told them it was their duty to start it up again when they were enrolled. Most of the legacies have traditions like these that they pass on to their kids. I was asked to be a part of it because, obviously, Theo is my best friend. Stewart and Daiki were brought in by Jasper. Theo brought in Ariel and Rand, from water polo. Ariel brought in Sebastian sophomore year, and Stewart brought in Kiara last year. Rand brought in Joyce." She pauses to roll her eyes. "And now I've brought in you."

"And everything is done exactly how it was when Mrs. Mahoney was here?"

"Yes—same rules about sneaking into the supply closet to deposit your contribution. All we've added is the pill bottle forced upon the loser. Sophomore year, Theo invited this girl Zara Wilmington to play—she was ultimately expelled, but she left her drugs in the collection box because to her that was a great reward, and she was banished from the school before she could claim her prize. It's been the loser's prize ever since, and the winner doesn't have to put anything in."

"How do people know what to put in as a prize?"

"All it has to be is something of value. So vague, right? That's why I encouraged your diamond earrings. Which reminds me—" She lets go of my arm and rushes a few steps ahead of us to catch up with Joyce and Kiara.

"She just means, if there's something you want from someone, ask them to put it in the box," Ariel says, stepping closer to me as the hall narrows.

Something I want? Interesting. Something wanted and something of value aren't necessarily the same thing. And sometimes you don't know how much value something has until it's exposed.

Six Months Later

I glance up at the tall windows above the awning across the street and see Mrs. Mahoney, Jasper, and Theo. They're standing at the windows, looking down at us. My father follows my gaze and looks up at them, too. I think they'll back away from the window at first, now that we're staring. But they don't. And we don't.

OCTOBER

Thirteen

If you listen carefully to what people say about Theo Mahoney, you'll hear all kinds of different things. He's a kind soul. He's a great dresser. He's charming. He's friendly. He's polite. He's funny. He doesn't beat around the bush. He's a good student. He's humble. A real team player. Someone reliable. Someone down-to-earth. Someone romantic—according to those who have dated him and those who want to. You'll hear all kinds of things about Theo Mahoney, and all of it will be flattering.

But what I have on Theo Mahoney isn't flattering.

It's suspicious.

Today is Saturday, and we're all at Viviana Prep in a town along the coast, but still a six-hour bus ride from Rutherford for away games and meets and matches. Ariel and Anastasia finished their swim meet early this morning. I played field hockey in the afternoon while Theo had a water polo match and Jasper played soccer. It's evening now, and we've retreated back to the Cool Water Inn, a modern hotel that greets you with a floor-to-ceiling waterfall against a clear blue glass wall. It backs up to the ocean, and even though it's chilly this time of year, there are raised wooden pathways leading to several decks—wouldn't want us stepping on the sand like commoners. Each deck is made of a lavender-gray wood and has matching Adirondack chairs surrounding gas firepits in steel-colored tapered bowls with flames that rise out of blue rocks. I like sitting out here, being so close to the ocean.

We've all won today. Viviana Prep is known more for its theater program than its athletics, but we still bask in our victories. We drink the oolong tea they served in the lobby as though we earned it.

Stewart, Jasper, and Daiki walk the paths to a firepit a few decks over. Stewart locks eyes with Anastasia, and she smiles and waves at him. But they don't join us.

"I'm surprised you and Stewart haven't hooked up before," I say. "Playing the"—I lower my voice—"*game* together all those years. I thought you guys would be closer."

"Not the case," Anastasia says. "It's a game. Tradition. Obligation, sometimes. Plus, I'm typically unavailable. He's probably been pining after me for years."

Theo, Ariel, and I exchange glances.

My phone vibrates. I take it out of my coat pocket and see a text from Meghan and Cadence. They were my best friends before I left. The people I'd always felt the closest to. But last time I talked to them, they were dressing up for spirit week. I'd just finished an exam on the Bay of Pigs, and they were contemplating putting pompoms in their hair and brainstorming slogans to iron onto their T-shirts. Their text right now says they're going to the movies. I'm sipping tea with an unobstructed view of the Pacific Ocean. Our worlds seem a million miles apart.

"You don't want to stay small-minded," Rosie had said when she was convincing me that I should attend Rutherford. But she wasn't referring to Meghan and Cadence. "Everyone is small-minded if they don't put themselves up against the fence, push their limits, face unfamiliar challenges, get out of their comfort zones." She spoke from a place of experience. Rosie had lived in six different countries by the time she was twenty-seven.

"If you went away to Rutherford, you're not the only one who would get the chance to grow," Rosie told me. And she was right. Mimi never got to have the kinds of adventures Rosie had. I was born when she was twenty-three. Mimi hadn't done much traveling since. An occasional trip to wine country with her friends. Sometimes we'd go into Chicago to see a show. She left the extravagant vacations up to my dad. Mimi's trips here and there weren't the same as the explorations Rosie was having; even I could see that. It was also obvious that between the two of them, Mimi had to act like the bigger person always, no matter how illogically Rosie behaved. Mimi was the practical one. The responsible one who did take pride in being responsible, but still got the claustrophobic what-if itch when she saw Rosie's photos on safari in Africa, having breakfast with a view of the Eiffel Tower, skiing in Japan, camping in Iceland, hiking in Colombia, surfing in Australia.

So now Mimi is traveling the world with Rosie, and I'm not speaking to either of them, not keeping tabs on them, and they're not keeping tabs on me while I'm here at Rutherford. And it doesn't matter that I didn't know why at first. When I think about what Rosie told me before I left, it all makes sense.

"We're all about to be exactly where we're supposed to be, and everything is going to be fine. I'll look out for Mimi while you look out for your dad," she had said, kissing my forehead as I got into my dad's car to leave for Cashmere.

"Who's the text from? Sebastian?" Ariel asks.

Immediately, with no time for me to play it cool, my cheeks get hot. Full-on blushing.

"No," I say, looking away. "From my friends from back home."

"Oh, I've got some of those," Ariel says as though we're talking about a pair of Wellingtons and not actual people.

"Do you miss them?"

She shrugs.

"I'm not homesick, but I do miss my friends sometimes."

I glance to Ariel and Theo to see if they have anything to add. But they stay quiet. They're looking at each other and at Anastasia. A kind of understanding between the three of them. I don't know if they're judging me for having this weakness of missing people; if they're thinking I haven't been away long enough to know what it's like; if they think they know something I don't about how friends from home can't compete with the world of Rutherford.

Sometimes when the three of us are laughing so hard I can barely breathe, or when Theo takes my arm in the hall and walks with me to class, or when Anastasia leans in close as she whispers details about random gossip she's learned, or when Ariel randomly comes to my defense on some inconsequential topic that Anastasia has adamantly disagreed with me about—like wearing white after Labor Day—I forget that they all have this other side to them. Something that I'm not a part of because they haven't known me for that long. They could decide to ice me out if they wanted. The game is a Rutherford tradition, and it's an honor they asked me to play. But it's not a sign that they've truly accepted me the way they've embraced each other.

I have to remember this. Every time I feel relaxed and happy with them and think it might be an option to ask Anastasia about the dirt I have on Theo, I have to remember how they're looking at each other now, cool stares over a steady flame. Proof I could be met with malice instead of information. It would risk them seeing me as the threat that I am. And then I'll never know the truth about Theo.

Fourteen

Sebastian walks up to our group and salutes a greeting. His eyes fix on mine.

"Want to go for a walk, Collins Pruitt?" he asks.

"Okay, sure." The words come out in this embarrassingly squeaky tone. Anastasia doesn't bother holding back her laughter.

He reaches out to help me up from my chair, and I take his hand.

"Bring her back in one piece," Theo calls as we walk off.

We follow the wooden paths to the edge and step onto the sand. It's a still night, and the sun is nearly down. Candles wrapped in birchwood are protruding from the sand, giving enough light that I can see Sebastian's every expression. The ocean roars, and the air smells sweet.

"So, Collins Pruitt." He says my name, and a wide smile spreads on his face. I glance around to see if anyone is looking at us. Everyone on the decks can see us, if they bother to look. Jasper turns in our direction briefly, though I'm not sure if he noticed me standing here with Sebastian.

Sebastian waits for me to return the smile before he continues. "Do you have a boyfriend?" he asks. "Or a girlfriend? Or both? Or is it one of those 'it's complicated' situations, even if you're technically single?"

I'm single, technically, yes. Here specifically for the education, to learn what Theo is hiding, and make Jasper fall in love with me. "It's complicated."

His face lights up, his brown eyes shining, his smile leaping off his face. "Is it someone from back home? It's always someone from back home. Or someone in college? You know you can't date someone in college while you're here, right? It never works out."

"It's none of the above."

He scratches his head. He's as animated as ever.

It's amazing, actually. His charm doesn't seem manipulative. It seems genuine. He talks like he doesn't think before he speaks, but in his case, it does him nothing but favors, pumping spontaneity into his every word. "What do you think of Rutherford, Collins Pruitt? You never did answer me about that. And I haven't forgotten."

I respond with a shrug again because this method of replying with a noncommittal response could intrigue him. But suddenly, I say, "I miss my friends from home."

He takes the smallest step toward me, looking at me like he's waiting to hear more. Like he wants to know all about it.

"I don't want to go home or anything. It's just the first time I'm not perfectly in sync with them, and it's—I don't know—"

"It's jarring is what it is," Sebastian says. "It's like you fall out of step with your old life and you're perfectly happy at Rutherford, but your former life is going on even without you there, and that feels like you're both being left behind and like you're leaving something behind."

"Yeah." I nod, surprised he knows precisely what I mean. "That's what it's like. Exactly."

"And it doesn't stop with your friends; it's almost worse with family, you know? You feel you're missing out on things you didn't even know you cared about. Cousins' birthdays and your sister's choir performances—things that were ordinary and sometimes boring before they stopped being part of your life. Do you feel it yet—that weird ache for ordinary and at the same time the agitation of having to readjust to it all when you go back?"

But I don't want to think about them. My family. I don't want to think about what's different, about everything I had no choice but to leave behind; about the position I was put in and the secrets I'm still keeping from my dad. How I'm protecting him—I have to protect him.

I glance toward Jasper. He's not looking at us. He's laughing, his head tipped back, no book in his hand. It's a rare sight. And now I'm not thinking of Rosie and Mimi and my father. I'm thinking of him, wondering what made him laugh like that.

"It's cold this close to the water," I tell Sebastian, and we start to walk toward the decks.

"Will you have dinner with me?" he says. "Back at Rutherford. One night. Come on. You have permission to go off campus, right? Let's take the bus and go to the Shrimp Shack in the square. Let's go. Have dinner with me. I swear it will be fun. Please?"

I want to say yes, I really do. But I think about how I felt when he told me about leaving his old life with his friends. How he has the potential to understand me perfectly. I think about being here without having to wonder what Jasper Mahoney was laughing at, or getting close to Theo. If I could use all the tricks Rosie taught me on Sebastian. It would be easy to see the good in him. It would be easy to reflect it back, to show him I believe in him.

"Look—okay," Sebastian says. "I know I'm a lot. I've been told I come on a little strong. But I think life is too short to beat around the bush. Don't you?"

He reaches for my hand, helping me step up onto the wooden pathway leading back to the deck.

In that instant, I remember that he formerly dated Ariel—*Ariel,* who is easily feared, but not easily moved. And even though she's made it clear that she's done with him and has no desire to be with him again and couldn't care less if I wanted to date him, I also remember the way he touched Joyce over Labor Day weekend.

"Why do you want to have dinner with me?" I say as we walk.

Without missing a beat, he answers, "Because we're trapped at Rutherford, where it's half prison, half paradise, and you're new and I don't know anything about you except your name, and that you're single, even if it's complicated." He's smooth in his bluntness; irritatingly so. "Well, all that, and I've got the strangest feeling we'd get along really well, and I'd be sorry if I never tried to get to know you."

This might be the nicest thing anyone's ever said about me. How do you say no to that? The answer is, you don't.

"I don't like shrimp," I say.

His eyebrows raise. "Is that a no? Because there are other things on the menu. But also, who doesn't like shrimp, delicious shrimp?"

I laugh, and he smiles that smile of his.

"It's not a no."

"Noted." I think Sebastian actually never gets nervous, and this causes me to want to make him nervous. "So dinner? Just us?"

"Oh, why not?" Except I know all the reasons why not.

His smile grows so large, I can't help but smile, too.

"Can't wait, Collins Pruitt," he says, dropping me off right where he'd picked me up, with Theo and Anastasia and Ariel, with Jasper two fires over, not even looking my way.

"I'm going to sit with Stewart," Anastasia says. She's only looking at me. "Do you want to come?"

"Yeah," I say, and as we walk over to them, she says, "So what's with Sebastian?" and I wonder if this wasn't really about Stewart at all; it was only a ploy to get me alone to ask me about Sebastian without Ariel's cynicism around.

"He wants to have dinner sometime."

"Of course he does." She waggles her eyebrows as we join Stewart and Jasper's group, taking the two seats next to Stewart. I'm across the fire from Jasper and unfortunately right next to Daiki. But as I sit in that circle, trying not to stare at the way the glow from the fire does wonderful things to Daiki's face, and waiting to learn what made Jasper laugh the way he did, I think, my friendship with Anastasia and the pursuit of nudging her toward Stewart is putting me closer to all of them. It's like Rosie said— I'm exactly where I'm supposed to be.

Fifteen

My favorite thing about Rutherford is that there is so much to do, you don't have time to think of anything else. Distractions have to take a back seat. Sebastian will have to wait. Dinner plans aren't real plans; they're an idea and a fantasy, and looking forward to them is like a fire burning on a distant shore, the promise of warmth once the destination is eventually reached. The purposefulness of my being here drives me. Even when I'm hanging out with friends, I'm there for a reason. I have a problem to solve. A secret to dig up and use to my advantage and threaten to expose.

It's unlikely that I'll get close enough to Jasper that he'll feel comfortable enough to tell me what Theo's hiding, the way he easily told me about Rob. But maybe I can pry it from Anastasia, since she thought I was close enough to them to bring me into their Rutherford tradition.

"We should go to the soccer game this weekend," I say the following week as we eat lunch in the courtyard, wearing sweaters and sunglasses because that's the kind of day it is. "We could eat at the square after." Since I don't have a field hockey game on Saturday, it would be a good time to go out with Stewart, Jasper, and Daiki, as our day passes for weekends will allow.

"Eh, let's not and say we did," Anastasia says.

"Sometimes you don't make any sense," Theo teases her.

"Wait—why not?" I say. "It's going to be a big game." I have no idea if this is true, but it sounds like something that might convince people to go to a sporting event. "Don't you want to see Stewart play?"

"I'm not really into Stewart anymore," Anastasia says.

"Since when?" Ariel says. This is my thought exactly.

"Oh?" I say. *Don't panic.* "Did something happen?" Just yesterday, Anastasia was sitting next to Stewart at dinner, with her whole body turned toward his, lingering on his every word and talking a mile a minute, something she does when she's really invested in holding someone's attention. I sat next to Jasper for five minutes, where he complained about the new library sign-in sheets and laughed at a joke I didn't understand. Still. Progress.

"She realized he wasn't her type," Theo says.

"But . . . why not?"

"Theo has not painted a flattering picture of him. Ergo, I'm not interested."

Theo's quick to support this accusation. "You all haven't been forced to spend as much time with him as I have. He's my brother's best friend; I've seen more than enough of him throughout the years. He comes on vacation with us every summer. Our Anastasia deserves someone less entitled. Less boring. Less obtuse. He claims to speak several languages, but have you ever heard him say anything except *very good* or *not good* when he casually, but purposefully, slips another language into conversation? He'd be a complete waste of her time."

"Stewart is not entitled," Ariel says. "Not compared to anyone else Anastasia has dated."

"*Excuse me,*" Anastasia says.

Theo turns to Ariel. "If you think Stewart is so great, you should date him."

"I don't have chemistry with Stewart like Anastasia does."

"In Theo's defense, I have great chemistry with a lot of people."

"And Stewart is also not obtuse. Come on," Ariel says. "A little vanilla, sure. And the *not good* thing is a little annoying. But don't make up awful things about him just because you don't want Anastasia dating one of your brother's friends, which is really what this is about."

I'm quick to get on Ariel's side. "For what it's worth," I say to Anastasia, "I did think you had amazing chemistry with Stewart, and he's in my contemporary writing class and doesn't seem obtuse at all."

"*For what it's worth*—please, Collins," Theo says. "You only want Anastasia to date Stewart because you need an excuse to talk to Jasper."

I do nothing but let my mouth hang open at this very accurate accusation. I hate that I'm transparent to Theo—to all of them.

"Really, Collins," Theo continues, "no matter how much you inch your way closer to him using Anastasia and Stewart, he's simply not the guy for you—and it has nothing to do with *you*, like I've told you before and you've probably noticed by now. And I know you know about him and Rob—the last person he was with—so you get that Jasper's not really that into dating. He's into his Dartmouth acceptance and keeping up his grade point average and playing lacrosse in the spring and not much else. Stick to Sebastian."

This last sentiment about Sebastian feels like he's saying, stick to shallow waters. Theo's so convinced he's right. He usually gives me the benefit of the doubt, and it's not lost on me that he'd be giving me one now, with Jasper, if there were one to offer.

"I want Anastasia to date whomever will make her happy, and I happen to know that Stewart isn't up to the job," Theo says.

Lon Davies, a fourth year on the water polo team, calls to Theo from across the courtyard, motioning for him. Theo leaves to see what he wants.

"Sometimes you let him boss you around," Ariel says to Anastasia.

"But he's right." Anastasia shrugs. "Stewart isn't a good match for me. Theo gets it because he knows me better than anyone. And because of Jasper, he knows Stewart."

We sit quietly until Ariel bites into her pita chip and emits a loud crunch.

"It's true what he said about Jasper, too, you know," Anastasia says to me. "You want to be with someone more fun anyway, don't you? Like Sebastian."

I nod, fake smile. *Right.*

There's a noticeable tension in the air now as we eat lunch without our usual chatter, glancing occasionally a few tables away to see if Theo might be coming back to join us. In a way, I feel closer to them than ever, that they're comfortable enough to bicker with me the way they do with each other. Especially Theo.

As I make my way to my next class, I pass Jasper in the hallway, but he doesn't even register me. Like I'm still no one to him, and soon I'll be less than that now that Anastasia has decided she's not going to pursue Stewart.

I can't count on either of them, not Jasper, not Anastasia. All I can do is use what access I've already been granted.

That evening, I skip out early for dinner and visit the business center. I print out the photo I have a scan of on cardstock. On the back of it, I print a copy of the nondisclosure agreement with Theo's signature.

And that night, when it's my turn to enter the storage room to make a drop, I put what I made inside the box along with another pair of white gold earrings shaped like rosebuds. Earrings recognizable as mine, as I've worn them many, many times.

We play Spades, and I lose. I keep losing. Distracted, I guess—even though I know I've done the right thing. The quickest way to find out about a secret is to shine a light on it in front of those who might understand its worth. A spark of fear can go a long way, and what I've done has the potential to release a quiet inferno.

Sixteen

As I'm changing after field hockey practice the next day, I get a notification that my test score in calculus has been posted. Per usual, I feel a thrill of excitement. My first big test score. Up until now, it's been only quizzes. Typically, I never do as badly as I think I did on a test, and seeing the grade comes with a wave of relief. And if I'm being honest, I'm often Jasper levels of pleased with myself and my ability to rock tests even when I feel unsure about the material.

When I open the results, they're not good. Not good at all. *Oh no.* There is no relief. My breathing picks up—not in the good way. All I feel is dread.

C-.

The minus especially stings.

I try giving myself all the pep talks I know. It's only one test. It's the beginning of the year. You'll have plenty of time to turn your grade around. *It's going to be fine.*

But then I see the rest of my grades.

Oh NO.

I haven't been stalking them like some of the other students do because not all teachers stay up to date anyway. Here they are, all up to date.

All unacceptable. In fact, I'm barely maintaining the average I need to keep my place at Rutherford. I launch into a full-on panic. I walk around the room shaking out my hands, trying to calm myself. I try breathing in for four counts and out for four counts.

If I get kicked out, that will screw everything up.

I have to shift focus. I can't be as carefree as Anastasia and Theo and Ariel. I can't be so free with my time, so social. I can't be flirting with Sebastian on the side. I'm not used to it here yet and I'm falling behind. Now I need to catch up. It's the most important thing.

This dark cloud of horrible possibility follows me around through the weekend. It haunts my dreams and intrudes on my days. A steady beating of *you're not good enough*. A swirl of questions asking why I ever thought I would be.

To make matters worse, I'm called into Dr. Libby's office, where he tells me I'll need to really *apply* myself if I want to stay. I say, "Yes, I understand" as he reiterates how I'm not keeping up.

On Wednesday, I skip breakfast to catch up on homework and spend lunch doing my assignment for contemporary writing before it's due in fourth period, and then I don't allow myself time to get a snack between school letting out and field hockey practice because I spend an inordinate amount of time in Ms. Simmons's office hours listening to her re explain the latest number theory lesson—something I still don't fully grasp in relation to how she wants us to complete the assigned project. And I can't rely on my usual *I think I've got this* mentality anymore. No more skimming, no more guessing, no more last-minute, *this is probably fine* essays.

During field hockey practice, I feel my energy running low. My head is dizzy, and my stomach is gurgling from being full of water and not much else. We're finishing up the second set of drills when I pull away to the sidelines and vomit the gallons of water I'd downed trying to stave off my wooziness onto the perfectly trimmed grass. I expect Coach Steger will want me to shake it off and finish practice. But she says, "That's enough for you, Pruitt. Hit the showers."

I pretend to be disappointed. Really—now that the initial embarrassment is over—I'm elated with relief. I could use the extra time to read the chapter on Cold War fallout in Austria.

As I round the corner to the girls' locker room, I feel it again, that intense nausea that indicates I'm going to be sick. I approach the garbage can at the side of the building, knowing I won't make it inside to the bathroom like a civilized person in time, but it's got a slot opening and would require me to stick my head in the trash to successfully get my vomit water into the can. The idea alone has me puking into the grass.

"Oh—shit," says a familiar voice behind me.

Great. Thankfully this vomit is the least offensive kind of vomit. But still. Not something I want anyone to witness. Especially not the person standing before me with perfectly messy curls and holding his shin guards and a bottle of water. He's sweating in a way that makes him glisten, and why does sweat make me look like a wet rat but make him look like he's about to do a shoot for Calvin Klein?

"Hello, Jasper." I wipe off my chin.

"Are you . . . okay?"

"Of course."

He stands there with that incredulous expression, like either I'm such a wreck that he can't look away or he's waiting for the real answer.

"I pushed myself a little too hard during practice," I say. "That's all."

"You look pretty pale. Like, not a normal pale."

"It's nothing. It will all be fool." *Fool.* The word that came out when I accidentally combined *fine* and *cool.* This normally only happens when Daiki is around, so something must be very wrong. I'm feeling light-headed now. A little woozy.

"Are you sure you're okay?"

Jasper doesn't like weak girls. He likes strong girls. The kind of girls that could lead him in an overview and revolutionize the field of medicine. Not the kind that are caught barfing because they were irresponsible and missed meals.

He hands me his water bottle. "You need this." Then he disappears into the locker room. I sit on the ground and sip the water. It tastes amazing. You wouldn't think I'd be so keen on water given all the water-vomiting, but vomiting also dehydrates a person, so it's a vicious cycle. Jasper appears again, this time carrying a protein bar. I frown when he holds it out for me. Chewy faux peanut-buttery chocolate is the last thing I want to eat. But I can't let him see that I'm too sick for even a protein bar, the kind intended to replenish. As soon as I take the first bite, I realize it was exactly what I needed—maybe the best thing I've ever tasted.

"Thank you," I say, practically a moan, my mouth full.

He smiles. Not enough so that I can see his teeth. But there it is. He's pleased with himself. He waits as I finish, not making it awkward, but staring out at the forest beyond the fields, like he's enjoying the view or something.

"Don't you have to get back to practice?"

He shakes his head and shrugs. "It's okay. I'll explain what happened."

I frown. Not exactly great for my personal reputation at this school. "Do you have to?"

The smile gets a little bigger. "I won't specify it was you."

"I appreciate that."

"Don't worry about it."

I take the last swallow of his protein bar and finish off his water, and miraculously, I do feel better. Still a little unsteady, but not like I'm going to fall over or get sick again.

He reaches out his hand when I attempt to stand. I pretend I don't notice and get up without his help.

"Sorry for drinking all your water."

"It's fine, Collins. We all have those days."

"Really?"

He shrugs. "Maybe at first. It can be hard here when you're not used to it."

"So I'll get used to it and one day it won't be so bad, is what you're saying?" Getting a compliment—a simple note of encouragement, even—from this guy is like squeezing water from a stone.

He shrugs again. I wait. "You'll get used to it, or you won't and you'll go home."

So much for encouragement. He's nothing but blunt honesty. I think of what he said to me during the overview about the concepts being very basic, the way he seemed put out when I asked questions. "Your faith in me is flattering. It really is." I cut around the corner on my way to the girls' locker room.

"Wait—" Jasper says.

But I do not wait. What's good about Jasper? He helps me but looks down on me for needing said help. He rescues me with water and protein but sees me as not being strong enough—or strong at all. Not cut out for this place. If he knew I was on academic probation and about to fail, would he even be surprised? Would he be able to see that I'm doing what it takes to stay here and doing what I came here to do? Even if getting him vulnerable seems impossible, the way you can't expect a vampire to fear death. I've managed to infiltrate Theo's inner circle, and that is something. It has to be.

I shower and change quickly in the locker room. I don't want to face the rest of the girls when they finish practice. I leave out the same entrance I came in, because that's the one that isn't visible from the practice fields. Jasper's still there, waiting for me.

Not knowing what to say, I can only shrug at him. Why did he wait? Is he worried about me? Is he upset that I snapped at him? Is it that important that he clear things up between us even though we are barely close acquaintances?

"You have my water bottle," he says.

Oh. I pull it out of my bag and give it to him. I do not look at him.

I walk up the hill to the girls' dormitory. I crawl into bed. I only leave to get dinner, but I don't eat in the cafeteria. I stay in my room and study. I go to bed at the required eleven o'clock. When my alarm vibrates at five minutes to 1:00 a.m., I'm startled. I'd forgotten. Tonight is the exchange. Tonight, I'll see how valuable my information is to Theo. To all of them.

Seventeen

When we enter the tunnel room, the chandelier is already lit up. Anastasia, Ariel, and I are the last to arrive. Anastasia is grinning like crazy as we get started. She's so excited she can hardly stand still. My nerves are rattled, imagining what will happen when people start choosing their prizes and notice the extra item I placed in the box.

Jasper presents the box. Stewart brings up the scores on his phone.

"Anastasia was the winner this time," Stewart announces proudly. "Très bon."

She releases some of her sealed excitement and lets out a squeal.

"Beginner's luck," Theo says, but he's smiling like he's happy for her.

Anastasia wiggles her fingers as she peers into the box. She bites down on her lip. She squints. Her brow furrows as she looks up. *Has she noticed it?* She looks at Theo.

"There are two keys in here," she says. She turns to Joyce. "Which set is the one we talked about?"

Kiara shakes her head. "You don't get to ask questions about the prizes. Just choose."

Anastasia glances around, waiting to see if anyone will object to this. When no one does, she lets out a whiny moan. She chews on her lower lip as she peers into the box, shifting from one foot to another as she debates what to take.

"There should be a time limit," Jasper says.

"Seriously," Ariel says. "Do it already."

Anastasia reaches in fast, like she risks getting bitten by a snake at the bottom of the box, and comes up with two gold keys.

She faces Joyce. Joyce nods; she looks down. Anastasia lets out a cheer and leaps to hug me since I'm closest to her even though I don't know what's got her so excited.

"Keys to the Manhattan penthouse Joyce's family is selling," she announces to the group.

"She's giving you her family's penthouse?" Rand from the water polo team says, his mouth dropping open.

"No," Joyce says quickly. "Only for the weekend after Thanksgiving."

Anastasia spins the keys on her forefinger. "I love New York in the fall."

"Rand, you're next," Stewart says.

Rand doesn't hesitate. He comes back with the other set of keys. He holds them up. "What do these get me?"

"My family's house in the Hamptons," Kiara says. "You can use it anytime before May."

Rand is ecstatic. He does an embarrassing little dance in celebration.

Kiara smiles at Joyce, who bashfully smiles back. I can feel Anastasia festering next to me, watching them, knowing now that she did not get the best possible deal, even though Joyce's keys were the ones she was after from the start.

"Is your family being forced to sell off all their property, too, Kiara?" Anastasia says. Retaliation.

Joyce's eyes fall to the floor. Kiara glares at Anastasia.

"*What?*" Stewart says to Anastasia, who's standing next to him. Across the circle, Daiki's mouth drops open.

"We're selling a lot of our things," Joyce says, still not looking at anyone.

"Joyce, you don't have to explain—" Theo starts.

"No, it's okay." Joyce looks up. "It'll be all over the news soon anyway. There have been some charges against my father. We're having to sell some of our assets."

"Charges for embezzlement," Anastasia says. Her voice is low enough that Stewart and I can hear her, but I'm not sure those across the room can. Theo is only two people away and gives her a look like he doesn't approve. "And possession of cocaine," Anastasia whispers. Stewart rewards her for this information by giving a small gasp.

"A little bird told me," she continues. "Joyce's cousin Felicity. I went to camp with her three summers ago." I remember last month after the exchange, when Anastasia ran to catch up with Joyce. I think of how she convinced me to put in my diamond earrings and wonder what she said to persuade Joyce to include the keys to her family's home in New York.

"You really are a treasure trove of secrets, aren't you?" Stewart says to Anastasia.

"Who's next?" Theo says.

"You are." Stewart nods toward him.

I watch as Theo gazes into the box. I hold my breath. What will he do when he sees the photo he's not supposed to talk about? Will he take it before any of the others have the chance to see it? He reaches into the box and comes out with a pair of designer cuff links.

Jasper is next to choose a prize. He'd know about the NDA, wouldn't he? Wouldn't he at least recognize the photo of his brother? Jasper pulls out a black stainless-steel watch.

Ariel goes next. Would she know Theo's secret? She walks away with a sapphire ring.

Stewart takes a signed hardcover of *The Rules of Attraction*. Kiara choses a vintage Louis Vuitton clutch. Daiki takes a pearl bracelet for his girlfriend, because of course he does. Sebastian chooses my earrings and winks at me. Ariel and Joyce roll their eyes almost in sync.

"Sorry, Collins," Stewart says.

I realize that I am the only person left.

"What?" *Shoot.* "Really?" I knew I had a terrible game, but I hoped someone from the other groups had played worse. Jasper approaches me with the box. I look inside as I reach down to retrieve the prescription bottle of illicit drugs. The box is empty aside from that. *Jasper.* It's his job to bring the box from the storage room to the exchange. He must know. He must've known, and he must've removed it.

My hand is trembling as I grasp the pills.

Does he suspect me? Would he have any reason to believe someone else in that circle wanted to expose Theo?

I try to look relaxed, flash them a grin, like it's funny to me. But I don't think I'm very convincing. The smiles they give me are full of pity. Except for Jasper, whose expression stays solemn with a hint of concern.

As we're about to leave, I feel a hand on my shoulder. I turn to see Theo.

Oh no.

I grip the bottle tightly to stop myself from fidgeting. I remember to keep breathing. Nothing looks as guilty as someone holding their breath.

"Allow me," he says.

"What?"

He nods to his hand, cupped to receive something. Low between us like he doesn't want anyone else to see.

"Give me the drugs, Collins," he says.

"But—?" I don't understand why he's taking the punishment from me.

"I'll keep them in a safe place. So you don't have to worry," he says.

For a second, I think it has to be a trap. It's a lot of power, letting him hide the pill bottle where he could easily set me up.

"It's okay," I say. "I can—I'll keep them hidden."

"Oh, just give them to him," Anastasia says. She takes them out of my hand and passes them to Theo. "You're already sort of losing it lately. One less thing to stress about. He'll take care of them."

"Oh, okay. Thanks."

Theo gives me a warm smile before he walks away.

"He does this for Jasper, too, whenever he loses," Anastasia says, taking my arm as we start toward the girls' dormitory.

I look back, before the boys disappear into the darkness of the narrowing tunnel. Jasper is looking back, too.

Eighteen

On Saturday, we're up at the crack of dawn to take buses to play soccer and field hockey against a nearby boarding school. Many others study as we ride, but I feel myself getting carsick and have to stop even though these are three hours that I really don't want to waste staring out the window.

At St. Paul's, I was great on the field hockey team—not the best player, but a decent one. Here, lately, I'm barely passable for varsity. Sometimes they put second years in before me. Between this and my grades, it's like my mind can't do what I thought it could, and neither can my body. I lose the ball twice while I'm dribbling, three of my passes are intercepted, and the one shot I take misses. We win, no thanks to me, and cross the complex to watch the end of the boys' soccer games. Sebastian owns this field for sure. Everything about how he plays is in contrast to the way Jasper plays. Sebastian looks like he's having fun. Jasper is intense and concentrating. When time is almost out, Jasper is given a blue card and taken out of the game. Daiki signals to him to calm down, but even as he sits there, I can see him simmering. Anger and frustration building within him. Even when they win, his celebration isn't sincere, like he's thinking that even though they won, he still lost, because he didn't play as well as he'd wanted to.

I still have no idea if he thinks I was the one who put the photo of Theo in the box, if he knows the truth behind it. But I have been avoiding him, just in case. It's not hard to do. Without Anastasia seeking out Stewart's company and with the game over with for the month, there's not much reason for our paths to cross.

On the way back to Rutherford, the buses drop us off at a burger place to eat. Instead of going inside, I step to the side, let the others file out around me. I lean against the bus as they disappear into the restaurant. I'm exhausted from playing and overwhelmed thinking of all the calculus homework I still have to do. I close my eyes and try to concentrate on my feet against the ground, my back steady against the wall of the bus.

"Are you okay?"

I open my eyes and see Sebastian standing a few feet away. The rest of the soccer team trails into the burger joint. He looks a little banged up and sweaty, but in that very appealing sort of way.

"Yeah," I say. "Had to catch my breath, I guess."

"Are you coming?"

Through the windows, I can see the mob of Rutherford students filling the restaurant. I should go in and have a burger with all of them. I should celebrate our wins. But that's what I've been doing since I got here. Taking the time to celebrate and socialize. Flirt. That's how I've fallen behind. Right now I don't have the luxury of trying to get closer to Jasper or getting the truth behind Theo's NDA. Everything falls apart if I get kicked out of Rutherford.

"No," I say. "I'm going to stay on the bus. I have a calculus test, and I'm way behind."

He nods like he understands but still looks disappointed—which I really appreciate. "I guess I'll leave you to it, then," he says. "Wouldn't want to be a distraction, Collins Pruitt."

I smile as he walks away. I drag myself back onto the bus. Coach Steger brings me a burger, fries, and a drink and tells me she doesn't mind if I stay in the bus to study but that I have to eat, and I thank her.

I work furiously, as fast as I can, before we leave, and I'll have to put the books away to avoid getting sick. Maybe I'll sleep. I'm sort of looking forward to it. But until then, I can feel the time passing too quickly, and me, moving through these equations at a snail's pace.

Out of the corner of my eye, I catch a flicker of movement. I turn, thinking the whole team is on the way back, but it's only someone on the bus parked parallel to ours. It's Jasper—identifiable firstly by his long gait and curly hair, secondly by his face as he sits, tilts his head back, and stares at the ceiling before he sighs and gets out an economics book.

For a few minutes, I watch him. He seems relaxed. Maybe this is catching him at a good moment, when he's calm like this, away from the crowd of people, dedicating himself to study-ing, which from what I can tell is his favorite hobby. I move to the row that lines up with the row he's in and slide next to the window. In my notebook, I use a Sharpie to write out one of the equations that I know I did right in large dark letters. Underneath it, I write, *I THINK I HAVE THE HANG OF IT NOW.* I knock on the window and wait for him to look over at me. He's at first irritated with the knocking, but when he sees me, he smiles. A good sign. I hold up the notebook and grin at him. He studies the equation and my message. Maybe he won't get it—won't even re-member that he gave me an overview in calculus at the beginning of the year. But then he takes out his own notebook and starts scribbling something. I get excited waiting to see what he's going to say next. Maybe this will show him that I'm similar to him in this regard—on the bus with my schoolwork instead of having a burger and celebrating. Maybe it will make him feel the slightest bit closer to me.

When he finishes, he holds up his notebook. It's my equation except—different. *Oh.* He corrected it. So it wasn't right after all. I write a new message to him and hold it up. He chuckles when he sees it. It's just the word *SHIT.* He scribbles something in his notebook and holds it up against the window. It says, *YOU WERE CLOSE.*

Noises erupt from the front of the bus as the rest of the field hockey team crowds the seats. Jasper's bus fills with the other soccer players.

When we arrive back at Rutherford, as we're getting ready to haul our stuff back to the dorms, Jasper comes up to me. He passes me a folded piece of paper.

"What is this?" I ask. He shrugs, smiles, but doesn't say anything.

I wait until I'm safely out of his view before I open the note. It's the equation—an explanation of what was wrong. It sort of makes me smile, how sweet it is. Even if it's a practical note. It feels unexpected.

That night, when I'm forced into bed at eleven o'clock, and still clueless in calculus and behind on my readings for English, and only five sentences into my essay on current pop culture as seen through the lens of generation X, I start to worry. Maybe I'm not cut out for this at all. Like, any of it. Not the academics. Not the rigorous schedule. Not living away from home. Not being with these kinds of people. Not getting the truth out of someone. Not for making someone fall in love with me, no matter what Rosie said.

"How important is your father to you?" Rosie asked me that spring, when she was living us, right after I'd been accepted to Rutherford. We were out on the porch even though it was early in the season and still a little too cold to be out there. We were bundled in blankets and the sun was setting, turning the sky a mild orange. Mimi was out at the barn. This was the kind of place she'd always wanted to live since she was a child, when she'd dreamed of living off the land—that's what she called it.

In case Rosie didn't understand that my father was important to me, since her father wasn't important to her, I answered, "Of course he is. He's my favorite person in the whole world."

"What about me?" she'd teased.

"Come on," I said, rolling my eyes. She knew I loved her, that she was a favorite also. "Why are you asking me that?"

She shrugged. "He's important to both of you, I know that." By this, she meant Mimi and me. "But what would you do if you found out he was keeping something from you?"

"Something—like what?"

"Something about his personal life."

"Oh. That's none of my business." I'd heard Mimi say this whenever pressed about why my dad lived in New York City, away from us, if he was dating, the places he was traveling. "Jake's personal life is none of my business," she'd say.

"What if he was in love?" Rosie said.

"Then good for him." I wasn't completely clueless. My dad was kind and charming and handsome—and single. I didn't assume he never dated. I'd figured that if he did date, it was not something he wanted to flaunt in front of Mimi or me. Because what would be the point? And honestly, I never thought he'd get serious with someone because he was so busy with work and with, well, being a dad to me—a job that required travel and time; a job that he took very seriously.

"What if it's changing him, messing with his head, and screwing with his priorities?"

I shrugged. Admittedly, I didn't like what I was hearing. I wanted him to be happy, yes. But I also wanted to continue to see him whenever I wanted. I liked looking up from a field hockey game to see him cheering on the sidelines and staying up late with him watching TV and hearing him on a conference call in the guest room, which doubled as his office in the middle of the day, whenever he stayed with us, which was so often it was less of a guest room and more just *his* room. I liked waking up hearing him and Mimi talking softly in the kitchen over coffee. They had a real friendship, and it comforted me. I didn't think he'd ever want to change what he had going with us. I didn't think a girlfriend would ever get between him and me, or him and Mimi. But I'd also never had to consider it before.

"You know he helps out quite a bit financially with you and with Mimi. You don't really think she makes much of a profit from those goats, do you?"

I didn't answer her. I could hear the goats bleating from where we were sitting. Mimi loved her goats. She raised some of them for milk, some of them for their wool, some of them for children's parties or for the goat yoga craze.

"You don't think he's going to support Mimi forever, do you? After you're grown up and moved out? Especially if he has someone else he needs to support."

I shrugged again because, like before, I'd never had to consider it.

"He's important," she said, "to you and to Mimi, and you have to fight for what's important."

"We don't have to fight for Dad; he's . . . he's ours." The only thing that made sense to me.

"Yes. That's true. But sometimes fighting for someone means protecting them. It can also mean saving them."

"Saving him from what? Some new girlfriend?" I pictured a woman who looked like Mimi but dressed in a fur coat and heels, who liked big cities and lived in a SoHo loft. Someone harmless. If she were really so important, we'd know about her. Until then, whoever she was, she was none of our business, and we were none of hers.

"People most often need to be saved from their own hearts, from where they follow their heart when it's bursting so full for someone that they can't hear their head. They don't always do what's best or what's right."

"How do you know he's in love, anyway?"

"I saw him when I was in New York."

I almost asked, "When were you in New York?" but it would have been a silly question because Rosie was always everywhere. "He told you?" I said.

"He didn't have to. I saw her. I saw *them* and the way they are together when they don't think anyone can see them."

I still didn't understand. "Maybe it's a good thing. It could be nice for him. I'm going to Rutherford, so maybe he needs this." It hurt a little, thinking about how infrequently I'd get to see him when I was away. But I didn't want Rosie to see this sadness in me. I wanted all the things she'd talked about when she'd convinced me to apply; I wanted something new. I wanted to show her I was as strong and capable as she thought I was.

"Collins," she said. She was quiet for a while. "The woman he's in love with is married."

My first instinct was to defend him. He wouldn't do that. There must be more to the story that we were missing. My dad has never been a liar. Or a cheater, for that matter.

"He can't help it," she said, leaning forward in a way that indicated that she could read how this news distressed me. "He's a fool, and she's a horrible person."

But I knew my dad was not a fool; that he never could be. Not even for love.

She took my hands. "It's going to ruin him. This situation is not good. I don't think it's a coincidence that your father makes nothing but good investments and this woman's family is drowning in debt. She has him wrapped around her little finger. The influence she has over him, it's unnerving."

"He's not the kind of person who can be manipulated." But I'll admit a little doubt crept in.

She let go of my hands to readjust her blanket. I could tell she was getting annoyed that I wasn't as offended by this news as she'd wanted me to be. "Well, whatever happens with him financially affects you and Mimi, too. You have to think about that."

"Did you tell Mimi about her?"

"I did. But you know your Mimi. She's not taking it seriously."

I knew my dad was a good judge of business opportunities, and part of that is being a good judge of character. He'd told me this, and I'd seen him in action myself.

"It's hard to believe he'd fall in love with a bad person," I said.

"They do have one thing in common. It's what binds them, makes someone like her irresistible to someone like him. Nothing is more important to this woman than her sons. She would sacrifice anything for them. That's part of the problem, really—the lengths she'd go to ensuring they had the kind of future she thinks they deserve. Even if she doesn't have the means to provide for them anymore." Rosie leaned in closer to me, the blanket falling from around her shoulders. "Listen to me, Collins. I'm telling you about this because it's not a small thing. And you're the only one who can save him from himself."

"If you're so worried about this, why don't you talk to him about it yourself?"

"I have. Believe me, I have." She shook her head. "Don't you get it? It's too late to talk to him about it. He can't believe she'd do anything to hurt him. He's not thinking that his relationship with her will get in the way of what he can supply for you and Mimi. He trusts her; he doesn't think she might threaten his reputation by exposing what they've done. He didn't perform a risk analysis on falling in love, Collins! Love is already a risk; letting someone get that close to you, it's the biggest risk of all. It leaves you most vulnerable. He knows that, and he knows the risks that come with falling for someone like her, and he let himself get involved with her anyway." She pulled the blanket back around her. Her cheeks were pink from the chill. "By now, she probably knows all his deepest fears. Exactly how to wreck him, bribe him, or blackmail him, whatever it takes for her to get what she needs from him. Whatever it takes."

It made my stomach flip, thinking of someone taking advantage of him. My dad was careful with how he conducted business. But people still accused him of things. Investigations were still conducted to confirm his moneymaking practices were legitimate. They always were and thus the press had never been involved. But one bad leak did have the potential to hurt him. And I didn't think he'd like the public knowing he was involved with a married woman.

"He's gone this far with it," Rosie said. "There'll be no going back for him. Not unless . . ." She stared at the barn. Mimi was on her way back, walking through the pasture in her rubber boots, pulling her sweater tighter around her, waving at us with hands covered in fingerless gloves.

"Not unless what?"

"Not unless something else was on the line."

"Like what?" But I had an inkling. "Me?"

She stopped watching Mimi and turned to face me. "You." She shrugged. "Or them."

Nineteen

They say you have to know your weaknesses. Self-awareness or whatever. They say that when you know your weaknesses, you can better figure out how to use them as strengths.

One strength I already know I have: I do not give up very easily.

Jasper walks quickly down the hall. It's hard to keep up with him and this brisk pace he keeps. He careens outside, getting ready to cut across the courtyard, by the time I reach him.

"Jasper, wait." I practically have to yank on his backpack to get him to stop.

He whirls around and looks at me. The weather in Cashmere is starting to turn, and now dark clouds constantly hover over the forest. The ocean is always gray. It's starting to rain lightly, and Jasper lowers his eyebrows, annoyed at having to stand here while the droplets fall on us.

"Hey," I say. *Smooth, Collins.*

He crosses his arms. His impatience is growing even though it's been approximately two seconds. This guy truly can't be bothered.

"You have to remember the reason you're there, the reason you need him. You'll be convincing because you have to be," Rosie told me before I left for Rutherford.

"Can I ask you something?" I say.

"Now?"

I nod. I feel the tears rising again. They are summoned at simply the thought of all the work ahead of me, how I might not be able to do it. And also, I think they're from shame for having to ask what I'm about to ask; fear that he'll say no; that it will ruin his image of me even further.

"You're crying?" He sounds confused but also a little concerned.

The raindrops come down harder, and I'm grateful they can mask some of my tears. He holds his backpack over his head to block the water, and I do the same.

"What is it?" he says, annoyance slipping back into his tone.

"Will you give me another overview?"

"What?"

The rain pounds down on us. The sound of the water splashing off the stones and brick grows louder. Other students rush past. We're the only two standing in place.

"Please," I say, raising my voice to be heard above the noise. "I'm behind. I'm so close to being on academic probation. You were right, okay? I'm having trouble keeping up. But I don't want to leave." I think of Mimi finally out of the country with Rosie and of how my friends back home have fallen into a new normal that doesn't include me, and I wonder what kind of home I have to return to anyway. A place that's already moved on without me. Mimi would have to come back. Rosie would say, "What happened? Why couldn't you do it?"

"I need you," I blurt out. And it's true. He won't like it. It's the wrong thing to say to him. But it's all I have to make him listen to me. "You're smart and you've got the hang of this place and you understand calculus. Please. Just a few times a week. Just until I'm not so behind. I wouldn't ask if I weren't desperate, you know I wouldn't."

I'm surprised when he nods as if he does know or he at least gets it.

"Meet me in the library twenty-five minutes into dinner."

"Thank you—"

He walks away before I can finish, without even confirming that the time he's proposed works for me.

That night, promptly twenty-five minutes into dinner, after I've inhaled my burrito while listening to Theo, Ariel, and Anastasia discuss whether or not Anastasia should cut bangs and then have a lively debate about the problem of the criterion, a fundamental problem of epistemology, I leave for the library to meet Jasper.

He's as no-nonsense as he was when we first met here, in the very room he reserved for us on that day.

"I'll explain the principles to you, and then we can work here until it's time to go back to the dorms. I've got my own stuff to do, but you can ask me questions as they come up."

"*If* they come up," I correct him before I can think better of it. He shrugs. He rotates the book my way and starts in on the first section I missed.

Questions do come up as I work on my own. A lot of them. So many that after a while I decide not to ask them anymore because I don't want to disturb him. He's a deep studier. More serious than I've ever seen him, which is saying something. As he types on his laptop, his eyes get this laser-focused gaze. Sometimes I'm not sure he's blinking regularly.

When we leave, we walk together. I think this must mean he feels sorry for me, more than it means he is interested in my company. Or maybe, because even though the school is well lit, it is still dark outside, and he simply thinks escorting me is the right thing to do.

"That was helpful for you?" he asks as we move down the stairs toward the main hall and the exit.

"Are you kidding?"

But he doesn't look like he is kidding. I have to remember who I'm talking to.

"It was very helpful," I say. "Immensely helpful. Incredibly helpful." Overdoing it a little, maybe.

"Meet again tomorrow?"

I nod. "Thank you."

The clouds have parted, and the sky is clear. I stop to look up at the stars. I can't remember the last time I saw them. From our house on the outskirts of Madison, I would watch them twinkling back at me all the time, maybe every night. Jasper keeps walking. I have to jog to catch up.

"So what do you do for fun?" I ask.

"What do you mean?"

"Come on. *Fun.* How do you have fun here?"

"I don't know. The usual ways. The social nights. The game. Soccer practice. And I like the work, so, I guess, helping you."

"But that's not fun." *Is it?*

He shrugs. We've reached the part in the path where I go right to walk down the hill to the girls' dormitory and he must go the other way. Rutherford dorms are built toward the bottom of a steep hill; the paved trails are really the only way to reach them and, purposefully, I believe, these pathways only converge on campus.

"Hey, Jasper." He turns around and waits for me to continue. "I used to go on long drives for fun. Down country roads. Fields all around. Passing silos and cows."

He watches me for a moment. This was probably the wrong thing to say again. But I want him to know things about me, small facts at least. Even if he forgets them as quickly as he hears them.

"There weren't a lot of cows where I live, but apart from the smell, that sounds nice enough." He waves once and goes on his way.

When I get back to my room, Elena is already in bed. She left the lights on at my desk. I still have to finish the reading for English, so I slide into my chair. *The Age of Innocence* is sitting on top of my laptop, not where I'd left it on the shelf. I pick it up. It's been tabbed with Post-its. I crack it open and see it's been highlighted. There's a note. It's in Elena's neat handwriting.

No use reading this whole thing when this is all you really need to read to draw themes for the assignment. The highlights. Get it?

It's the nicest thing anyone has done for me since I moved here. And I didn't even have to ask her. Maybe catching up academically won't be as bad as I think. Maybe this is a challenge they've all been through, and this is Elena, throwing me a life raft. I'm not going to waste it.

Five Months Later

"It doesn't matter now, does it?" he says.

It's easy to say it doesn't matter now when he doesn't know what I'm about to do. I start to talk, but my voice hitches.

"I want to say something to you," he says. But I shake my head—can't tell him not to say it, because deep down, I want him to say it. I do, and I don't. If it's *I love you*, this is the worst possible time. If it's *I love you*, how will I respond?

"Please," he says like he's begging me. I go still in his arms, except for the trembling that I can't help. "I want you to know," he whispers, pulling me to him. "There was nothing before you."

I kiss him one more time. And when it's over, I take a deep breath, I brush away the last of my tears.

NOVEMBER

Twenty

I get this stomach-dropping doubt that creeps in at the same time nearly every day. Right when I'm walking up the steps to meet Jasper in the library.

"You are so smart; you can do this," Rosie had said. She never told me that I was beautiful, but I know she thought I was because I looked like her and Mimi, and a lot like my dad, and I know she thought they were both beautiful. It was obvious in the way she'd gaze at them, watch them when they weren't looking. You didn't observe someone so closely if you didn't like the view.

"You are so smart, and making someone love you is a challenge you should be up for, especially while you're young." I watched her long fingers, freshly painted red nails, twisting around the stem of her wineglass, and the way her eyes were so steady and relaxed as she spoke; her voice so assured, her mouth always serious. She was the most glamorous person I'd ever known. I believed with my whole being that she had made many, many people fall in love with her.

This is what I think about as I climb those stairs to meet Jasper. What if I'm actually not smart enough to do this? I'm barely passing here at Rutherford. What if I'm not good enough?

"Let me see," Jasper says as I sit down across from him in our usual study room. I'd managed to finish my calculus assignment during the break between school getting out and field hockey. I try to get the assignments done, skipping any that totally stump me, before meeting him so he can check them over. This is the first time I've ever completed the assignment without having to bypass some of the problems.

He checks it over, with a red pen and everything, while I pull out *Fences* and start my reading assignment for English.

The two of us have sort of a routine for these study sessions.

"Good," he says when he's done—something he never says.

"Good?" I snatch the notebook from him. He smiles. It's covered in red marks, but most of them are the word *OK*, which is basically a gold star from Jasper. "I only messed up three of them?"

He nods. "Very impressive." He doesn't sound at all impressed, but I've learned that while his tone may not show it, he never says anything he doesn't mean.

"This is a relief!" I say, holding the paper to my heart. It would usually take me an hour or more to complete the corrections. It might only take thirty minutes this time.

"Pretty soon you won't even need me at all."

"Wishful thinking." I smile at him, and he smiles back. We're friendly, but I don't know how to push past it; don't have the slightest clue how to twist it into something more, how to intrigue it out of him or do what Rosie says and be the reflection of all his good qualities that he can't look away from. And again, I don't have the time to think about this when I've only just gotten my head above water in the pool of Rutherford academics.

As we're packing our things to leave, he says, "I can't meet tomorrow."

"Oh." *Don't panic.* "Why not?"

"I'm going to try to sleep—to nap."

"Huh. That's not what I was expecting you to say."

"What were you expecting me to say?"

"That you had a hot date, maybe?" Why not try to bring it up?

He chuckles. We walk out of the library. Per usual, we're the last ones leaving.

"I figure, I've got the time, I should nap."

"I get it." We descend the stairs. "If I had extra time, I would definitely nap."

We move down the hall, past the B wing.

"I think the next section on Taylor polynomials is going to be a real problem for you."

"I love how confident you are in me."

"I mean, we should get ahead of it. I'll make you a study sheet."

"You'd do that for me?" I bat my eyes. It makes him smile a little, as he always does when I'm being silly, more for my benefit than his amusement.

We walk outside. The air is frigid, but at least it's dry. I exhale to test if I can see my breath, and sure enough, there it is.

"I probably won't be able to nap anyway," he says. He yawns.

"I believe in you," I say as we reach the landing where the path separates.

"Good night," he calls as he goes his way and I go mine.

I don't know if comfort is a good thing to have with a person you're trying to make love you. I've never been in love before. Not the real kind. Only the achy kind that comes from longing for someone you can't have. I don't know about the actual feeling, if it does require comfort and ease. Or if it needs intensity and fire and butterflies. I don't know how I will ever learn about this unless I fall in love myself.

Twenty-one

"Dinner tomorrow?" Sebastian says as I'm on my way to the library after spending a mere ten minutes eating with Ariel and Anastasia and Theo. Jasper was right about how hard I'd find this calculus section. I could barely complete the first problem on the assignment. "You've been like a Rutherford whirlwind for the last few weeks—hard to catch. But if you're free—"

"Are you free, Sebastian? Just breezy and laid-back and *available*?" I'm thinking of the calculus assignment I don't understand and the paper on modern fairy tales due in my contemporary writing for media class that I need to make some serious progress on.

"Come on, say, 'Yes, Sebastian, I'd love to take some time off to have dinner with you,'" Sebastian says, walking quickly alongside me. "We can eat in the B wing, under the windows. They open it up when it gets too cold to eat in the courtyard, and the sun lights up the stained-glass—"

"Tell me the secret." I stop abruptly in the middle of the staircase. Sebastian's eyes widen. That earth-smashing smile of his follows.

"Secret?"

"Yes. How do you do it all here? How do you study and finish your assignments, and fill out college applications and play on the soccer team and run the international club, *and* have time to eat and sleep and even date? And you have friends. And you get to hang out with them. And spend dinner actually eating dinner. And you play *the game*. How? How is it possible?"

"Whoa, Collins Pruitt. I think you need a recharge."

His answer is so ridiculous that I start laughing. Frankly, my mind doesn't know what else to do. A recharge. If only! If only anything were that simple—if only such a thing were possible and all I needed was a reboot, a little time plugged in. Sebastian at least seems to understand that my hysterical giggling isn't actually funny.

"Come with me," he says, offering his hand.

"I can't come with you. I have to redo my entire calculus assignment and then write a paper on the 1989 Russian landscape and finish reading *Cold Mountain* and complete an essay about modern fairy tales." But all the while he's taken ahold of the sleeve of my itchy gray Rutherford cardigan and is leading me through B wing and out the side doors.

We walk outside, and the air has a chill to it, a bite from the ocean breeze and for being so high up. But he leads me to the edge of the courtyard, past all the tables and statues, past the open grassy area, right to where the retaining wall drops off behind a short hedge. You can't see the shore from here, but you can see the ocean, the roaring water in the distance. The lowering of the sun. The green block of the forest cast in a shadow. He gently takes my backpack off, pries the history book I was clutching out of my hands, and sets them down on a nearby bench.

"Just for a second," he whispers. I stare at him, he's full of sincerity.

I close my eyes to collect myself and take it all in. The pine smell. The cool, fresh air. The proximity of him with his arm lightly touching mine. I open my eyes and admire the view. It's breathtaking.

"It reminds me that I like being here," he says, gazing out, too.

I feel a flood of gratitude for him, thinking of me, seeing my hysterics and trying to make me feel better. And for this place. The way the forest has a foggy quality to it in the morning and how quiet the ocean is before noon. The intricate stained-glass windows lining the halls, the cathedral ceiling in the library. And the classrooms with that used-book smell and the teachers who came from all over the world. The smell of fresh-cut grass in the fields before practice. The view from my bed. The shared giggles in the morning as we all get ready together in that lavender-smelling bathroom with the heated floors. I think of how Elena tried to help me study by marking up my book, for no other reason than she's my roommate. I think of how nice it is having Anastasia and Ariel and Theo, to be able to take them aside in the hall and talk about nothing. I think of my father the weekend he dropped me off, sipping red wine in the square, his face lit up by twinkle lights as he told me, "Don't go easy on them, kid."

"See?" Sebastian says. He grins like he knows he did a good thing.

I nod. I feel tears in my eyes and feel embarrassed. I cry so much here, way more than I cried before. I'm blaming the altitude, but it's probably the sleep deprivation and the stress. He leans in toward me and squeezes my hand. He kisses my forehead so casually and quickly that I almost don't realize it's happening.

"It'll be okay," he says quietly. He lets go of my hand and leaves me there with the view. I take another full breath before I walk to the library.

Jasper is waiting in the private study room. He nods at me as I take my usual seat across from him. I try to be quiet as I get out my stuff so I don't disturb him from whatever he is reading so intently.

"Where were you?" he asks, not looking up from his book.

"I was . . . I got held up."

"For a second, I thought I had it wrong and we weren't meeting today." When I don't say anything, he looks up from his book. There's something in his expression. Expectancy. This is an opportunity.

"I could give you my number in case you ever think you mixed up the dates again. And you could give me yours."

He blinks at me, then says, "Yeah, okay."

We take out our phones, even though they are technically prohibited in the library, and trade numbers.

"Look at you breaking the rules," I say as he hands back my phone.

He doesn't look at me as he says, "Some rules are worth breaking."

If not for the lack of eye contact, this would be downright charming.

We work until the library closes, as usual. On the walk back to the dorms, Jasper yawns. I think he probably gets as little sleep as I do, but he seems more depleted than usual.

"Are you all right?" I ask him.

"I'm not sleeping well," he says.

"I crash every night. I don't even remember closing my eyes or lying down all the way before I'm asleep."

"No need to brag."

"You could try having hot milk before bed."

He makes a face. "You're from the dairy capital of the country; of course this is your solution."

"You could count sheep. Or count backward from one hundred."

"I was thinking of cutting out caffeine."

"That should help, too."

"My mom uses meditation apps." He sighs. "I'm sure eventually something will work."

"Well, good luck."

"Thanks."

I'm halfway down the hill when my phone buzzes.

A text from Jasper. "See you tomorrow."

I confirm this with a smiley face. Much to my surprise, he sends one back.

Twenty-two

Next week, after taking a test in number theory and knowing every single answer for once, I fly through field hockey practice with such confidence that Coach Steger asks me where this enthusiasm was for the semifinal game last weekend.

I'm still riding so high from my first totally successful Rutherford test experience, I decide that I deserve to spend the entirety of dinner eating. I truly relish in this opportunity. Anastasia, Theo, and Ariel make me laugh so hard I almost have basil-infused water coming out my nose. It's the first time I have calmed enough to really let loose since those first weeks I was here, before the Rutherford schedule got to me and I fell behind.

I send Jasper a text letting him know I won't be able to make it today. I'm not sure he'll check his phone between now and when he wonders where I am in the library, but I watch him across the cafeteria as he fishes his phone out of his pocket and glances at me. Wow, he looks awful. The past few days, his trouble sleeping has gotten worse. He didn't even have to tell me; I could see it on his face. This heavy exhaustion. The life draining right from his eyes.

Jasper walks toward the exit, slumped over like he's not even strong enough to lug around his bag. He stares at the ground as if the cascade lighting is too bright for him, and he stumbles into a trash can trying to weave past a group of second years. I shouldn't be worried about him. He certainly wouldn't be worried about me.

"Hmm," Ariel says.

Anastasia and Ariel sit across from me, their heads all slightly tilted to the left—the tilt of judgment, I call it—they're watching me watch Jasper. Theo is making the rounds, greeting his subjects.

"Still find him mysterious, do you?" Anastasia says.

They know I've been studying with Jasper. But I don't think they realize how often we meet.

"He looks awful, right?" I say.

"Maybe a little more sunken in than usual," Anastasia says, touching her cheeks as she studies him.

"It's like Theo's always saying. He's obsessed with school. Kinda like you are, but usually he doesn't seem as desperate."

"Thanks for that." Except—*wait*. It is kinda like me, the difference being I'm forced to be obsessed with schoolwork. It's true that I'm desperate. I'm scared. I'm a mess. But I think back to that day when I was so behind, I had to study on the bus after the field hockey game. Jasper was there, too. On the soccer bus, studying also.

"I have to go," I say, gathering up my food, my bag, rushing as quickly as I can while they stare back at me, confused.

Maybe it's really not as much of a coincidence as I think. Maybe I've missed the signs. Maybe all along Jasper has been having a hard time at Rutherford, too. Maybe he, *too*, is constantly worried about failing, not living up to his past successes. Maybe all the times he warned me I would have to get used to it or go home were actually warnings to himself. It's a revelation.

When I burst into the private study room, he hardly even glances away from his laptop screen.

"I think I know what will help," I say.

I wait for something from him, anything really. An eye roll or a scowl. A *"What are you talking about, Collins?"* or a *"What's that, Collins?"* But he doesn't even register that I've spoken to him. He's wilted to one side, his forehead pressed into his fist, which seems to be holding his head upright. The bags around his eyes are dark, and his lids are heavy. His face seems sharper and paler than when I studied with him two days ago. Even his curls look flat.

"Hey. When's the last time you slept?" I sit down next to him, and that at least makes him look away from the screen. He shrugs and rubs his eyes.

"I don't know," he says, his voice strained.

"This isn't good, Jasper. Come on, get your stuff, I know what will help—"

"I'm not finished yet." He runs his hands over his face and props up his head in front of his computer.

On the screen, I see several tabs open on his browser. Each one contains information about state laws—trials, subpoenas, witness testimonies.

"What class is this for?"

He quickly shuts the laptop. "It's not—it's nothing."

"You want to be a lawyer?" Maybe this is how he daydreams about the future. He looks up state laws and fantasizes of the day he can prosecute a trial of his very own.

"Absolutely not."

"Then what—"

He slides his laptop into his backpack and stands up. "Fine. What did you want to show me? How long will this take?"

"Not long," I say, suddenly very unsure about bringing him to the edge of the courtyard and telling him to *take it all in,* the way Sebastian helped me.

He follows me outside, and when we reach the spot, my regret is all-consuming. I was desperate when Sebastian brought me out here, frazzled and overwhelmed, and it really did help. But what makes me think this will calm Jasper the way it calmed me?

I attempt to take his backpack the way Sebastian took mine, but he squints and pulls it back.

"Set it down." I motion to the bench. "For a minute."

He eyes me as he reluctantly places his bag on the bench. I do the same. I stand next to him. I look out at the ocean in the distance, the sun splintering over the gray waves; the forest lit up by the last of the light. The air smells fresh right now, and there is only a slight breeze carrying the scent of pine and jasmine through the already chilled air. The lawn and shrubs before us are a lush green. This kind of peace is contagious. I can already feel it catching.

"So what are we doing?" Jasper says.

"You don't feel . . . ?" Of course he doesn't feel refreshed and peaceful; why did I think this was a good idea? "We're taking a moment. Having a recharge."

"A *what*?"

A recharge is what Sebastian called it, and yes, I'd laughed at first and thought it sounded like a huge waste of time. But it'd worked; I'd felt better—almost serene—more settled afterward.

"I'm trying to help you!"

"This is really patronizing, Collins."

"Well, you're not sleeping, and you look terrible." He sighs—irritation bubbling up—but I keep going. "You're studying yourself sick the way I did, and when I felt like I was drowning, *this* is what helped me remember why I was here, what I liked about being here. It reminded me how lucky I am to be at Rutherford and that I wanted to keep fighting to stay."

He looks me over carefully with his bloodshot eyes. "You and I are very different people." He takes a deep breath and looks to the ground, and I know what this means—this is a move he often makes, the look-down. It means he has more to share. He's only getting started. "I'm not studying myself sick. I'm not *drowning*. I don't need a reminder of how much I like it here or how lucky I am. I *get* it. I already know I love it. I already know that my graduating from here solidifies my Dartmouth acceptance. This isn't even the best view at Rutherford."

"Okay, well, you spend as much time as I do studying and you look like you're struggling, and this is the only idea I had to help you." If I'm laying out my weaknesses, I'm laying out his, too.

"My only issue is that I can't fucking sleep. I don't need a recharge. I need a shutdown."

"Then I guess I should've gotten you warm milk instead. My mistake!"

Jasper sighs and takes the few steps toward the bench. He sits down beside our bags. Then he starts laughing. It doesn't sound hysterical, like he's losing it. It sounds like a release. I haven't seen him laugh like this since that night at the inn, around the firepit.

"I did try warm milk," he says.

"And?"

"Not good." He looks up at me and smiles. I walk over to him, and he moves our bags to the ground so there's room for me to sit next to him. The bench is cold against my tights. "Nothing works, really. I'll have to get a sleeping pill from the infirmary eventually, I guess."

"That's hopeful."

"It'll be the last resort. I hate not having control over when I sleep or when I wake up."

"Controlling is one of your top five traits. I've noticed."

"That doesn't sound good. But it does sound like me, unfortunately."

"Self-awareness is important." I watch him smile as he looks ahead, out at the view. I think it's catching in him, too. If only a little.

"You're nice," he says. "That's one of your . . ." He pauses to make sure he's saying it right. "Top five traits?" I nod. "You're kind, I mean. It was thoughtful of you to bring me up here even if it's pointless. Very nice of you."

"I'm not always nice."

"Good." He nods again once. "I should be more like you."

"You definitely should." We're both half smiling, the way we're only half joking with these things we're saying to each other. These are his weaknesses, unspooling. He's exhausted enough to reveal them.

"So why can't you sleep? Do you know?"

It's quiet for a bit; I wait for him to answer.

"There was this thing Theo used to have me do sometimes when I was stressed out. It helped until—it helped for a while."

"Well, what is it?"

He turns to me, and he seems a little more alert than before—less irritated for sure. "I think it might help you, too," he says. "Do you want me to show you?"

Twenty-three

We meet Theo at the gate leading to the athletic complex. It's dark when we arrive except for the path lights and the tennis courts, lit up for a group that's either practicing or has signed up to play for fun. We follow Theo through the side doors of the gym and down the hallway to the boys' and girls' locker rooms. Theo's already in workout clothes and waits while Jasper and I change. He leads us farther down the hall, past the weight rooms and yoga and dance studios, until we reach the last door on the right. It opens, and the water polo coach, Mr. Simon, is standing there, twirling his keys. He nods at Theo and eyes the three of us.

"Okay," he finally says, sighing. "You've got forty-five minutes. Put the gloves and bags back when you're done." He leaves, and the door clicks shut behind him.

Theo walks to the far side and pulls out hand wraps from a bin. Jasper grabs three sets of red boxing gloves.

"Don't tell me we're about to fight each other?" I'm kidding, but also waiting for some kind of reassurance.

The two of them do not laugh. They're walking over to the other side of the room, where the mats are rolled up against the wall. They take hold of three freestanding boxing bags from the piles, scooting them to the center of the room.

I stand there feeling useless, so I start to wind the wrap around my hands. I don't know what I'm doing, but I figure there can't really be a wrong way to prepare your hands for boxing. When the bags are in place, Theo comes over to me, takes my hand, and undoes the wrap. Jasper and I listen as he instructs us on the proper way to wrap our hands, though it's obvious Jasper has done this before. He's always a few steps ahead of the instructions, but he concentrates, examining his and Theo's against each other, so careful to get it right. Theo helps us both with our gloves, which doesn't seem like something one would need help with, but once one glove is on, it's tricky to squeeze on the other one.

"And now what?" I say, taking position next to a bag, which is what Jasper's doing.

Theo syncs his phone with the speakers, and suddenly the room fills with loud, fast music.

"And now you hit the bag, Collins," Theo says.

He and Jasper go to town, their fists slamming against the bags. I swing my arm and make contact, but the pushback is uncomfortable.

"Use your whole body," Jasper calls to me. He shows me his punch, the way he positions his feet and twists his body. I nod and copy him. It does feel much better.

Theo explains the different kinds of punches—jab, cross, hook, uppercut, overhand—and tells me to punch from my core, which doesn't make sense until I really get going and feel the power in this. Next, Theo directs me in the proper way to kick the bag, how to position my foot so that I don't get hurt.

Jasper is focused on his bag, hitting it, kicking it, circling it like it's his opponent. It seems like it might be working for him, the way Theo intended. He's out of his head. He's coursing with adrenaline. He's wearing himself out—maybe enough that he'll be able to sleep. Theo is different with his bag; he's concerned with form and technique. He does an ordered sequence of punches and kicks over and over again before he changes it up, like it's a choreographed set.

I try it Theo's way first, making up a sequence—kick, jab, cross, uppercut. But I keep messing up. I like the punches the most. The jabs and the crosses make me feel the best. With each punch, there is a power I'm releasing, as well as a tension. A mounting anger and then an impactful release.

You're so strong. I hear Rosie's voice in my head. *You can do this. You won't let us down.*

She's turning out to be wrong—isn't she? Here I am alone with the Mahoney brothers and I still have no idea what Theo's being paid to keep quiet about, and Jasper finds my gestures to move our relationship beyond that of study partners to be patronizing.

Rosie took me out to dinner, just the two of us, after I officially got into Rutherford. To celebrate, she claimed. But by then, it'd been over a month since I was accepted and I'd already learned there was another reason she wanted me there.

It was during a dinner of prime rib and rosemary potatoes that she pulled out her phone and showed me Jasper and Theo.

"These are her boys, Collins. All she cares about. The reason she's secured your father as insurance for when her debt catches up with her."

I stared at the screen, scrolling through the photos Rosie must've collected from various social media accounts and publications, at their polite expressions, the list of all their accolades. The backdrops of their photos—grand staircases, lawns with perfectly trimmed grass, ocean views, and European skyscapes. And Rutherford. The stained glass of the B wing. The stadium lights of the athletic complex. The cathedral ceiling of the library. I had photos like this, too. A life on sprawling, green land, charming through and through. Trips to Hawaii and Europe. Summers on the coast. Telluride winters. And now I would have Rutherford, too. This is what Mrs. Mahoney was supposedly fighting to preserve, getting involved with my father.

My first instinct was to worry that it would be awkward to walk the halls with them, knowing what I did about our parents; wondering if they knew, too. But Rosie assured me that it was a best-kept secret, too risky for Marylyn Mahoney to let anyone know about it, especially her family.

"I could ask him to stop seeing her." I'd floated this idea by Rosie before. Her answer was always the same.

"You could. But he didn't believe me. And even if he listened to you, then it'd be you who was depriving him of the happiness and love he thinks he's getting from her. It shouldn't be something you have to ask him, a burden you'd have to carry." I thought about an ultimatum, *stop seeing her or else*, if he didn't believe me that she was bad for him. But what proof did I have of that except what Rosie told me? And what could I possibly threaten *or else*?

I looked at the photo of Jasper and Theo again—a family portrait from when they were younger, where it really stuck out that they had their mother's eyes and their father's smile.

"She'd risk breaking up her family?" I asked.

"Her priorities are squarely with money, and that's what she thinks is best for her boys ultimately."

I nodded. As I sat there, I thought there was nothing we could do. But over the next few days, I started to get ideas.

"What kinds of things do you think would make her break it off with him?" I'd mused. Rosie and I were sitting outside the capital building waiting for Mimi to finish up with her meeting downtown and meet us for lunch.

She stayed quiet, like she knew I had something specific I was getting at.

"Since I'll be at Rutherford with her sons and they're all she cares about besides my dad's money, then maybe they would be able to help with this."

"How so?"

"Like if they knew, they might ask her to stop seeing him. If she cares what they think, maybe she'll do it."

"Would they believe you, though, with these accusations against their own mother, someone who's always been there for them, who puts their own happiness above her own? And if they asked her, she could always lie." She shook her head. "Besides, that would backfire. They always shoot the messenger, Collins."

At the time, I hadn't believed her.

I punch the bag hard over and over again, thinking about how wrong I'd been. How much I'd hated the messenger and didn't care if it was unfair. I think of the broken glass on the floor. Mimi's voice escalating into this helpless cry while Rosie yelled. How frozen and numb I felt while it was all happening. The first and most shameful thought that kept surfacing was this: I love my father, and I don't care what he's done, but how am I supposed to forgive the two of them?

My skin is covered in sweat, and it's starting to feel tight around my chest and neck. A tingling sensation with a shortness of breath. I peel off the gloves. They bounce lightly when they hit the gym floor. My hands are shaking as I attempt to untangle the wrap from around my hands and wrists.

"What are you doing?" Theo says, out of breath.

Jasper stops hitting his bag and leans against it, waiting for my response.

"I remembered I have something to do."

Theo pulls off one of his gloves. "I can walk you back if you need—"

But I'm shaking my head, already taking fast steps toward the door. "It's fine," I call to them. "I just have to go."

It's too cold to be outside in only my workout shorts and a tank top, but I don't stop by the locker room to get changed. I'm half-way up the path when it starts to rain, light wispy drops that sting because of the wind, and I'm soaked by the time I reach the girls' dorm. I'm still shaking. My mind whirls. I reach for a distraction, try to remember all the work I have to do. But all I see are Mimi's sad eyes, her sullen expression, promising me she'll give me the space I've asked for, telling me it's fine if I don't want to talk to her for a while. Rosie squeezing my hands before I left, whispering, "I know you'll do what you have to do. We're counting on you."

I race to the third-year bathroom and rush straight into the shower. My teeth chatter until the hot water comes down around me and I'm enveloped in steam and that replicate lavender smell.

Rosie didn't just have photos of the Mahoney boys' lives. She had that photo of Theo and six other boys at Camp En Tous Lieux, which was French for *everywhere* or *in all places,* and, in my opinion, impossible to pronounce. She had the nondisclosure agreement saying he couldn't speak about being there. She had the record of that year's groups, where the names of those six boys were expunged from the record. She knew one of the other boys' fathers—which is how she found out about the NDAs. How she got ahold of Theo's, she wouldn't say, but Rosie was gifted at getting whatever she wanted. The names of lawyers representing each party were on the agreements, and my guess was that's where she'd started.

"He was supposed to have a summer full of hiking around the world, through mountain ranges, a professional guide leading the group," she said. Camp En Tous Lieux was an exquisite experience, taking a group of boys and girls who could afford their high prices on unforgettable summer long outdoor excursions that would test their limits and show them they could do the impossible—according to their website. "But he was back from their trip after only two weeks. All the boys were." She showed me photos posted to his profile during that summer he should've been with the camp, where he was instead vacationing with his family or with Anastasia. "Something happened on their trip. Something so terrible they can't talk about it, and Theo is at the center of it."

"How do you know?"

"I have the other NDAs." She pulled them up on her iPad. "For all the other boys in that group, the price of silence is $2 million. For Theo, it's $5 million."

I didn't know how to argue with this.

"If you find out what it is, then we can use it. We'll ask Mrs. Mahoney what's more important to her, this information getting out about whatever her son was involved in at that camp, or your father."

"How will I find out what it is?"

She gave me a proud smile. "You'll think of something. And if you don't, there's always Jasper."

"What did he do?"

"Nothing yet." She pushed my hair behind my ear, a rare gesture of affection from her. "Maybe instead we'll tell Mrs. Mahoney that she has to choose between your father's broken heart or Jasper's."

The warmth from the shower and the steam surrounds me. Rosie went through all this trouble for me to be here. She told me things no one wanted me to know. She wouldn't've done all that if she didn't think I could help her; if she didn't think getting me to Rutherford to save my dad would be worth it. I feel my head clearing, the panic subsiding.

When I come out, I smell as good as the air and feel fresher than a daisy. Joyce and her friend Neveah are sitting on the benches by the vanity. I wave to them. Joyce is crying. She wipes her eyes and shakes her head. "It's nothing," she tells me. A clear lie. News reports have continued to circulate about Joyce's father, the extortion and the cocaine, plus more trouble from the prostitutes he was having affairs with. The things our parents do trickle down to us, and it's not fair, but there's no getting around it.

"I'm sorry," I say on my way out.

I pause when I reach the door and turn back to face her. "This thing that happened, it's not going to define you," I say. I think of Mimi, her hand pinching my chin, forcing me to look up at her. The stern look in her watering eyes. "Don't do it, Collins," she said. "Don't let this be it for you. This isn't everything. This does not define you." For that moment, I do miss her; wish I wasn't too mad to call her, see where she is in the world, and if its vastness was living up to her expectations.

"Thanks," Joyce says, her quivering lips forming a true smile. Neveah nods like she's seconding this random plug of advice.

Mimi was right, and she was wrong. Something can define you and also strengthen you. A horrible burden can be blown into something new, something better.

I sit at my desk and open my laptop. There's a new email from my dad, a forwarded invitation from Robames for a corporate retreat at the Hylift complex in Canada. The retreat is for the board members, key investors, and company executives only. For people like my dad and the Mahoneys.

The invitation reads: *Bring your families and join us for less work and more play at Hylift resort this holiday season!*

My dad's message says: *It's probably going to be more work and less play for me, but we'll still have a blast. What do you say, kid? Since Mimi and Rosie are staying in Buenos Aries, I figure we deserve a vacation-bound holiday, too.*

I write back and tell him that I'm excited and can't wait to spend the holidays with him at Hylift.

This news that over winter break I'll be staying at the same mountain resort as Jasper ignites me. Gives me a second wind, so to speak. Because Rosie was right about me. I am strong and smart, and I'm not giving up.

Twenty-four

When I get off the plane for Thanksgiving break, my dad cries. It's the first thing I see when I exit the terminal, a sign that says *Welcome Home* and his large tears.

"You're such a baby," I say as I hug him.

"It feels like yesterday when *you* were just a baby, and now here you are flying by yourself across the country." It gets him crying again.

"Are you going to be okay?" I lean back and look up at him.

He nods. "This is much better. When you were a baby, there was always so much spit-up."

I laugh and lean into him again and am hit with the familiar smell of his John Varvatos cologne and the French roast coffee he drinks throughout the day. Oh wow, I really did miss him.

The first thing I do when I get to his Tribeca penthouse is fall asleep on the couch while the 1994 version of *Little Women* plays on the television. I tried to stay awake until Laurie professed his love to Jo, but fell asleep right after Jo cut her hair.

When I wake up, the movie is off. The television is back to its normal streaming of stock prices and Wall Street news, on mute. The room is dark except for the screen of the television and light coming from my father's open office door, a few feet from where I'm lying. I can hear him talking on the phone. He's speaking in a gentle voice.

"I know, Marylyn, believe me, I know," he's saying—his tenor like he's comforting someone. "I miss you, too. But it won't be much longer."

This is the first time I've heard him on the phone with Marylyn Mahoney, though over the summer when we were in Barcelona together, I saw him on the terrace outside our villa, pacing, talking on the phone. I assumed it was her because of the way he was smiling to himself, the way he couldn't stand still, the way he nodded as he listened, covered his mouth at some of the things she said. I watched him lean against the side of the villa as he said goodbye to her. He tipped his head back after he hung up, his face to the sun. I'd never seen him look so exposed and helpless.

"I hate it when you're stressed," he says to her now. "I don't want you to worry. I'm doing everything I can. I'll take care of it; I'm trying." He's quiet where she must be talking. "Okay," he says. "Okay. I promise. I've got it covered. I love you. Goodbye."

I hear him sigh, and I know he's probably dropped his hands to his sides and sunk into his desk chair, like saying goodbye to her requires some sort of recovery.

After a few minutes, I get up and go to my room, waving as I pass his office. It's normal for him to be awake at odd hours.

The next day, we both wake up around 11:00 a.m. He makes us a coffee and tea while we wait for the French restaurant around the corner to deliver the brunch he ordered. But a different delivery arrives first. A large bouquet of roses, two dozen of them, in a tall crystal vase.

Admittedly, I first assume they're from Marylyn. Flaunting her feelings in the most flagrant way in my father's apartment. Second, I decide they must be from any one of my father's business partners or clients, sent as a thank-you or a gesture of goodwill. And then I wonder if they're from Mimi, since this is the first Thanksgiving I'm spending without her.

My father sets the flowers on the counter as he reads the card. He frowns. "So who is Sebastian?"

"Hey, excuse me!" I snatch the card out of his hands in such a panic that he starts to laugh.

"Who is Sebastian, and why does he miss you?" my father teases me.

I die of embarrassment as I see the card does in fact say: *Have a good holiday! Miss you already. Yours, Sebastian.*

"Yours?" he continues, chuckling. "What exactly does he mean by that?"

"This isn't up for discussion." I rush into my room, the sound of my father's laughter fading behind me. Once I'm safely inside my room, I smile. I've never received flowers from a crush before. *Yours* is quite embarrassing, yes. It's also making my face hot, my stomach flutter.

There's a light knocking on my door, and I jump. I press my hands against my cheeks as I say, "Yes, come in." My father is very good about only entering my room when invited. I relax my expression, get rid of my smile.

"Thought you might want to admire these while giving them proper sunlight." He sets the bouquet down on a small round table next to the French doors that lead to the terrace.

"You want them in here so you don't have to look at them while we eat."

"Don't want to lose my appetite," he says.

We spend the rest of the day together, except instead of going to the movies like we usually do, I break to catch up on my English reading.

"You know if you don't like it at Rutherford, for any reason, not only this ridiculous amount of homework," he says, "I will pull you out of that school so fast. I mean it."

"Did they tell you I was almost on academic probation?"

"Mmm-hmm, I did get that call. I said I was fine with it. One school's academic probation is another's honor roll."

"Aren't you proud that I've pulled myself out of it?"

"Of course," he says. "But if it's too much . . . don't you want a normal, carefree childhood, girlhood, whatever?"

"No," I tell him. I really mean it. "Not anymore."

The next day, our Thanksgiving dinner arrives from our favorite Mexican restaurant. I squeal with delight. Mimi hated typical Thanksgiving food. She loved to cook but disliked boring food, and the usual turkey, gravy, stuffing, and mashed potatoes were uninteresting to her. Our turkey last year was mole-roasted, basically covered in a chocolate sauce, and served with masa stuffing and spicy chili gravy on the side. Our stuffing was made with rice and, naturally, goat cheese; our potatoes were roasted crisp.

This isn't exactly the same as our usual Thanksgivings in Wisconsin, but eating burritos and nachos feels more like our normal than if he were to order a carved turkey or attempt Mimi's recipes himself. He does make the dessert, though—a cherry pie he started when I was still asleep. Together we make pumpkin tarts and peach cobbler.

My father would always help Mimi in the kitchen when she was prepping the food, and one thing I do really miss is the way they'd banter, Mimi taking such delight in all of us cooking together, my father dressed down, usually the most relaxed we'd see him all year because he'd have his phone off and spending time with us was the only thing on his agenda. It was moments like those that I often wondered if they might fall back in love. I couldn't see then that their love came from respect and was forged out of necessity, because of me. There was no falling back; they'd never been there in the first place. It wasn't Mimi who knew how to make someone fall in love with her.

Twenty-five

The next morning, I get a text from Anastasia asking if I'm going to spend the weekend with her and Theo in the penthouse from Joyce that she won in the game. I explain to my dad my friend Anastasia Bowditch is in town, and he tells me I can hang out with her until 11:00, when he will send the car for me.

"Collins," he says as I wait for the elevator on my way out. "I'm glad you're making new friends." I smile at him as the elevator dings its arrival and wonder if he'll be seeing Marylyn tonight. The Mahoneys spent their Thanksgiving with Mr. Mahoney's sister upstate, and she could easily take a train down to Manhattan the way Theo is to join Anastasia tonight.

When I arrive at the penthouse, it's nearly completely empty. Its white walls and beige carpeting and floor-to-ceiling windows make for an eerie setting. All that remains are a few blankets, stacks of decades-old magazines, wooden barstools with tall backs, blue-tinted champagne flutes with jeweled bases, the Game of Life!, a record player with speakers, and a single record, Madonna's *Like a Prayer*.

Anastasia tells us she screamed in horror when she first saw it and promptly went out and bought blow-up mattresses, six-hundred-thread-count sheets, a large charcuterie platter, cases of pamplemousse-flavored LaCroix, and an apricot-and-dry-earth-scented candle. By the time I arrive, one of the mattresses is made up in the master, the gas fireplace is flickering, the room smells like an orchard, and Anastasia is sipping sparkling water out of a champagne glass and eating brie, staring out at the neighboring skyscrapers and city lights, while Theo hooks up the other air mattress to the air pump and watches as it inflates.

"We didn't get one for you since you're not staying the night, but if you decide you want to, Theo will share his." Theo unhooks the pump and begins dragging the fitted sheet over the edges of the mattress. "Mine will be otherwise occupied." She jumps up to pour me a glass of sparkling water. "Do you have a New York boyfriend?"

"A New York boyfriend?"

"Someone you see only when you're in the city. Like a Manhattan hookup."

"No—"

"But you half live here," Anastasia says. "I really recommend it. I don't even half live here and I have one. Theo had one, too, until he moved to LA."

Theo sighs. "Broadway wasn't good enough for him. He had to be on television, too."

"It's fun to have some romantic attention around the holidays when it's all family, family, family, you know, Collins?" Anastasia hands me a full glass of LaCroix.

"Why are you blushing like that?"

"Like what?" Why does Theo have to notice *everything*?

"You have someone in mind already, don't you?" Anastasia points at me. "Who is it? Someone who interns for your dad? A Midtown barista?"

"I don't have anyone here in mind. I mean, anyone in mind at all. Or in general."

They eye me. They're on to me because I am the easiest person to be *onto* when it comes to having a crush.

Fine. "Sebastian sent me flowers," I confess.

"Of course he did," Theo says. "He's full of moves."

"Unoriginal moves," Anastasia says. "The ladies at Cashmere Flowers probably recognize his voice on the phone."

"He orders on their website," Theo says. "What? I asked him once."

"That's so lazy."

"Or is it incredibly efficient?"

The two of them look at me, like my opinion suddenly will be the tiebreaker on Sebastian's laziness. "It was nice to receive flowers, regardless of his ordering methods. Besides, it was forever ago when he asked me to dinner, and I'm always too busy to go."

"Oh, that's got to be driving him crazy." Theo snickers, and Anastasia nods. "I bet he gives her back her earrings on the date." So that was a move, too, one they've both seen before undoubtedly with Joyce and Ariel as part of the game.

"I bet he takes her behind the angel," Anastasia says.

"Behind the what?"

Theo and Anastasia smile at each other.

Theo explains, "Behind the angel. That statue in the courtyard of the angel spreading her wings."

"Or *his* wings—it's not clear," Anastasia says.

Theo continues, "It's in this perfect position that blocks the view of the courtyard and the cafeteria and the B wing windows."

"He takes girls there to kiss them," Anastasia says.

I can feel myself blushing again. The urge to smile is strong—even if it's cliché, even if it's one of his moves.

Anastasia's phone chimes, thankfully taking the attention off me and my tomato-red face.

"Oh no," she says, her eyes scanning the screen. "Daniel is going to be late." She downs her sparkling water and frowns.

"Sometimes New York boyfriends are unreliable," Theo says.

"He even convinced me to take an earlier flight, and now he's late. That's rich," Anastasia says.

Anastasia's mother is from Florida, and her father is from England. This Thanksgiving was spent in Orlando and, as Theo explains it, Anastasia was anxious to get far away from the humidity as soon as possible. But from what I can tell, Anastasia and Theo rarely spend more than a few days apart, regardless of where their families' take them for the holidays.

If Theo and I being there tonight serves the purpose of killing time for Anastasia while she waits for Daniel, her unreliable New York boyfriend, who Theo reveals is "a whole year younger and five inches shorter than Anastasia," it doesn't feel like it. We slide Theo's mattress so it's pressed up against the window, and when we sit on it drinking LaCroix out of overzealous champagne flutes, it's like we're at the precipice of the city. Eventually, we put on the record, turning it up as loud as we can. We dance and sing along to *Like a Prayer*, and when it starts to get dark, we turn down the lights so nothing will impede our view out the windows. Next, we get creative, sliding the stools around the mattress and using the sheets to make a fort. We flip through the magazines from 1998 and 2004 and laugh at the fashion choices and headlines. People in 1998 were preparing for the year 2000 like all the computers would explode. People in 2004 were astonished at the high rates of music being downloaded as iTunes sold its two hundred thousandth song. Tobey Maguire was Spider-Man. Martha Stewart was in jail.

"What a world," Anastasia keeps saying, another phrase that—according to Theo—Anastasia is borrowing from her mother.

When Daniel arrives, Anastasia whisks him down the long hallway and into the master, taking whatever's left of the charcuterie board with her.

"How's your bruise?" I ask Theo. Jasper and I continued to meet him in the gym after that first day. It's actually helped Jasper sleep, and I like it because it lets me release any dormant stress and stomp out the doubts that crowd my thoughts, the unpleasant memories from the summer that keep resurfacing. I don't even mind that it cuts dinner short. The three of us have started taking turns wearing punching mitts, meant for catching punches. Theo taught us how to use them, and we're getting better at doing his sets. Absorbing a punch is satisfying all the same.

"It's fading fast," Theo says, rubbing the place under his arm where I hit him. I hooked when I was supposed to jab and missed the mitt. Theo flinched at first but then laughed, so I didn't feel too bad, until the next day when he showed me the mark I'd left. He promised me it didn't hurt. "You can really throw a punch, Collins. You're a natural."

"Or do I have a good instructor?"

"Take the compliment," Theo says. It's things like this that make Theo so beloved, popular by default. He's generous with encouragement and doesn't let you get down on yourself. Not even a little bit.

"Jasper needs boxing so he can sleep. I need it because I'm so stressed out. Is there a reason you need it?"

He shrugs, looks away out the window.

"I mean," I ramble, "I know you don't have much to be stressed about, but—"

"I have plenty to be stressed about."

"Like what? The usual Rutherford stuff? Seems like you have that mostly under control. More than under control, really. You breeze through that place. You own it. Everyone loves you. And I know it's not only because of your charm. I know your grades are good, too—"

"You know that, do you?"

"Everyone knows that. The way the instructors treat you, your class rankings . . . it's pretty obvious."

"You know what everyone loves more than academia, more than charm?"

I shake my head. Theo gets the grades Rutherford wants their students to get. And he has the talent of finding something in common with anyone, making him that rare human with connections to everyone; a million friends that feel bonded to him no matter how well they know him.

"Of course, you don't notice it," Theo says. "Because you have it and it's never going away. You're swimming in it. You've never known a life without it, and it'll always be there."

"What are you talking about, Theo?"

"I'm talking about money," he says.

"But you have that, too. Everyone at Rutherford does. I thought—" But I remember what Rosie said. The reason Mrs. Mahoney was so interested in my dad. She knew how to use love to get what she wanted, and that's what she was doing with him.

"My parents haven't worked in their entire lives," he says. "When my father is 'on business,' it's really him having dinner with his friends or some golf tournament he doesn't want to miss because he doesn't think he deserves to miss it. They call it *keeping up appearances*. They've recently started taking investment advice and expanding their portfolio, but they're not doing the best. They have a lot of debt. It was my great-grandparents who made the fortune, and then the next two generations did nothing but spend the money and live the good life. Jasper and I have known since we were kids that we'd have to actually work. We had a front-row seat to assets being sold, the way my parents scramble to make sure we can at least afford Rutherford and the lavish vacations that, according to them, are as important as our education. Jasper and I see what's wrong. How fast money can disappear. We've always known we won't live like them, and we're not afraid of hard work the way they seem to be."

"I'm sorry, Theo."

"It's not really their fault, I suppose. Their parents didn't work. They were never told they needed to. They weren't led by example or by instruction."

I nod because I don't know what to say. I'm not sure why he's telling me this. Maybe so I'll know what stresses him out and come to understand him better as a friend.

"So it's a good thing that I'm charming and friendly and good at school and that Jasper wins lacrosse championships and decathlons." He looks at me with a serious expression. "I know it may seem like we have everything going for us and like our family could afford to cover a $5 million NDA lawsuit, but really, we can't."

My blood stills, and my throat dries up. Five million dollars. He's talking about the NDA. His secret.

"Collins. I know it was you who put the photo in the exchange box," he says.

"I—" Damn it. What can I possibly say—how can I explain why I know or why I'd thought exposing it to that trusted group would somehow leak the information? "How did you know it was me?"

"I picked up the box to bring it to the exchange. According to tradition, it's supposed to be Jasper's job, but he was stressed out, so I did it for him. You were the last person to make a drop. You went right after me, and there was no photo in the box when I put in my item. So either someone sneaked in between the time you left your earrings and the time I picked up the items or it was you."

I cover my face. "Theo, I'm sorry. I'm so embarrassed."

"It's okay," he says.

"It's okay? But it's not. It's really not. I can explain."

"Where did you get it? The same person who told you I was taking steroids?"

"I wanted to know what you were hiding. I thought if you were forced to face it in front of everyone playing the game, you'd reveal what it was. It was a shitty thing to do, and I'm so sorry."

"I understand why you'd be curious about me," he says.

"You do?"

"You're new at Rutherford. I can imagine how Jasper and I must've seemed to you. And I know you're afraid."

I wait for him to elaborate.

"What—what am I afraid of?"

"I don't know," he says. "But there's something weighing on you. I can see it. Maybe you're afraid of getting kicked out and looking for leverage. Maybe you were intimidated by the gossip constantly flowing from Anastasia and saw how she used her information to get what she wanted—like this penthouse, for example. She knew Joyce's parents were going to be forced to sell it, and she told Joyce to put it in for the game under the pretext that she wouldn't tell the whole school about it. Useless deal that was, considering Anastasia can't keep a secret to save her life." I think of how Kiara put her parents' Hamptons house in the exchange both to confuse Anastasia and take away her power over Joyce. "But we're friends now. So if there's something you want from me, just ask."

"It's none of my business." I look to my hands, too ashamed to meet his eye.

"It was a forest fire," he says. "The reason our group at Camp En Tous Lieux was sent home. The reason for the NDA. One of the counselors accidentally set off a flare gun in the dry season. The fire burned fifty acres before it was contained. There were no injuries or casualties. But that's not the kind of thing Camp En Tous Lieux wants getting out, as you can imagine. My NDA was for more than everyone else's because they thought my price for silence needed to be higher, given my family fortune." He rolls his eyes. "I trust you," he says. "I know you won't say anything."

I smile, grateful that he trusts me. Sort of honored that our friendship is at this place. I try to decide if this is a valuable secret, something I can use to threaten Mrs. Mahoney. It's another small secret, like Jasper's former involvement with Rob James and the truth behind the reason he got his internship. If I were to tell Mrs. Mahoney that I knew about the Camp En Tous Lieux fire and that I was going to expose that Theo broke the NDA when he told me, there would be no proving that Theo was the reason I knew about the fire. When Rosie revealed that Theo had a secret, she'd assumed the truth would be something Theo had done that I could use as leverage to keep Mrs. Mahoney away from my father. But the onus here is on the camp, not on Theo.

"You didn't have to tell me that," I say. "You don't owe me anything as part of our friendship."

"Maybe not," he says. "But you're helping Jasper, so maybe I do."

"But it's all selfish, Theo. I'm helping him because I like him. And really he's helping me." And that was selfish, too, saying this to Theo, trying to intrigue him regarding my involvement with his brother. Weeks of studying together and boxing together, and I'm closer to him, yes, but only by inches. Theo might be able to help with this, too. Looping Theo in feels like the best option. Ideally, he'll offer some insight.

"Why?" Theo says.

"What?"

"Why do you like him?"

"Because he's . . ." I can feel my face getting red again. All I can think about is Anastasia talking about Jasper, saying *those curls and that bone structure*—but I can't say this to Theo.

"Mysterious?" Theo says.

"I thought he was mysterious, yeah, and I used to like that. But now it's as if . . . he seems impossible to know. That was intriguing at first. But it's not anymore. Now it's maddening."

"That's my brother, okay? He's closed off and focused and chooses responsibility over fun every time. You haven't picked up on that by now?"

"I've noticed all that about him, Theo, but he's also undercover witty and incredibly self-aware about everything except that he can be witty. He has a good sense of humor, and he won't laugh at something unless he really thinks it's funny—same with questions; he won't bother asking you something he already knows simply because of small talk, even though sometimes it makes him come across as rude. And his mind is immaculate, like there's an order to his brilliance that's so interesting it makes you want to shave off all his perfect hair and cut into his scalp to have a look."

Theo stares at me.

"What?" I finally say. "The thing I said about his scalp was an exaggeration, I don't really care to see his brain."

"No, I got that. But—" He sighs. "You wouldn't want to be with him right now anyway, trust me."

"Why not?"

"All he's searching for lately are distractions."

"Distractions from what?" But then I have another thought. "Is that why he's helping me with calculus?"

"And why he agrees to meet me in the gym to box. Though to your credit, he was uninterested in coming until he thought you might like it. Does it really matter? You're getting a calculus tutor out of it, and now I've got not only one sparring partner but two—one that's a real natural." Theo pats my leg.

"But . . . what does he need the distraction from?" I think of the way he was slumped over his laptop, propping his head up, how he's been having trouble falling asleep.

Theo shrugs. "Life in general."

"*Life in general* is the reason he can't sleep?" I wonder if he's troubled about his family's financial situation, the way that Theo is.

"If this is something you're worried about, why don't you ask him yourself?" Theo says.

"Maybe I will."

Anastasia and Daniel enter the living room laughing. She kisses him goodbye and then plops down on the air mattress next to us.

"He's leaving so soon?" Theo says.

"He has a curfew. So lame, right? No offense, Collins."

"None taken."

My curfew comes up swiftly after Daniel's. As I'm leaving, Theo says, "Wait."

I turn around in the doorway. "Yeah?"

"You really like him?" Theo asks.

I nod.

"Getting him isn't just something you have to prove to yourself, because he's not falling all over himself for you the way Sebastian is? It's not for any other reason than all those things you listed off before you got creepy and said that thing about his brain?"

"Yeah," I say. My dad once told me it's easier to lie to someone if you don't have to look them directly in the eyes, and that's how he could tell I was lying to him when I was little, because I'd stare at his hairline. Right now, I'm finding that's not the case. "I really like him."

Theo gives me a small smile and lets the door fall shut. I can't tell if he believes me or if he looks at me and only sees a girl he can trust because she's carrying an impossible weight.

Twenty-six

We return to Rutherford that Monday, and I meet Theo and Jasper in the gym for a boxing session, picking up right where we left off. The weather is unruly, raining harder than ever, and we can hear thunder clapping in the distance as we scoot the bags out from their corner and wrap our hands.

We've barely started warming up when Theo says he has to go.

"I totally spaced. I'm supposed to meet Ariel to watch the rest of that documentary on junk science and unsolved crimes. You guys stay. Sorry to bail; I completely forgot."

This seems like the most obvious lie and not even a good excuse. I think it must be because of what I said to him at Joyce's penthouse, and this is his way of giving us time alone. I wonder if he told Jasper anything I said about him.

"You're leaving . . . to watch television?" Jasper doesn't seem to buy it either.

"I'm meeting one of my closest friends because I promised her I would." He unplugs his phone, sucking the music from the room. "Have fun," Theo calls as he tosses his hand wraps into the bin and heads toward the door.

The door drags closed with a low bang.

This is what I wanted, I remind myself—the chance to be alone with him without our schoolbooks; this is good. To break the tension, I start hitting the bag. Jasper glances at the door one more time like he thinks Theo might come back, then does the same. For the next several minutes, it's only the sound of our breathing getting heavier, the dull thud of our gloves hitting the bags, and the occasional blast of thunder.

After a while, we're both out of breath. We break for water at the same time. I know I'm supposed to say something to him, that I should be taking advantage of it being only the two of us.

I decide to come out and say it—ask the thing I most want to know. "Theo told me you're helping me with calculus because you need a distraction. What's going on? What do you need a distraction from?"

"That's not the only reason I'm helping you."

Not what I was expecting him to say. My heart is already pounding because of the workout, but now I feel jittery, nervous.

"What are the other reasons?"

"I don't want you to get dismissed from Rutherford. I want you to be here, and I like teaching you calculus and studying with you and walking with you when we're done at the library and meeting you here for this." He looks away and scratches under his chin with his wrist, using the hand that still has a glove on since his other hand is holding his water. I stand there in disbelief. This is the most he's ever said to me that wasn't directly related to calculus. "And I don't mean to be hard to get to know—" He pauses to take another small sip of water. My gaze jumps to the floor, to my hands, anywhere except looking directly at him. Theo told him what I said about how I don't like the mysterious side of him anymore. I close my eyes for a second, hoping Theo didn't say verbatim about me wanting to look at his brain. Jasper continues, "I haven't—in a while—and it didn't turn out so well—the last time."

"The last time you got to know someone?"

I get brave enough to look at him, and I watch as he tries to put one hand on his hip, forgetting that he's still wearing the glove on that hand. It's sort of adorable, his awkwardness right now.

He yanks off his other glove and meets my eyes. "The last time I liked someone."

This confession from him surprises me. About making someone fall in love with you, Rosie said, "If he knows he has you, he'll be less afraid of giving himself over, too." Thanks to my confession to Theo, Jasper knows I like him, and now that knowledge has put him on the spot; forced a decision. He says he likes me, and that's what I wanted, but it's only the start. I'm going to need more from him than this. There's still a lot I need to uncover about him to make his feelings toward me stronger.

"You mean Rob." The last time he liked someone. Anastasia said he definitely hated her now. But that's leaving out a lot. "What happened between you guys?"

He begins to speak, but the thunder sounds again, louder and closer than it was before.

"It should've never happened, the two of us," he says, sliding on both his gloves. "I wasn't thinking clearly."

"I hear that can be a side effect of love."

I maneuver my second glove on, though I'm not ready to go back to the bags yet.

"I wasn't in love," he says quickly. "It wasn't a relationship. It was an infatuation. And I regret it all."

Following his lead, we walk over to our bags.

"All of it?" I say.

"All of it," he says with no hesitation. He starts punching his bag, and I do the same. We listen to the thunder getting farther and farther away from us.

In a few weeks, I'll be at a luxury ski resort with Jasper and Rob James. He says it wasn't love, but even so, whatever happened with them changed him. He's going to be cautious about falling in love now. He'll question it. He'll want to have no doubts that love is really what he's feeling.

Four Months Later

He leans forward and kisses me like he can tell that we don't have time, like he knows it's running out. He puts his hands on either side of my head and stares at me like he's getting a last look.

My kisses are to fill him up. They aren't to promise anything, because they can't; they never could.

DECEMBER

Twenty-seven

Winter is setting in at Rutherford, leaving frost on the grounds every morning and a bone-chilling wind cutting through the air every night. Studying for finals takes over everyone's schedules. I don't even have time to wonder when Sebastian will try another one of his signature moves on me, and even if I did, he wouldn't have time to make them. We cancel the game for the month of December because no one has room in their schedule to be social, let alone time for sneaking into the storage closet or to the tunnel between the dorms. Theo, Jasper, and I hardly have availability to meet in the gym. The library is so crowded that reserving a private study room every day is next to impossible. Jasper and I are lucky to get seats at the same table, and sometimes he has to kneel next to me when we go over my calculus problems.

It helps that field hockey is over and all I have to do to fill the activities requirement is pick from a list of offered sports alternatives. I choose yoga because the boxing classes are already full of the fourth years, who have priority. But it turns out I like the sereneness of sitting in silence.

Even still, as I finish my last final, and the bell rings loudly, letting us all out for winter break, I feel this pit in my stomach. It stems from a fear that I've spent all my time studying and not enough of it getting closer to Jasper, and pressure from knowing that this break would've presented me with the perfect opportunity to tell Mrs. Mahoney the reasons she needs to stay away from my dad. But because Theo's secret isn't the scandal I was hoping for, and Jasper doesn't love me, so I can't threaten a broken heart, now this vacation is a scramble to get closer to Jasper, to get him to feel something more for me.

"You have to tell me everything," Elena says as we pack our suitcases. Word's gotten around that a handful of Rutherford students whose parents are prime investors in Rob James's company will be at the winter board meeting in Hylift.

Elena's best friend, Ruthie, who leaves nothing to the last minute, finished packing earlier this week. She sits in Elena's desk chair chatting with us while we fold clothes. "If you see her wearing any other colors besides white and gold, photo documentation is required," she says.

"I doubt I'll see her that much."

"Um, yes, you will." Elena tosses me the gray sweatshirt of mine that she always borrows. "Even though you're not attending the meetings or whatever, I'm sure you'll see her at some of the dinners or around the resort. Hylift is a giant mansion. It's only one building. Bumping into people is a given."

I'm counting on that.

"When Jennings & Jennings held their retreat at the Wellington, I saw the Jennings brothers all the time," Ruthie says. "At dinner, at breakfast, in passing, in line to the bathroom, at the pool—all over."

"You saw Muriel Jennings at the pool? In his bathing suit?" Elena and I both stop what we're doing to wait for her answer. Muriel Jennings is always included in the annual list of New York City's most eligible bachelors—something I know because of the times my father was also on the list. In his late twenties, Muriel Jennings is young for a billionaire. He works out a rumored three times a day, even keeping a treadmill and weights in his office for quick sprints or lifting sessions while he does business, and it shows. You can see his muscles through his suit.

"I sure did," Ruthie says.

"That's when photographic documentation is most required!" I say as Elena screams, "Why didn't I know about this!"

Ariel and Anastasia knock on the already-open door to announce their arrival, and Elena and I yell, "Ruthie saw Muriel Jennings in his bathing suit last year!" instead of giving them a proper greeting. Ariel is predictably bored by this news, but Anastasia shrieks, demands all the information from Ruthie, and then starts frantically texting Theo to tell him.

"Are you excited about Hylift?" Anastasia says. I know she's brought it up so she'll get the chance to casually let Elena and Ruthie know that she'll be going there, too.

"I'm excited."

"Me, too."

"You're going?" Elena asks, falling right into her trap, and Anastasia explains that she'll be arriving at Hylift later in the month because "Theo's family is basically my family, and I can't go the entire break without seeing him."

Since it's such a destination spot, a lot of the board member families are extending their stay, though this seems to be encouraged since Robames is throwing a New Year's Eve party. That's what Dad and I have planned—staying the whole break. That's what the Mahoneys have arranged, too, according to Theo.

I finish packing, say goodbye to Elena and Ruthie, and walk with Anastasia and Ariel to the Rutherford front gates, where there is a cluster of students either waiting to catch a shuttle to the Cashmere airport or waiting for a car service to take them down the Cashmere cliffs and into the next town, where there is a much larger airport.

I scan the row of cars until I see a sign with my name.

"That's interesting," I muse as I read the paper the driver is holding.

It says:

PRUITT, COLLINS
MAHONEY, JASPER & THEODORE
LAING, STEWART

"It makes sense," Ariel says, noticing the sign. "Since you're going to the same place."

I hug the two of them and tell Ariel goodbye and Anastasia that I'll see her soon.

The driver helps me with my bag, and I climb into the back seat. A few minutes later, the doors open. Jasper and Theo climb in.

Theo takes a seat next to me, and Jasper bypasses me to sit in the third row. He gives me a quick smile instead of saying hello, then puts on his headphones.

I can hear Rosie's advice, clear as day, what she'd say to me if she knew I was about to be trapped in a mountain resort with Jasper, free from Rutherford obligations and from Rutherford rules. She'd tell me there's no excuse now. She'd tell me to find a way to get closer to him. *Let him see that you're the one who shines a light on the good parts of himself and makes him forget all the bad parts.*

"Are you as excited for us as the rest of the school seems to be?" Theo says.

Theo and I chat for a while, until Stewart arrives and joins Jasper in the very back. We're exhausted from exams and don't talk much as we're hauled off to the closest international airport.

By the time we arrive, it's dark. We check our bags and go through security. We have four first-class tickets. According to the seat assignments, Jasper and I are next to each other, and Theo and Stewart have the opposite row.

"Are you okay with the window?" Jasper asks me as we board.

I nod. I'm not sure if we're going to switch seats so that Jasper can be next to Stewart and I can sit with Theo. But when we board, we all take our assigned seats.

There's a wide console, an armrest that's easily shared between us without our arms touching. Jasper and I might as well be seated in different rows. As the plane takes off and the cabin lights go out, I wonder if he'll try to sleep. He takes out his tablet, puts on noise-canceling headphones, and watches a movie. Clearly, not wanting to be interrupted. I try to watch a movie, except I fall asleep. I wake up an hour or so after I drifted off to use the restroom. Jasper politely gets out of his seat to let me pass, instead of having me squish past him, which I'd be more than happy to do. When I return, his tablet is dark. His headphones aren't on. He fidgets as I get situated next to him. I can tell he has something he wants to say to me. After I've got my seat belt back on, he leans in my direction. Right as he gets out the first syllable, there is a chime. The captain comes on the overhead speaker to announce we're beginning our descent. By the time we're prepared for landing, Jasper has his headphones back on and his eyes closed. Probably listening to the same music he sometimes puts on when we're boxing—music for decompressing that, for Jasper, has a loud, repetitive beat and a catchy, melodic chorus.

After we land and disembark from the plane, we rush to the correct gate. We have to go outside to board our next plane. It's very cold. The wind blows hard and biting against my face. My breath comes out in thick steam. We're surrounded by white—snow and ice-covered mountains and a cloud-filled night sky.

"Right this way." An attendant motions for us to follow him. But where he leads us isn't to another airplane at all. It's to a helicopter, its engine roaring, its blades whipping through the air. Stewart, Theo, and Jasper climb right in like they've done this a thousand times. I freeze. I've never been in a helicopter, nor have I ever wanted to be in one. Many times my father has tried to get me to take a helicopter tour of Manhattan—my answer is always a resounding *no*. I preferred a shark tank to the helicopter tour option when we were in South Africa. When my father told me I'd be coming straight to Hylift, he failed to mention exactly how I'd be getting there.

"Come on." The attendant holds out his hand for me. But I can't do it. I can't move. I look up to see what Theo and Jasper are making of this, but I can't see them—until Jasper suddenly appears. He's climbing out, coming toward me. *Good.* Maybe he doesn't want to be in a helicopter either and they'll make new arrangements for us to ride on a real airplane. He grips my shoulders when he's in front of me. "You've never been on one before?" he says, yelling over the noise. It's so loud I want to cover my ears.

I shake my head.

"I haven't either." Right when I think we're going to weasel our way out of this, he says, "I've done some research, and it's going to be fine."

I keep shaking my head, but my feet take a few steps closer. He lets go of my shoulders and grabs my hand.

"I don't want to," I say. He taps his ears to tell me he can't hear me, and I move closer to him, so my mouth is by his ear. "I'm scared."

"They won't let anything happen to us," he says into my ear.

"That's not good enough," I say. He has too much faith that simply because people are being paid to get us to Hylift safely, they will. Come ice or snow or wind or engine malfunction.

"If you get in, they'll give us headsets. I can talk to you the whole time."

"How is that going to help?"

"Because I'm going to explain to you why you don't have anything to worry about. Come on. I'll tell them they can't take off until you're comfortable."

This gets me on board, and through the headsets, Jasper has the pilot promise they won't launch until I say I'm okay. But now that I'm strapped in, I'm shaking. Tears are stubbornly encroaching my eyes, and my bottom lip won't stop trembling. It must hurt, how hard I'm squeezing Jasper's hand.

"What are you afraid of?" the pilot says to me through the headset.

"The bad weather," I say, picking this to start with in my long list of terrors.

The pilot starts going on about weather patterns and how the helicopter can handle all of it. Jasper cuts him off. "What are you really afraid of, Collins?"

I completely unload. "I'm scared something will happen to the blade. I don't think I'll like the up-and-down motion that will make it feel like we're falling. I don't want a scenic view of the mountain right as we're crashing into it."

Jasper nods, but then he pulls out his phone.

"Look at this," he says. He holds it so I can see it, flipping through different screens that show numbers—*no*, statistics that pertain to helicopter crashes with this particular model, with these particular weather conditions, coming from this particular airport. The statistics do indicate that my odds of surviving this ride are very, very good.

"Can we try to take off now?" he says.

"Hold my hand during the up and down." Theo reaches for my free hand. "And if you don't want to see outside, close your eyes."

"But it's going to be beautiful!" the pilot chimes in.

Jasper glares at him even though the pilot is facing the other way. "Only if you want to, Collins. Also, remember this flight is only twenty-five minutes long; it'll be over very quickly."

"It's the only way to get to Hylift," the pilot adds.

Theo nods to confirm, but for some reason, it takes a nod from Jasper before I truly understand that this is our lone option.

"Okay," I say. "Let's get it over with, then." I squeeze both of their hands and pinch my eyes shut. As predicted, I do not like the feeling of the takeoff, the wobbly lift into the air as though we are levitating, but at an incredible rate. Nor do I care for how it feels as we propel forward or when we have to make a turn. But I run the numbers over and over in my head. The odds are in our favor. This makes me think of *The Hunger Games,* and for a second, I'm distracted. But a moment later, I remember where I am again. The helicopter jerks to the side. I tighten my grip on their hands. Suddenly, I hear a low voice singing in my headset. Theo. He's singing "Like a Prayer." Jasper joins in. Stewart, too. I'm impressed they know all the words. I slowly start humming along. This does help. I can't seem to resist singing when they start on the chorus. We keep singing as the helicopter takes another uncomfortable curve. And then a new voice joins—that of the pilot. He's way more into it than we are, singing in a falsetto, belting out the lyrics. I can't help but crack a smile, like a reflex. I dare to open my eyes. Theo is gazing out the window as he sings. Jasper is looking at me. They are both smiling. I see past Jasper, out the window. It's breathtaking—beautiful like the pilot said it would be. A dazzling skyful of stars and snow-covered mountains lit up by the full moon. I stop singing to gasp.

"I told you," the pilot says. I nod—I have to give him that. And suddenly the jerking movements that startled me before don't seem as bad. I don't mind the corners so much, and I even manage to stay calm as we land.

Another car service picks us up from the helicopter landing

pad. The landing pad is on Hylift property but still a ways from the resort. We climb into the SUV and trek through a snow-covered road with snowbanks so high on each side that I can barely see the forest behind them. Large snowflakes tumble down. When we come upon Hylift, it's like a beacon, all lit up, with a large front porch and smoke rising from the chimneys. It looks like your typical cabin in the woods, but fifty times the size, with a wraparound porch that we can't see the end of and a roof that is multiple stories tall.

Inside, the lobby is expansive, a fire roaring in the enormous, stone fireplace and giant wreaths decorated with colorful ornaments hanging on the walls. The ceiling is so high I have to crane my neck to see it. Large streams of silver tinsel dangle from the beams.

We're informed at the front desk that our parents' flights were canceled coming out of Chicago but that they will likely get in tomorrow. They provide us with the keys to our rooms and tell us the kitchen has stayed open, in case we're hungry and wanted a hamburger. A hamburger doesn't even make my top-five favorite foods, but in this moment, it sounds like an absolute dream. Jasper and I both answer emphatically, "Yes." Theo says he's too tired to eat and retreats to his room. Stewart says he's also too tired. As I tell them good night, I thank them for singing to me on the helicopter ride.

I have to thank Jasper, too. But as we sit together at the booth they've prepared for us in the corner of the closed restaurant, right up against a large window with a view of the snowy mountains and the full moon, I think about the way he jumped out of the helicopter to get me and the way he offered me his hand and didn't let go for the whole ride. I feel shy about saying it.

We're quiet as we inhale our dinner.

"That was the best burger I've ever had," I say.

He smiles. "They could've served Spam and it would've been the best meal I've ever eaten."

I laugh.

"That made the helicopter ride almost worth it." I take a deep breath. "Thank you, by the way. For, you know . . . without you—" I'm so bad at this—but why? Why is it so hard to tell him this, to admit it? "I never would've—"

"It's okay," he says. "I looked up those statistics when we were in the car on the way to the airport. They made me feel much better about riding in the helicopter. I'm glad they made you feel better, too."

"Yeah, that really helped." *And when you came after me, and when you gave me your hands.* "And the singing. That helped, too."

"Theo knew exactly how to distract you." He looks away, out the window, and I get the sense that he has something to add. He sighs. "He knows you so well. But I—I don't think you're that easy to know either."

"Maybe you're right."

He stares at me like this response surprises him.

"I am right," he says.

"So we're both hard to know." It feels like he wants me to admit this, like it's what he was waiting for.

"But Theo knows you."

"Theo knows a lot of people. That's how he is."

"But you and I—" He cuts himself off, and I wait for him to continue. "You and I have spent a lot of . . . we should know . . . I should know as much or more about you than he does, given everything." I'm startled at how agitated this makes him. "I want to know you more. And I want you to know me. But—" He looks away again.

"But what, Jasper?"

Before he manages to speak, the server comes to collect our

plates. The lights dim. A clear hint to remind us that the restaurant is open specially for us but ready to shut down officially now.

We walk down the corridor and get into the elevator. He presses the button for floor ten, and I press the button for floor eight. Piano music flows from the speakers.

I can feel the night winding down and coming to a close, and now that I'm full, I feel exhausted and ready for sleep. But Jasper brought it up again, us getting to know each other, what I said about him to Theo over Thanksgiving break that Theo shared with him. If he wants to let me in little by little, I'll have to pull as much from him as I can.

"Are you going to be able to sleep tonight?"

He looks altogether disheveled. Not quite as bad as when he wasn't sleeping at all, but he does seem beat, physically and mentally. His guard might come down a little simply because he's too tired to keep it up.

He crosses his arms, like even though he says he wants me to know him, he doesn't like that I asked this about him, a branch of something I've learned about him already. "No. Probably not for a while."

"I bet I won't be able to fall asleep right now either since I slept so much on the way here. Not to brag."

He smiles as he nods. He looks down at his watch as he says, "I was planning to swim."

"The pool is open?"

"It's open all night."

I wait to see if he'll invite me. I can't tell if he likes the prospect or if it makes him nervous.

"Can I meet you?"

"Yes," he says without hesitation.

Twenty-eight

When I arrive, Jasper is already there. He's sitting at the edge of the pool with his feet dangling in, leaning back on his palms, watching the falling snow stick to the slanted glass panels that make up the roof. The back wall of the room is made of glass, too, with a forest encroaching on the other side. The room is dark except for the dim blue lights under the water, so we can see outside through the windows, instead of our own reflections.

When Jasper notices me, he smiles, gives a small, awkward wave, and then eases himself into the water. His shoulder are broader than I thought and he's defined in a way that shows off how participating in all those *athletics* are doing him favors under his Rutherford uniform. I'm human, so I notice. I feel the slightest bit shy as I peel back my robe and join him in the pool. He tugs on a swim cap and goggles.

"Oh, you wanted to really swim. Like, actually swim." It makes me giggle that I didn't figure this out. Of course when Jasper said he wanted to go to the pool, it wasn't to lie listlessly in the water as I'd thought.

"I brought extra goggles and an extra cap in case you wanted to use them." He motions to the ledge of the pool where a blue cap and goggles are resting.

"That's okay." I'm far too tired to swim the kind of intense strokes that would require a cap or goggles. Instead, I put my hair up and casually do the breaststroke, keeping my head above the water.

Jasper pushes off the wall and swims freestyle. He goes fast, chasing the goal of wearing himself out.

The water is crystal blue, thanks to the underwater lights. It was cold at first, but now it's refreshing. Originally, I'd planned not to get my hair wet, but as I glide through the water, I think, *Screw it.* I plunge below the surface, moving my arms to keep me under. When I can't hold my breath anymore, I come up. Next, I float on my back. I stare up at the glass ceiling. The snow has covered most of it, but since it's angled, there are patches near the peak where the snow has slid away, and I can see the tops of the trees in the surrounding forest and bits of the night sky. It's calming, all of it. Even the soft splashes in the distance from Jasper swimming. And then suddenly, I can't hear them anymore. I stop floating and stand upright. He's breathing heavily at the ledge as he peels off his goggles and swim cap, freeing all his damp curls. He turns and stares at me.

"Did it work?" I say.

He sinks down into the water so it's hitting his shoulders and runs his hands over his face. "I think I have to try something else." He slowly swims over to me. "That didn't make me tired. It woke me up even more, if that's possible."

"Really?"

"Yeah. Pathetic, isn't it?"

I catch sight of a bin in the far corner of the room, where there is a bundle of foam pool noodles. "Hey, I know what might work."

He asks, "What?" but I don't answer him as I get out of the pool and walk to the bin. As my feet smack against the cement, and I feel the coolness of the air against my wet skin, I realize how exposed I am and hope he's not looking me over the way I looked him over when I first arrived. There are not only foam pool noodles but also kickboards, sleek and rubbery, not like the chipped foam we had to use for swimming lessons when I was a kid. I start tossing items into the pool. A few kickboards and several of the foam noodles come raining into the water. I jump in after them, getting excited.

"Maybe instead of trying to wear yourself out, you need to subdue yourself into relaxing."

"Maybe." He sounds unconvinced, but he follows along with me as I instruct him on how to make a proper floatation device out of the kickboards and foam noodles, with noodles positioned under our legs, backs, shoulders, and heads, and kickboards for our arms and feet. It's almost perfect, except it's hard to keep the kickboards in place under our feet, and each time we try, they loosen and go shooting through the air. We laugh so hard, I feel almost as awake as Jasper does.

Eventually, we settle into our contraptions, each of us holding on to the edge of the same noodle, so we can pull each other away from the wall when one of us floats too close.

"Are you relaxed?" I say.

"I guess."

"Then you must be doing something wrong. Are your muscles unclenched? Are you slowing your breathing? Is your mind clear?"

He floats toward the wall, and I pull him closer. We bob and weave as our noodles gently collide before the water calms again.

"I'm thinking about—actually, never mind."

"Oh, come on. Tell me."

It doesn't take much pushing to get him to spill it, and I decide that's a good sign.

"You know when the boards under our feet flew through the air?"

"Okay, yeah?"

"Well, I'm—" He lets out a short laugh like he's embarrassed. "I'm trying to calculate how big the board would have to be to launch one of us into the air. But it's kind of relaxing, thinking about this."

"Math is relaxing to you?"

"It's actually physics—" He cuts himself off as though he can see the expression I'm making or he knows me well enough to know I'm rolling my eyes. "But it's sort of relaxing, yeah."

"Relaxing because it's a distraction?"

"Yeah."

A few seconds pass, and he doesn't say anything. I'm dying to pry, but I don't want to be annoying or too pushy. Mostly, I want him to know that I get him, that I understand why trying to solve a physics equation is relaxing for him.

"Is Rutherford really all that stresses you out?" he says.

"Oh, sure, it's only the most challenging academic program in the country—*only* that."

"I mean, there's nothing else?"

"Nope. My life is perfect."

I glance over at him. He nods, and I can tell by the way he's looking at me that he knows this isn't the case.

"Was that—was Rutherford what you were thinking about the first day we started going to the gym?"

"The first day?" I'm not sure what he's talking about.

"Yeah. You were hitting the bag really hard, and you had this faraway look like you were somewhere else. And then you seemed like you were going to cry or scream or, I don't know, explode, and you suddenly told us you had to go and ran off." He gives me a small smile. "So that was only about Rutherford, about exams, about math?"

My throat gets tight, but I manage to smile. It surprises me that he'd noticed I was losing it that day, and that he remembered. "It's actually calculus."

Sometimes you have to show vulnerability to get vulnerability back from someone—I knew that even before Rosie told me. It's the reason you have to kneel on the ground to get a skittish goat to let you get close enough to put a lead on it. But Jasper's already seen my weaknesses in adjusting to Rutherford. He doesn't need the rest. He doesn't need to know what happened to me the week before I met him or about the memories that made me run away from the gym that night. They're mine to churn over, mine to live with.

I tug on the noddle to bring him closer to me, even though he's nowhere near the wall. He pulls me closer in return.

Twenty-nine

Jasper and I are side by side in the water, the noodles under our heads colliding. We're unbelievably still. I let the tension settle around us; allow him to fully feel how it's both comforting and unnerving to be near me like this.

There's a noise then: a low hiss of the door to the pool opening. We sit up, using the boards to support our arms. Rob James herself is standing there. Except she looks unlike I've ever seen her before. Her hair is in a high ponytail, stray pieces dangling past her forehead, her bangs pulled back. Her face is bare, no foundation or eyeshadow or mascara or lipstick. It reminds me how young she is, even though right now she's dressed like a grown-up. She's not in her trademark white and gold; she's in a black silk robe that cuts off at her thighs and fuzzy red slippers. Her bodyguard isn't with her. She stares at Jasper, glances only briefly at me.

"I was hoping to catch you alone," she says, her voice not at all timid. "Can I talk to you for a second?"

Jasper gets untangled from all the foam noodles and lets go of the boards. "How did you know I was here?" He sighs, aggravation showing on his face. "You can't have me followed, Roberta."

Roberta.

"I only need a few minutes." She stays stoic, but there's a hint of distress in her tone. A dent in her armor.

"Now's not a good time. We were about to leave." He starts gathering the foam noodles and moving toward the ladder, glancing back at me to make sure I'm following him. I collect the foam noodles and boards, and I swim toward the ladder.

I feel her eyes on me as I climb out of the pool behind Jasper. She watches as Jasper hands me a towel and holds my robe for me as I slip it on.

"Are you going to introduce me to your guest?" she says, her voice cheery but still firm.

"This is Jacob Pruitt's daughter," Jasper says.

"Oh, of course." She smiles at me, and it's warm and genuine. "Your father is an integral part of our investment team. We're so glad you could join us here at Hylift. Thanks for spending your holiday with us and lending your father's time. You know how quickly things are moving at the company. We have to take advantage of this momentum!"

I find myself smiling back, telling her I get it. "You and the company can have him every holiday if it means we get to vacation here," I say. She has this effect. I want to reassure her that I understand the importance of what she's doing—innovative, life-changing stuff. At the same time, I want her to know that I'm grateful, both for this destination spot and for her courage, building this company that's going to make the world a better place when so many told her she was too young and too naïve.

"It's really great to meet you," she says. She holds out her hand for me to shake, carrying herself like she's in one of her white-and-gold power suits and not in a slinky robe.

"Collins Pruitt," I say.

She smiles and nods at me like she already knew this, though I don't think she did. "I take it you go to Rutherford with Jasper."

"I do," I say.

"It's a great school." She beams at us like she's a proud alumna, excited to see the fellow legacies coming up behind her. "I hope to see you both around. We should hang out—if I *ever* get any downtime, that is." She laughs, and I laugh because she's laughing—her full and demanding schedule is hilarious in this instant since she's declared it so. Jasper, however, does not laugh.

After another friendly wave, we leave her in the pool area. But as I start toward the elevators, I realize Jasper's not with me. I turn around and see him standing next to Rob, her hand gripping his arm.

"Please," she's saying to him, her voice so low I can hardly hear her. "You have to talk to me sooner or later." She sounds young as she says this. There's no desperation in her voice, but something defenseless in the way she's staring at him—her whole being softening.

The look he gives her is so cold. "No, I don't."

Her hand drops from around him, and I quickly exit, hoping she didn't notice that I'd been watching.

She was absolutely mesmerizing. I forgot, for a moment, to see this encounter for what it is. She's here, in the middle of the night, looking for Jasper. She's wearing a short silk robe. She was hoping to catch him alone.

Jasper and I walk hurriedly to the elevators. He hits the button aggressively, like he's worried she's going to come out of the pool area before the elevator arrives. But when she emerges through the double doors, she doesn't try to approach us. She passes us, giving me a tight courtesy smile before she continues down the hall and disappears around the corner.

The elevator opens, and we step inside. I ask him, "Why won't you talk to her?" I think of the way he'd bristled at her touch the evening she'd spoken at Rutherford and the regret he'd spoken of in the gym, how he wants to take back everything with her— someone so beloved by most who meet her, a genius and a star. In truth, I don't want him to talk to her. That can't be good for my cause. But I do want to know what they have to talk about—what she wants to tell him, what she believes is still between them.

"It might make you feel better," I say. "Closure or whatever."

"There's nothing left for us to say to each other," he says.

"I don't know, Jasper. She seemed like she had something she wanted to say to you."

He stares hard at the front of the elevator, making his irritation obvious.

"She knows how to work a room," he says, his eyes shifting to me for a moment. "No matter how small the audience."

I frown and cross my arms so he'll understand that I picked up on his subtle insult—the insinuation that she performed for me just now and that whatever she did made me want to be on her side. Even if he's right.

"You don't know her like I do," he says. "She brings out the worst in me. If you knew what I did when I was with her, what I was like, you would tell me to stay as far away from her as possible."

What he *did* when he was with her? I'm dying to know.

"Maybe if you tell me," I say, keeping my voice casual, "I'll reassure you it's not so awful. It really might not be that bad. In the grand scheme of things."

He's quiet, and for a second, I think it's worked and he's going to tell me whatever horrible thing he did when he was with her that's probably part of, if not *the* reason he wants to take back their entire relationship, or whatever it was.

"But what if it is that bad?" he says.

"Maybe I'll have advice."

"Maybe." I think he's only saying this to be polite.

"Why did it end between you and Rob?" According to Anastasia, it's common knowledge that he hates her, but what's not known is why.

He doesn't say anything. The elevator stops on my floor.

"You aren't going to tell me?" I say. "Even if it means we don't get to know each other any better?"

I step out of the elevator and turn around when I hear him say my name.

"Collins?" He sounds as unsure as I've ever heard him. "I'm sorry."

The doors seal closed.

Thirty

I have a lot of questions rooting around in my head about Jasper and Rob James. To get closer to him, I feel like I need to understand this—whatever was between them and whatever makes him harbor so much regret. She was giving him his overview when it started. She was a senior when he was a sophomore, though I have seen his sophomore-year photos, and he'd had his growth spurt and a full jaw chisel by then. But what happened in the meantime, between when they got together and when it officially ended over the summer, to make him hate her. What did he do when he was with her that he's still ashamed of? What makes him want to take back the whole thing? Is it something he did with her, or for her, or to her?

A little after noon, I text Theo to meet me in the sky lounge. It's the top floor of Hylift, connected to the aerial tram that takes skiers to the closest mountain. Theo's sitting on a stool, eating fries at the counter in front of a window. I take a seat next to him.

Our parents, as well as a slew of other board members who were also derailed in Chicago, arrived this morning. I had brunch with my dad, but he has meetings the rest of the day, so I'm pretty much on my own. Theo and Jasper are, too, even if the Mahoneys aren't as involved in the company operations as my father is.

Theo and I catch up for a bit and rejoice about how excited

we are to be done with Rutherford finals. Neither of us mention that we have reading lists we could be tackling to prepare for the upcoming semester. I wait a while before I bring up what I really want to talk about.

"What happened between Jasper and Rob James?"

"You think I know any more than you do?" he says.

"Theo." I pat his hand. "I think you know all about it."

Theo takes his time swiping a long, greasy fry through a pile of ketchup. "I understand that Jasper and Rob James makes for some juicy gossip, but don't you think it's a little awkward to be discussing that now, when it's completely over, and we're *here,* at a gathering for her investors—a.k.a. our parents—who have lots of money tied up in her company?"

"I'm not asking because I want to gossip." A little too defensive, maybe. Theo gives this infuriating *yeah, right* kind of look as he shoves two more fries in his mouth. "I'm worried it's not completely over."

His forehead scrunches with concern. "Why do you say that?"

I tell him what happened at the pool last night.

"What the hell?" he mutters, shaking his head. "She can't do that. It's not allowed."

Not allowed? "What do you mean?"

"It's creepy!" Theo says. "She shouldn't be tracking his whereabouts just because she can."

"She was very eager to talk to him. Alone."

"I'm sure she was." Theo rolls his eyes.

"But why?" I say, not caring that I might be coming off too pushy.

"Listen, everyone falls all over themselves for her and thinks she's brilliant, but that's—that's by design. Do you get it?"

"Not really." Except I was completely under her enchantment last night, the way I had been when she'd spoken at Rutherford.

But what's so wrong with thinking a brilliant businesswoman is a *brilliant businesswoman*?

"She's got a great new invention and a whole company to develop it, the richest people in the country tossing money at her, but what really skyrocketed her to success is that she has this persona that draws people in. People want to believe in her. They want to root for her. They want to be a part of whatever she's created or is going to create. She's like a magician. But with Jasper . . . the spell is broken. She can't stand that." He looks over my shoulder and starts waving. I glance behind me to see Jasper and Stewart walking toward us. "Does that make sense?"

I'm nodding as Jasper and Stewart join us at the counter.

The four of us finish off another plate of fries, and after we sign the bill to our parents' rooms, we head to the aerial tram that goes to the mountain. The ski runs are closed because of too much snow, but the tram continues to operate, taking guests to the exceptional views.

We have the tram to ourselves, and when we file in, Jasper stands next to me instead of at the other side of the tram, not spreading out the way that Theo and Stewart are. He puts his hand right next to mine on the railing as we glide above the forest to the neighboring mountain.

Because the mountain isn't open for skiing, we aren't allowed to leave the docking station, but we can walk on the covered deck to take in this view, which is even vaster and more extravagant than the view from the sky lounge. I stay near Jasper as we look out at the mountains in the distance, and the snow falls down around us in large flakes. He leans against a pole at the end of the deck, and I lean on the other side. Carefully, I place my hand around it for stability. Jasper lets his hands wander up and down the sides, and it seems like a nervous fidget at first, but when his hands stop moving, they rest next to mine. An inch away or less.

I like this game more than I care to admit. It's an afternoon of almost-touches, and I wonder if he's holding back on purpose or if this is all he's brave enough to do in front of Stewart and Theo.

When we return to the sky lounge, it's noticeably more crowded. People surround the corner of the bar area. The three of us look at each other quizzically, wondering what's gotten everyone gathered. The answer comes to us through the speakers.

"I'd like to thank you all for joining me at Hylift this holiday season." Rob James's voice booms throughout the room. She sounds like the Rob James I'd expect, a confident and friendly voice. A tone that makes you want to hear more. "In the meetings to come, we'll discuss the great strides we've made in this innovative breakthrough that's going to revolutionize the way we treat so many diseases. Our research has come a long way. We are making waves in product development."

At this, some people in the crowd start to clap. I can hear that she's smiling even though I can't see her through the thick sea of people around her. "I'm so pleased that you're all here to learn more about where we're headed and to celebrate the new deals being brokered, ensuring that our product will have a place in the market sooner rather than later." She pauses, and the whole room holds its breath, waiting for her to go on. A glassful of sparkling water rises in the air, a few feet away. The hand holding it has clear but perfectly polished nails and a golden chain dangles from the wrist. "Hear, hear!" she says.

The room erupts so suddenly it makes me jump. I spot my father in the group. He's got his champagne flute in the air like everyone else, but the expression on his face isn't joyous. It's set in concern. And when he brings the drink to his lips, he finishes the entire glass. Across the crowd, I look for Mrs. Mahoney and find her on the other side of the room, standing with Mr. Mahoney. They clink their glasses together before they drink, laughing and smiling.

After the toast, the crowd thins, and I catch a glimpse of Rob. She looks radiant, like her face on the cover of *Vanity Fair* come to life—her hair wild but still contained, pulled back with a golden ribbon. She's in a long white coat and a thick gold necklace. With her looking so sophisticated and otherworldly, effortless in the way she captivated the room, it's hard for me to picture her dating Jasper—any boy at Rutherford, really—and hard to reconcile what I saw of her in the pool, the expression on her face when she was pleading with him.

She moves through the pack, stopping and clinking her glass with those she passes as she smiles that megawatt smile and thanks them for coming.

I turn around to see what Jasper makes of this—of Rob James getting closer to us. But it's only Stewart and Theo standing next to me. Jasper is gone.

Thirty-one

Later, when the sun's going down, I take photos of the mountain backed by a brilliant sunset from the sky lounge and send them to Meghan and Cadence. We don't have this view from the outskirts of Madison, and I think they'd like it. They text me back a selfie of the two of them at Meghan's house, where they are eating popcorn and watching movies and sitting in front of a blazing fire. This is how we used to always kick off winter break. I'm staring at the familiar, distant scene when they call me.

"Hello!" they shout into the phone at the same time.

I move into the hallway near the elevators so I can hear them better. They're talking so fast, telling me about their plans to sleep in and go sledding every day and asking about Hylift and Rob James.

"You are coming back eventually, right?" Meghan says.

"Eventually, yeah." Though I don't know when.

"Oh, good," Meghan says, her voice full of relief.

"We saw the For Sale sign at your house and got super worried," Cadence says.

"What are you talking about?" This has to be some kind of mistake—I don't believe Mimi would leave the country with Rosie without knowing her home would be there waiting for her when she got back.

They respond at the same time. "We can't believe your mom is selling the farm!" and "You didn't know?"

"Mimi would never sell the farm. There's no way."

"Um, we saw the sign, Collins!"

"Kimberly's mom is the Realtor."

This sudden urge to prove them wrong, to get confirmation that it can't possibly be true, surges through me. A mix of panic and determination.

"I—I have to go. I'll call you guys tomorrow." I hang up quickly, even though Meghan is midsentence in protest. I ignore them when they call me right back. I don't check the message they left. I'm too busy searching for our address online, watching as our house comes up on all the real estate listing sites. Our farm, for sale.

It doesn't make any sense. Why would she do this? I tear back into the sky lounge, approach my father where he's in a friendly conversation with some man dressed like he thinks we're at an ugly sweater party.

I show my father my phone, the sites with the farm posted for sale, not caring that I'm interrupting in the rudest way possible.

"Did you know about this?" I demand as my father smiles and apologizes on my behalf to whoever he was talking to. He takes my arm gently and leads me to a less crowded area.

"Mimi didn't talk to you about this?"

I shake my head. "Cadence and Meghan told me." He still doesn't know Mimi and I haven't been speaking.

"Well, this is something she needs to talk to you about herself."

"Why is she doing this? She loves the farm and that house." *Our house.* "It was her dream."

"Dreams change, Collins."

"So traveling the world with Rosie is her new life now? She doesn't care about having a home anymore?"

"This is a conversation you need to have with her yourself," he says as calm and cool as ever. "I don't question your Mimi when she makes up her mind. If she hasn't told you yet, then maybe she's waiting to do it in person."

"Is this because of you?" My heart starts going wild as soon as the words come out, and my father's expression turns shocked. I don't like making his face change like that. I don't like bringing conflict into our relationship when we've never, ever had a reason to fight. But I don't feel like I have any other choice.

"Why would you assume this has anything to do with me?"

I can think of many reasons that her selling the farm is centered on him, starting and ending with him being the one who gave her that farm in the first place.

"It's technically your farm, right? Since you're the one who bought it. You're the one who pays for the upkeep." I know it hurts him, my talking about the farm like it's his property that he was simply allowing us to use, when it's never felt like that's the case and he's never done anything to make it feel that way. But that was before he fell under the spell of Mrs. Mahoney and before I knew that he was hiding things from me.

"That's your Mimi's farm." His voice gets stern. "I might have paid for it, but the deed is in her name. It's hers alone. Period. It's her business if she wants to sell it."

I hate the tension between us, hate that I can see how it hurts his heart the same as it does mine for us to have this kind of back-and-forth—me pressing him, him having to defend himself about his place with Mimi in our family. His eyes search mine, like he's waiting for me to confess the truth about where my accusations are coming from, the way I always do eventually with him.

"He would be crushed if you said the things to him that you said to us," Rosie had told me that week before I'd left, after she and Mimi and I had all calmed down as much as we could. After

I'd turned shocked and stoic and Mimi's crying had leveled out even though her eyes were swollen. The pieces of the plates she'd thrown at Rosie had been swept up and put in the trash. Mimi got a distant look in her eyes, and I knew she was thinking about how my dad wouldn't be able to handle any of this because the only thing that could truly break him was my hating him the way I'd claimed to hate the two of them. It breaks my heart thinking about it. About losing him. Shattering the life he'd thought he'd had with us, the way it was shattered for me. Sure, it wasn't fair that he was as guilty as the two of them were, but he hasn't had to suffer the consequences of my refusing to speak to him like they did. But I'd lost Rosie and Mimi in a sense that day, the way I'd lost a part of myself. I don't want to lose him. I can't. Not when he needs me now more than ever.

"I understand," I say to him. His eyes turn relieved before his stare travels past me. I don't even have to turn around to understand he's made eye contact with Mrs. Mahoney, like he needs to see her in this moment of disagreement between us as much as he needed me to tell him I understand that Mimi selling the house has nothing to do with him. I think of the way my dad and Marylyn didn't talk much in the sky lounge this evening, but wherever my dad was standing, he always had a perfect view of her.

"I'm in shock," I say. "I'm sorry I yelled at you."

His gaze returns to me. His demeanor changes back to the calm and cool dad I know so well. "You don't have to say sorry. Come on, kid; I get it." He puts his hand on my shoulder. "It must've been quite a surprise. But look, if you want to, talk to your Mimi about it. Now that you're at Rutherford . . . maybe she has something else in mind."

We get a table a few rows away from the Mahoneys. After our drinks are served, I catch Mrs. Mahoney stealing glances at my father, subtly shifting her eyes in his direction as she sips on her

white wine, whenever Jasper, Theo, and their father are participating in a conversation that doesn't involve her. I catch Jasper
stealing glances at me, too. He is less inconspicuous. He outright
stares. Smiles when I look back at him. I think my father notices,
the way I hear his chair creak as he shifts in his seat, suddenly
finding himself uncomfortable, needing to fidget. I think Mrs.
Mahoney must pick up on it, too. Her eyes trail Jasper's whenever
his attention is away from the table.

She sits in between her sons at a corner booth. Rosie was right
when she said that Mrs. Mahoney adored them the most in the
world. Her eyes light up when they speak. Theo gets passionate
talking about something, and she leans toward him, placing her
hands over his as they pound against the table. She nods, encour-
aging him to continue, and shushes her husband when he interrupts. She turns sad when they broach some topic that has Jasper
sulking. She lifts his head, placing her fingers under his chin, a
worried expression on her face as she examines his eyes, red from
lack of sleep. She even orders him a whiskey, like she thinks this
might help, and when he doesn't touch it after the first bitter sip,
she lets her husband have it.

"You're still going to help him?" Rosie asked the day before I
left for Rutherford. "You're going to do what we talked about?" I'd
nodded and told her I would try. "You can do it because I've done
it," she said. "Now you know."

Thirty-two

My father wakes me up the next day by blasting "Build Me Up Buttercup" through our suite. He comes in my bedroom and pulls back all the curtains, filling the room with light.

"It's too early." I glance at the clock on my nightstand. It's 10:00 a.m. It would be a reasonable time to wake up if I hadn't stayed at the sky lounge until 1:00 a.m. "Leave me alone." I pull the covers over my face.

"But I'm ready to go!" He tugs away the comforter. "Come on, I presented my proposal to the team this morning and don't have meetings to attend again until after Christmas. We're not going to waste this holiday sleeping! You can sleep when I go back to work."

I glare at him as he takes my hand and drags me up, all the while singing along with the music. He leads me to the tableful of breakfast food and pours me a cup of coffee.

We spend the day on the snowshoeing trails, hiking through the trees and past frozen lakes. Firepits are lit at night, when the snow lets up for a while, complete with a hot chocolate stand and a s'mores bar. We roast marshmallows by the fire and reminisce about the last time we did this, camping near Maroon Lake. At a neighboring firepit, the Mahoneys are preparing their s'mores. I watch over the flames as they talk and laugh, teasing each other when their marshmallows catch on fire. They seem very close and as though they actually like each other. Even Mr. and Mrs. Mahoney. He stands behind her with his arms wrapped around her, warming her in front of the fire, and she leans into him with reassurance, smiling and holding his hands. Being with my father might be helping secure them financially, but would she really want to risk losing this?

On Christmas, we stay in our suite and open presents in front of our own roaring fire. My dad has us call Mimi and Rosie, and the three of us do a great job of pretending it's not the first time in months that we've spoken. There's a wild relief and lots of emotions in Mimi's voice, even as she tries to cover it. But my dad doesn't think this is that out of the ordinary since it's our first Christmas apart. We don't bring up the farm at my dad's insistence that this is something Mimi will discuss with me when she's ready, on her own terms.

I'm awoken the next day around seven in the morning to my dad's voice, getting angry as he talks on the phone. I move closer to the door to hear what he's saying.

"She thinks rejecting my proposal is a viable option," he says. "But she's going to have to reconsider. I've gone over this a thousand times, and it's the only solution! She's managed to convince you and the rest of the board that this lawsuit isn't going to crush Robames—but, well, I've seen how this can play out before, and they're very wrong. Go over it again—tell me if you come up with anything better!"

I hear a thump and imagine he's thrown his cell phone in frustration. He sighs, and a few seconds later, his phone rings.

"Hello," he says, sounding calm. "You know I can't tell you that right now. I don't know where you heard that, but—yeah, I understand. I get what's at stake for you with Robames and this lawsuit." He takes a deep breath. "I don't want you to feel like that.

I'm sorry. My hands are tied. No—I'm telling you, my proposal and the response to the lawsuit has nothing to do with that. I can't—yes, I know. I do know how important your family is to you, come on. And I know this complicates things for you. I hope it'll be okay, but there's no guarantees. Yeah. Okay. Sure thing."

I hear the hanger in the closet collide against the wall as he grabs his coat and then the low thud of the door closing.

His voice was soft on that phone call. Like he was talking to someone he cared about. Like her. But why would whatever troubles Robames Inc. is having *complicate things* for Marylyn or her family?

With the idea that I'll find his proposal—or something akin to it—that will tell me more about the lawsuit, I trudge up the spiral staircase to his loft. I heard him say last summer that Robames was under investigation—not uncommon from what I understand, as many companies have rocky starts. According to that angry phone call he was on before Mrs. Mahoney called him, it's still happening, now in the form of a lawsuit. But what does that have to do with the Mahoneys? *I do know how important your family is to you,* he'd said to her. This couldn't be at all related to how Rob and Jasper were involved, and Jasper's internship, could it? That seems too small and too hard to prove—not something that would require my father to present some big proposal to the other investors about.

I stand in front of the desk where he has his files neatly organized, though none of them are labeled. I open the one closest to me. It's pages of research and development, lab tests and conceptual models of the Roba-Fix. The next file I open is full of legal memos, but it's mostly about deposition times and dates, with only a case number referenced, no clues as to what the lawsuit is actually about. I glance at my dad's legal pad, full of scribbles in this very specific inky-blue pen that he likes to use. Mostly, it's numbers, calculations, and percentage markups, random and nonsensical because I don't know the context. In the corner of the page, there are rows and rows of items, all crossed out and unreadable, except for the item that's circled. It says:

Sell all research data and close before trial.

I turn back to the folder with the legal memos and flip through it again. This time, it jumps out at me—*Jasper Mahoney*. His name appears in a list with about twenty-five others. The list is labeled: *Candidates for Deposition*. The memo is dated in November— around the time Jasper stopped being able to sleep.

My heart begins to race. I search again, frantic to find the name of the lawsuit or at least something that references it that would help me understand why Jasper is being deposed for it. But there's nothing here, not with his hard copies anyway. The information I want is probably on his computer. His locked-in-a-briefcase, password-protected computer.

I don't know what I've uncovered, but it feels like something that draws me closer to understanding more of why Mrs. Mahoney is risking her reputation, her family, to be with my father. Her boys are her first priority. Maybe it's not entirely about my dad's money but his influence that she's after.

Thirty-three

Theo, Jasper, Stewart, and I hang out by the pool in the afternoon, and later, after separating briefly to have dinner with our parents, we meet in the sky lounge. We sequester ourselves in a large booth in the corner and order fries. We find classic board games stacked on the shelves near the bar and spend the next few hours playing Sorry! and Chutes and Ladders. It's late when we head to our rooms for the night, but when I get back to my suite, my father isn't there.

I send a text to Jasper: *Are you asleep?*

Never. You?

We decide to meet at the pool again, but this time when I get there, he isn't in the water, and he didn't bring swim caps and goggles. He's in the resort-provided robe, lying on a lounge chair and staring out at the forest behind the glass wall. I recline in the lounge chair next to him in my matching robe.

"This is really peaceful," I say. I try not to yawn, but it's no use.

He smiles. He nods. I can see that he is still not at all at peace. Rosie said that keeping secrets prevents people from being close—something she was very right about. So I decide not to beat around the bush. Plus, my curiosity about this has been eating away at me all day.

"I saw your name on the deposition list," I say. "For the Robames Inc. lawsuit."

His head snaps in my direction, surprise morphing his expression.

"How did you see that?"

"I looked at one of my dad's files."

He frowns. I should've known that snooping wouldn't be something that Jasper Mahoney finds attractive.

"It's probably nothing, and they're only bringing you in because you interned there," I say.

"Right," he says. "Do you—do you know what's going on with that lawsuit?"

I shake my head. "Do you?"

He doesn't answer right away. "I don't really know, either."

"Are you worried they're going to find out about you and Rob and how you used to be involved? Are you worried that will expose the real reason she hired you as an intern?"

"That's not something they can really prove," he says.

He's right. He was the ideal candidate—someone with good grades, who broke records in that year's decathlon. Dartmouth accepted him early. Why wouldn't those be good enough reasons for Robames Inc. to bring him in as an intern? I've already considered this, so it's more than likely he has, too.

"But if they ask you about it, you'll have to tell them. Lying under oath is a felony."

"I know that." He turns away from me and stares straight ahead, his jaw tensed. I can see the frustration rising within him. This deposition has really gotten to him. What's he so nervous about? It has to be more than just revealing that he used to hook up off and on with the company's founder.

"What are you afraid they're going to ask you?"

He still doesn't look at me. "Nothing," he says. "They can ask me anything they want. Should we get in the water?"

"I don't care," I say. Interesting how he changed the subject so suddenly. "Jasper?"

"Hmm?"

"You seem very on edge since I brought up the lawsuit."

He licks his lips, exhales. "It's not that. It's being here at Hylift. We can do whatever we want out here, and we don't have any schedule to follow, and, I don't know, isn't it kind of irritating after a while?"

"Ah, you miss Rutherford. A packed calendar, all that structure. It hasn't even been that long since we left."

"It's like a disease," he says, "but it's always like this during breaks—after the first week or so, I'm dying to get back to Rutherford."

"You have a condition. You hate relaxing. Your body flat-out rejects it. You like the regimen of Rutherford. There's nothing wrong with that. It's been your life for four years."

"I guess. You're dreading going back, aren't you?"

I nod. "I never thought I was bad at school until—"

"You are not *bad at school*," he interrupts.

"Well, that's nice of you to say. But honestly—and you have to tell me the truth—do you actually retain anything that you learn there?"

"I think I retain most all of it."

I search for signs that he's being sarcastic or at least exaggerating. He's not. Of course.

"I don't remember a single thing I learned in number theory class," I say.

"That's because number theory is boring."

"But I do remember that up until 1920, tug-of-war was an

Olympic event. And I don't even know where I read that, only that it's true."

"Huh," Jasper says. "Do you know who won the gold medal for tug-of-war that year?"

"Great Britain."

"Whoa—okay, so you actually know the answer." He laughs. "What else do you know?"

"Jupiter is twice as big as all the other planets combined."

"Oh, yes, I've heard that, too. Did you know Buzz Aldrin's mother's maiden name was Moon?"

Not a clue. "Everyone knows that, Jasper."

We crack up. He stops laughing before I do, his eyes slowly closing.

"Marie Curie's notebooks are still radioactive," I say in a soft voice. I yawn and shut my eyes.

"If you traveled at the speed of light, time would stop." His voice is getting lower.

"Dogs have around seventeen hundred taste buds."

I don't know if he drifts off first or if I do, but when I wake up, it's no longer dark in the room. Jasper is still in the lounge chair next to me, fast asleep. Outside, the sunrays glint over the trees. It's so beautiful, I'm tempted to wake him. I watch the sun stretch past the forest, changing colors with the morning while Jasper sleeps. He only wakes up when a family with pre-teen children comes barreling in, excited to start their day with a morning swim.

"That's all it takes?" I say as we walk to our rooms. "Only a view of the snowy woods and night sky, muted blue lighting, a soft robe, and useless facts?"

"I slept like a rock." He yawns again, and I wonder if he'll fall back asleep when he gets to his room.

Since the snowfall has finally subsided, that afternoon they open the mountain for skiing. Theo, Jasper, Stewart, and I squeeze onto the aerial tram with the other excited skiers and snowboarders toting all our gear, ready to hit the slopes.

Truth be told, none of us are very good at skiing. This makes us the perfect group. We stick to the beginners' runs, occasionally trying out a harder track, where we fumble our way down the hill, laughing at our own clumsiness. We're at least skilled enough not to get seriously injured. Either that or we've been lucky.

Jasper's pleasant mood and renewed energy make for a notable shift. I like watching him race Stewart. I like watching him laugh. I like that he can enjoy skiing without his usual intensity that stems from trying to be perfect at it or hoping to wear himself out.

"Whatever you did, it worked," Theo says to me at the base of the mountain, nodding at Jasper, who's in a snowball fight with Stewart a few feet away. One of their snowballs bursts at our feet, and I pack the snow into a ball knowing full well this is going to rope Theo and me into their skirmish. We breach the woods, so we're out of the way of everyone else, and weave through the trees as we hurl snowballs at each other. The snowballs shatter into a million snowflakes when they hit one of us.

Jasper zeroes in on me, lobbing snow at me until I'm backed into a tree. He approaches, and I take cover, my hands over my head, waiting for the final blow. When he's standing in front of me, he doesn't douse me in snow. He peels away one of my arms, and then the other, and when I look up at him, he's staring at me with this huge smile on his face. He looks deliriously happy. He seems like he's going to say something, but a quick laugh comes out instead. He does this when he's nervous, I remember. He locks eyes with me, and my heart beats faster and faster. This is unexpected. I think he wants to kiss me. I hold my breath, waiting to see what he'll say next.

But he doesn't say anything. He smiles again. Stewart calls our names. We look in his direction at the same time, and he tells us the tram is coming soon. We rush over to join him and Theo, jogging clumsily in our ski boots. Jasper stands next to me on the tram, and I catch him watching me instead of the view as we move over the forest on our way back to the resort.

Everything I've done hasn't worked yet, I think. *But almost.*

Thirty-four

"You don't have to kiss someone to get them to fall in love with you; you make them fall in love with you so that you get to kiss them." That's what Rosie said. Back when it was still spring and I didn't know about Jasper and Theo, or Mrs. Mahoney and my father. Or any of the other secrets. But now, as all the other things she's exposed swirl around in my mind, I question if it's that simple. If I'm allowed to want a kiss from Jasper, if I'm allowed to take one, if I'm obligated to.

A kiss could be confirmation that he's closer to loving me—closer to trusting me. It could be proof that I can slither my way into someone's heart—that I'm strong and smart and determined enough to pull it off. It could be . . . nice. I think of the way he looked at me during the snowball fight and know that, yes, kissing him wouldn't've been all that bad.

Plus, I bet his mother would hate it.

That night, since we're weary from the day of skiing, we decide to watch a movie instead of hanging out at the sky lounge. We meet in Theo and Jasper's room—a suite with a wall entirely of windows and a bedroom for each of them. We deliberate about what movie we want to watch and decide on a horror film. After a quick trip to get popcorn, soda, and licorice from the store in the lobby, we settle in and start the movie. I'm on the end of the couch, next to Jasper, with Stewart on the other end, and Theo lounging in the armchair next to Stewart.

I'm more nervous than usual to be sitting so close to Jasper in the dark. He leans toward me, resting on one of the over-stuffed throw pillows. He smells like the hotel soap—like oranges and flowers. His curls are still slightly damp from his post-ski shower. His hands twist around the corner of the pillows whenever there's a tense scene. Whenever something startling happens on the screen, Theo reaches over to grab Stewart's shoulder. Sometimes it scares him so much that he flings his popcorn across the room. One thing that's been apparent these past few days is that Theo downright enjoys Stewart's company. He doesn't mind spending every waking moment with Jasper either, even though he'd indicated otherwise when Anastasia was interested in Stewart. I'm curious to see what happens when Anastasia arrives and if Theo will suddenly care about sharing his time with her.

"Why do you keep falling for this?" Theo laughs after Stewart is so surprised during one scene that he spills soda down the front of his shirt.

The jumpy parts hardly get to me because I can't stop glancing at Jasper—at his hands around that pillow. I remember the day he took hold of me at the helicopter landing, his hands holding my arms before he took my hands in his. I can still recall what it felt like, his hands on me, and can't stop imagining what it would be like to reach out and hold his hand now, feel his palm squeeze into mine—or his arm around me, his hand cupping my shoulder. Or brushing past my cheek, holding my face.

Pull yourself together. This is what Theo would say if he knew what I was thinking.

I'm glad the movie is nerve-racking so I have an excuse for seeming uneasy. I start to feel paranoid about sweating, and I can't stop jiggling my foot. But I still want to kiss him, and more than that, I want him to want to kiss me. Toward the end of the movie, I shift so that instead of leaning on the armrest, I'm resting on his pillow. He notices me right away and adjusts so that there's room for my arm on the pillow—though not leaving so much room that our arms aren't touching. I take so many nervous sips from my soda that by the end of the movie I'm dying to use the bathroom.

After I'm done, I check myself out in the mirror. My face is a little sunburned, not too much, but there is a faint outline of my goggles, if you really look. I shake out my hair, trying to give it more volume. I sniff my armpits to make sure all that sweating didn't overwork my deodorant. I turn sideways to examine my profile, the view that Jasper had of me during the movie. If I were just another student at Rutherford, Jasper probably wouldn't've looked twice at me. He's spent the past two years on and off with Rob James, after all. If not for all the regret, maybe it would still be going on between them. And if not for my agenda, he wouldn't be sitting on a couch with me in the dark watching a movie, giving me almost-touches on the tram rides, falling asleep next to me at the pool. Right now, that doesn't make me feel strong or smart. This is the part of deception that's disheartening—the lines between manipulation and truth get blurred.

The bathroom rests in an abrupt hallway between the two bedrooms. When I come out, I can hear Theo and Stewart laughing in the living room. The light to Jasper's room is on, and his door is open. I step closer so I can see inside. He's folding a few stray shirts, putting them in the dresser. Other than that, his room is immaculate—though I don't give him too much credit for this since I'm sure housekeeping is mostly responsible.

I knock on the open door to alert him I'm here.

"Hey," he says. He turns around and leans against the desk as he refolds the blue shirt he was putting away. "This is where I come to *not* sleep."

I smile and take a few steps into the room.

"Thinking of going back to the pool?" There's a strain in my voice—my nerves running rampant being in here alone with him.

"Maybe." He looks away, fidgets with the shirt in his hands. This almost makes me feel better, that he's starting to show signs he's nervous, too.

"Where else can you get that view and that blue light?" I get an idea. "Can I try something?" I step toward him, and he straightens very quickly, startled by my sudden proximity. I take the shirt from his hands. I turn off the overhead lights but leave on the lamp at his desk and drape his blue shirt over the shade. Then I move to the windows, walking back the curtain to expose a view of the star-filled sky, the tops of the forest trees.

"Now all you need is a robe."

He looks around the room at the new atmosphere I've created, and I watch his smile get larger and larger. When his eyes meet mine, it seems to break him from his daze. He moves past me toward the closet and yanks not one robe but two from their hangers. The second one he tosses to me. He slips his on and goes to the other side of the bed. My hands tremble as I untie the tight bow the hotel tied to hold the belt around the robe. I slide the robe over my shoulders and secure it in front, then join him on the bed. From where I'm lying, I can see a stack of books on his desk next to his laptop.

"You brought Rutherford with you," I say. "How many books from the assigned reading list have you read since we've been out?"

"Only two."

"That's respectable."

"Glad to have your approval." He laughs lightly. His voice is getting lower, the way it did when we fell asleep by the pool. My eyelids start to grow heavy. I'd thought the robe would be too hot over my clothes, but it's very cozy.

"Tell me the most boring thing you learned in those books. That's sure to put us both to sleep."

"There was this study done once about how likely people were to lie given certain situations, like if they saw a little kid steal a piece of candy from the store, would they say anything; or if they witnessed their best friend blatantly lying to someone, would they call them out in front of the person they were lying to."

"Jasper." I turn on my side so I can see him. Talking to him like this makes the knot of nerves in my stomach dissipate. "That's the opposite of boring. That's fascinating."

"You think so?" Until he turns on his side, too, and we're face-to-face and the knot dispels and turns into a fluttery sensation.

"What was the outcome of the study?"

"It was inconclusive," he says. He puts his hand over the pillow, holding it down so it doesn't impede his view of me.

"I wouldn't lie in either of those situations," I say.

"I would've lied in both of them."

"I hate secrets," I say, adjusting so I'm lying on my back. I try to take a deep breath. "Even something that seems small. Why hide it, or cover it, or lie about it, you know?" I can feel the ground coming out from under me now—just like on the day I learned the truth. I hate how easily it sneaks up on me, this awful feeling; how the memory can flood me, suffocating me, without any warning, when I've been doing such a good job of pressing it away.

I see him turn toward me out of the corner of my eyes. "Hey—are you okay?" he says.

"Yeah, fine." My voice betrays me; it comes out high yet raspy.

"Collins?"

"I'm fine." I pinch my eyes closed and try to steady myself. It takes every bit of my concentration to breathe.

"I read about this other study that examined situations where one person was upset and they didn't want anyone to know why. All subjects conclusively ended up admitting the reason they were unhappy because they knew it would ultimately make them feel better."

I open my eyes and turn to look at him. I feel a few tears slip down my cheeks.

"Subjects in Group A at first resorted to yelling and storming out of the room. Subjects in Group B's initial reaction was to shut down entirely. But subjects in Group C admitted to their feelings immediately. Group C's life expectancy was the greatest out of the three groups."

"Really?" I say.

He hesitates. "No." The slightest smile forms on his lips. At first I'm very confused. Then, I get it.

"You *made up* a psychological experiment?" I feel myself smiling, too, the sudden urge to laugh taking over.

"Did it work?" He shrugs. "Do you feel better?"

His hand brushes up against mine. I squeeze his fingers. Fabricating a research study because he thought it might cheer me up might be as romantic as Jasper gets. He noticed I was losing it and took it upon himself to try to straighten me out.

"You don't have to tell me what's wrong," he says. "But I don't like it when you do that—you get this look on your face, like that day in the gym, like you're—I don't know, like you're unraveling or something."

I study him for a moment, his concerned expression, his proximity. My chest still feels tight, but I manage to take a breath deep enough that air swells in my lungs.

"I don't like it that you can't sleep," I say.

"I slept last night," he says. He shifts slightly and puts his other hand over mine. I think it's weird at first, but then he says, "You're shaking," and I realize he's using both his hands to try to keep mine steady. "What's wrong?" he whispers.

I think about telling him, letting the words go. Getting them out and letting him tell me how maddening it all is—letting him see. But then would I think of it every time I looked at him? Or would I find solace in him, the way I do now, and instead of remembering the secret and forgetting how to breathe, I'd think of his kindness, his hands covering mine?

Weaving my fingers through his, I turn to the side, toward him. He leans in my direction at the exact same moment. *This is it,* I think. *This is when he'll kiss me. It's the perfect time for him to kiss me.* I close my eyes. They fly open again when I feel him move, the heat of him next to me suddenly gone.

He's sitting up. He looks out the window instead of at me. I sit up also, hot with embarrassment, my heart racing with confusion.

He clears his throat. "We shouldn't," he says.

We shouldn't. All the moments that got us here are compounding in my mind—the almost-touches, the hidden smiles, the easy conversation, the way he looked at me after the snowball fight today. How he was holding my hand tonight, how I'd helped him finally relax enough to sleep last night. I was trying to make him love me, but I was helping him, too—wasn't I? The way he'd been helping me? I'd hoped I was; I'd wanted to.

"Why—why not?" I say. Maybe he can sense it, that I come with strings attached. And after whatever he's been through, I know he deserves someone who doesn't have the baggage that I come with or all that I'm going to inflict on him. Maybe since he's already been ruined once, getting involved with the wrong girl, he doesn't want to risk it again. But the thing I was counting on was Mrs. Mahoney sparing his heart—promising to leave my dad alone, and I'd carry on with Jasper for as long as we wanted, until Dartmouth would inevitably pull us apart. It'd be an easy split—I promise myself that now, watching as he glances at me, then turns his attention nervously to the sleeve of his bathrobe, that whatever happens, I'll make it easy on him. One of the lingering, leftover tears cascades down my cheek. I try to wipe it away before he sees.

He shakes his head but doesn't say anything.

"I'm nothing like her," I say. I want him to know; I don't want him to be afraid of this, whatever is between us. "Being with me would be nothing like being with her."

"I know that," he says quietly.

"Then why—" But he's shaking his head again.

"All right," I say. I get up and take off the robe. "I guess I'll just see you tomorrow. Good luck sleeping."

"Collins, wait—"

And I do *wait*. I turn around, and he's standing there like he's helpless, his palms out like he's ready to explain. But he still says nothing.

So I leave, and this time he doesn't try to stop me. My heart is hammering hard in my chest when I get back to my suite, and I can't fall asleep, no matter what I do. I keep thinking about it. How suddenly he moved away from me on the bed. If he doesn't love me, he doesn't love me. It's so embarrassing—why did I ever think he could? I'm a Rutherford near failure who goes from laughing to unraveling in minutes. He fell asleep next to me at the pool, and I took that as a sign we were getting closer. But it was probably his weariness catching up with him, the tranquil environment, the coziness of the robe. It's certainly not proof that he's falling for me.

Rosie told me the secret so that I would know I could do this.

But she was wrong. I'm not like her, not in the ways that she thinks I am, not in the ways that I want to be.

I understand that things can change in an instant, and that's both hopeful and discouraging. They can shift outwardly—like forcing your aunt and mother on an expedition out of the country while moving 2,200 miles away to attend an institute with a study schedule and plan to save your dad that crowds your thoughts, makes you forget. And you hope that will be enough. But change can also make things corrode inwardly, and you find yourself up all night because of one instant, one mention of secrets and lies, and you're brought back to the moment you tried to forget because of a boy you're supposed to be able to conquer—but here you are, three in the morning and you can't stop shaking and pacing, hyperventilating into your pillow so your father won't hear, trying to pull apart and bury the way it made you feel. The way it still makes you feel.

Thirty-five

It was a few days before I left for Rutherford when Rosie let the secret out. I've debated in my head a million times if she'd planned it all along or if it was an impulse decision—she was either suddenly desperate for me to know or she wanted to punish Mimi and knew this was the deepest she could cut.

"I want to show you something," she said to me out on the back patio. The weather was still hot and sticky. We were due for rain. I was dreaming of the ocean breeze that was promised to dance across the Rutherford campus.

Rosie sat down next to me on the bench swing. She was holding a beat-up copy of T. S. Eliot's "The Waste Land."

"This was a gift. It's a first edition."

"Wow."

"Do you know who gave it to me?"

I shook my head, readying myself for anything. With Rosie, it could've been anyone. A relative of T. S. Eliot. Some Parisian politician like the one she'd traveled to Croatia with. Maybe a renowned Harvard professor who had fallen in love with her when she'd spent that summer living in Boston.

"Your father." She cracked open the book and pulled out two photos that were stashed in between the pages. They were Polaroids. She handed me the first one. It took a moment for me to really understand what I was seeing. In the photo, my father and Rosie were squished together on a love seat, their feet up on an ottoman. They were much younger. They were relaxed and happy, wearing big smiles, and they were looking at each other. The first thing I noticed was the intimacy of the photo, their proximity and how comfortable they seemed. Whenever I'd seen them together, they were friendly, but in this photo, there was a tenderness between them. The second thing I noticed was the protruding stomach under Rosie's shirt. And even when I registered it, I contemplated if it really was what I thought it might be. A pregnant belly.

She handed me the second photo. It made me drop the first one. Rosie was with my father again, this time in a hospital bed. Rosie's hair was damp, and she was dressed in a hospital gown. She was holding a tiny, crying baby. My father was in scrubs, one arm around her, one arm under the baby. They were both looking down at the baby, their mouths slightly open in awe.

Rosie grabbed my hand. I looked up at her, but I couldn't fathom that she was there or what she was saying. I only saw the photos flashing over and over again in my mind.

"Collins? Collins?" She tightened her grip around my hand. "Do you understand?"

I couldn't speak as the possibility mounted itself within me as a reality, the lie still swirling in my head.

"I'm your mother," she said. She smiled. There were no tears in her eyes. Her voice was strong, assured. The same tone as when she'd asked me if I knew who'd given her the book. "Do you understand? You and me, we're the same."

Mimi came out and realized quickly that something was wrong. She saw my unresponsive face; then she noticed the photos, one resting on my lap, the other scattered to the ground.

"Collins? Collins—it's not—it's okay—I'm so sorry—" She was

panicking, too, and I still hadn't found my voice, though I could feel myself shaking, could feel tears encroaching.

That's when the fight started. I'd never seen Mimi crying so hard, screaming so loudly. I'd never seen Rosie so defensive, her voice on fire. If we'd had neighbors, surely the police would've been called.

"We were supposed to tell her together, all of us, when the time was right," Mimi said.

"The time was right tonight; it was my secret to tell," Rosie countered before she walked away.

Mimi following Rosie into the kitchen, saying, "Make a mess, then leave, that's what you're good at."

"My *messes* are the best thing to ever happen to you, Michelle!"

"You're right—Collins is the best thing to ever happen to me, and you ruined it because you put this lie between us—"

"No one forced you to lie to her!"

"What were we supposed to do? You disappeared for seven years! She was born, and the next week you were gone! We didn't hear from you for seven years while you were living large, traveling the world! Jake was scared shitless and didn't know what to do. I was her mother because there was no one else. I loved her the way you didn't know how to."

"I wasn't only talking about Collins!" Rosie shouted back. "I was talking about Jake—about the money. This house, your whole life! A rich man and a wonderful daughter and new house where you could do whatever you felt like doing, spend the day however you pleased, raise goats to entertain yourself."

"Our life is so much more than that!" Mimi cried. "And maybe it would've been different if you'd have stuck around to see it—to be part of it."

"He enabled you—that's the truth, and you loved it. You've always been a coward. More than happy to stay in your sheltered life and never go outside of your comfort zone. Never change or grow or experience new things, or take risks with your heart."

"Loving you was risky enough for a lifetime."

"You liked being a mother; you were grateful that I made you one. You never would've allowed yourself to get close enough to anyone to have a real relationship where you'd have a baby of your own. And you liked playing house with Jake—don't tell me that you didn't. You knew you weren't bold enough to ever find someone like him—someone that interesting and kind and wealthy. I gave you your fantasy life—and hey, look, Collins had a great life, too—so don't act like in this scenario I ever did anything but make you happy, giving you exactly what you wanted."

Mimi shrieked. The first plate went soaring through the air. "Don't you dare stand there and tell me you were thinking of anyone except yourself when you left us!" Another plate went flying, and at the third plate, Rosie left the room.

Mimi stood shaking in the kitchen. Crying harder than I'd ever seen anyone cry.

I was frozen on the patio, my eyes wide with disbelief, my hands shaking.

When she noticed me, she tried to steady her breathing. She wiped her face with her sleeve. She stepped carefully around the broken pieces of glass and walked through the open door. She knelt in front of me, grabbing my hands.

"Jake and I didn't want you find out like this," she said. "I'm so sorry this is how you had to learn about it. I'm so sorry we lied to you—but we were scared. We tried to do what's best for you; we never wanted you to feel abandoned. It might've been the wrong thing to do—"

"It *was* the wrong thing to do," Rosie interrupted, coming from around the side of the house, stepping into the glow of the patio lights.

"The wrong thing to do, Rose, was spring this on Collins now, without talking to me or Jake, right before she's about to leave for Ruther—"

"Stop it!" I shouted. Right then, I felt a flood of madness from deep inside of me. I didn't care if Mimi was only trying to do right by me, that she never wanted me to feel deserted. I felt tricked. Like I should've figured it out somehow. I'd known my whole life that I looked like Rosie, but Rosie and Mimi looked alike, too. I hated that they both knew this truth about me and talked about it behind my back, so many discussions that didn't include me that were about me.

"I'm so glad I'm about to leave!" I screamed. "How am I supposed to trust either of you ever again? I hate what you've done, hate everything about being here and hate that of all the people who could've been my mother or acted as her stand-in, I'm stuck with the two of you!"

I said things to them that would've ruined my father, not caring if it destroyed them. Because in that moment, I only wanted my father. Maybe that wasn't fair to them. But I wanted to shut them out and pull him closer, and that's exactly what I did. One of them had left me and one of them had used me, and all he'd done was be my dad, the best he could, which was pretty damn great. They'd lied to me about who they were to me, but he didn't lie about who he was. I needed him. And I couldn't bear to lose him. Not to this secret and certainly not to Marylyn Mahoney.

Thirty-six

When I meet Jasper, Theo, and Stewart in the sky lounge to take the tram to the mountain the next morning, Anastasia is there. She envelops me in a hug.

"You look terrible," she says.

"It's nice to see you, too, Anastasia." I tug my beanie down farther. I don't want them to know that after I left Jasper's room, I barely slept. I want them to think everything is fine—wonderful, even. Normal, at least.

Anastasia is mortified that none of us are great skiers. She's been skiing since she could walk and can't fathom how slow and awkward the four of us are. For the last run of the day, Anastasia convinces us to do one of the more reclusive trails that cuts through the forest, insisting she can coach us through it and that it's not as steep as the other advanced runs. There's also a map we've pulled up on our phones, and there are tracks in the snow from skiers who've been there before for us to follow.

I like this route the best because it's gorgeous. It's isolating, but in a very good way. No sounds except the swishing of our skis against the powder and our own laughter.

"Let's split up," Anastasia declares when we come to a fork in our path and have two trails to follow, one to the right and one to the left. According to the map, they both let out in an open valley that curves like a bowl before it lets us off at the base of the mountain.

"Shall we race?" Stewart asks. He smiles at Anastasia. "You don't count since you'd wipe the floor with us."

She looks down at her feet. Her crush on him is still in full effect, I've noticed.

"She's such a show-off," Theo says, pushing her playfully. It backfires, and instead of sending her sliding forward, he sails backward and has to fall to stop himself.

"Let's race," I say. To prove to them I'm up for anything even if I seem somewhat listless today.

"I'll take Stewart," Theo says.

"*Sehr gut.* Fine by me," Stewart boasts with confidence because really Theo is the fastest out of the four of us, even if he also falls the most.

"On your mark!" Anastasia yells. Theo and Stewart quickly scoot over to their side of the trail. "Get set! Go!" They take off with Anastasia trailing behind them barking orders.

Jasper and I don't move. He grinds the end of his pole into a patch of icy snow. He watches as it chips away at the crystals.

"I like you," he says. "And I'm tired of subtext. But . . . it's complicated."

I should play this cool, take the *I like you* as hope, enjoy the warm feeling it gives me. But instead, I say, "How? How is it complicated?"

"You said last night that you think it's pointless to lie no matter the situation."

I nod. There's a heap of things he hasn't told me—won't tell me. Not about why he pulled away from me last night or what goes on in his mind when he can't sleep, what he needs a distraction from. He didn't tell me he was being deposed for Rob

James's lawsuit. Or what happened that makes him regret ever getting involved with her. And the worst part is I was tempted to spill everything last night, tell him all about Mimi and Rosie, about my dad.

"The problem is," he says, "it's not my secret to tell."

He might not deserve this kind of rage from me, but it gets blasted at him anyway as I think back on what Rosie said that night—*It was my secret to tell*—and how both she and Mimi used that as an excuse for never coming clean to me about who my real mother was. I can't help the sternness in my voice as I say, "If you know the secret, then it is yours to tell."

"You really believe that?"

"Yeah, I do."

I don't wait for him to come up with something before I take off down the hill without him. He keeps up easily because we're both slow, and I'm rushing so, I fall down more than he does.

We reach the end, where the hill is curved. Theo and Stewart and Anastasia are at the base shouting up at us, letting us know they beat us by several minutes.

We descend the slope, skimming the edge in a wide turn to loop around and ski into the base. But halfway down, I decide to shift in direction. I plunge straight forward. Bending my knees and keeping them closed for maximum speed and to prevent myself from flailing. I trip a little at the base, but I manage to stay upright as I come to a stop.

"That's my girl!" Anastasia high-fives me.

"Very impressive, Collins," Theo says.

Sometimes it feels good, taking a risk that no one expects and watching as it works out fine.

When we get back to the sky lounge, Rob James is there. She's dressed in a white fur coat with gold snow boots. She's making her way through the crowd, meeting the families of her board members and investors as she sips on a pink drink in a martini glass.

Jasper, predictably, excuses himself and goes back to his room, keeping with his goal to stay as far away from Rob James as possible. But the rest of us find a high-top table available and order fries. Stewart offers to get us sodas from the bar since the lounge is slammed and we're all parched from skiing. Anastasia volunteers to help him carry the drinks.

"Look at them," I say to Theo, nodding at Anastasia and Stewart. They're by the bar talking and laughing, standing close. I'll admit, I'm feeling a little antagonistic.

"Anastasia likes to flirt," Theo says. "With anyone willing and able."

"You like Stewart—the whole time we've been here, you've had a great time with him. You enjoy yourself around him. You think he's fun. Muy bueno, très bon—as Stewart would say. It doesn't make any sense that you told Anastasia all those things about him when you yourself don't believe them for a second, on top of them not being even remotely true."

"*Fine,*" he says. "Stewart's great. Sehr gut. You're right. They should date. I'm staying over here, aren't I? Out of their way. I haven't said anything to her about him since she arrived. If they want to fall madly in love, I'm not going to be the one to stop them."

"Good." It's sometimes really unsatisfying to go off on someone about how they were wrong, only for them to turn around and agree with you so quickly.

"She needs someone to kiss on New Year's Eve anyway."

"Who are you going to kiss?"

"I'm going to surprise myself. You?"

"Probably no one. Keeping with tradition."

"You've never had a New Year's Eve kiss?"

I shake my head.

"Do you want me to talk to Jasper for you?"

"No—seriously, no."

"He's difficult," Theo says. "He's determined not to get involved with you *like that,* and once he sets his mind to something, good luck changing it."

"Why, though? Why is this something he's decided?"

Theo's lips part like he's about to tell me. Instead he shrugs. "If anyone can talk sense into him, it's usually me. Want me to see what I can do?"

"Thanks, but it's okay."

"You really like him, huh?"

"Theo, you know I've been interested in him since I first got to Rutherford. Don't embarrass me."

"I remember," he says. "I thought it was strange that you chose to zero in on Jasper."

"Why? He's gorgeous and brilliant."

"And boring and anxious and competitive and school-obsessed." He shrugs. "But if you think he's *allegedly* gorgeous and brilliant, I guess I'll believe you."

I throw a fry at him. "You guys look very similar, you know?"

"Thanks?"

We laugh.

"So on a scale of one to ten, how much do you like him?" Theo asks.

I pop a fry in my mouth as an excuse not to answer. When I'm done chewing, I say, "On a scale of one to ten, what are the odds of me still having a shot with him?"

"Ten."

"Even with his *determination?*"

Theo smiles. "You've got very good odds."

Thirty-seven

"It's New Year's Eve! We have to look perfect for the extravaganza!" Anastasia barrels into my room, her hair in rollers, toting her dress, a case of makeup, and a curling iron, the cord dragging on the floor. Anastasia's been referring to the Robames New Year's Eve party as *the extravaganza* since she arrived.

While we get ready, Anastasia tells me all about people I've barely heard of who will be in attendance tonight. Debra Skye, who goes to Vassar and whose family came into money late; Kyle and Rick Singer, from St. Jude's Boarding School, who have both been kicked out of the sky lounge for being too drunk and whose parents invested their trust funds into Robames hoping to quadruple them; Judith and Ian Vander Holms, twins who graduated last year from Rutherford, whose dad is about to take over their company because granddad Vander Holms is dying of colon cancer, though the family refuses to make it public, and Anastasia only knows because she caught Judith crying in the bathroom; Connie Cho, head of a media conglomerate, and according to Anastasia, "a legit queen"; Raymond Copper, who is, as she puts it, "West Coast–movie-producer famous" and is *for sure* sleeping with the famous actress Mya Rhodes, who happens to be his twenty-eight-year-old daughter's best friend from her sorority.

"What have you heard about my father?" I ask as I apply a final coat of lip gloss, curious if his reputation has at all been tarnished by Mrs. Mahoney or if it's truly a locked-tight secret.

"Not much, Collins. Only that he's East Coast–businessman famous and on that most eligible New York bachelor's list with Muriel Jennings. Except he's, you know—*so old*." She whispers the last part like it's a secret.

"You girls look wonderful! You're as beautiful as your personalities," my father says to us when we emerge from my bedroom, fully dressed and made up and ready to ring in the new year.

"Is that supposed to be a compliment?" Anastasia asks me as we get together in front of the fireplace for a photo.

"Yes," my father says, probably clueless that he was being spoken about but not spoken to, the way Anastasia likes to talk about people. "You have a sparkling personality, Anastasia. Does that clear it up?"

"You look good, too, Dad." And he does, dressed to kill in a black tuxedo, his hair combed back, held in place by some kind of product.

We pose for a few photos and then a few dozen more, trying for one that Anastasia approves of before we take off for the party. My dad's almost as excited as Anastasia; I can sense the elated urgency coming from him as we ride the elevator. He rolls on his heels. There is a small smile playing on his lips.

The first part of the party is on the lobby level, in the restaurant, which has been transformed completely, arranged with rows of long tables with white centerpieces, tall ivory candles, and gold-plated dishes and silverware. No one is seated yet; everyone stands near the bar, in the area that's been cleared under a giant chandelier, mingling as drinks and appetizers are served.

A caterer hands my father a martini. He scans the room as he sips on it. They stop on Mrs. Mahoney. She's alone at the end of the bar, and she smiles when she sees him. Like she was waiting for him.

I glance at Anastasia to see if she's noticed, but she's pointing across the room to where Stewart and Jasper are standing.

"Go ahead, I'll catch up with you in a minute," I tell her.

My father smiles at me and gives me his arm. We move around the room for a while making small talk. He proudly introduces me to his colleagues, until Anastasia calls to me from the punch fountain.

"She's your most demanding friend yet," he says. "But she seems like a lot of fun."

I nod.

He squeezes my arm. "Have a good time. I'll see you when they serve dinner."

On my way, I stop by the drink cart to get another sparkling cider. My nerves are jumping at the prospect of talking to Jasper. Though both of us have been acting perfectly normal around one another, it still doesn't feel that way. I look back and my father is gone. He's moved toward the end of the bar, like the second I left, he walked a straight line right to her. He kisses Mrs. Mahoney on the cheeks as if he's greeting an old friend. But he's standing very close, and his hand lingers on hers a little too long. They drink martinis at the bar as they talk. She plays with her left earring as she listens to him. And her smile is very large. But his is larger. Even from across the room, I can see how enamored he is.

In that moment, I wonder if I'm really capable of going through with Rosie's plan. Even if Jasper starts to fall for me, even if Mrs. Mahoney can be bribed in this way, it's not going to change how my father feels about her—how he'll look at her across the room, how he'll want to be there for her no matter what, how his heart will break when she lets him off the hook. And maybe I don't have what it takes, and it'll end like this: She'll jeopardize her marriage, and he'll jeopardize his fortune and his reputation, and Mimi will sell the house, and Rosie will ask me why I couldn't stop it.

I watch as Mrs. Mahoney and my father communicate with their eyes. When a man they must both find annoying comes up to them, talking exuberantly with his hands, patting my father incessantly on the back, my father and Mrs. Mahoney exchange looks. The man leaves, and they smile at how awkward the exchange was. She leans in close to talk to him, and he elbows her gently. She rests against him for barely a second—it's so subtle that if I weren't someone intent on watching them, I wouldn't have noticed. My father's face flushes at her touch. I scan the room, wondering where Mr. Mahoney is and if he might be witnessing this. But he is on the other side of the room, talking boisterously to a group of men who reward him with hearty laughter.

"I think the adults are getting drunk," Theo says, startling me so badly I almost spill my drink. "Well, the adults and Stewart."

He nods to the corner of the room, where Stewart is taking a half-empty champagne flute off the tray in the corner, set up as a place for people to discard their drinks, and pouring it into his empty water glass. He has to act fast before one of the servers clears the tray, which they do at an incredible rate to keep the party from looking cluttered. Anastasia and Jasper are shaking their heads at him but seem amused nonetheless.

I hear the unmistakable deep and uproarious laughter of my father, where he's still standing with Mrs. Mahoney. She's keeping it together better than he is, though her eyes are watering and her hand is over her mouth and her shoulders are shaking. She leans forward and whispers something in his ear that gets him going again. I can't think of what someone like her could've possibly said to make my father laugh like that.

"Shameless, aren't they?" Theo says.

This is exactly what I was thinking, but—

"What?" I say. "What are you meaning?" My attempt to act casual is thwarted by a usually Daiki-induced symptom—my brain couldn't decide between saying, *What do you mean?* and *What are you saying?*

"What do you mean?" I try again. My father is friendly and his mother is friendly and they know each other through various business dealings. That's what this could be from an outsider's perspective. A perfectly reasonable friendship.

He presses his lips together like he's trying to hide his smile. "Oh, never mind. Nothing."

Wait a minute. "No . . . no," I say. "What did you mean by that?"

He studies me as he takes a sip of his punch. "Well, this is awkward, Collins."

I cut another quick look toward the two of them and, *ugh*— they're being even more *shameless,* her fingers dancing along his arm as she tells him what would appear to be the most fascinating story he's ever heard.

"I knew it," Theo says, pointing at me. I shake my head— playing dumb, playing it cool, trying for anything, really. "I knew it! I told Jasper he shouldn't worry so much. I told him that I was sure you already knew about them." He gestures in the direction of our parents. "I knew it," he mutters, taking another drink.

"But—how—how do you and Jasper know about it?"

"She's our mother, Collins. And besides, our parents have always been like this."

"Like what? Like, unfaithful?"

"Exactly—but, eh, is it really called *unfaithful* if they're honest about it?" I don't know what to say or what he means, so I stare at him blankly. If they're *honest* about it, does that mean Mr. Mahoney is aware of what's going on between them?

"My parents have had this sort of arrangement since I was little," Theo explains. "For as long as I can remember, it's been like this. My dad dates other people, and so does she." He watches as his mother nudges my father again, and their laughter slows until they're left smiling unabashedly at each other. "Usually, they try not to be so obvious—it's not exactly something any of the parties involved want people to know about—but, well, let's give them a break. They've been working very hard since we got to Hylift, and tonight, the cocktails are flowing."

I can't believe what I'm hearing. I guess it makes sense that my father would only get involved with a married woman if he could do it without going behind her husband's back, without having to lie. But it's still a secret to most people, and if it's like Rosie said and Mrs. Mahoney is taking advantage of him, this would be the best way to do it: away from scrutiny from outsiders. And if she's involved with my father for her own gain—for money or the good of her boys or both—with this arrangement she's in with her husband, which she's been open and honest about with her sons, she doesn't stand to risk anything.

Theo squints at me like he's trying to gauge my reaction, like he wonders why I've been stunned silent. "Why does this bother you so much? He hasn't been with your mother for years, right? Your dad is documented as one of New York's most eligible bachelors."

"Jasper knows, too—about them?"

"Of course. Jake came with us to St. Barths last summer. Not like he stayed with us; he was at the neighboring villa. But still. It was obvious why he was there."

Jake. I nod again, still taking it all in. I don't remember my dad ever mentioning a trip to St. Barths.

"But you can't blame Jasper for not saying anything," Theo says. "He didn't want to be the one to tell you your dad was sleeping with our mom. He was afraid it would somehow tarnish your dad in your eyes, his being involved with a married woman, even though it's part of an arrangement. And he didn't like keeping it from you. But he was *determined*. Even when I told him that it wasn't the worst secret to have and that you probably already knew anyway. Which you did. Because I'm always right."

When Jasper said that things were complicated, this is what he meant. And when he spoke of a secret that wasn't his to tell, he was referring to this—our parents' secret about being involved with each other.

Now I can tell Jasper that I know and all he was worried about will be behind us. My breath catches a little thinking about how he won't have any reason to hold back with me after this.

"I would've told you myself about the affair, the arrangement, the whole thing. Put my brother out of his misery." Theo takes a long sip of his punch.

It sounds like he's leaving something out, and I wait for him to continue.

"So why didn't you?" I finally ask.

"Like I said, I was pretty positive you already knew. And I couldn't help but find it odd—in fact, I still find it odd—that you knew our parents were involved, you even thought they were having a proper affair, and yet, you still chose to hyper-focus on Jasper. Right from the start of the year." My face flushes. I don't know what I'm supposed to say to this or where he's going with this accusation, what he's trying to prove. "You were the one who asked him to help you with school, weren't you?"

Shoot. "Because I desperately needed it."

"Everyone knows your roommate, Elena, is a bona fide genius; she could've helped you."

"Why would I bother her with that when I knew Jasper didn't mind tutoring me?"

Theo considers this but doesn't seem convinced. "There were a lot of other resources you could've gone to for help."

"It's not like I nearly failed out of school just to get close to him—I wasn't *hyper-focused* on him, as you say." I keep going, rambling on. I'm not sure what answer Theo's looking for from me or why he's suspicious of my interest in Jasper.

"Collins—"

"I don't know what you're accusing me of or what else you want me to say about it, Theo—I didn't find out about our parents and then go and fall for your brother on purpose."

"Collins," Theo says, louder this time.

I hear someone say, "Whoa," and glance over my shoulder to see Stewart standing there. Theo's got a slight grimace on his face. I turn around again and see Anastasia and Jasper are there. I flinch in surprise. And then I feel a rush of mortification. What did they hear? Everything I said? Between the soft alternative playing over the speakers and the condensed sound of everyone talking, maybe they didn't hear anything I was saying. I couldn't even pick up on the sound of people approaching—I was as surprised when Theo came up to me earlier—so, really, how much could they have heard?

According to the uneasy expression plaguing Anastasia's face: everything. Stewart stares at me with wide eyes—he's definitely drunk. Theo is giving me a one-shouldered shrug. Jasper is looking at his feet.

"The acoustics in this restaurant are terrible," I mutter before leaving.

"Collins. You don't have to run away," Theo calls after me.

I pretend I can't hear him.

Thirty-eight

I hurry out of the restaurant, and instead of going to the closest bathroom, somewhere Anastasia could most definitely find me, I head to the other end of the lobby, toward the bathrooms by the east exit. Through the clear doors leading outside, I see that it's snowing again, hard and heavy like before, slanted sideways from the wind.

As I'd hoped, this bathroom is completely vacant. I slump down on the couch in the sitting area as one of Mimi's favorite songs to sing with her girlfriends on karaoke night, "Eternal Flame," plays lightly in the background.

This is not how I'd planned to start the New Year's Eve extravaganza. Not with Theo accusing me of having an agenda, spurring a rogue confession with no immediate indication of how Jasper feels about what he'd heard. I don't know what to make of what I just learned either. Did Rosie know that my father's relationship with Mrs. Mahoney was part of an agreement—something her whole family knows about? Or was she as in the dark about the real situation as the rest of the public? And if she was wrong about their affair, what else has she gotten wrong? What else might she not know?

I decide to go back to the restaurant, face Jasper and the others. They'll probably tease me. Jasper will hopefully greet me with a short, nervous laugh and the kind of smile that he can't help. It makes my palms sweaty, thinking about what he'll do now that he's realized I know about our parents and that's not something he has to worry about keeping from me any longer.

I open the door to leave the bathroom and—he's standing there, in front of the exit, the snow falling down in large clumps behind him. I smile. He came after me. He heard me say I was falling for him and he came after me.

As I push the door open farther, I nearly crash into a large, tall man in a suit. It's Rob James's bodyguard. And he isn't alone. Since he didn't see me, I step back. I let the door swing closed, cracking it open just wide enough that I can see the two of them. Jasper and Rob. She's in a long white dress with bell sleeves, a gold choker resting around her neck. Her hair is down and wild; her makeup is dark, with gold outlining her eyes.

"Remember how it used to be?" she says to Jasper. "We did things for each other all the time—for no other reason than we wanted to. Because we wanted what was best for each other."

He looks away, shaking his head. "I told you already," he says, his voice brusque and deflated. "I said I wasn't going to say anything, and I meant it. You don't have to worry." For a second, when he looks at her, I see sadness in his eyes. A hint of longing. "I'm sorry. But I don't want to talk or reminisce. I just want to move on and forget it ever happened."

She straightens, and any friendliness in her demeanor vanishes. "Thank you for letting me know that I don't have to worry about what you'll say when they question you during the deposition," she says. "Keeping quiet is the least you can do."

"The least I can do?" An expression of complete astonishment covers his face.

"Because you owe me, Jasper." There's madness in her voice.

"Don't forget that when you're *moving on.* Don't forget about all I've done for you, what I've risked for you when I didn't have to."

"It's impossible to forget, the way you keep holding it over my head." He drops his tone like it's hard for him to keep from yelling. "How long are you going to keep doing this?"

"For as long as I want," she says. "Because I can still see it—how it could be for us—don't you?"

He shakes his head and covers his mouth. But he looks upset, sad all over again. "It's too late, Roberta."

"It could be different for us in the future." She reaches forward and grabs his hands. He lets her. He stares at her fingers gripping his. "When this is all behind us. If you don't throw it all away. You'll be at Dartmouth next year. And we could still use your brilliant mind at the company. You know I'll always want you as close as—"

"Stop. I can't do this again; it's too hard." Jasper winces and lets go of her hands. He turns and walks quickly out the doors, into the storm.

Her mouth drops open. She goes after him, pressing the door open and running outside. Her bodyguard follows. I leave the bathroom and rush to the door. I stare through the glass as Rob James reaches the end of the pavement and stops. She calls his name, but he keeps going. She throws her hands in the air as Jasper takes off through the trees, into the forest. Her bodyguard removes his jacket and holds it over her like an umbrella, trying to shield her from the snowfall. She clasps his arm, using it to support her as they move up the stairs, returning inside. She hugs herself against the cold and pinches her eyes closed as she cries.

They walk inside, and Rob heads straight toward the bathroom. She stops when she sees me. She wipes away the mascara streaks her tears left slicing down her cheeks.

"Collins," she says. "I value honesty, so I hope you'll know that I mean nothing but respect when I say don't get too attached to him. You seem like a bright girl. I'd hate to see you get hurt."

She goes into the bathroom before I can respond.

I stare outside at the pounding snow, the thicket of trees that Jasper disappeared through, and then I charge out into the storm after him.

I hold up my dress to keep it from getting soaked by the snow on the ground and squint against the cold breeze that blows snow-flakes directly in my face as I rush past the paved and shoveled part of the driveway, and into the forest after Jasper. He didn't go too far, only a few feet through the dense trees to a small clearing.

"Jasper?" I shout. It's freezing, and my breath fogs back in my face. "Jasper, wait."

He's pacing. He shakes out his hands. He rubs his neck as he trudges through the layers of snowfall. I hate that she was able to get under his skin—and hate most that she can still have such an effect on him.

"Jasper, stop—" I put my hands on either side of him to keep him still. His fists are clenched. His eyes crazed with fury. Snow-flakes are sticking to his eyelashes. They dot his hair and dust his shoulders.

"I saw you and Rob—"

"I was coming to find you," he says, the words tearing out of him. "After you ran off. But she followed me, she cornered me, she—she's never going to leave me alone." His breath comes in and out in fast, quick bursts of steam against the cold air.

"Jasper." I squeeze his arms, trying to steady him. "You can't let her do this to you." *Why can she still do this to you?* "What happened with you and her? You said it was over, but if you need closure—"

"I don't need closure, I need to get away from her!" he explodes.

"She's a liar and a fraud, and she's guilty of everything they're accusing her of." He shakes his head frantically. "And she's going to get away with it!"

"She's lying to her investors?"

Jasper nods, catching his breath.

I've heard about other CEOs endangering their own careers by embellishing their expected revenue. She was caught, and instead of making her pay, letting Rabames go to trial, my dad has found her an out, a way to save the company, everyone's investments, with whatever is in his proposal. His eyes focus on mine through the snowfall. "I'm a liar and a fraud, too. I'm getting away with as much as she is. The truth is, I'm helping her. She's all that stands between me and my future the same way that I'm all that stands between her and hers."

My teeth start to chatter, and a shudder runs through me as I take in what he's saying—what I think he's saying.

He removes his jacket and tugs it around me, pulling me closer to him in the process. "Shit, it's so cold," he says. But neither of us move to leave, even as the snow belts down hard, blanketing the woods around us. When Rob cornered him by the bathrooms, he told her she didn't have to worry about what he would disclose during his questioning. He said she was holding something over him. And now he's confessed to me in the middle of this storm that he's helping her. I think I understand what's happening. Rob knows what he most regrets, whatever makes him want to take back every second he spent with her, and she's using it against him to make sure he lies for her in the deposition.

With one hand holding his coat closed around me, I stretch out the other and grab his arm.

"What does she have on you?" I say.

He shakes his head, but I tighten my grip on him.

"It's okay," I tell him. I can see how scared he is, how this has been corroding him and he's desperate to let it go, set the words free, the way I felt in his room other night, wishing I could tell him the truth about Mimi and Rosie and my dad and how I feel tricked and foolish and sad all at once.

"I cheated in the decathlon," he says, a stream of fog emerging as he lets the sentence out in one gasping breath. "That's how I broke the record. That's the reason I got an early acceptance into Dartmouth. That's why I can't say anything when I'm questioned for the lawsuit."

His eyes trace over my face, searching for clues about how I'm going to react. I can see that he's very afraid of what I'll do next, what I'll say. But this is how it works, isn't it? Falling for someone, trusting them with things you hardly trust yourself with.

I know he wants me to speak, but at the same time, he's scared of what I'll tell him now that he's revealed the worst thing he's ever done and admitted it's spiraling into something even worse. I unclench my grip around his arm and grab his freezing hand.

"I won't tell anyone," I say.

Thirty-nine

Drenched and shaking, Jasper and I take the elevator to the tenth floor. He gives me a spare set of pajamas from his drawer and tells me that I can have the first shower. But after I've thawed myself under the hot water and changed into the flannel pajamas, I find him in sweats sitting in front of a blazing fire. His pajamas are too big for me, and that makes them all the cozier. I roll up the bottoms so I don't trip as I walk. He smiles when I join him on the couch. There are a few bags of junk food strewn out over the coffee table.

"Since we missed dinner," he says. Room service is undoubtedly not an option while the restaurant is busy catering for all the party guests, and Robames rented out the entire resort.

The electric kettle beeps, and Jasper gets up and pours us two steaming cups of hot water, which we mix with hot chocolate. We hold the warm mugs close, letting them warm us as we sit in front of the fire.

"About what I said at the party," I say. "I don't know how much you overheard—"

"Collins—" he interrupts. "You don't have to explain yourself. Not to me. I get it. How it's been with us—it's—I mean, I feel the same way."

Something swells inside me that I can't quite place. Like relief or happiness—maybe both. He's smiling at me, and I must be smiling back; I think I must've even smiled first. My mind is foggy, and my stomach is fluttery, but I still wait for some sort of self-satisfaction to burst within me. I was caught saying I was falling for him, and he admitted that he feels the same way. But there with the sweep of unbridled happiness, is a current of fear—this abrupt awareness that now that I have this, whatever it is, I could lose it. I'm supposed to gamble it.

Jasper sighs. "I'm so glad you know about our parents." He leans back, peeks at me through his curtain of curls. "And you don't care?"

"It's a little weird." He nods in agreement. "But not enough that I want to stop."

I take my first sip of hot chocolate and let out a moan as it hits my lips. He watches me and smiles. He sets down his mug, and I can see in his expression that he's as happy as I am about our confessions but that he's also aware of the distance between us because of what else he revealed tonight.

"Tell me what happened," I say.

For a second, he stares at the fire and doesn't say anything, and I worry that he's already slipping away, locking up the things he hates about himself in case I'll hate them, too. But then he turns toward me, letting his arm line the top of the couch, and I know he's going to come clean about it all. The real reason she's his biggest regret.

"Rob was in town for the decathlon. I was in her hotel room the day before the competition, waiting for her to get back from some meetings and using her laptop because it had this new graphics program that I wanted to use to complete an assignment in my digital artistry and media language class. Right when I was getting started, I noticed the official questions for the decathlon, sitting there next to her laptop. I didn't know how she got them—

figured since she knew people on the committee they'd, I don't know, given her a copy. It doesn't make sense, thinking back on it, and I should've known it was a trick."

"What do you mean *a trick*?"

He chews on his lip before he continues. "I was working on my assignment, but I couldn't stop thinking about the decathlon questions. They were *right there*. And I kept thinking about what she'd said earlier that week, that if I did exceptionally well at the decathlon, it would make me a more feasible Robames intern candidate. She told me that if there were something incredible on my résumé that set me apart from the other applicants, we could spend the summer together and no one would think twice about it."

He was not only on the team that won the national decathlon, but he also broke records for questions answered correctly and the time it takes to complete the final round. A definite résumé booster.

"So I did it; I looked at all the questions and spent the rest of the day figuring out the answers. When it was time to compete, I was more than ready. She was in the audience, and all I could think about was how impressive I must've looked to her—how I was really coming through for us so we could be together that summer. But also—" He shakes his head, and the way he glances away from me for a moment, I can tell this is the part he's most ashamed of. "I also thought that maybe while she was watching me up there, she was thinking I was as smart or as quick on my feet or as magnanimous as she was. There was so much about her I didn't see because of how I felt about her—this infatuation. But none of it was real. Not the way I felt about her and definitely not the way she claimed to feel about me. Everything she does is calculated. Because of course, she went out of her way to get those questions from the people she knew on the committee; of course, she planted them exactly where she knew I would find them. She was counting on me using them. She thought I would do anything to be with her, but she wanted to really make sure. She wanted assurance. Proof. So she'd know I wasn't a liability. And she needed me to screw up so she'd have protection in case I ever became one."

Protection. "But—why?"

"She wanted me to intern at Robames, working closely with her, but she knew I might question what I saw going on at the company. And that's exactly what happened. I noticed very quickly that things weren't right. I started thinking clearly; I started seeing her for who she really was—and for who she wasn't."

"But she can't prove you cheated; it'd be her word against yours."

"She does have proof," he says. "When I confronted her about some of the stuff I'd witnessed, questioned what she was doing at Robames, and told her I thought she was wrong and that I knew she'd been deceiving everyone, she showed me the recording. Her laptop camera had been on the whole time. It's clear as day in the recording: me, flipping through the official questions of the decathlon."

"She set you up."

He nods. "She never really cared about me. I was only an opportunity to her. She saw me and knew I was someone she could control. Someone easy to manipulate. That's the only reason I was appealing to her."

I think of the way she was crying after their fight and wonder if he's got it right about this. If it was losing him she was crying over or if it was the fear of losing the company she'd built. If she only spoke to him about their future to ensure he didn't change his mind about lying in the deposition.

"That's the only reason she wanted me at Robames. She thought

I'd lie for her. And if I said I wouldn't then she had a way to make me." He leans forward and looks down.

"Only because she threatened you."

"But I was an easy target. Walked happily into her trap."

"If the lawyers knew about how things were *romantic* between you and Rob, wouldn't it discredit you, take you off the deposition list? Then you wouldn't have to lie."

"She doesn't want anyone to know about what happened with us. She's always wanted it a secret, saying we'd make it public when I was in college, afraid she wouldn't be taken seriously if her investors or colleagues knew about it."

"Since you've been at Hylift, she keeps trying to get you alone—"

"Yes, exactly, *alone*. And it's not to start things up with me again. All she wants is reassurance that I'm still afraid she'll expose me, that I'll lie for her. There's no way to prove we were involved. Right now it's nothing but rumors and hearsay. She graduated the semester after it started between us, and once she was gone from Rutherford, I only saw her once in a while. Our communication wasn't consistent. She'd email me when she was near Cashmere or in Seattle visiting her uncle, and I'd email her if I was touring colleges in the east. We'd make plans to meet up. But it wouldn't read like anything more than former classmates arranging to get together to catch up."

Without meaning to, I've scooted closer to him on the couch, and with my legs bent the way they are, our knees are nearly touching.

"The only way out is to come clean," he says. He glances down, and I think he, too, is noticing our proximity. "And I don't know how to do that. I don't know how to tell everyone I've let them down." He rests his hand on his leg, right near mine. "It's probably cowardly or selfish, but I can't bring myself to do it."

"I understand." I want to grab his hand. But I can't find the courage. It seems perverse to feel this tenderness toward him growing even stronger now that I've learned all this about him— all about the worst parts of him, the most horrible mistake he's ever made, and how he's doing nothing to repent. I know what keeps him up at night, what he tries to beat out of his mind when we go to the gym with Theo. I should feel powerful. But instead, I feel protective. They feel like my secrets, too, now.

"Do your parents know why you've been deposed?" I ask. "Do they know what it's about?"

"They've seen my name on the deposition list and think I've been included because I interned there. They're nervous about the lawsuit, the way all the investors and board members are. But—" he says, shaking his head. "It gets complicated because of the money my parents have tied up in her company. They've been clear they do not want to talk about it with me, and actually, that's been sort of a relief. I haven't brought it up either."

"My father is very good at his job, and he's not going to let any-one lose their investments," I say before I really think about if this is the kind of thing I should be telling him right now.

"I've heard that," he says, a small smile on his face.

My stomach makes an embarrassing gurgling noise, and Jasper raises his eyebrows.

"You're hungry." He laughs. "Me, too."

We dig into the junk food. We rip into Cheetos and peanut M&Ms and salt-and-vinegar chips and gummy bears and Fritos. It's unbelievably comfortable, sitting here in front of the fire with him like this, chowing down on my favorite snacks.

"This might be better than filet mignon," Jasper says.

"We're having our own gourmet dinner," I say. "Cheetos confit."

Jasper laughs. "Hershey's brûlée."

He seems more carefree, lounging next to me. I wonder if he feels like a weight's been lifted since he doesn't have to keep our parents' relationship from me anymore. He's also confessed all his regrets, and I'm still here, happily eating a junk food dinner with him.

I thought Theo was the one with the secrets. But what Jasper's hiding is more damning than I ever could've imagined. Keeping this quiet would be worth more to Mrs. Mahoney than my father. But Jasper smiles at me, and I wish we could stay forever like this. I wish there were a way to get his mother away from my father that didn't involve him or the two of us, together.

Forty

Jasper stares at me, watching my every move, scanning my face, the way my hands break off a hunk of chocolate before putting it in my mouth. And then he zeroes in on my lips.

"Why are you looking at me like that? Do I have chocolate on my face?"

He smiles at me. "I think you're really incredible," he says. His arm is along the back of the couch, and his hand is near my head. There's nothing I want more than to kiss him right now. He really is beautiful, and he wants to be kind, the way he thinks I am. It's a mystery to me still, that I know all the bad things about Jasper but can only see all the reasons someone would want him. I can't help but cherish this strange way he makes me feel. A bag of chips rustles as I move closer to him. This makes his smile get even bigger. But he moves closer, too, and places his hand on the back of my head. I rest my hand on his shoulder.

As he leans toward me, the door opens with a bang. It makes us both jump. My hand retreats from his shoulder, and his drops from behind my head, sliding down my arm. We turn toward the door behind us and see Theo standing in the entrance with Stewart slumped against him.

"A little help, please!" he calls.

Jasper rushes over and takes Stewart's other side.

"Bathroom, now," Theo instructs, and the two of them steer Stewart to the right, through the doors leading into the restroom.

A moment later, they both come out, sans Stewart. But I can hear the very faint sounds of him vomiting.

"How much did he drink?" Jasper asks.

"He was having a very good time at the party," Theo says. "Until suddenly he wasn't."

"Did his parents see him like this?" Jasper asks.

"Or Anastasia?" I blurt out.

"I got him out of there before any serious damage was done," Theo says. "But speaking of Anastasia, she's been texting you like crazy, Collins—" He pauses as he looks us up and down like he's finally registered that we're no longer in our party clothes. "And not to interrupt whatever you two have going on in here that looks suspiciously like a boring night in, but I left her to fend for herself at that party while I took care of Stewart, and she's been frantic trying to reach you. I'm sure she's in dire need of rescuing."

"You should go." Jasper nods at me.

"You should both go," Theo says.

"It's okay," Jasper says.

"No, no—Stewart's already got throw-up on my suit jacket, and there isn't anyone at that party I'd be caught dead kissing at midnight anyway. You two should go." I think Theo winks at me, but it happens so quickly, that I can't be sure.

"You can go back to the party," Jasper says to him. "I've helped Stewart out like this before. He's *my* friend, and—"

"He's my friend, too," Theo says sharply. "And so is Collins, and I'm not going to let you stay cooped up in here using Stewart as an excuse just because you want to avoid Rob James when you could take a fantastic girl to a sensationally overdone party. Stop hiding and enjoy the damn night!"

Jasper glances at the ground, blushing. "Okay," he finally says. "You're right."

"I'm always right."

We decide not to change, since our party clothes are still wet, and arrive at the *sensationally overdone* New Year's Eve party wearing pajamas and slippers. Jasper takes my hand as we walk through the silver streamers marking the entrance to the party in the sky lounge. It's been transformed the way the restaurant was revamped for the dinner portion of the night, the tables sequestered in one side of the room with plenty of space to mingle around the bar and a stage with a band playing and a dance floor full of people on the other end. The ceiling is covered in silver. The rest of the décor is black. Everything is dark with muted purple lighting. It's quite the contrast to the usual white and gold that makes up most Robames events.

As we look for Anastasia, I see my dad. He's standing with three other people near the tables, chatting casually. Mrs. Mahoney is on the dance floor, swaying to the music with her husband. We finally find Anastasia talking exuberantly with Kyle and Rick Singer. She does not seem in dire need of being rescued but throws her arms around me when we approach.

"You and Jasper sure look *comfortable*," she says into my ear. I smile instead of answering her. "Have you seen Rob James?" she says. "I thought she'd be in black to match the party, but I should've known better."

It's not hard to find her. She's dancing with a group of others who seem about her age, like maybe they're her friends from Yale or her class at Rutherford that she invited to be here with her. She's in a slinky dress, white and iridescent that almost looks silver when the lights from the stage hit it at certain angles. I know Jasper must've noticed her, too. But he keeps his gaze on me.

"Let's dance," he says, stepping closer and tilting his head toward me to be heard over the music. He takes my hand and leads me to the dance floor. We move away from Rob James and the rest of the crowd and find a spot toward the side of the stage, out of view from most of the party, including our parents, which is the point.

"I'm a terrible dancer," Jasper says as we start. But after a few seconds of him twirling me around and pulling me close as the band sings Elvis's "Burning Love," I have to respectfully disagree.

The rest of the room melts away. All the songs are for us. We're dancing like no one is watching and laughing even though we can't hear ourselves above the music. We're every cliché that's ever existed about two people falling for each other, and I don't care.

I was so at ease with him sitting on the couch a short while ago, and yet, now, every time our hands are clasped and he pulls me toward him, for those brief seconds when we're nose to nose, shoulder to shoulder, hip to hip, my heart starts to race and I feel this thrill that's unlike anything I've ever felt before.

The countdown starts without warning—an abrupt cut of the music, and a screen on the stage behind the band displays the numbers in the style of a flickering old film. The whole room chants the countdown, voices growing louder and more excited as the numbers get lower. Jasper and I face each other, and soon I'm not looking at the screen or the lively crowd; I'm only looking at him. His hands grip mine, his fingers tickling my palms. He shifts toward me, his hand moving to my waist. I pull him closer with my other hand, and his face moves so near mine that our foreheads are almost touching. *Why is this countdown taking so long?* He must be thinking the same thing, because on three, he leans down and kisses me. I can't hear the crowd or the rest of the countdown. I can't feel my feet on the floor or the flannel against my skin. I can only feel his lips on mine, his hands on my back, his heart drumming under my fingertips. We don't notice the wild cheering around us or the poppers going off or when a burst of silver confetti rains down from the ceiling, until I don't know how much time has passed and the lights start to flicker. A purple glow floods the room, and the band announces that the party is over. Jasper and I stare at each other, silver confetti stuck to our hair and clinging to the fabric of our pajamas. I think even if I fail at everything I'd promised Rosie I would do, it'd be worth it.

Three Months Later

He steps toward me, his hardened expression slipping.

"Please take the trade, Collins." There's desperation in his voice. "Please. I don't want to blow up my whole world. We can all go back to how it was before."

Back to when? Was it ever simple when all along, this is what we had lurking beneath the surface? Vials that we'd created ourselves that could be used to poison us.

"If I do it," I say. "Then I need your help with something else."

JANUARY

Forty-one

Anastasia stays with me after the party since Stewart's passed out in the bed Theo and Anastasia were sharing. We spend the morning in bed snacking on muffins, and she peppers me with questions about Jasper.

"Are you guys, like, a couple now?"

"I don't know," I say over and over again to her inquiries.

"Is he an amazing kisser?"—the only question I do have an answer to. A resounding *yes*.

"You look drunk and happy and also a little sick," she says. "That's how I know you're completely into him."

"I'm completely into him," I tell her.

She leaves to have brunch with the Mahoneys, and I stay in bed. I feel weird. A strange mix of delight and dread. It's easy to conjure how it felt to kiss him, to be close to him. I keep replaying it in my head like an impulse I don't have control over. I want to forget the reason I decided to make Jasper Mahoney fall for me in the first place. I shouldn't want to forget.

He told me everything he hates about himself, confessed the things he finds most shameful. And they're things that people would happily crucify him for. They're things Mrs. Mahoney would want to stay hidden. Wouldn't she? Or would she cut me loose to hurt him myself, if it meant protecting what she has going with my father?

Rosie told me their affair was illicit—but now I know it's not. She told me my father was being manipulated because Mrs. Mahoney was using him for his money to settle the debt from her bad investments and reckless spending, and Theo confirmed they are indeed having money issues. Rosie claimed that his involvement with Mrs. Mahoney would tie up his money and that Mimi might not be able to rely on him financially anymore, which would explain why Mimi was selling the farm.

I don't know what to believe anymore. There seem to be pieces I'm missing, and I can't decide if they're things Rosie was missing, too, or if she didn't tell me the whole story on purpose.

When I come out of my bedroom, my dad is sitting in the living room reading the newspaper, a fire ablaze in the fireplace, all the curtains pulled open, showing off the damage of last night's snow. Except today the clouds are gone, and the bright blue sky stares back at us.

"I missed you at dinner last night," he says. I make myself a cup of tea and fill a small plate with biscotti and scones. I notice his hot water is low and refill his mug.

"So, Jasper Mahoney, huh?" he says as I sit down next to him.

I pretend to concentrate on dipping my biscotto into my tea. "So, Marylyn Mahoney?"

He coughs and sets down his mug.

"Sorry it's awkward now," I say. "But I know about you and . . . Mrs. Mahoney. I know all about the arrangement and your trip to St. Barths with them."

"St. Barths was a business trip," he says quickly. He rubs his face with his hands. "I guess I shouldn't be surprised that you know about this since you're friendly with the Mahoney boys . . . I'm sorry you didn't hear it from me first. But I didn't think—"

"Dad, I don't care that you're involved with her. As long as you're happy." He'd seemed like he was when I saw the two of them laughing at the bar before the New Year's Eve dinner. "And you are, right? Happy, with her?"

He has a few false starts as he tries to answer me. Finally, he shrugs. He smiles. "I'm happy, sure."

"Then I'm happy for you," I say. "Do Mimi and Rosie know about you and Mrs. Mahoney?"

"That isn't really the kind of thing your Mimi and I discuss."

I nod, the image of Mimi shaking her head, saying, "Jake's personal life is none of my business," flashing through my mind.

"What about Rosie?" Rosie made it sound like she watched his affair from afar—an accidental run-in in New York when she coincidentally chose to eat at the same restaurant as they did. But what if that's not how it happened at all?

He hesitates. That simple pause tells me the answer must be yes, and he doesn't know how to explain the reasons Rosie knew and Mimi didn't.

"Rosie knows," he says. "But don't be upset with her for not telling you about it." Not the thing I was expecting him to say. "Rosie was, well, she wasn't happy about it, to say the least, so I asked her to please not say anything to you."

"Because Mrs. Mahoney is married?"

"I explained the arrangement to her. But that wasn't what concerned her, no."

"What concerned her?"

He scratches his chin, his fingers rubbing the light stubble of his unshaven face. "Rosie is a naturally suspicious person, that's all."

"Because Mrs. Mahoney needs your money?"

He's about to bite into a piece of biscotto, but he leans away in surprise. "What—why would you say that?"

"I'm close with the Mahoney boys, remember?"

He tosses the biscotto on the plate in front of him, his eyebrows raised. "They told you I'm with Marylyn because she *needs my money*?"

"Okay, so they never said that. But Theo did tell me that their family isn't exactly thriving financially. I just thought that maybe . . . money was a factor."

"Because otherwise why would she be interested in someone like me?"

"Dad—no, that's not what I meant at all." This isn't going quite the way I'd hoped. "I've seen your most eligible New York bachelor write-up; I get that you are quite the catch." He crosses his arms as I continue. "But she's not. It's an arrangement, not a relationship. You can't do things with her that you'd be able to do with a regular girlfriend. You have to be careful when you're out in public with her. You can't take her out to dinner or to the movies or dancing. You couldn't even kiss her on New Year's Eve."

"That kind of stuff isn't important to me."

"Dad." I try to read his face, search for signs he's lying. "Should I be worried about you?"

He laughs. "There's no reason for you to be worried. I'm perfectly happy. I like my life. I'm comfortable with the arrangement with Marylyn. I'm less comfortable with you dating one of her sons." He holds up his hands. "But that shouldn't stop you."

"What does Marylyn think about it?"

"Believe it or not, that is not our favorite topic to discuss."

"She wouldn't do anything rash like tell Jasper he has to stop seeing me, would she?"

"Of course not. Why would you even ask that?"

Rosie said Mrs. Mahoney put her sons' happiness before her own. If she thought I genuinely made Jasper happy, she'd want me to be with him. Wouldn't she? Part of Rosie's plan counted on this.

"Do you get to see her today?"

He glances at his watch. "In a little while."

I wrinkle my nose. "You should shower first."

"Hey!" He ruffles my hair as he stands. His phone rings, and he takes it out of his pocket.

"Hi," he says quietly, answering the call. "Okay. I don't know who told you that, but like I said before, it's not up to me, I don't have control over—Hello? Hello?"

He sees me watching him and shrugs. "Bad connection." He sets his phone down on his desk and plugs it in to charge before he disappears into the bathroom.

He must've silenced the ringtone, but I can hear it vibrating aggressively against the top of the desk. Message after message after message.

When I hear the shower going, I walk over and pick up the phone. It vibrates in my hand as the messages pop up on the screen, continuing to come in. They're all from the same person. *Rose*.

By now, I guess I should've figured out that Rosie and my dad keep in touch. But it still surprises me to see so many texts from her when she's in Buenos Aries with Mimi.

You say you have no control, but you're the one who wrote the proposal.

You said your hands were tied, but that's not true.

You said there were no guarantees, but you're all that's standing in the way.

You know I've put everything into Spectacle Barkley.

Let the Robames lawsuit play out, Jake. Don't screw me over.

I know you don't believe me, but my family is the most important thing to me.

I gave you your family. Don't forget.

If you care about us, you'll pull the proposal for consideration.

We're your family, not her. She has her own family, and they aren't your responsibility.

I can't afford to lose what I've put into Spectacle Barkley, but you can afford to lose Robames Inc.

You're not thinking clearly because of her.

You'd do this for me if you weren't with her.

I know you think you love her, but she's using you.

If you don't withdraw your proposal, you'll be sorry.

Promise me you'll stop pushing your proposal on Robames Inc.

I won't ask you for a single thing ever again, I swear.

Something about the wording in these messages is familiar. *You said your hands are tied.* And the parts about family being important, the phrase *no guarantees*. It reminds me of the phone call I overheard my dad having with Mrs. Mahoney when we first arrived at Hylift. Unless he wasn't talking to Mrs. Mahoney like I'd thought, and it was Rosie he was on the phone with.

During the other phone call I'd heard him on that day, he said his proposal was all that could save Robames from the lawsuit. But he'd also said that Rob wasn't accepting it. He'd wanted to convince her. And here Rosie is telling him to drop it. But why?

I put my dad's phone back where I found it and take out my own phone. I search for Spectacle Barkley to try to understand what Rosie was talking about, why she kept bringing it up. I'm directed to a home page advertising a company that takes the DNA of those with chronic illnesses and tells them the best way to eat to preserve their health according to their genetic makeup.

This information doesn't exactly answer my questions or give me any more insight into why Rosie wants my dad to pull his proposal for consideration and let Robames collapse under the fallout of the lawsuit.

But there is one thing that's clear to me now. Rosie blames Mrs. Mahoney for why my dad isn't doing what she's asking. I get that, even though I don't understand why she's demanding he drop the proposal. She's not worried about him being with someone who's using him. She's not worried about me or about Mimi. She's only worried about herself. And she's using us to threaten him.

I think of the dishes clattering to the floor, splintering the day Rosie told me who she really was to me. The sound was almost as loud as Mimi's screaming. Rosie had looked at me from the kitchen window. Her expression was stable—flippant, even. She appeared confident, like she stood by what she'd done. She'd wanted me to know that she was my mother so that I'd understand why I was capable of doing all the things she wanted me to do at Rutherford. She unveiled the truth she'd helped cover for so many years because getting my father away from Mrs. Mahoney is *that* important to her. But not because she's afraid of my father being taken advantage of and how that might affect Mimi and me. She wants him to withdraw the proposal and thinks Mrs. Mahoney is the only reason he won't do what she asks. *You'd do this for me if you weren't with her.*

She didn't reveal the whole truth about why she wanted to break up my father and Mrs. Mahoney, only a truth she knew I would get behind; that she was counting on me to save him.

And it'd worked. After she'd told me she was my mother, it made me feel like I could trust her—like she might be the only one who'd ever tell me the truth because she dared to expose the deepest buried secret, regardless of the risk. I believed her blindly about my father and Mrs. Mahoney and what I had to do, because with the new knowledge that I was actually hers, I not only thought I could pull it off, I also really, really wanted to.

My phone chimes. A text from Jasper.

What are you doing right now?

Now I see I was being manipulated. Rosie's agenda is entirely self-serving. She tricked me, and I fell for it. But I don't have to go along with her plan. Not anymore.

I text Jasper back.

Nothing. I'm free.

Forty-two

Jasper Mahoney sneezes whenever he eats a peppermint. He's almost never hungry for breakfast food and hates the taste of coffee. When he laughs, he gets this expression on his face, as though he's surprised that something in this world could be so funny. He has a constellation of moles decorating his back that spread along his shoulder blades. I try to find a pattern in them, touching my fingers to the points, but they're arranged in perfect disorder. When he falls asleep, he does so with his whole body; as his eyes close, his shoulders curve in, and he becomes so incredibly still that I have to fight the urge to put my hand over his chest, to check if he's still breathing. It's like this every time he falls asleep. Be it a quick nap after skiing or at night, when I'm lying next to him, as I am for each remaining night we're at Hylift, promising my dad he has nothing to worry about, pretending half the time I'm staying with Anastasia.

Jasper and I stay up talking until we are too sleepy to make sense of words anymore. We whisper under the sheets, his hands sliding along my skin, my fingers trailing down his sides. We kiss until our lips are numb or we lose our breath or it becomes too wonderful and too overwhelming all at once that I have to stop and turn away from him but still need his arms around me, and I can tell that something wonderful and overwhelming is happening to him, too, by the way he's slightly shaking as he holds me, the way he'll whisper my name as he hangs his head against my shoulder. He sleeps better when I'm there, and so do I because when I awake right before dawn with a start—thinking it was all a dream—he'll groggily drag his arm across me, pulling me to him.

"I'm not ready to go back to Rutherford," he tells me on our last day at Hylift, as the first signs of sunlight send streaks through his bedroom window.

"Let's stay here forever, then."

He smiles like he knows I'm only half kidding.

We go for one last ride on the tram. I lean against him, taking in the view. The sky lounge is nearly empty when we get back. But Rob is there, sitting in a corner booth, surrounded by older men and women, my father among them. Jasper's hand tightens around mine as he quickens his pace. My father pushes his hair back, a sign of stress. No one at the table looks very happy, a sea of black suits surrounding Rob in her white blazer and gold headband. For the first time, I wonder what it must be like to be in charge of a company that large, to have the vision and the idea and all those men and women with their money to appease. Maybe it would make anyone desperate—paranoid enough to want to have leverage over even the people who're supposed to be closest to them.

After we've packed up our things and said goodbye to our parents, we walk with Anastasia and Theo to the helicopter. Jasper keeps his arm around me and whispers statistics into my ear. Right before I climb on board, he kisses me.

They all sing for me again as we soar over the mountains, this time with Anastasia belting even louder than the pilot, and I stare at them, wondering how I got so lucky. Can you worm your way into people's lives, get to know all sides of them, without also starting to feel close to them? The helicopter takes a sudden dip, and I reach for Jasper at the same time that he reaches for me, draping his arm over my lap like he knows I need both something to grab hold of and something to make me feel steady in my seat.

"That's adorable," Stewart says.

At the same time, Anastasia says, *"Gross."*

We burst out laughing.

It doesn't seem possible to filter through people's lives and not begin to care about them; it seems as impossible as making someone fall in love with you without falling for them right back.

Forty-three

When the five of us arrive at Rutherford, it's dark outside. The outline of the forest is a shadow against the gray and clouded sky, and the ocean can be heard in the distance, each determined wave barreling into the shore.

We've missed most of the welcome-back social event, but we still have to drag ourselves to the common room to make our drops in the storage closet box and play a quick round of Go Fish to determine the winners of this month's game.

I greet Elena and Ruthie and catch up with some of the girls on the field hockey team. I don't know what to say when they ask me what's new. They casually glance at Jasper, who's sitting two sofas away with the lacrosse team, like maybe they've already heard. I shrug and say, "Not much," but I look in Jasper's direction while I say it so that maybe they'll pick up on my small smile and I won't have to say I'm dating him, words that sound too regular for the way I feel about him.

When the whole group is ready to start the game, I tell Elena and Ruthie I'll catch up with them later, and sit down at the large round table. My phone alarm vibrates in my pocket during the third hand, signaling it's my time slot for depositing my item in the box. I excuse myself and head down the hall, slinking into the storage closet as quickly as I can.

I move fast, setting in my brooch shaped like a statue of the three graces, something my father gave me three Christmases ago when I was really into dressing up my sweaters. Just as I've made the drop, I hear the door click open and shut. I see a tall figure moving through the shelves. Taking a deep breath, I remind myself that the faculty can't come in during the socials because the locks have been changed. No one else doing their drop tonight ran into an ounce of trouble either. The person who entered steps into the light at the end of the row and walks slowly toward me.

"Sebastian, you scared me," I say. "Sorry—do I have my time wrong? I set this alert back in November and—"

"You don't have the time wrong," he says as he approaches me. "I wanted to see you alone, and, well, judging from how close Jasper was sitting to you around the table, and the way he put his hand on your knee, and that kiss he gave you before you arrived at the social—don't think no one saw that because he had the audacity to do it right in front of the main hall windows—I'd guess it'll be a long while before I get the chance to be alone with you."

"Jasper and I started dating over break," I say.

"So it would seem." He smiles as he looks away, slightly shaking his head. "Anyway, I wanted to give these back." He reaches out and hands me the earrings he'd taken during one of the exchanges. "I had something more fun planned for giving them back to you, but it doesn't seem appropriate anymore. It was going to be cheeky."

"Okay." I shrug. "Do it for the next girl, I guess." I regret it as soon as I say it. It doesn't sound playful, like a joke, the way I intended.

"What's that supposed to mean?"

"Surprising someone with an item they lost during the game is one of your moves," I say to his incredulous expression. "Like kissing behind the angel and sending flowers. It's not like it's a secret; you do it with everyone."

He frowns. "And now you've chosen a boyfriend with no moves at all, so let me know how that goes." He turns to leave and immediately spins around and comes back. "Shit, sorry. It's just—I was so excited to see you. And then when you walked in with Jasper . . . it was a shock."

"It was kind of a shock to me, too, if you can believe it. I didn't know I would fall—feel this way about him."

"It's that serious?" He leans against the shelf and puts his hand over his heart. "Ouch."

He gives me a small smile, and I roll my eyes. "Oh, come on. It's not as though you spent all of break thinking about me."

"Except I did spend all break thinking about you."

He's probably exaggerating, even though being forthcoming and transparent has always seemed entirely genuine from him.

"But I never heard from you. Not once since we left Rutherford."

"And I didn't hear from you either."

He's right. "Because nothing had happened between us—"

"Yet," he adds, interrupting. "The start is the best part. When you have no idea what's coming; you just know you are very, very, *very* interested in finding out." The way he says this makes me blush. "Plus, Collins Pruitt, I didn't want to seem needy. And okay, fine, I was having a blast over break and keeping busy and there wasn't always reception where I was, but I still thought about you and the what-if between us constantly. I'm talking every day. We've never even had a date, and now I guess we won't get to until—" He cuts himself off, but there's a shadow of a smirk on his face.

"Until what?"

"Until Jasper goes to Dartmouth. Or until things go sideways. Still plenty of time for that."

I remember what Sebastian said at the beginning of the year. *You know you can't date someone in college while you're here, right? It never works out.* He's honest to a fault, unafraid of letting his truths come out, no matter how humiliating. He must really believe that no relationship can sustain that kind of distance. I believed it once, too, and it was going to be the way Jasper and I would part slowly, no heartbreak involved. But now I don't like to think about it. Now I know it wouldn't be that simple.

"Some things do work out, Sebastian."

"Just not you and me, I guess. Pity that we'll never know." He grins; he knows that's a good line.

"Save it," I tell him, smiling as I move past him.

He catches me by the arm. "I'm not happy for you. But I'll pretend I am until he's gone."

The door opens quickly. I must've taken too long and am now cutting into someone else's turn. Theo enters, his hands on his hips. His expression is flat as Sebastian walks past him to the exit.

"He cornered me," I say.

"I'm sure he did."

The door shuts with a low thud as Sebastian leaves, sealing the room in silence.

"I can trust you, can't I?" Theo says.

"I'd never do anything to hurt Jasper, I swear."

Theo reaches inside the box, leaving something in a blue box behind.

"That's not what I mean," he says. He's nervous and distressed. I can see it in the furrow of his brow, the way he keeps biting at his thumb. "Over Thanksgiving, I told you how much my family needed the money from the Robames investment. You wouldn't want anything getting in the way of that, would you?"

He watches me, like he's skeptical of what I'll say.

"Theo, what are you talking about?"

"Your dad has this proposal—an idea that would limit the effects from the lawsuit and keep it from going to trial."

When I nod, Theo looks relieved.

"So you know about it?"

"Sort of," I say. "But I heard Rob hates his idea and won't accept the proposal." My father told Rosie that his hands were tied. No guarantees.

Theo sighs. He rubs his temples. I've never seen him so worried before. Theo, the epitome of cool. "It's unreasonable that she's not even willing to consider it. And more than that, it's not fair."

"She doesn't seem to be at all nervous about this lawsuit. Your dad is the only one who can see clearly what this could do to her company. I mean, public perception alone will be hard to recover from."

I nod. "I'd like Robames to avoid the lawsuit so that Jasper can be kept out of it. And I trust your dad. He's made his living this way. He knows when to revive a company and when to kill it and when to change it."

We hear the door open again—this time with a hearty swing. It falls shut slowly as the noise of shuffling feet approach us.

It's Stewart who turns down our row. He steps back when he sees us, like our presence has startled him. "Collins—what are you doing here?"

Or just my presence, apparently.

"You're early," Theo says to him.

I glance between them, trying to gauge if it's simply Stewart's turn to make his drop and that's why he's here or if Theo was waiting for him because they were meeting.

Stewart studies his watch. He flicks it, then puts it up to his ear like he's trying to hear if it's still working.

"Well, did you ask her?" Stewart says to Theo.

"I was about to."

"Ask me what?"

"We need your help with Jasper," Stewart says. I hold my breath, wondering if, since they know about the proposal, they also know about Jasper being on the list of those deposed.

Theo nods. "We need Jasper to convince Rob James to accept your dad's proposal and—"

Stewart continues, talking over Theo. "It's the only way to salvage her company and protect our families' investments, thanks to this serious lawsuit—"

"She's caught up," Theo says.

"Okay, so what do you think?" Stewart asks me. "Will you help us with Jasper?"

"Have you tried asking him yourself?"

"Sure did," Stewart says. "But damn if that guy hasn't made staying away from her his first priority. And he's really sticking to his guns on this one. Won't listen to me or Theo, doesn't even seem to care how much money his family will lose if the company goes under. No bueno."

"But we think he'll listen to you," Theo says. "If you tell him to reach out to Rob, we know he could talk her into making the changes to her company that your dad laid out in the proposal to save it."

"Tell him you're not going to get jealous and dump him if he calls her," Stewart adds. "Tell him you don't want your dad to lose his investment either."

"Lately he likes to stay out of our parents' mess," Theo says. "But if you're worried about it, too, maybe he'll reconsider."

"And you really believe he'd be able to convince her?" I think of the way Rob had looked at Jasper at Hylift, the way she'd said she always wanted him close and her promise that it could be different in the future for them, how she was crying after he'd run into the storm to get away from her. They might be right about Jasper having a good amount of sway.

"She had him *followed* at Hylift," Stewart says.

"She still cares what he thinks," Theo says, and I remember what he'd told me, about Rob hating that Jasper was no longer under her spell.

But I don't think the two of them know what she has on Jasper or that he has incriminating things to say about her if this ever goes to trial that he'll be forced to lie about. They have no idea that it's much more complicated than an old romance that didn't end well.

"Why the hesitation?" Theo says.

"Unless you've got loyalties elsewhere?" Stewart says, and he and Theo exchange a glance. Is Theo still suspicious of me and my reasons for liking Jasper in the first place when I knew about our parents?

"What do you mean by that?" I glare at them, then zero in on Stewart. "Why do you care so much? What do you have at stake?" I can't get over the strangeness of this meeting, their plan to ask to me to help. It feels like there's something they aren't telling me.

"My parents and my grandparents will lose money. We'd have to sell our home in Tuscany if this deal falls through," Stewart says. "I can't lose that. It'd be molto brutto."

"Everyone has different priorities, right?" Theo says to me, shrugging.

"Regardless," Stewart says. "Getting Jasper to talk to Rob is really the only chance we've got to convince her to do the right things to save her company and our parents' money. Will you help us?"

Forty-four

There are these old cabins in the forest, off the path that leads to the water. They used to be rented out to tourists during the peak season, but I'm told that about six years ago the road to reach them washed out due to heavy winter rains, and the owners never replaced it. The cabins have been vacant ever since.

"Cabin seven is supposed to be the nicest," Anastasia says as we walk to the cafeteria for lunch. She overheard Theo and me talking about the cabins and instead of telling her the truth, that we're going to the cabins to listen in on a phone call between Jasper and Rob James, he tells her that I'm going there to be alone with Jasper. It's clear Theo doesn't want Anastasia to know what we're up to, the only secret he's keeping from her as far as I can tell. When I asked him about it, he said that he didn't want to risk a leak and get the four of us busted for wandering off campus where we aren't permitted to go.

"Cabin five is said to be the most spacious," she continues. "I've heard rumors that cabin nine is infested with raccoons."

"I like cabin three," Ariel says.

"I've heard cabin three smells like mildew," Anastasia says.

"They all smell like mildew."

"Well, how would I know?" Anastasia tosses her hair over her shoulder. "I prefer not to hike five miles to hook up with some-one."

"It's half a mile."

"Whatever. I prefer not to hike *at all*." We get in line for the toasted sesame noodle salad, my eyes scanning the cafeteria for Jasper. "But you should totally go, Collins. If you and Jasper don't mind the hiking or the smell or the raccoons."

That evening between dinner and the first night checks, I go to the gym. It will appear regular, me going to the gym, but once I'm there, I leave out the back exit and walk to the edge of the woods, where Jasper is waiting for me.

We trudge along the path as the sun goes down. The rays slice through the trees with the sounds of the ocean's waves lapping at the shore in the distance. When we reach the third big curve in the trail, we leave the path, going right instead of left, and walk toward the birch trees a few yards away. We go straight until we're past the birch trees and come to the thicket of younger pine trees. Brushing through them, we see the wide clearing, with a few small one-room cabins. Theo said to go in the one with the blue door—cabin two.

The door sticks on the first attempt to open it, but Jasper puts his weight into it, and it pops open. Theo and Stewart are already there, sitting at a small square table with a lantern in the middle. On the opposite side of the room, there's a short couch that's been covered with a plaid blanket. The floor is dotted with dirt and dried leaves, and it does smell like mildew. But Theo lights a can-dle and sets it on the counter of what would be a kitchenette, if all the appliances and cabinet doors weren't missing. The smell of oranges starts to fill the room.

"I do what I can," he says, nodding toward the candle. He turns to Jasper. "Are you ready?"

"I still don't think I'm the answer," he says. "But sure."

"Just tell her what she wants to hear and you'll be golden. Très bon."

The four of us sit at the table, around the glow of the lantern. Theo thinks we should all be there for the call, to hear in real time how she responds to Jasper's pleas and to guide Jasper in how to steer her toward accepting the proposal, depending on what her arguments against it are. Jasper's phone is positioned in the center. Theo has a notepad and pen for communicating with Jasper while he's on the call.

"She's expecting you?" Theo asks—something he got clarification on before we came here, when Jasper texted Rob to ask if they could talk and made the arrangements. It's the first clue that Theo is in fact very nervous about how this will turn out.

"Yes," Jasper says. "This is the time we agreed on." He glances at me and I give him the slightest nod so he'll know I'm ready. From inside the pocket of my sweatshirt, I hit the button on my phone, setting it to record Jasper's conversation with Rob.

Jasper and I have our own plan.

"Let's get on with it then," Stewart says.

Jasper dials her number and puts the phone on speaker.

"Hey," she says, answering on the second ring. "I'm glad you wanted to talk."

"Me, too," he says. "Is this still a good time?"

I'm struck by the casualness of their tones. Her voice isn't rigid, overtly professional, nor is it dripping with desperation. His is void of the usual defensiveness he exhibits when he talks to her.

"Yeah, now works," she says. "What'd you want to talk about? Calling to tell me you've reconsidered? You still think about what I said about the future? You know I hated every second I saw you with Jacob Pruitt's daughter at Hylift. Did you do that on purpose to drive me insane? Because it worked."

Jasper moves uncomfortably in his chair, his eyes shifting to meet mine. He's thinking what I'm thinking: she's walking right into our trap. We want what Theo and Stewart want, for Rob to accept my father's proposal. But we also want her to stop blackmailing Jasper.

"Speaking of Jacob Pruitt," Jasper says.

Theo covers his face with his hands like he doesn't think Jasper is being smooth at all.

"Oh, *what*?" Rob says. "Did you finally figure out your mother was sleeping with him?"

Stewart's eyes get big. Theo shakes his head at him, but I know they'll have to explain it to him later.

"Her latest *arrangement*. Did it upset your new girlfriend?"

Jasper pinches his eyes closed. "No, nope . . . that's not what I'm calling about, Roberta."

"I assume you're calling to apologize."

Jasper takes a deep breath. Stewart and Theo are nodding profusely at him.

"That is why I'm calling," he says. "And to say, I miss you."

Rob doesn't say anything right away. All of us hold our breaths waiting to see if she takes this bait. Theo and Stewart are hoping his confession will soften her, make her more likely to listen to Jasper's suggestion about the proposal. Jasper and I have something else in mind.

"Well, you know Jasper, you were a great intern. You've got an innovative mind and you're very intuitive. I still see a future for you at Robames."

"With you," Jasper interjects.

"The company could always use someone like you," she says without missing a beat.

Shoot. Jasper looks at me, sharing in my frustration.

Theo taps him impatiently on the shoulder. He scribbles

BRING UP THE PROPOSAL NOW on the notepad and holds it up to Jasper.

Jasper nods at Theo. He says, "From what I've heard, you won't have much of a future at all because of this lawsuit." She inhales sharply. He continues, "I didn't mean that to sound like a threat. I want to help you. I want you to get out of this unscathed, you know? I still believe in you." Theo and Stewart are nodding their approval. He glances at me, and I nod also. He's doing exactly what he's supposed to do. "If you accept Jacob Pruitt's proposal and enact his ideas, that should get the Justice Department off your back and spare you from going to trial. They wouldn't have the chance to publicly tear down everything you've built. You'd get to keep moving forward with Robames. You'd still be doing what you love, and that's what I want for you."

It's quiet for so long on the other end that we all lean forward, straining to hear if she's still there. Finally, Jasper says, "Hello?"

"I'm here," she says. Then she laughs. "That's what you want for me, is it?"

Jasper looks to us when he notices the new harshness in her voice. Theo and Stewart start nodding emphatically, instructing him even though he doesn't need it from them. Only from me. Under the table, I link my ankle around his.

"Yes," Jasper says. "Is it so hard to believe that I want you to be happy? Would you believe that I still love you—doesn't a part of you still love me?"

Theo grimaces like he thinks Jasper said the wrong thing again, maybe took it too far. But this is the confession we need from her in case Jasper really can't convince her to authorize the proposal.

"It is very hard to believe that my happiness is something that crosses your mind," she says. "Especially because not going to trial would sure make your life easier, wouldn't it?"

Jasper starts in quickly. "It would make your life easier, too," he says. "It would be better for both of us. Now and for the future."

"Did she put you up to this?"

"Did who put me up to this?" There's malice in his words because she's either talking about me or his mother, and either way, he doesn't like it.

"Or was it your brother? Worried for his family's crippling debt and trying to be the hero you could never be?"

Jasper lets loose. "If authorizing Jacob's proposal can get the lawsuit dropped, I don't understand why you won't do it. It doesn't make any sense."

"Do you even know what's in his proposal, Jasper?"

"Yeah, I do," he says. But he sounds unsure. He hasn't seen it. Neither have I. Theo writes *RESEARCH* on the notepad, but Jasper shakes his head. We aren't sure what that means or what he's trying to say.

"You have no idea what it's asking of me," she says. "And it doesn't get the Justice Department off my back or dissolve the lawsuit. All it does is stop it from going to trial. Protect the precious company image. But I'll have to give up my own life's creation."

"You're twenty," Jasper says. "You have plenty of time for another *life's creation*. You have time for ten of them! Maybe next you'll choose to invent something that's actually feasible."

Jasper's hand flies over his mouth like he's startled at what came out. He's still seething, though, his other hand gripping the edge of the table as he talks to her. The three of us stare at him, a new heaviness to the air now that Jasper is becoming unhinged.

"And you have plenty of time to apply to other colleges," she says. "If any of them will take you after they find out what you've done."

Theo drops the pen he's holding. He's starting to understand how complicated it is between Jasper and Rob, how there are things Jasper hasn't told him.

"At least I go down alone," Jasper says, abandoning the plan Stewart and Theo came up with to convince her to accept the proposal, abandoning our plan to get her to admit that she was involved with him. "You're screwing over so many people. It's incredibly selfish."

"I believe in fighting for what's mine," she says. "Something I used to think you understood. But now I know you don't. You're a coward. Have a great life, Jasper. Don't try to reach me anymore; I won't be taking your calls. If you want to talk to me about this again, you're going to have to discuss it with me in person."

She hangs up.

Jasper stands aggressively from the table, knocking over his chair.

Stewart tries dialing her back on Jasper's phone, but it goes straight to voice mail.

"I told you that wouldn't work," Jasper says.

Theo folds his hands over the notebook. "So she's blackmailing you," he says calmly.

Jasper looks down. He lifts his chair off the floor and straightens it in front of the table. He nods.

"And you knew about this?" Theo says to me.

"She's the only one who knows," Jasper says.

"Dude, what does she have on you?" Stewart says.

No one says anything, and I wonder if Jasper will be forced to confess to them about cheating in the decathlon, if they'll demand to know the entire truth.

"I was recording the call," I say quickly, revealing our plan because what's the use now that it didn't work. "If we could get Rob to say something about her and Jasper being involved, something to support all those rumors and hearsay, it would discredit him as a witness. He wouldn't be asked to testify. She wouldn't be able to blackmail him into lying."

"She doesn't want anyone to know about me—about us," Jasper explains. "She never did. Not until I was in college. She wants to be taken seriously, and her involvement with me jeopardizes that."

Theo watches Jasper with sad eyes. He's putting together that it was more than the stress of being on the deposition list that made Jasper have such a hard time sleeping.

"I guess the real question is, what do you have on her?" Theo says. He reaches out and touches Jasper's hand resting over the back of the chair. "It's all true, right? What they're accusing her of? And you know because you interned there?"

Stewart groans and puts his head on the table even though Jasper doesn't answer.

Jasper told me Rob was a liar and a fraud. Guilty of everything they're accusing her of.

"Why wouldn't the proposal dissolve the lawsuit?"

"Robames isn't being sued," Theo says. "The lawsuit isn't against the company. It's against her."

"Oh."

"She lied about everything," Jasper says. "I saw what she did. She lied about money. She'd fabricate results. I saw the reports saying her invention wouldn't work. No amount of additional research will change that."

Rob's speech over Labor Day fills my thoughts, how she spoke about believing in yourself, about never giving up. And I think of what Theo said about people wanting to trust in her, and that it's this persona she emulates that got so many investors behind her. They believed in her idea, but they also believed in her—her direction for the company, for the Roba-Fix. My father is almost never wrong—and he's certainly never *this* wrong.

"The Roba-Fix isn't real," Jasper says. "It seems too good to be true because it is. It's an impossible invention."

My heart starts to race.

"Do you get it now?" Stewart says.

I nod slowly, disoriented from the news and the weight of how dangerous Jasper really is to Rob if he's allowed to testify, why she has to be savage to make sure he lies. And why revealing their former relationship is not an option for her.

"You don't have to worry," Theo says to Jasper. "I've read the proposal many times, and it's really her best option. Even as stubborn as she is, she can't deny this. We'll figure out a way to convince her. If you have to meet with her in person like she wants, so be it. It was a good idea to try to discredit yourself. But our family still needs this investment."

"I don't know if anything I say will make a difference to her," Jasper says.

"You have to try again," I say, suddenly filled with panic now that I know the whole story, the real pressure Jasper's under. "Call her or email or her something—say you'll do it, you'll talk to her about this in person. And when you're alone with her try again telling her you believe in her and getting her to confess that you used to be involved. Pretend you still want her. Tell her you want that future with her and that you still love her. Remind her of all the good things you bring out in her. If she won't admit to a past love affair, we'll set her up for a current one. Let her see that you're the one who shines a light on the good parts of her and makes her forget all the bad parts." The words are heavy in my throat. It's not my advice. It's Rosie's. "We'll record it or we can plant cameras or—"

"Are you losing your actual mind?" Stewart says. The three of them stare at me with wide eyes, but my thoughts are still reeling, still producing ideas to save Jasper from this no matter the cost.

"Imagine if we had tangible proof that Jasper's not a credible witness," I say. "Proof of something she doesn't want anyone to know about. We'd have more leverage to bargain with her."

"You mean threaten Rob?" Theo says.

"She started it," I say.

"This is messed up, especially coming from you, Collins," Stewart says.

Theo tentatively looks at Jasper, unsure how Jasper will react to it. Jasper agreed to charm her over the phone, to try to get her confession by saying whatever was necessary. It would be different in person; we all understand this.

I hate to think it, to admit it, but I can see so clearly how to get what we want from Rob. The trap we'd have to set. More proof that I'm Rosie's daughter after all. Scheming and sneaky, taking high risks to get what I want. Rosie doesn't want Rob to authorize the proposal, and this to me is another reason we should do whatever it takes to force her to authorize it.

"If we have real proof that Jasper's an unreliable witness because he's romantically involved with Rob, then we'll give her a choice. Either she accepts my father's proposal or we expose her relationship with Jasper. If she doesn't agree, then it discredits Jasper for the trial, but more importantly, it discredits her in the eyes of her team, her investors. There'll be no getting around those rumors that she hired him as an intern to be with him. We present her with those options and she'll have no choice but to authorize the proposal to save face, even if she has to lose her *life's creation*."

There's an edge to the way the three of them are watching me, like they're shocked there's this viciousness inside of me, that I would put Jasper on the line like this. But I'm waiting for them to see that this ruthlessness comes from caring about Jasper. I'm waiting for them to also realize it's what's best to keep their families' investments. Jasper leans toward me, his expression opening, like he can see that this desperation, these wild ideas, really are a representation for how much he means to me.

"It was worth a shot," Jasper says. "But what if she matches our threat with one of her own?" He's worried that she'll retaliate by releasing the recording of Jasper cheating.

I don't have an answer to that except to say that she went so far as to have him followed at Hylift, and even if it was only to catch him alone to threaten him, I saw pain in her expression when he ran out into the storm to get away from her, the way she cried, like something about him still gets to her. But I don't say that. I don't say anything.

"I'll think of something else," Theo says. "I promise."

Jasper nods. "Okay." He sounds like he actually believes Theo. Like maybe he's relived for the alternative to my plan.

We leave shortly after, heading outside into the dark to make our way back to Rutherford. Stewart holds the lantern as we traipse through the trees. I thought Jasper and I were blindsiding Stewart and Theo by having our own plan to record the call. But I missed a lot about the entire situation. The details of the lawsuit. And the proposal.

"Could I see the proposal?" I ask Theo. He said he's read it many times. He said it's the best option. "You have a copy, don't you?"

Under the low blaze of the lantern, I catch Stewart eyeing Theo.

"I'd like to see it, too," Jasper says when we've taken a few steps and they still haven't answered me.

"All right," Theo says. "I'll send it to you."

"Are you sure?" Stewart says to Theo, keeping his voice low.

"Yes," Theo says, irritated.

"How exactly did you get the proposal?" I ask. Neither of their parents were privy to the meetings where my dad was presenting it.

"Collins, how do you think?" Theo says. "It's probably against protocol, but your dad gave my mom a copy. Special *privileges,* I guess."

"Okay, okay, I get it," I say.

"Theo, was that really necessary?" Jasper says.

"So you're dating, and your parents are dating," Stewart says, chuckling. "We'd better do something about Robames so they can afford all the therapy you're going to need."

We reach the path to the dormitories and let Stewart and Theo go ahead of us.

"I'm sorry," Jasper says, slowing his pace.

"What are you sorry about?"

"It's all my mess. My shitty past with Rob. My family's horrible debt. My parents' awkward arrangement."

"But I don't care about any of that."

"Are you sure? You don't think less of me for cheating—for not coming clean about it? You don't think I'm a horrible person?"

"I don't think that at all."

Sometimes I want to tell him everything. Let my own secret out into the ether. I know this terrible thing about him, and I still can't help how I feel toward him. But my secret is different from his. If I told him the truth then he'd know that the person who was supposed to love me no matter what left me for seven years and only told me the truth when she could pad it in lies and because she needed something from me. And I fell for it, I fell for all of it. How am I supposed to lay out all the proof I have that love is contingent on money and security and success and status and expect him to believe me when I tell him that I don't care about any of those things when it comes to him?

"Are you okay after talking to Rob?"

"I hate who I am with her. Even during that short call today, I was unhinged. I don't want you to see that side of me."

"I want to see every side of you."

He grabs my waist and leans down so our foreheads are touching. I brace his shoulders with my hands.

"I want to see every side of you, too," he says. "Promise me you'll show them to me."

I nod. I tilt my head upward and kiss him as my answer.

But there are things I don't want him to ever know. The parts of me that are unlovable. The part that was easy to use and easy to erase and easy to leave. Whatever it was about me that Rosie didn't want, I hope to hide from him for as long as I can. Forever, maybe.

Forty-five

My dad's Robames proposal is long and boring, and as Jasper taps absentmindedly on my leg as he reads next to me, it's hard to concentrate. We're in the common room sitting on one of the couches facing away from the hall. We sit close so we can both see the proposal on my laptop screen. It's early—classes don't start for another thirty minutes—and we're the only students here.

"It's essentially saying that they want to take the Roba-Fix off the market and turn Robames Inc. into a research facility," I say. Jasper makes figure eights over my tights.

"It's a very good idea."

"You think it could work?" I lean into him. His fingers stop moving, and his hand lies flat against my leg.

"Absolutely." He scrolls back a few pages. "I mean, look at this. Thanks to all the research Rob insisted on, she's built one of the most advanced facilities in the world. They've collected thousands, if not millions, of DNA samples from people with these specific chronic illnesses—the kind that the Roba-Fix was designed to help."

"It doesn't look like any other company would be able to compete with her in this arena either," I say, scanning the screen. The warmth of his hand spreads through me. I turn so I'm angled against him and watch as his body responds by turning toward me, too.

"She wouldn't be directly responsible for a medical revolution, but selling this research to pharmaceutical companies might help give someone else headway into creating one."

"Not to mention, the amount they'd pay for it." I point to the graph of forecasted sales. They aren't in the billions like the Roba-Fix was projected to make, but they're in the millions.

"With hardly any competition," Jasper says. He lays his arm across me, and I feel like an electric current is shooting through me.

I read the chart of similar companies, and he's right. According to my dad's calculations, Robames the research company would be able to offer more than any of the other businesses.

"Wait," I say, my finger hovering over a familiar company listed as a top competitor. Spectacle Barkley—from Rosie's messages to my dad. *I can't afford to lose what I've put into Spectacle Barkley, but you can afford to lose Robames Inc.* I don't understand. "I thought Spectacle Barkley was a company that told chronically ill people what they should eat to stay healthy based on their DNA. Why would they be considered a competitor?"

"Oh yeah," Jasper says. "That's just the service they offer to get DNA samples. Spectacle Barkley's real profits come from selling their research to pharmaceutical companies that need them for testing when developing drugs."

This explains Rosie's motives, the details of the money she was seeking all along. If Rob accepts my dad's proposal and turns Robames from a retailer into a research facility, it will put Spectacle Barkley out of business. Rosie would lose her investment. If Robames were to collapse under the lawsuit, Spectacle Barkley would stay the leading research facility in its field.

Rosie wanted me to get Mrs. Mahoney away from my dad because Rosie thought he would do what she asked and let Robames fail if Mrs. Mahoney wasn't so dependent on it. *You'd do this for me if you weren't with her.* And she wanted to put me right in the middle to entrap Mrs. Mahoney by using her sons' secrets and their happiness to threaten her.

"What's wrong, Collins?" Jasper says. "It's a perfectly legal practice."

"Oh, I know," I say, forcing a smile. "So there's no real competition, then." The ideas in the proposal are sound, which means that if we were to try again to convince Rob to accept it, we have even more selling points to offer. If Rob decided to suddenly listen to reason. "Perfect." I yank on his tie, and we both glance over the back of the couch to confirm the hallway is empty. I grab him as he kisses me, holding him to me as we fall back on the cushions.

What would he think if he knew what I'd agreed to do to him, to his brother? What would he say if he knew it was the reason I'm here with him right now, like this? Would he believe that I never would've been able to go through with it after getting to know him?

These thoughts follow me around like a haunting.

That night, Theo leaves us ten minutes early from the gym, which is nice of him but also gets him out of cleaning up the equipment. The second the door clicks shut, Jasper pulls off his gloves and presses me against the bag, and I don't even mind that the wrap still around his hands is rough and sweaty.

I don't deserve any of this, I think.

And when we study in the private rooms of the library, which aren't really private at all because of the glass panels on the doors and the casual strolls down the corridor Ms. Lata does every once in a while, it's all ankles hooked under the table and finger squeezes across a smattering of books and notepads. Sometimes we'll sit next to each other and I'll be thinking of nothing else except his hand on the back of my chair, almost touching me, the way I can feel the heat from his body and smell his laundry detergent, and an hour will pass and I'll have only read one paragraph and won't remember what it said and I'll have to do the reading under my covers with a flashlight after the eleven o'clock check-ins, but I won't even care because being near him was sixty minutes that I didn't deserve, not when I'm only this close to him because I wanted something valuable to take away from him. He always notices when I'm tired the next day, and he'll quiz me so I can study through the fog of his slow smile and the sandalwood scent of his shampoo and the way his hand occasionally grazes my knee.

It should be freeing to put Rosie's plan behind me, to abandon her the way she abandoned me. All Jasper will ever have to know of me is what's happened between us. And whatever will keep happening between us. But it's no use. I can't stop wondering: I know all his secrets, but what would he say if he knew mine?

I'm often jolted awake right before dawn, with this overwhelming sense of displacement.

"What's wrong?" Elena says when my jerky movements wake her.

"Stress," I tell her.

"Are you still worried about failing out? I thought you were doing so much better."

"I am. I don't know what's wrong with me." But the nightmares aren't about failing out of Rutherford anymore. They're only about losing him, waiting for the moment when this will all expire. I don't know when it'll end with him. But it will end, won't it? Doesn't it always?

When Rosie told me to make him love me, is this what she'd had in mind? Can you sweep someone else away without getting swept up yourself? What are you supposed to do when you're the one who cast the spell but not the one who has the power to break it?

I know the secret to his undoing, but I fear that he's the answer to mine. Because sometimes in the bad dreams, the thing I'm losing feels like it's something I've already lost—like Rosie and Mimi—and I wake up wondering if he was ever mine at all.

We all get the email about Rutherford's upcoming Open House on a Monday morning. No one talks about it because it's boring, a weekend for our parents, for potential students. But there are pointed stares between Theo and Stewart across the courtyard. A solemn nod my way. Jasper's hand stiff against my back. We don't talk about it. But we all saw it. We're all thinking about it. It follows us around. The possibility and the hopelessness, both existing together. Theo doesn't finish his dinner and knocks over his drink, spilling iced tea across Anastasia's beet and goat cheese salad. Stewart forgets his lacrosse stick in his locker for practice. Jasper sighs against my neck behind the athletic complex as the sun goes down. Rob James is coming for the Open House. A guest—the main event. She'll be at Rutherford in no time. And what are we supposed to do? What can we do?

Two Months Later

It pains me, the way he slumps to the ground. The way he caves in on himself.

"You know this is all more complicated than you think," he says. He begs. "You know you don't have to do this. All you have to do is stop. I *know* you, and I know this isn't going to sit right with you. Go back on your word, forget the promises you made before you knew me, before you knew *us*."

But he can already see it in my eyes—because it's true, he does know me—that I'm not going to stop. No matter how much it puts him at risk. I'll make good on everything I swore I would do. Every last thing except for the millions of small, unspoken promises I made to him, each day that I spent getting to know him.

FEBRUARY

Forty-six

There are two times a year when Rutherford likes to show off. The first one happens during orientation, and the second at the end of February, when Rutherford hosts spring sports opening tournaments and displays students' artwork at the galleries in the square and the theater department wows with a musical production and the choir and orchestra and band dazzle with their performances. And successful Rutherford alumni come to talk about how Rutherford shaped their very bright futures.

This is what will bring my father and Mrs. Mahoney to Cashmere tomorrow. And Rob James.

"There'll be a surprise," my father tells me on the phone, not sounding all that happy.

"I like surprises." I try to be upbeat, like maybe he's afraid his surprise isn't good enough.

We're walking back from the athletic facility after practice when I tell Anastasia, Ariel, and Theo what he'd said. They try to guess what the surprise could be.

"He's finally going through a proper midlife crisis and has bleached his hair," Ariel says.

"He's revealing his identity as a CIA operative," Anastasia says. "What? I know a girl who that happened to."

"He's probably bringing you flowers or chocolates or maybe just plain money," says Theo.

We reach the courtyard, and the parents have already started filtering in, observing us students like we're part of the show, taking photos of the Rutherford view and the architecture and the statues like this is a tourist destination. I wave as we pass Jasper where he's stationed in the courtyard under a maroon canopy with a lacrosse display, handing out pamphlets, answering questions. It's cloudy today and windy, and the weather is still chilly, though mild, not dropping too far below forty degrees or rising above sixty degrees.

At first, I think my mind is playing tricks on me when I notice them standing there near the edge of the courtyard.

"I thought your dad wasn't getting in until Friday," Theo says.

"Hey, who's with your dad?" Anastasia says, seeing them also.

I stop walking. Anastasia, Ariel, and Theo take a few steps before turning around, realizing I'm no longer keeping pace with them.

"What's the matter?" Ariel says.

"Collins?" Theo calls. But I'm already running away, ducking into the nearest entrance. The problem is there are people everywhere; the hallways are overcrowded. I rush up the stairs and into the library. Only after I'm closed off in a private study room can I finally take a breath. I fist my hands, press them together. They're shaking so hard, terror pumping through me.

What are they doing here? Mimi and Rosie strolling through the campus arm in arm with my dad. *Why are they here?*

I don't want to see them, I don't want to see them, I don't want to see them.

I startle when my phone buzzes in my cardigan pocket. Jasper.

Hey, are you okay? Where'd you go?

There's a light knocking on the door, and I jump. My phone falls to the ground. Sebastian is on the other side of the glass. He steps into the room.

"You ran in here like a bat out of hell. Thanks to you, tomorrow the library is going to be crawling with those WALK, DON'T RUN signs that hang around the pool."

I try to smile at him, give him the laugh he deserves. But I start to cry, sobs charging out of me, a flood of tears.

"Whoa, hey," he says, coming toward me. "It was a bad joke; you don't have to cry, Collins Pruitt."

I cover my face and try to pull it together. He puts his hand on my shoulder and squeezes. Then his hand moves to my back, rubbing up and down. I lean forward and start crying against him. He hugs me, and I let myself go.

"What happened?" he says.

I don't know why it all comes spilling out of me. But I tell him the truth—sound bites of the most important parts. The three of them lied. Rosie is my mother, and she had no problem leaving me when I was born and didn't come back for seven years and left a hundred times after that. Mimi pretended to be my mother because it gave her everything she'd ever wanted—a house and a purpose and the company of my father. Rosie only told me the truth because she wanted to use me to get something from my dad.

"Money. It all comes down to money," I say. He nods. He keeps his arms around me, and I keep going, crying, telling him how mad I am, how I've barely spoken to them since coming here. All Sebastian has of me is this fantasy, a what-if, and who cares if I ruin that, who cares if this scares him, who cares if he hears this and he no longer sees me as someone he wants to pursue? I need him to see all the things that I'm not. The things I'll never be. And

I can trust him because he says whatever's on his mind the second it's on his mind. He's without a filter and full of genuine truths, no matter what. A rejection from him could never hurt me, and that makes him the safest person I've met at Rutherford.

My phone buzzes again. Sebastian retrieves it from where it landed on the floor and hands it to me. A text from my dad comes through: *Cat's out of the bag because we ran into Jasper and Theo. I'm a day early, and your Mimi and Rosie are here. Surprise! Mimi's dying to see you! Get back to us when you can. Love you.*

"I shouldn't've told you all that," I say to Sebastian. Maybe it wasn't fair to unload on him like this. Especially when I don't want anything from him—when I could only do it because I don't need anything from him. "I haven't told anyone else. My dad isn't even aware that I know the truth."

His eyes get wide because he is that honest and cannot hide his reaction of surprise.

"That's messed up, Collins Pruitt. I don't think that's the kind of thing you're supposed to keep bottled up."

He gives me another hug, strong arms around me that feel like forgiveness. I close my eyes against him and hear the door open.

I don't think it looks that guilty, our hug. It's arms draped over shoulders, not waists. Jasper still frowns.

Sebastian says, "I told a bad joke, and she did not take it well." He playfully punches Jasper on the arm. "But she seems to be done leaking tears for now at least." He turns back and gives me a wave before he leaves us alone.

"What the hell?" Jasper says. There's no anger in his voice, only worry.

I use the sleeve of my cardigan to dry off my face and wipe away the last of my tears.

"Jesus, Collins—what's going on?" Jasper pushes the stray hairs out of my face. He lets his thumb brush lightly over my cheek. "Please talk to me. What's the matter?"

I want him to know everything about me. But not this.

"It's nothing—I don't know why I freaked out—Sebastian was in the library and he saw me—I don't know what happened." He deserves more than this lame lie, this transparent excuse. But I don't know how to give him that.

"Really? Because from where I was standing, it sort of looks like you saw your dad with your mom and aunt and ran away."

"*Oh.*" My stomach drops a little. He noticed this. What else has he noticed? Maybe I can unspool all those secrets I'm ashamed of with him the way I did with Sebastian. Maybe he's already started to unravel them himself because he really sees me.

"Is this because of the surprise? Did you not want to see them?" I feel the nervous flutter of his fingers tapping against my collarbone. "Is this because of my mom—you're worried that with your mom here at the same time it'll be weird?"

"It's not that." The lie comes out smoothly. "I was shocked, yeah. That's part of it. They're supposed to be traveling the world. I don't know why they came back just to see me."

"*Just to see you?* Are you kidding? That's your family. Of course they'd stop their worldwide expedition to visit you."

"I know. You're right. I should be glad they're here. It was an overreaction. I'm fine now. I can go see them." This room feels small and hot suddenly. I move around him to get to the door.

"Collins." He puts his hand against the door, keeping it closed. "You don't seem fine. Please tell me what's going on."

I don't say *it's nothing* because I don't want to lie to him again. Instead, I peel his hand off the door and take it in mine. I move closer to him.

"Jasper," I say. "Let's go. They're waiting for me."

Sometimes when I close my eyes, I can see Rosie's face, her

expression full of disappointment because I couldn't go through with what she'd asked of me. Even though she wasn't protecting Mimi and me or my dad; everything she wanted me to do was about protecting her investment. And now I have my own something to protect. What would I do to keep from losing it? Or maybe the real question is, what wouldn't I do?

Forty-seven

It's not fair that they can show up like this, without warning. How easily their deception flows into the scene to look normal, regular. How Mimi sobs when she sees me just like a mother whose daughter is living away from her for the first time would do. And Rosie pats me heartily when she hugs me, like a proud aunt.

Rosie asks Jasper if he'd like to join us for dinner. He's excited when he says he'd love to, even though if we meet them, we'll have to miss the exchange for the game and will therefore have to forfeit to last place. Theo will take the drugs on our behalf and hide them for us. *The Mahoney boy, right where we want him,* I assume she's thinking.

He holds my hand as we walk to the restaurant. He tells me something funny, gently leaning into me as he whispers in my ear. He watches me carefully as I order—so curious to see if I'll get what he thinks I'll get, and as we eat, he watches how I react to certain stories shared across the table like it's his favorite pastime. Throughout dinner, he rests his arm on the back of my chair and sneaks squeezes of my hand under the table. I don't know if Rosie notices, but I hope she does. I want her to see how much he loves me. So much that he would never leave me.

Except it isn't Jasper's fault that he adores me—and I bet she can see that, too. I had to try, had to push, had to show him why and how he should fall for me.

As the night winds down, Mimi asks if she can come back and see my dorm.

"I'd love to see it, too," Rosie says.

"Maybe tomorrow," my dad says to her. "Let them have some time together."

Rosie stands next to my dad on the curb as Jasper, Mimi, and I take the car service back to Rutherford, watching as we drive away.

In the car, Mimi tells Jasper stories about me when I was small, the way I used to pretend to be a dog, my head hanging out the window as we drove the long roads that led from Madison to our house on the outskirts, and about the time I tried to bake a mud pie in the kitchen oven at 425 degrees, believing that the heat would transform it into a real, edible pie.

Jasper says good night and leaves for his dormitory, and when Mimi and I get to my dorm room, it's empty. Elena is still out with her parents.

"I like him," Mimi says about Jasper. "He seems nice and so smart and like he cares profoundly for you."

"Yeah, we're really happy," I say, an unintentional defensiveness in my tone.

Over dinner, Mimi and Rosie had regaled us with stories about their travels. It warmed me a little, thinking of Mimi out of her comfort zone—the place she never leaves—climbing mountains and taking trains across countries and seeing the originals of the artwork she's loved in history books her whole life. Is she running away now—the way Rosie does?

"Why are you selling the house?" I ask her. She's more like Rosie than ever before; she has no home to return to. Maybe no reason to come back at all.

She turns from where she's looking at the corkboard holding my schedule, various *Reminder!* Post-its, my field hockey medal, and a photo of Dad and me before the New Year's Eve party.

"Jake said you were concerned about that," she says. "I'm sorry to spring that on you. I wanted to tell you about it in person when the time was right."

I wonder when she'd thought the time for this would be. And if it was her idea to come here to surprise me or if my dad pushed it. Maybe if it were up to her, she'd still be in Peru, taking in the Saqsaywaman.

"I thought that was your dream house," I say.

"It was, at one point." She runs her fingers over the sweater on the back of my desk chair, feeling the Rutherford maroon woven fabric. "When I was twenty-three, that's all I wanted. Somewhere to be with you, to raise you. But that was a long time ago."

"What about the goats? What about your business?"

"I enjoyed it all," she says, nodding. "But, Collins, none of it was really mine, you know?"

It was ours, I'm thinking. I don't get it. I thought that since Dad had a vested interest in keeping her happy because she looked after me, she was more than willing to take whatever he gave her.

"After you learned the truth about Rosie," she says, "I wasn't sure you'd ever forgive me or that you'd ever want to come back, and when Rosie told me what a trip to another country did to help her clear her mind, I thought, screw it, why not? I was going to try anything to forget how awful I felt, to keep myself from calling you every hour on the hour the way I so desperately wanted to, trying to respect your wishes and give you space from us."

There's a sting in my throat, like I want to cry.

"You and me, our home, that was all I wanted." She takes the sweater off the back of my chair and folds it neatly. She places it in my drawer, third from the bottom where the sweaters at home are kept. "But things have changed now, with you away. I'm starting to picture my life differently. And I want to make something of myself, something new, something for me."

"You took care of me for him so he could work and stay in New York—I thought you'd want him to support you the rest of your life in exchange for all you did for him."

She shakes her head. "Raising you was a privilege, don't you see? Not because of the house or the goats. It was my dream because you were there. It was a luxury that your dad could give me whatever I thought was best for you and lucky that he agreed with what I wanted for you and trusted me to take care of you." She wipes a few tears away. "But without you, that house is just a house. You're so independent now, and I'm very proud of you. It's inspiring, really."

She reaches into her purse and pulls out a thumb drive. "There is something I need to show you," she says. "I want you to know I don't blame you for the way you left for Rutherford, for being mad, for what you said, for not wanting to speak to me. It wasn't right, keeping the truth from you. Jake and I, we could've done it differently; we could've been honest with you from the start. Maybe we should've been. I think we were both living in this sort of fantasy world—making this great home for you, thinking it would distract you until your mother came back. But after seven years, there isn't really a coming back, and for that, I'll always be sorry."

I start up my computer for her, and she inserts the thumb drive. She sits next to me on the bed, holding the laptop so we can both see the screen.

"I want to make sure you know you were born out of love. And you were born into love, too."

She presses Play. She shows me clips of Rosie and my father, scenes from their life as a couple where they were happy and smiling. Snippets of them camping along the river, on safari in

South Africa, having a picnic in Central Park. My father looked the most excited, though, during the clips when Rosie was pregnant, both his hands on her belly, a full smile on his face. Moments of her asleep, him leaning over her, singing to her stomach. And then some I've seen before, of Mimi and me and my dad, the two of them clamoring when I took my first steps, gathered around my high chair when I tried real food for the first time, anxious to see what I'd like and what kinds of faces I'd make if I didn't like something.

When the recording finishes, we both have tears in our eyes. I've looked at Mimi my whole life and thought she was my mom. That doesn't go away overnight. Maybe not ever. And I don't think it should have to.

"What do you want to do, then," I ask, "if you don't want that house, if you want to sell the goats?"

"I was thinking of taking a page out of your book and going back to school." She shrugs. "Maybe get an apartment downtown, start taking classes. I don't know yet what I want to study, but I'm ready to start reviewing my options."

"And you don't want Dad to help you with that?" I say, on the brink of understanding. "He'd do that for you, you know."

"I know," she says. "But I want to do it. For me. And the good news is the house sold last month. The new owners aren't moving in until early summer, so there's still time for you to make one last visit if you want. And the goats were surprisingly easy to sell."

"I think you'll be great." I like imagining her out in the world, getting to see how her dreams as a little girl have changed and what's possible for her, knowing she'll always have me, no matter what. "And the money from the house will be enough to get you started?"

"Not yet, but it will be," she says. "Rosie had a new investment opportunity that seemed very promising. Nearly a guarantee. I bought in with the money from the sale."

My whole body goes cold.

"All of it?" I say.

She nods. "The money from the house and what I had in savings from the small profits the goats provided."

No. My chest gets tight. Rosie took Mimi's money—the entirety of it—and invested it in Spectacle Barkley because she was counting on me to ruin Mrs. Mahoney and my dad, thinking that if not for his attachment to Mrs. Mahoney, he'd let Robames crumble under the lawsuit, securing her investment with Spectacle Barkley.

"Did you ask Dad what he thought?"

"I didn't," she says. "Rosie's reports looked great to me. And you know how you dad is always telling us to trust our gut?"

"But Rosie is a liar." She did this to punish my dad so if he put Spectacle Barkley out of business, it'd be Mimi's investment he was losing, too. I wonder if he knows. I wonder if that will change his mind about pushing the proposal, or if he'll give up and let Rob have her way. "She's selfish and conniving."

"But she's also my sister, and despite it all, she wants what's best for me. She wants what's best for you, too."

If I tell Mimi the truth, how Rosie convinced me to come here and what she set me up to do, she'll see it as one more thing she didn't protect me from regarding her sister and the lie they upheld. And this isn't her fault.

"Can I stay with you at the hotel tonight?" I say.

She nods and smiles, as though she also can feel things snapping back into place between us.

I don't want her to know that she's being used by Rosie to manipulate my dad. I don't want her to know what Rosie wanted me to do at Rutherford. And I don't want her to know that I'd agreed to do it.

Forty-eight

When we arrive back at the hotel, Rosie and my dad are sitting outside sipping wine on the patio of the hotel bar under a heating lamp when we approach them. They don't look like a formerly in-love couple. They seem like strangers, not sitting close, hardly talking.

"I'm crashing with Mimi," I say, holding up my overnight bag.

"I should've guessed." My dad smiles. "Don't stay up all night talking."

Mimi and I sit on the patio with them, chatting for another thirty minutes before my dad heads to his suite. Mimi yawns, and I tell her to go up to the room without me, that I'll be there soon. She smiles as she gets up to leave, looking at Rosie and me and our similar eyes, a peace about her like she's happy to give us space to be alone together.

We're the only two patrons at the hotel restaurant who haven't gone inside. The air has turned wet with a misty rain.

"I know the real reason you wanted me to break up Mrs. Mahoney and my dad." There's nothing else I want to say to her, nothing else I want her to know except that this time, I figured out the truth on my own.

She leans back in her chair and looks out at the dark, deserted street. It's still and slick, and the rainfall is only visible under the streetlight.

"I know about Spectacle Barkley and my dad's proposal," I continue, "and that you think if he weren't dating Mrs. Mahoney, he'd let Robames fail because it's what you want."

She takes a slow sip of her wine. "I don't think that, Collins, I *know* it for certain," she says.

"No, you don't." She's so full of lies, and I can feel her readying to feed me another one.

"He's done it for me before," she says.

"What—*when*?" That can't be true.

"Sixteen years ago," she says. "Your dad can resuscitate any failing company. But he let one die for me because I asked him to, because it would make my investment worth more and he knew it was what I'd been counting on. He really did love me once. He didn't know I'd use the money to disappear, but now he's used to me being gone. I didn't leave him entirely alone, anyway."

The blood drains from my face. *Sixteen years ago.* She used the money to get away from us, and there must've been a lot of it, enough to sustain her for seven years. She left us, and she wouldn't've been able to do it without him.

"It's not that I didn't love you, Collins." She studies me, picking up on my distress. "I would've made a horrible mother. Michelle was so good at it. I knew I was leaving you with the best possible people. People better than I was."

"You're right," I say. My heart is pounding in my ears. "They're much better than you."

"Your father loves you far more than he ever loved me," she says. "But he feels indebted to me. He always will. I gave him his only daughter." She looks me over again, searching for how I'm going to react to this. She wanted me to provide the leverage to hold over Mrs. Mahoney, but I was always the leverage she used against my dad. "Pulling the proposal is something he would've done for me in a heartbeat, if not for Marylyn and her money problems. Your father is an intelligent man, but he's oblivious when he's in love. He allows it to take all of his strength, and he loses himself in it, lets it cloud his judgment." She pulls her coat closed against a sudden breeze. "I hope he didn't pass that trait down to you."

"He tries to take care of the people he loves. I don't think there's anything wrong with that."

"I wish you would open your eyes," she says. She leans toward me, resting her elbows on the table. "It's obvious that Jasper is in love with you. You did it. You can get Marylyn away from your father for good and that's what you must focus on now. He still needs you to save him."

"I don't believe you. I've got no reason to believe you."

"Why would I lie to you about this when I've already got what I want?" she says.

"What do you mean?"

"While you and Mimi were visiting your dorm, I told Jake about Mimi's investment in Spectacle Barkley. He didn't agree to pull the proposal, but he did agree to stop pushing so hard for it. He's stepping back for now; he even canceled the meeting that was scheduled for tomorrow with Rob and her investors to go over it one more time. He's going to let her make her own child-ish mistake. And my sources tell me Rob James never seriously considered Jake's proposal anyway. So there you go. I'm getting what I want whether or not he lets Marylyn Mahoney dictate his every move. You can take Spectacle Barkley and the proposal and my agenda out of the equation. I don't care anymore if he lets Marylyn walk all over him. But the fact still remains that she is rotten and greedy and bad for your dad. It's up to you now, if you still want to save him."

"He's happy with her. He doesn't need saving."

"Maybe he's happy. But how long will it last when she's a

colossal drain on his income? It's only going to get worse when the Mahoneys take this big hit, losing their Robames investment." She swirls her wine before taking a sip. "Not only that, Marylyn's also taking information he's told her in confidence and selling it as stock tips. It's called *insider trading,* and it's extremely illegal. Not something your dad would want to be caught up in. It could ruin him if she's ever caught, even if he was unwittingly involved. Like I've said before, I've tried to warn him about her. He won't listen to me and he won't listen to you."

"But how do you know that Marylyn is doing that? Where's your proof?" When she was telling me about Theo's secret, she had the camp photo and a copy of the NDA. And for these accusations against Mrs. Mahoney, she's got nothing? There's a reason my dad didn't believe her—he knows he shouldn't; she had nothing to show him as evidence, and she had something she wanted from him. She's not credible. She never has been.

"You'll have to trust me on this one." She finishes her glass of wine and lifts her purse off the back of her chair and straps it to her shoulder.

"How am I supposed to believe you after everything you've lied about?"

"On the contrary." She stands. She puts her hand under my chin, forcing me to meet her eyes. "I'm the only one who's ever told you the truth."

She leans down and kisses my forehead, then walks into the hotel, leaving me alone in the hazy rain.

Forty-nine

Mimi and I stay up late brainstorming about what she might study and the different schools where she could enroll, and the next day, Rutherford's open house kicks off with a string of events. Breakfast in the square followed by a track-and-field preview and sports scrimmages.

My race finishes right in time for me to watch the end of Jasper's lacrosse game. But before it's over, he's ejected for too many fouls, which isn't like him at all. He storms off the field. I follow him.

He walks to the edge of the woods and throws his stick. He rips off his equipment and sits on the ground, his elbows resting against his knees. His hair is sweaty and clings to his forehead.

I pick up his stick from where it's landed a few feet away. I take a seat next to him. He smells like sweat and freshly cut grass.

"It's getting to you, isn't it?" I say. Rob James is here in Cashmere and even though we haven't seen her, the air is rich with the question of what we should be doing about it, if we should bother, if we're desperate enough.

He nods.

Mimi was so determined and happy last night, excited for the future in a way that everyone deserves to be excited about big life changes. I don't want her to lose all her money. I don't want her to have any more setbacks.

But I don't like the rigidness of Jasper's back, the redness in his eyes from lack of sleep, the sharp inhale that occurs whenever he thinks about it too hard; the way he was on edge today while playing lacrosse.

"I want to meet her. If she agrees to it," he says. He doesn't look at me. "I'm going to beg her to authorize the proposal, save my family's investment. Why not, right? I'll leave my pride at the door and say please until I'm blue in the face." He runs a grass-stained hand through his damp hair. "It's going to be different this time, when I talk to her."

He absentmindedly picks at the grass, pressing it in between his fingers and then yanking on it.

"Why will it be different?" I say, not a clue as to what his answer will be, but uneasy about it all the same.

"She's not going to be able to blackmail me anymore."

"Jasper, no—not an option." I pull on his jersey to get him to look at me and finally he does.

"Yes," he says. "I've thought about this, okay? I cheated. I messed up. So if she won't authorize the proposal, then I'll give a damning testimony and she'll lose the company all the same. I'm going to tell her she can release the recording, tell whoever she wants that I cheated. She can't use it to control me anymore."

"But what about Dartmouth, what about—"

"I have to, Collins, don't you get it?" He untangles my hand from his jersey and takes it in his. "I don't want to live with this anymore. Every day I wonder how you could possibly care about me when you know what I'm getting away with and that I'm still lying about it."

"There's more to you than this one stupid mistake."

"Stupid mistake is putting it nicely. But I've thought about this."

"Have you really? Because if you give an unfavorable testimony at the trial, you do damage to Robames. That's not good for your family's investment either."

"I know." He concentrates on my hand, brushing his thumb over my knuckles.

He's trying to do the right thing. But the result is also him giving up. Letting the chips fall where they may, annihilating Rob and losing his family's money in the process.

I squeeze his hand until he looks at me.

"Theo will never let you do this."

"That's why you can't tell him."

Best case scenario, Rob James agrees to authorize the proposal, fearful of Jasper's testimony now that he's no longer cooperating with her blackmail. She never releases the recording of him cheating and Robames is saved thanks to Rob giving her blessing to ditch the impossible Roba-Fix and take her company in a new direction as a research firm per my father's proposal.

Worst case scenario, Rob James makes it public that Jasper cheated in the decathlon, Jasper gives a damaging testimony putting Robames out of business, Rob loses her company, everyone loses their investments, and Jasper loses his scholarship.

The potential outcomes are extreme. It's very risky. Theo would never agree to it.

The lawsuit, whether Jasper gives the honest, disparaging testimony or not, will be the kiss of death to Rob and, by extension, Robames. If the Roba-Fix is impossible and she's been hiding this from her investors and clients, then why wouldn't she want to avoid a lawsuit at all costs? If the choice is between giving up her dream or going down in flames, why is she choosing the latter? Why doesn't she think this is worth fighting for? Why does she think she'll get away with it?

"You should meet with her," I say. "But it has to be on your terms."

What I really mean is, it has to be on *my* terms.

One Month Later

"We'll see you later tonight," Theo says, waving to us.

I nod. My throat constricts. I want to cry. I want Jasper to say something or at least make eye contact with me. But he continues down the path with Theo and Stewart and doesn't look back.

"Something weird is going on," Anastasia says. "We're going to find out what it is."

MARCH

Fifty

On Saturday night the auditorium is filled for the production of *Newsies*. This is the most popular event at the open house, aside from the speech Rob James gave the previous evening. The Rutherford campus is practically deserted.

This is what we were counting on.

We get to the common room around 7:45 p.m., giving us just enough time before Rob arrives to meet Jasper.

"How does this angle look?" Theo stands on a chair, positioning a small camera on top of a bookshelf in the corner of the room.

"Turn it on," Stewart says. "Let me make sure it connects." He sets up his laptop on the large round table.

Setting up a meeting between Rob James and Jasper on my terms involved telling Theo, because as the eyes and ears of this school, he knew the best place for them to meet—the upperclassmen's common room, somewhere both public and private—and he knew the best time for them to do it—during the main event of the open house, when the rest of Rutherford's population would be occupied. We included Stewart because we needed him to get us cameras from the video production and media development department at Rutherford, where he has access as vice president of the Modern Media Club.

Theo and Stewart don't know the whole truth, though. They don't know that Jasper isn't going to fight her on the blackmail.

As far as Stewart and Theo are concerned, Rob and Jasper are meeting for one last try at convincing her to authorize the proposal. The cameras are there to catch her admitting that the Roba-Fix is a lie or confessing romantic involvement with Jasper—a final attempt to have something on her that she doesn't want the public to know about. One last shot at leverage and a chance to discredit Jasper as a witness.

And Jasper wants all these things too; so do I. But I also want to know what Rob will confess to Jasper when she's backed against the wall after Jasper tells her that he doesn't care if she exposes that he cheated in the decathlon; what she'll reveal about why she won't give up even though her invention is impossible.

"I'm having some trouble with the program," Stewart says. Theo climbs off the chair, sets down the cameras, and pushes Stewart aside so he can mess with the software. "*I'm* the one in the Modern Media Club," Stewart says as Theo slaps his hand away when he reaches for the keyboard.

Jasper is across the room pacing. His shoes make shuffling sounds against the wood floors. It really is eerily quiet at Rutherford right now; every small noise is magnified.

We all hear it at the same time. The loud clicking of heels coming from the hallway. Jasper stops; Stewart and Theo straighten. The footsteps get louder, closer, coming right for us.

"Roberta . . . she likes to be early."

"*Nicht gut.*"

Theo taps furiously against the laptop keyboard, the cameras still not connecting.

Soon the footsteps reach the door to the common room.

"It's only Anastasia," Theo says as she walks into the room.

We all sigh loudly in relief. Anastasia frowns.

"Nice to see you all, too," she says. She puts her hands on her hips. "Thought you could all sneak off during 'The World Will Know' and I wouldn't notice?"

"We're doing a project—" Jasper starts.

Stewart nods. "For school." An unnecessary addition to Jasper's lie.

Theo and I know better than to attempt to explain this scene to Anastasia. We need to get her out of there before Rob arrives.

"Stewart, can you handle the cameras?" Theo says as we steer Anastasia toward the door.

"Cameras?" She whips around and walks toward Stewart and the computer.

"It's for the Modern Media Club, Anastasia," Theo says, his voice tight with impatience. "Can we go now?"

"But why are you involved?" she says to Theo. "You hate the Modern Media Club."

Stewart shakes his head as he continues to mess with the software. "What'd we ever do to you?" he mutters.

"I don't see any cameras," Anastasia says, growing more suspicious by the second.

"We'll tell you about it while we walk back to the auditorium," I say.

The plan was that Theo, Stewart, and I would monitor Jasper and Rob on Stewart's laptop from the storage closet around the corner where we make the drops for the game, in case he needed rescuing, or if she says something to press his buttons and we need to intervene. But if Theo and I must return to the auditorium and watch the final act of *Newsies* to keep Anastasia away, then that's exactly what we'll do.

"Is that a camera?" She points to the small camera hiding in the corner of the pool table.

"Damn it, Anastasia, we're going to miss the play," Theo says.

Her eyes scan the room, on the hunt for more.

"There—that's one too." She points to the camera nestled next to a stack of board games. "It's like this room is under surveillance. So who are we spying on?"

We. In typical Anastasia fashion, she's quick to insert herself into this situation.

"*A school project.* I'll explain it all on our way to—" Theo's mouth snaps shut. Anastasia's eyes get wide. Jasper sucks in a breath. Stewart takes his hands back, away from the keyboard. A chill travels down my spine.

Oh no.

Rob James is standing in the doorway. She's not dressed for the theater like we are, but she still looks nice. She's in a casual white tank top and baggy white linen pants. She has large gold cuffs on each wrist and wears tall golden pumps. She's got her hair pulled back, and her face is completely made up.

She takes her time walking into the room and makes eye contact with each of us as she passes. When she reaches Stewart, she leans forward, examining the screen.

"You're absolutely right," she says. "Surveillance indeed."

"You of all people can appreciate this," Jasper says. His expression has darkened.

Rob works on the laptop and, by the way Stewart's mouth turns down, I know she must be disabling the cameras. She shuts the laptop and smiles at us.

A smile like this, tight but genuine, is not what I was expecting at all from her. She's still the most powerful person here and she knows it. Leisurely, she crosses the room and takes a seat in a large leather chair.

"I guess . . . I guess we'll leave you and Jasper to it, then," Stewart says with an unsteady voice.

But without the cameras, there'll be nothing to record her

admitting the Roba-Fix is a pipe dream or catch a confession about their past that might get Jasper out of testifying. And Jasper will be laying it all on the line in hopes she'll be more afraid of his testimony than she is about altering Robames, according to the proposal, without any leverage or backup.

"No need to leave," Rob says. "Whatever Jasper has to say to me, he can say in front of all of you. *Clearly*."

She glances around the room, assessing the upper hand she's earned simply by being early.

"Please sit." She gestures to the couch in front of her and the two chairs angled towards her. "This concerns everyone, right? Since you all just happened to be here setting up *surveillance* before the private meeting I had scheduled with Jasper."

We do as she says. Jasper and I end up in chairs on opposite sides of the coffee table, with Stewart, Theo, and Anastasia on the couch.

Her eyes skip around the room, stopping the most on Jasper. What does she see when she takes him in? Someone she used to care about? Someone she still wants? Or does she simply see a threat?

"Phones off," she says. She takes her own phone out of her pocket and turns it off. She sets it on the coffee table and waits as we do the same. She watches as each of us power down our phones, holding up the screens so she can watch them go dark. Chapter titles from her book flash through my mind. Controlling the Narrative. Managing Outsider Influence. Commanding Attention.

"I suppose this is about Jacob Pruitt's proposal," she says when all the phones are off and in the center of the coffee table, and Jasper finally looks at her. At the mention of my father's name, her gaze flickers over to me. She takes a deep breath and looks to the ceiling. "You know, this room hasn't changed. Not a bit. When I went to school here, we sat in this very spot. So many memories. Talking for hours. Lots of fun games." Her eyes lock on to Jasper's. "So you tell me, what game are we here to play?"

Fifty-one

"It's not a game to us," Jasper says. "It's our families' money. Our future."

"It's sort of cute," she says. "All you privileged teenagers afraid of no longer being spoiled. What are you so scared of?" She pouts, mocking us as she continues. "One less yacht in the harbor. Platinum American Express cards instead of Black. Maybe you'll have to skip St. Barths for a year or two."

Theo rubs his forehead nervously; it'll be much worse than that for the Mahoneys.

"But you're the one who stands to lose the most," Jasper says.

Rob scratches her chin like she's thinking hard—another gesture meant to insult Jasper—before she speaks. "What's the saying? You can't lose something you never had? I was nineteen when I started Robames. Not a penny of my own money went into the company."

"The lawsuit is going to destroy you, regardless," Jasper says.

"I understand why you're afraid of this lawsuit, Jasper," she says. "But I'm not afraid of it. Not at all. As long as everyone co-operates and does what they're supposed to, it should be fine."

"What about public percept—" I start to interject so Jasper doesn't yet reveal that he's not willing to lie under oath no matter what she does with the recording of him cheating.

Rob cuts me off with a laugh. "Public perception? Fixing that is the easy part. Winning people over has never been hard for me." She crosses her legs and leans back, especially relaxed as she tells us, "I'm not done yet. Not with this company. Not with the Roba-Fix."

"This is off the record, Roberta. You have our phones. You disabled the cameras." Jasper's doing very well, keeping his demeanor calm and his voice friendly. "You can admit that the Roba-Fix is dead. You should at least . . ."

He doesn't finish and I watch the effect this has on her. The way she holds her breath like she thinks he still will. The sternness in her voice when she says, "I should at least *what*?"

Jasper makes her wait before he tells her. "You should at least admit it to yourself."

This makes her shoulders go rigid. "It's not dead until I say it is."

"How are you going to raise the funds to keep an impossible product going after this lawsuit exposes the truth?" He's leaning forward as he speaks to her, the only tell that he's under stress.

"There are plenty of options," she says. "I can mortgage my assets, buy some more time. Plus, it could take years to sort out the details of the lawsuit."

"But it will eventually get sorted out," Jasper says. "And you know they have a case. A very strong one at that."

"Right now," she says. "*Right now,* they think they have a case." She leans on the armrest and moves one hand as she talks, her gold cuff sliding up and down her wrist. "But they're not big-picture people. They're driven by deadlines and rules, and they abide by a narrow point of view." She's speaking like she's addressing an auditorium of people, some of that Rob James magic flaring up. "Progress doesn't happen with deadlines and rules and narrow points of view. It happens when we put faith in new ideas. It happens when we embrace courage, when we take risks. So who knows what Robames can accomplish if given the space and freedom and time."

"Come on, Roberta." His tone stays gentle and he gives her a small smile. "You're a dreamer, but you're also a realist. Jacob Pruitt wouldn't've written a proposal changing the foundation of Robames if he thought there was a chance in hell you could win this lawsuit. He was protecting his investment, yeah. But he was also protecting you."

"Don't stick up for him just because she's here." She nods in my direction. "Maybe *the* Jacob Pruitt is not as brilliant as we've all been led to believe. Maybe he's as shortsighted and greedy as the rest of them. Did you even read the proposal?"

"I did," Jasper says. "I think it's a great solution."

Rob shakes her head. "If I accept the agreement under his proposal, I'm basically a bartering tool between Robames and the Justice Department. I'll be forced to buy back shares." Her voice turns stern. "They'll tell the investors that I can't pay back a lien on my assets, on *my* patents. My ideas. They'll strip me of my voting rights for the company I created myself."

"But have you considered the alternative? You could end up in jail," Jasper says. "Is it worth the risk?"

"Plenty of people still believe in me. Plenty of people know I'm going to do great things for this world." She makes a point not to look at Jasper and stares at the coffee table, at our pile of phones. But I wonder if he's who she most wants to hear this—of all the people who have given up on her, she wants him to know she's not alone. It makes me think that she must be more alone than ever. "You don't get it," she says, frowning. "I would be banned from being an officer or director of any public company for a decade or more. What am I supposed to do in the meantime?"

"You could do anything—a million other things," Jasper says. "You could go back to Yale?"

"I hated it there. I like it out here. I like putting a dent in society and making changes. Improving things. I like growing a company and boosting the economy. I like having a hand in steering the ship of progress."

I understand what she means—the importance and freedom of doing something on your own, the way Mimi wants a fresh start to make a road for herself instead of continuing down the perfectly paved path my father laid out for her.

"You can still do all that. One day."

"But not with the Roba-Fix, and I'm not done with it yet—I'm not ready to give it up. It's a product the world needs." She twists in her seat. "My mother was very sick, you know."

"I know," Jasper says quietly.

"A device like the Roba-Fix would've really improved her life." She leans back, her eyes shifting to Jasper.

"I remember the day you got back from her funeral," he says, his voice softening, "when we were sitting in the courtyard and you told me you were going to do something so that no one would have to suffer the way she did ever again."

Rob looks down and nods. "Since in the end, I couldn't save her . . ." Her face creases like she's about to cry. She puts her hand over her forehead, trying to shield us from seeing. I'd wanted to know what was driving her. It's fear. It's loss. It's grief. It's complicated.

"Roberta, don't." Jasper's voice is almost a whisper. It's full of sympathy and pain. He gets up and crosses the room. For a moment, it's like the rest of us aren't there, it's just the two of them and everything they went through together in the past, so much he's not told me that's just between them. It hurts him to see her upset, I can tell. Jasper kneels in front of her. Whatever he's saying to her, he's saying it too quietly for the rest of us to hear. She nods as he speaks, and eventually she leans forward and hugs him. He holds her with an arm around her shoulder and his hand against the back of her head, the way he sometimes holds me.

It's pretend, I tell myself. *It's only for show.* But the cameras are disabled and our phones are turned off.

Jasper finally lets go of her, but he doesn't return to his seat. He stays next to Rob as she wipes her eyes, pulling herself together like she's just remembered we're all sitting there.

"None of you understand the things I'll lose if I accept the proposal." Her gaze falls on Jasper. "Or what I've already lost."

Jasper doesn't say anything, though he's staring at her like he wants to.

When the silence has stretched on for too long, Theo says, "With this proposal, Robames will still revolutionize medical research."

"But it won't be mine anymore, will it?"

"It will always be yours because it would never have been possible without you," Theo says.

Jasper closes his eyes for a second, like he knows this won't be enough for her.

"It doesn't matter," Rob says. "The proposal is off the table, anyway. The investors have stopped campaigning for it."

"What do you mean?" Stewart says, his voice tight and urgent.

"Jacob Pruitt had a meeting scheduled this weekend to argue again for the proposal. But he canceled it at the last minute and hasn't made an attempt to reschedule it. I think they've finally accepted that I'm not giving up; that I'll never give up."

"So you don't care that what you're doing is wrong? Or what it costs our families?" Stewart says. "You're delusional if you think it's not going to ruin you, too."

Jasper glares at him—a warning to stop. Anastasia frowns. The hostility coming off him is hard to understand given how little this loss will affect his life, especially compared to what the Mahoneys will be losing.

"My mind is made up," Rob says. "There's nothing any of you can say to change it." She squares her shoulders and straightens her posture. "Sorry for wasting your time. You can all go."

Stewart snatches his phone from the table and storms out of the room, leaving Theo to collect the cameras and his laptop. Anastasia and I help, fishing cameras off shelves and out from behind books. Jasper stands, but doesn't leave her side.

I think that maybe he still wants to talk with her after the rest of us have left, but when Theo, Anastasia, and I are about to walk out, he joins us.

"Collins," Rob says. We turn to face her. "Can I speak with you alone?"

Fifty-two

Rob James stands next to me in the doorway, watching Theo, Anastasia, and Jasper walk down the hall, leaving us alone in the common room. When they round the corner and are out of sight, she closes the door.

"What's your phone number?" she asks, taking her phone out of her pocket. She inputs the numbers as I dictate them.

My phone chimes with a message from her. She watches as I open it. It's a recording. I press play and see Jasper in a hotel room. I don't have to watch more than a couple of seconds before I realize what it is.

"Why are you giving this to me?"

"Don't you want to watch it all the way through?" But she doesn't wait for me to answer and comes to her own conclusion. "So he did tell you."

"About how you're blackmailing him—yeah, he told me."

"I didn't force him to cheat."

"He never said you did." Anger flares up in me. Is her plan to show me this recording to make me think differently of Jasper, to get me away from him? Or is it a test, to see how much I'd be willing to overlook?

"Why did you give this to me?" I repeat, letting the malice come out in my voice this time.

She smiles. "It's yours now." She holds up her phone and I watch as she deletes the video. "See?" she says. "That's my only copy. I promise."

"With everything I know about you, how am I supposed to believe that?"

"Because I promised."

It's a silly answer, especially coming from someone like her, who can command a room and persuaded many people to finance her company based on an idea.

I need her to know I am utterly unconvinced. "Why wouldn't you give this to Jasper yourself?" *Why include me, like some kind of intermediary?*

"I don't trust him with it."

She doesn't trust *him*. Well, that's rich. "What do you mean?"

She sighs before she speaks, like she's thinking of exactly what she wants to say. "Let me guess, he told you that nothing between him and me was real, that it was only an infatuation?"

"He might've said that." The pleasant expression on her face would indicate that this answer from me is some kind of win for her, so I add, "He also said he regretted everything that happened between the two of you; that he'd take it all back if he could."

She nods to herself, a smile forming on her lips—another reaction from her that I wasn't expecting. "Do you think that he'd be this upset with me—this hurt—if what he felt for me wasn't real?"

"I don't know, Rob. You set your laptop up to record him and left the decathlon answers out, as if you knew what he'd do and you wanted to catch him doing it so you'd have something to hold over him."

"That's not why I did it."

"Oh, really." I don't believe her at all. "Then what? You were testing him?"

"Of course I was testing him," she says. "How else was I supposed to know?"

"Know what?"

"He told me he was in love with me," she says, the words rushing out of her. "How do you know if you can believe anyone when they say that? How do you know who to trust?"

"If he *didn't* cheat, that would've proved he loved you? How?" Her logic doesn't make any sense to me.

"No," she says. "If he cheated, then I'd know—I'd know what he'd be willing to risk for me. For us."

"But he didn't mean to break a record. He didn't know being the decathlon champion would result in an early acceptance to Dartmouth."

"He knew that winning the decathlon would make him an ideal candidate to intern with me. And of course he knew it would help with Dartmouth. Dartmouth was always our plan. Why do you think I put Robames headquarters so close to its campus?"

"He did it to impress you." I want her to feel the sting of this, of what he was willing to do for her. How can she possibly feel okay using it against him?

"And he did," she says, stars in her eyes. "And I finally believed him when he said he loved me. I finally trusted him." Her smile falters. "But then, when he interned for Robames, he started to question things about the company. He doubted me, second-guessed what I was doing. He didn't understand why I had to lie. I watched him fall out of love with me. I felt him pull away. And the worst part—" Her voice cracks. "It was obvious he was wracked with guilt over what he'd done. I could tell he'd started to hate himself for doing it and couldn't even enjoy the good things that were happening to him, like he didn't think it was worth it. He didn't think *I* was worth it."

"You proved him right the second you used the recording to blackmail him. It didn't matter to you why he did it or that it was exactly what you wanted him to do." She shakes her head. Another nonanswer that isn't good enough. "So, what, am I supposed to thank you now? Do you think Jasper is going fall on his knees in gratitude that you suddenly had a change of heart after torturing him for these past months?"

"No, not at all," she says, but I still have more questions.

Why is she playing the hero now, giving Jasper his life back? Why she is using me to deliver the news? There has to be a catch. There always seems to be one when it comes to her.

"Why did you send me this recording instead of Jasper?" I ask.

"Because I don't want him to have it," she says. "Collins. If you really care about him, you'll delete the recording the second you leave this room. You'll tell him I gave it to you and that you destroyed it. If he trusts you, he won't need to see the proof. He'll just believe you."

She's planting doubts; she thinks that since I witnessed the way Jasper responded to her when she spoke about her mother, how caring he was toward her, that I'm in a weaker position. She's not wrong entirely, but I won't let her get to me.

"I don't need to test him the way you did. I'm going to tell him however I want."

"I've always known there was a time limit on how long I could blackmail Jasper," she says. "I know how he thinks. I saw how guilty he felt. It was only a matter of time before he'd try to turn himself in. If you don't get that about him, then perhaps you don't understand him as well as you think you do."

I don't want to stand here and listen to her anymore, hear her boast about how well she knows him and how all the tests she performed to get him to prove how much he cared worked in her favor.

"If there's nothing else, I'm going to leave."

"So leave," she says. "But if you really care about him, you'll listen to me. You won't risk that he could get his hands on it, because he'll only use it against himself."

Fifty-three

Jasper, Theo, Stewart, and Anastasia are waiting for me in the end of the B wing. Dim light from the lamppost in the courtyard streams in through the stained-glass windows, giving the hallway a sort of glow.

The air crackles with tension as I approach; they're still edgy from the meeting with Rob, since it didn't go in our favor.

"What did she want?" They all must be wondering this, but it's Stewart who says it. "Is she going to reconsider the proposal?" he adds.

I shake my head as I move toward Jasper. "She deleted the recording. I watched her do it." I take his hands and squeeze them, anticipating the excitement and relief he's going to feel. I don't care that Anastasia is standing there, her head whipping back and forth trying to catch up after all that she's witnessed tonight. Theo will have to fill her in however he sees fit. Right now I only care that Jasper knows he's free. "She's not blackmailing you anymore."

Jasper's eyes get wide, then his gaze lifts and he looks past me, like he thinks someone is at the other end of the hall. But no one is there and I try to quiet the voice in the back of my mind telling me that when he heard she'd let him off the hook, the first thing he did was search for her.

"That's great news," Theo says, patting Jasper's back.

Jasper looks at me and smiles. He squeezes my hands. He whispers, "Are you sure?" and I nod.

"So nothing about the proposal, then?" Stewart says. "You didn't think to try to convince her when she was letting her guard down and doing the right thing for Jasper?"

"No, I—" *Is that what I should've been doing?*

"Roberta's mind was made up," Jasper says. "There's nothing Collins could've said to change that."

"Maybe not," Stewart says. "But she could've at least warned us that her father had stopped pushing for it. Canceling that meeting and everything."

"How would she have known about that?" Jasper says. But now they're all looking at me.

"Did you know about it?" Stewart asks.

My hesitation is enough to make Stewart toss his hands in the air and shake his head at me. "My father had already failed countless times to convince her."

This is good enough for the rest of them, but it isn't good enough for Stewart. "Are you kidding me? You were alone with her and you didn't even try to make a case for the proposal. You only cared about getting her to stop blackmailing Jasper. Was that because you already knew that since your father had given up on the proposal, it was a done deal?" He zeroes in on Theo. "I told you—I told you we couldn't trust her!"

"Setting up the cameras for Jasper's meeting with Rob was my idea!" There's a fire flickering in my chest. *I told you we couldn't trust her.* What is he talking about?

"Oh, who gives a shit about that?" Stewart says. "That was no better than the idea to try to catch her on the phone. Bottom line, you knew your dad had stopped pushing the proposal and you didn't share that with us—how do you explain yourself?"

"Why are you freaking out, Stewart?" Jasper says. "You really care that much about losing a house in Tuscany?"

This question is plaguing me, too. Why is Stewart this distressed when his family stands to lose the least? Why does he care so much about what my father is doing with the proposal that he thinks I betrayed them and withheld information on purpose?

"Why don't you trust me?"

"Oh, please, Collins. *I know*, okay? *We know*."

I look to Theo, who's being suspiciously quiet. "What is he talking about?"

Theo hesitates. He bites the inside of his cheek. Anastasia pinches her lips together.

"What is he talking about, Theo?" Jasper says.

Theo shakes his head. "It's not a big deal—" he starts.

But Stewart is red-faced. "Spectacle Barkley," he says. He looks at me as he continues. "Rose Olsen."

My throat fills with dust. There's a hardening in my chest. Jasper stares at me, and I don't know if he recognizes the names.

"We know your mother is an investor in the firm that will undoubtedly go out of business if Rob accepts the proposal," Stewart says. The words blow out of him like releasing air from a balloon. "Don't lie. You only cared about stopping Rob from blackmailing Jasper, you didn't care at all about convincing Rob to accept the proposal. And what do you know—if Jasper tells the truth at that trial, Robames goes under and Spectacle Barkley flourishes, and that's what you wanted all along, isn't it, Collins?"

"But her dad has money in Robames," Jasper says. "And Rose Olsen isn't her mother; that's her aunt."

Theo pivots toward Stewart, and I can tell he means that as some sort of warning for Stewart to stop, but Stewart keeps his eyes trained on me.

"Not according to her birth certificate."

The edges of the hall blur. My heart starts pounding in my ears. My face gets hot.

"What were you doing with her birth certificate?" Jasper says.

"Just doing our due diligence," Stewart says.

I close my eyes. Their voices sound far away. It was my secret, and they're fighting about it like they can't see that it tears me up, having it exposed. I feel hands against my shoulders, a slow pulse of a squeeze.

"You're an asshole," Theo is saying.

"How did you—" Jasper is saying.

"I'm sorry, Collins!" The proximity and loudness of Anastasia's voice makes my eyes fly open. The hallway snaps back into place. She's the one with her hands on my shoulders, her face full of concern. "You know how Sebastian is when he gets talking; he'll let anything spill out as long as you ask the right questions. And I always do. It's a gift. Sometimes a curse." She looks over my shoulder, shooting a glare at Theo. "You didn't have to tell *Stewart*. That was told to you in confidence, the way all the secrets I tell you are."

"How did Sebastian know?" Jasper blinks at me, and I watch as his expression turns cold. "The first day of the open house, when you were crying—after you ran away from the courtyard . . ."

I turn to Theo because it's too hard to look at Jasper. I don't know how to explain it. How will Jasper understand that he mattered too much to be honest with? None of them understand how raw this makes me feel, that they all know I was left, that my mother wasn't my mother. They don't understand that she might've been doing what was best for me. They only see a complicated, scandalous story. And reasons why I'm the liability in our situation with Rob.

"I know she's an investor in Spectacle Barkley," I confess. Maybe I should tell them that Mimi has money tied up in it, too—

the woman who is most like a mother to me. Maybe they already know. The truth is, it did cross my mind that getting Jasper out of testifying might be good enough. That it wouldn't be the worst thing if Mimi got a return for the money from the house, enough to start her new, independent life. "Both of my parents know that investments are risky. Whatever happens to their money is their own fault. I don't care if either of them lose their investments. But I care about Jasper. I didn't want him to be blackmailed into lying. And Theo. I don't want their family to lose their money."

Theo's expression turns soft. Stewart's next to him looking at his feet, and I can't tell if he believes me. I wait to feel Jasper's hand come down around mine to steady the trembling. But he doesn't move. Anastasia drapes her arm around me; she rests her head against my shoulder.

We're quiet as we walk back to the auditorium until Anastasia announces that her feet are killing her and she needs to go back to her room to change shoes.

"Come with me," she says, tugging my arm. She hasn't left my side since it came out that she was the source who revealed that Rose Olsen was my mother.

"We'll see you later tonight," Theo says, waving to us.

I nod. My throat constricts. I want to cry. I want Jasper to say something or at least make eye contact with me. But he continues down the path with Theo and Stewart and doesn't look back.

"Something weird is going on," Anastasia says. "We're going to find out what it is."

Fifty-four

Anastasia and I go back to the girls' dormitory. But we don't go to our rooms. We use the tunnel to go to the boys' dormitory. It's as deserted as the rest of the campus as we climb the stairs, move down the hall, and enter Theo's room. She has a key to his room because of course she does.

Anastasia is meticulous as she searches Theo's desk drawers and thumbs through his things. She opens his laptop. She powers it on and types in a password. There seem to be no secrets between Anastasia and Theo; I wonder what she expects to find tonight.

"What exactly are we looking for?"

"I have no idea," she says. I watch over her shoulder as she opens his browser, and automatically his Rutherford email and his personal email open as tabs.

"Don't you think it's strange," she says, "that Theo told Stewart the secret about your mom? He never betrays my confidence. And especially not to Stewart. Stewart's closer to Jasper than he is to Theo." She squints as she leans forward to examine the screen, flipping through his emails. "Or so I thought."

"What do you see?" I ask.

"Nothing—I don't know." She shakes her head. "Stewart and Theo have only exchanged a few emails. They're about pizza."

Sure enough. A group email, even, where they debate what kind of pizza they're going to eat during some big playoff game they were all getting together to watch.

Anastasia lets out a groan of frustration. She slides the chair out from the desk and stands.

"What were you expecting to find?" I say.

"I don't know. It was also bizarre that Stewart was so worked up over the proposal when all he's losing is that house in Tuscany. Theo will lose a lot more and I think that's what Stewart actually cares about. So I'm looking for proof that they're in love or something."

"In love?"

"That's the only conceivable explanation," she says. "He and Stewart are lovers; therefore, they keep no secrets from each other. Even if it's very disloyal to me."

I take her place at the desk in front of Theo's computer as she moves onto his dresser.

"I guess that's one possibility." Theo's computer pings. A notification pops up.

Would you like to accept a message from Mom?

A second notification slides across the message, a banner that says: *This message is protected by Cyber Anonymous.*

Cyber Anonymous makes your internet activity untraceable. It's curious that Theo would've invested in this. And that it would be used when messaging with his mother.

"It's the *only* possibility," Anastasia is saying, her arm elbow deep in the bottom drawer of Theo's dresser.

I click on Yes to accept Mrs. Mahoney's message.

This is not good, she writes.

She sends another: *No one wants to pay for our information because they're hearing rumblings that the Robames lawsuit is moving forward. If Robames goes under they'll never trust us again. If they think our tips are bad, we'll lose all of them.*

I stare at her message, remembering what Rosie said about Mrs. Mahoney being involved in insider trading, selling stock tips. What if it's not only Mrs. Mahoney who's selling them? It's also Theo. Both of them, working together.

"Theo being in love with Stewart would also explain why Theo didn't want me to get with Stewart," Anastasia continues. Theo's clothes are strewn around her.

Mrs. Mahoney says, *So there was no luck when you met with Rob today?* Followed by, *Hello?*

"And if Theo and Stewart are *a thing*," Anastasia says, "that must be the reason he stayed with him on New Year's Eve instead of coming back to the party after Stewart got too drunk."

Hello, I type. I press Send. I want her to keep talking.

"When do you think it started between them?" Anastasia says. She's standing in the closet, rooting through the pockets of Theo's clothes. "And why didn't Theo tell me about it? He tells me everything."

Stewart said some payments were late? Did we get payment from the account ending 6815? Pls check now. From Mrs. Mahoney.

Stewart. This explains why Stewart was so invested in getting Rob to change her mind about the proposal. He thought we'd be able to get her to agree to it and was telling their clients to ditch Spectacle Barkley, thinking Robames would put them out of business. A bad tip given Rob has no intention of accepting the proposal or stopping the lawsuit, no matter how much she's been warned that her company will never recover.

"I don't know," I say. "But I don't think they're in love."

They're in business together—Stewart, Theo, Mrs. Mahoney. Selling tips. Rosie was right. And if she's right about this, then she's probably right about Mrs. Mahoney using my dad, being involved with him only for the way he'll support her financially.

I jump as another message pops up.

I don't blame you for not coming back to the theater, I'm killing time in the bathroom hoping it will be over soon.

Not coming back to the theater? Maybe she didn't notice when he returned with Jasper and Stewart after our meeting with Rob, or maybe—

Behind us, we hear the door creak open. And then it slams shut.

Fifty-five

"What the hell are you guys doing?" Theo says, his eyes scanning the room and all his things scattered on the floor.

"Theo, it's okay—you can't help who you love," Anastasia says.

Theo stares at me, at his computer with an open message. He comes toward me, like he's going to yank his laptop off the desk. I beat him to it. I shut it and hold it close to me.

"Insider trading is a felony, Theo." It might not be the smartest move to show him all my cards, admit that I know what he's really been hiding. But I can't stop myself. Rosie was right about the insider trading so that means I can probably trust what she said about Mrs. Mahoney only being involved with my dad for her own financial gain. Did Theo know about that too? And if he knew, how could he call himself my friend and not tell me?

"It's not what you think," he says. He smiles like he's trying to brush it off, like maybe he doesn't think I understand what I saw. But there's something off about him. His smile is tense and his eyes are wide. He's nervous.

"So you aren't selling stock tips with Stewart and your mother?"

He opens his mouth, but no words come out. I've caught him off guard.

"Excuse me?" Anastasia says.

"That's not—no," Theo says. "Come on, you can't honestly think that."

"But that's exactly what I think. And I wonder what my dad will think about it too, when I show him what's on your computer." This is risky. I don't actually know if there's incriminating evidence on Theo's computer. But he's using a security program to make his internet activity untraceable. Mrs. Mahoney felt comfortable speaking freely using the messenger app. And she asked him to check their accounts, like she assumed that since he was at his computer, he had access.

"Collins, *please*. You are not going to steal my computer, seriously." Theo laughs, but his voice hitches. Anastasia hears it too—I see the way her eyes snap up to look him over. He reaches out, as though he thinks I'll hand the laptop back to him.

I have it pressed against my chest, both my arms around it. "I thought we were friends," I say as I start walking toward the door.

"Collins—wait—wait—please." Theo's voice trembles. He grabs on to my jacket as I'm leaving, then steps in front of me.

"Theo, *stop it*," Anastasia says. "Get out of her way."

He bites his bottom lip like he's thinking this over. But he doesn't move. I try to step around him, but he blocks me.

"Give me my computer and then you can leave," he says to me.

"Theo," Anastasia says, a little louder this time, with more annoyance in her voice. "You can't hold her hostage in your room."

"She has my laptop," he says. "It has my essay on it for macro economics and my notes for the theoretical physics test on Monday."

"I'm not giving it back."

"So access them using the cloud," Anastasia says. "Let her go."

"This is bullshit," he says.

"If it's bullshit then let her take your computer. If you have nothing to hide, who cares? She'll be proven wrong and you'll get it back."

Theo's face is turning red as he struggles to keep it together. His eyes start to water. His lower lip shakes. "It was going to hold us over until Robames accepted the proposal, but then—well, you heard her for yourself today. She won't agree to it and she's freed Jasper up to disparage her in court."

"So you gave a bad tip," I say. "And now no one trusts you."

"It's probably over for us. We won't have that extra income. We don't get a return on the Robames investment, all we'll have is—" He cuts himself off, shaking his head.

"Is *what*, Theo?"

"Nothing," he says quickly. "We'll have nothing."

"What about my father?"

He bites down on his lower lip to stop it from trembling. "What about your father?" Theo looks away, still shaking his head. He seems deflated though, and it tells me that I'm getting closer to the truth and Theo knows it.

"She's using him, right? That's the reason for the arrangement, isn't it?"

He rubs his hands over his face, trying to collect himself. "It's called survival," he says. "It kicks in when you have no other options."

It hurts that this is the truth, the thing Theo was really hiding. He knew that his mother was using my father, taking advantage of him, involving him in her illegal scheme to make some money on the side, and he still let me get close to him. He treated me like a friend. And I'd thought he was.

"Let me go," I say.

"Please, don't do this to me," he says, tears falling down his face. "If you show that to your dad, he's going to dig deeper; he'll bring what he finds to the authorities. Really think about this, Collins. About what this could do to me, to my family—to Jasper."

I was warned, I think. I was told. Rosie reveals the truth only when she needs to, only when it works in her favor. But it was there all along; she gave me an undercurrent of what I needed to know about my dad and the Mahoneys.

"My dad has to know the truth, Theo."

A loud scream cuts through the room. Anastasia is standing in front of Theo's open nightstand drawer. She's holding a composition book, her face red with fury.

"What is this?" she shrieks at Theo. She throws the tattered book at him.

He lets it hit him, doesn't even try to move out of the way.

"You wrote down everything I told you!" she yells. "Made lists of things I found out—added notes about the companies that might be connected." She looks between us, and I'm not sure how much she's picked up on while we fought, but from the way her whole body is rigid with anger, I'd guess everything. "You were using me for some illegal bullshit and to screw over Collins's dad!"

"Anastasia, wait, please—come on—I was desperate."

"I don't want to hear it, Theo." She charges toward him. "How could you do this to me?"

"Don't act like you're above this," he says to her. "This is the reason you worm your way into other people's lives, the reason you pry and ask questions. You use people, too—you exploit their secrets to your own advantage. Like Joyce! You used all that information you got from her crying in the bathroom to get her to give you her family's penthouse."

"Well, you used it to break the law. You used *me* to break the law." She steps away from him, her eyes welling with tears. "I trusted you with everything. More than I've ever trusted someone before."

She shoves past him and leaves.

Theo closes his eyes at the sound of the door slamming shut.

"I can't keep this from my dad," I say. "I have to get her away from him. I made a promise."

It pains me, the way he slumps to the ground. The way he caves in on himself.

"You know this is all more complicated than you think," he says. He begs. "You know you don't have to do this. All you have to do is stop. I *know* you, and I know this isn't going to sit right with you. Go back on your word, forget the promises you made before you knew me, before you knew *us*."

But he can already see it in my eyes—because it's true, he does know me—that I'm not going to stop. No matter how much it puts him at risk. I'll make good on everything I swore I would do. Every last thing except for the millions of small, unspoken promises I made to him, each day that I spent getting to know him.

Fifty-six

Anastasia says she wants to be alone. Jasper says he's going to bed early. I tell my dad and Rosie and Mimi that I'm too tired to get tea with them after the musical, and we make plans to meet for breakfast before they leave. I'm going to give my dad Theo's laptop and tell him everything first thing in the morning. I'll go to his room before we have breakfast with Mimi and Rosie.

Around midnight, Theo texts and asks me to meet him in the tunnel.

I have a new offer, Theo's text says. And: *You're going to want to hear this.*

When I arrive in the tunnel, the chandelier is turned on. Theo is already there. He's dressed in a jacket and pajamas like I am. We're slow to meet in the middle.

"I want to make a trade." He takes a deep breath. "This month for the game, you and Jasper skipped the exchange because your parents came to town a day early and you wanted to have dinner with them."

I nod.

He wipes his hands on his pants.

"Since you missed it, your names got moved to the bottom of the list."

"Okay. So?"

"So you're the loser this month, Collins. The drugs are your responsibility."

"But—" I close my eyes. I know exactly where he's going with this. Every time Jasper or I get stuck with the drugs, Theo helps us out and keeps them for us so we don't have to run the risk of them being discovered. "You wouldn't, Theo."

He takes another deep breath. He doesn't look at me as he says, "If you don't give me back my computer, I'll tell the faculty where the drugs are. I'll tell them they're yours."

He never once shared his hiding spots with me and I didn't ask. And who's to say he'd even put them in his typical safe spot, if he's trying to get me busted for them? Maybe Jasper and Anastasia would vouch for me, explain the game and how Theo had access to the bag of pills and cocaine to set me up. But that's part of the game—keeping it a secret. We could all get in trouble for having illegal substances on campus.

"I'll need my computer back tonight," he says. He swallows hard. "Okay? Say you'll agree, come on."

I look down at my hands, which have turned so cold I'm surprised they're not blue or void of color altogether.

"That's the trade," Theo says. "Give me my computer, I'll keep the drugs hidden. If you don't, I'll turn you in. You'll get kicked out of Rutherford."

He steps toward me, his hardened expression slipping.

"Please take the trade, Collins." There's desperation in his voice. "Please. I don't want to blow up my whole world. We can all go back to how it was before."

Back to when? Was it ever simple when all along, this is what we had lurking beneath the surface? Vials that we'd created ourselves that could be used to poison us.

"If I do it," I say, "then I need your help with something else."

Fifty-seven

I'm groggy the next morning. I couldn't sleep so I get up with the sun and take a long shower. After I've dried off and dressed, I notice Anastasia sitting at the vanity on the other side of the partition, brushing her hair. I'm surprised to see her up this early. But maybe she's like me and couldn't sleep either. She smiles at me and I take a seat on the bench next to her.

"I just wanted to say again that I'm sorry I told Theo about your mom, your aunt," she says. She rubs her nails together, like she's nervous I won't forgive her, and that breaks my heart a little since the whole reason I reached out to be her friend was because I had a hidden motive.

"It's okay. I know you tell Theo everything." But after how angry she was with him last night, I wonder if that will still be the case.

"Why did you tell Sebastian?" she says. "Why did you trust him and not . . . anyone else you were close with at Rutherford?"

It's not easy to admit, to say it out loud. Is it going to sound silly now that they know the truth and didn't think less of me the way I thought they would?

"I was ashamed, I guess. And I was scared it would make people see me differently. Sometimes it's easiest to be open with people who can't hurt you. Does that make any sense?"

"Oh yes. That's why most people make the mistake of telling

me their dirty laundry," Anastasia says. "That, and I have kind eyes." I feel a wash of relief that Anastasia understands the reason I was afraid to talk about it—the reason I'm still afraid. "So I spoke to Theo," she says. She slips on one of Theo's sweatshirts over her camisole, and I can't tell if she is mourning their friendship or on her way to forgiving him. "He says you guys came to an understanding and you gave him back his computer."

I nod.

"Theo's not a bad person." She runs her fingers over the Stanford logo on the sweatshirt. "He was in a bad position. He did a bad thing. But he's not—" She shakes her head. "He can't do anything about his mom lying to your dad to secure financial help, or whatever. But he's going to stop selling tips. He's actually forced to stop because no one will trust them anymore after they said Rob would be accepting the proposal, and she didn't. Even though all the other information he got from me was damn perfect."

"And you believe him? You really think he'll stop?"

"Of course," she says. "He promised me."

It reminds me of what Rob said to me when she gave me the recording of Jasper cheating, when a promise was supposed to be good enough. I think of Rob James in a roomful of investors being told that her idea was the best idea they'd ever heard, of them actually listening to her the way that no one ever listens to young women with grand ideas, and how hard it would be to discover that your great idea will never come to fruition. She started by offering them a promise and they all believed her. But now they've caught her lying. Her word is shot. How will she ever get it back?

Despite it all, Anastasia still sees Theo as someone she can count on, someone she wants to protect. They have years of friendship to fall back on. I'd guess she's already tucking away this story to be retold in twenty years: *Remember the time you used me for insider trading?*

I get the text from Theo that I was expecting. *We'll be ready for you in twenty.*

Okay, see you soon, I text back.

I dry my hair and make my way to campus. It's foggy this morning, the sky is gray and darker. The path is covered in dew and the wind is wild. It's earlier than most Rutherford students get up on a Sunday, so I don't see anyone else on the path, until I reach the end. Jasper is leaning against the gate near the opening leading to campus. He straightens as I approach.

"Theo said he was meeting you, so I wanted to try to catch you on your way."

It's a relief to see him after he didn't answer my phone calls last night or return any of my texts. For a moment my heart swells, knowing he probably couldn't sleep either, knowing he's been here, waiting for me.

"I'm sorry I didn't call you back," he says. "But I wanted to say this to you in person. It was selfish of me to get angry that you told something private to Sebastian and that you didn't tell me. It's just—" He shakes his head. "There's no excuse. I was jealous because I knew you were keeping something from me, and I couldn't understand why you'd want to tell him about it and not me. But it doesn't matter. You don't owe me an explanation."

But it feels like I do. Especially since there's so much more I'm keeping from him.

"It's a strange thing to find out everything you knew about your family was a lie. I would fall apart every time I thought about it."

His eyes shift down to my hands like he knows they're shaking even where they rest buried in my jacket pockets.

"You can fall apart in front of me, you know," he says.

"It changed how I saw myself," I say. "I was afraid it would change how you saw me, too."

I wonder if he thinks this is the last of the secrets between us or if he can feel that there are still others waiting to emerge.

I pinch my eyes shut and tears creep out, down my cheeks. I hear the crunch of the gravel as he steps toward me. I feel his fingers brushing against my cheeks, and then his lips. When I open my eyes, he's so close, right in front of me. I memorize his face. His eyes scrunch at the corners when he smiles his biggest smiles. There's a spot above his lip that is constantly nicked, like he always hits that single place at the wrong angle. His eyes are a deep brown that makes me think of coffee and chocolate and the wet sand at the Rutherford beach, and I like them best staring at me in the early morning light. The way they are right now.

I try to picture my life at Rutherford without him. What it would've been like if I didn't have to worry about love—about proving that I can have it whenever I want it.

It's almost unfathomable how some relationships are held together. How easily they can be blown apart. I know enough to ruin Jasper, and he knows enough to ruin me, and all that keeps this together is trust. Trust that I don't deserve.

He leans forward and kisses me like he can tell that we don't have time, like he knows it's running out. He puts his hands on either side of my head and stares at me like he's getting a last look.

My kisses are to fill him up. They aren't to promise anything, because they can't; they never could.

"I tricked you," I say. "I tried to make you want me on purpose."

"That's funny." He gives me one of his slow smiles. "I thought I was the one who'd tricked you."

"But, listen—"

"It doesn't matter now, does it?" he says.

It's easy to say it doesn't matter now when he doesn't know what I'm about to do. I start to talk, but my voice hitches.

"I want to say something to you," he says. But I shake my head—can't tell him not to say it, because deep down, I want him to say it. I do and I don't. If it's *I love you,* this is the worst possible time. If it's *I love you,* how will I respond?

"Please," he says like he's begging me. I go still in his arms, except for the trembling that I can't help. "I want you to know," he whispers, pulling me to him. "There was nothing before you."

I kiss him one more time. And when it's over, I take a deep breath, I brush away the last of my tears.

"I have to tell you something," I say. He leans in closer. He smiles. So much trust built up around us that he hears *I have to tell you something* and he's not worried. He thinks that since he's asked me to reveal more about myself to him, I'm finally doing it. He isn't imagining that what I'll tell him will betray him in the worst way. "When I met with Rob and she deleted the video, she also—she also sent me a copy."

He nods as his eyebrows lower; confusion covers his face. But I keep going. I owe him this, even if it ruins everything.

"She said she recorded you because she wanted to know how far you'd go for her."

He frowns. "I wasn't thinking clearly."

"Because you loved her." He shakes his head. "Jasper, it's okay. It's okay that you loved her."

"No, it's not," he says, his voice getting cold. "Because how could I . . . how could I have loved someone who would do that to me."

"You can't help who you fall for," I say, something I really believe. Something I hope he remembers. "She recorded you to spy on you, to see if she could trust you."

"Don't let her manipulate you, too," Jasper says. "She made the recording because she knew trust was something she couldn't offer me when she'd built a billion-dollar company based on lies and false promises. She gave you the recording because she doesn't understand trust. She wanted you to have something you could use against me like she did because she doesn't understand that when you really care about someone, you don't need proof that they care about you too."

"I deleted the recording," I tell him. The second I left Rob in the common room, I deleted it. I didn't think twice about it. All I cared about was getting rid of it, erasing it before Jasper knew it existed and was possibly within his grasp. I want him to know this, before I tell him the rest.

He nods, a small smile on his lips, like he's not surprised. Like he knew I would do the right thing when it comes to him. This is the kind of person I wish I could be. That's the kind of relationship I wish we could have. It would be easier to keep pretending, but he deserves to know everything. The truth about why we're here, the truth about why I'm meeting Theo.

"I knew about our parents when I came to Rutherford. Everything I've done since I got here was to get close to you—and to Theo. I learned all about the two of you. I thought there was something to uncover about Theo. I thought he was hiding something horrible. When I found out what it was, I was going to use it to blackmail your mother."

His eyebrows spring up, and the rest of his face goes slack.

"I don't expect you to believe me, but she was using my father for money." He looks down for a moment and I can't tell if this is conceivable to him or if it's so out of left field that my secrets are going to sound delusional. There's a reason Mrs. Mahoney involved Theo and Jasper's best friend in her insider trading scheme, but not Jasper. "I needed something that would hurt her, that I could use to threaten her with to get her to stay away from my father. I was told the best way to hurt her was through you and Theo."

He concentrates, taking it all in. The wind whips at our hair and sends a shiver through me that has me crossing my arms. Jasper steps forward like he wants to put his arms around me—what he would normally do to help warm me. But he puts his hands in his pockets. He looks toward the ocean as he asks, "And . . . why—what did you want from me?"

It's easier to tell him the truth, when he's staring at the view instead of at me. "If I could convince you to love me, I could threaten to break your heart. Your mom would have to choose between your broken heart and my father's."

Now when he turns to me, his expression is a mess of shock and disbelief. He takes another step back, away from me.

"And? You're still planning to blackmail her?"

I nod because my throat is tight with nerves. It aches like I'm going to start crying again. I wish I could say I was calling it off, that I could come clean about this as if it were a mistake, a misunderstanding that brought us together but wouldn't be able to tear us apart.

"What do you have on Theo?" His voice is small. I never wanted to be the one to make him feel like this.

"Not enough."

He nods and takes a breath to steady himself. "Well, you have me right where you want me. I guess your plan worked like a charm."

"No, it didn't," I say. "Because I never figured out how to make you fall in love with me without falling in love with you right back."

"So I lucked out, is what you're saying?" He smiles, but it's not nice. There are tears in his eyes.

"I don't want to do it," I tell him, as if that matters. "But I don't know what else to do to get my dad away from her." It's the only defense I have, except: "It won't change what's going on between us, because she's not going to let anything happen to you."

"Are you sure about that?"

I don't mean to hesitate before I start nodding, but I do and he notices.

"So if she doesn't agree, then what? You're going to break up with me?"

"I don't know," I say, telling him the truth. But he's on a roll.

"Better make sure this breakup stings harder than the last one! How much do you need me to suffer for this to properly affect my mother?" He's looking at me like he's moved past anger and on to disgust. "This is something your father knows, but my parents have never learned—when you go *all in* on a risk, you have to be willing to take a big loss. You have to be prepared to lose everything. And you are, aren't you?"

I shake my head, holding back my tears. The problem is, he's right. I told him this not so I'd be absolved, but because I didn't want to lie to him anymore. I didn't want to come back from the meeting Theo set up for his mom and me this morning and smile at him like nothing was wrong, kiss him like I hadn't just threatened my relationship with him to save my dad; even if it's the only thing left I can do.

"It doesn't matter that this wager tips in my favor." In *our* favor, I want to say. "It's that you're willing to take this chance in the first place—that you're still going to take it."

"Whatever it takes to get my dad away from her." I don't tell him I wanted to prove I was lovable, that I wanted to have the kind of control that Rosie told me I could have. "Your mother is using him, and I have to break them up, and this is the only way I know how to do it."

He looks at me like he feels sorry for me. As if he can see that I'm like Rosie; that I made myself this way because I thought it would make me stronger, impenetrable the way I thought he and Theo were, along with everyone at Rutherford with bright futures and lush lives.

"I know the kind of people my parents are," he says. "I'm not going to argue with you about what my mother's capable of when it comes to getting money. I'll say whatever you want me to say, act however you want me to act." He shakes his head, looks to the view once more before he stares at me. "But between you and me, you've lost your leverage, because you've already broken my heart."

Fifty-eight

Jasper leaves me alone at the top of the hill. He takes the path back to the boys' dormitory. I'm supposed to meet Theo and Mrs. Mahoney on campus. That's what we arranged when I gave him back his computer last night and he agreed to do something for me. But I send Theo a text telling him never mind.

I need to be alone. I need to clear my head. I walk to the entrance of Rutherford and start down the paved drive toward the heart of Cashmere.

The frustration I feel is insurmountable. I'm mad that I couldn't go through with Rosie's plan—but at the same time, I don't know why I wanted to; why I thought I could. What drove me to do this and why can't I see another solution? And I'm alone in this entirely. Rosie doesn't care about getting my father away from Mrs. Mahoney anymore since Robames is going under. But I still care.

Theo keeps texting me, confused that we're not meeting when I was so adamant about it last night. So I turn off my phone.

I'm rounding the first corner on the path when a black car pulls up next to me. From the back seat, Theo rolls down the window.

"What are you doing?" he says. He notices I'm crying and frowns. "Get in." The car stops, but I keep walking.

"I want to be alone."

"It's only me," he says. "Come on, tell me what happened. Get in, Collins."

"I feel like walking."

The car creeps up closer and then stops. I move past it. Behind me, I hear the sound of a door opening and closing. The car drives away. I don't turn around, even though I know Theo's gotten out. He jogs until he's next to me.

"I don't want to talk about it," I say.

"Okay," he says.

He walks beside me down the winding road, not saying a word. The fog starts to clear and the sky gets patchy with clouds, the glow of the sun peeking through. Soon more cars are traveling along the private driveway connecting Rutherford to downtown Cashmere. Theo reaches out his arm every time a car passes, to make sure the cars see us in the curves of the road. We're keeping a good pace, and it gets hot after a while. Theo removes his jacket, and I do the same. He offers to hold mine for me, and that pushes me over the edge.

"Stop being so nice to me!"

He puts his hands in the air. "Sorry," he says.

"I'm mad at you." I resituate how I'm carrying my jacket, and the annoyance of holding it eggs me on. "I never should've given back your computer," I shout at him. "Now I have nothing to show my dad so he'll know the truth. Why did I care about getting caught with drugs? Who cares if I get kicked out of Rutherford? I don't even want to be here anymore now that Jasper hates me."

A car takes the corner a little tight and Theo and I are smashed together against the brick lining. I have to grab hold of him to steady myself.

"I can promise you, my brother does not hate you," he says.

"I told him what I was going to meet with your mother about."

But Theo doesn't know why I wanted to meet with her either, only that it was part of the deal when I returned his computer.

"Does he know you canceled the meeting?" he says.

"That's not going to matter to him." The damage is already done. Like Jasper said, it's the loss that I was willing to risk.

"What were you going to say to my mother?"

I sigh. Here we are on the side of the road, the morning sun beating down on us, making us sweat even in this cool morning weather. Jasper might not ever forgive me now that he knows the truth. I had the proof to get my dad away from Mrs. Mahoney, and I gave it up in order to stay at Rutherford. What do I possibly have to lose anymore?

"I was going to threaten her—tell her that if she didn't leave my father alone, I was going to break Jasper's heart."

"Are you serious, Collins?" His jaw drops open, and he studies me like he's waiting for me to tell him I'm kidding. It's quiet around us, until a car swerves past, the noise of its engine roaring then fading. "I didn't think you'd involve him. I thought he mattered too much."

"I don't know what's wrong with me," I say. I start to cry. He opens his arms and waits, asking if it's okay for him to hug me. I let myself fall against him.

"What's wrong with all of us?" he says.

I can't help it. I start to laugh. Theo smiles at me.

We walk together down the drive and through downtown Cashmere, into the square, the morning sun shining down on us as the clouds give way. When we approach my dad's hotel, we see him having his morning coffee and reading the paper, alone on the patio. There's a chill in the air, which must be why there's no one else out there except him.

I approach him and Theo follows. He smiles when he sees us, but he's also confused by our appearance. Theo and I are sweaty and warm from the walk, and we're holding our jackets.

He offers us a seat and asks if we'd like to order anything.

"I thought we weren't meeting for another hour," he says to me, checking his watch. "Is everything okay?"

Theo and I exchange a look.

"I want you to stop seeing Mrs. Mahoney," I say. "She's using you, she always has been. She's only involved with you for what you can do for her financially. And she's not being honest."

My dad frowns. He glances at Theo, and I think it must alarm him that Theo isn't jumping to her defense. "Collins—this isn't appropriate." He clears his throat. "I know it must be uncomfortable for the two of you, given how close you are to each other, and because of what's going on between you and Jasper—"

"That's not it," I say. "I'm worried about you—"

He shakes his head and folds his paper, slamming it down on the table. "Rosie's been speaking to you about this?"

"You should listen to her, Dad."

"Damn it, Collins—" His voice is stern and his face is turning red.

"She's telling the truth," Theo says, interrupting him.

"This is none of your business," he says, evening out his tone.

"She's been asking lately about some of your other investments—about specific companies, right?" Theo asks.

My dad doesn't answer, but he clenches his jaw. A subtle tell that Theo's made him uneasy.

"And she recently suggested you unload stocks from a certain digital media group, like she did?"

My dad still doesn't move. But he doesn't protest either. He lets Theo finish.

"Their CEO is about to check himself into a recovery program and cash out the business. We know about this, that's why she's cutting her losses. But she's been investing according to your information, too. Though you must know, that's not enough. Has she already started talking to you about helping alleviate the funds we'll lose when the Robames lawsuit kicks in and the company dies?"

"We help each other out, your mother and I." But he's looking down, into his coffee cup.

"But you shouldn't be helping her at all," Theo says. "It's not equal, and she doesn't care about you the way you care about her. You're not her only arrangement, though I'd guess she hasn't shared that detail with you."

My dad shifts in his seat. I know he doesn't like this, us talking to him about this private part of his life. I don't know if he'll have any reason to believe us, the way he didn't believe Rosie, or if the things Theo's saying are actually reaching him.

"You kids stay, have breakfast," he says, standing. "I'll see you later, when we meet up with your Mimi and Rosie," he says to me.

He walks across the street to the hotel next to the park with the tall windows and blue awning out front.

"Is that where your mother is staying?" I ask.

"Yes," Theo says.

"You know, you didn't have to do that. You didn't have to throw her under the bus."

"Yes, I did," he says.

"Are you nervous about what's going to happen to your family if my dad's not around to help?"

"Yes," he says. Small birds gather under the table next to us, scurrying for crumbs. They scatter as quickly as they arrived, and we watch them fly into the air, disperse in different directions. Theo sighs. "For now, breakfast is on your dad, and I earned it. I'm going to enjoy having pancakes and tea with my friend, and be glad we aren't threatening to send each other to jail anymore." He reaches across the table and squeezes my hand.

Fifty-nine

My father misses breakfast with Mimi and Rosie and me, and he's not there to wish them farewell when they leave to catch their flight. But I go back to the hotel and wait for him on the curb, watching the blue awning, waiting for him to exit.

Finally, a little after noon, he comes out. He looks terrible. Everything from the way he's standing to the way he keeps checking his watch and running his hands through his hair tells me that it's over between them. I'm relieved. I wasn't sure he'd do the right thing. I haven't believed this about him since the moment I learned he was keeping something from me. This is my fault. I have to start by trusting him with the past.

"Dad." I pick up my pace as I walk toward him. I hug him when I reach him, and even though it surprises him at first, I feel him squeeze back and bury his face in my shoulder.

I glance up at the tall windows above the awning across the street and see Mrs. Mahoney, Jasper, and Theo. They're standing at the windows, looking down at us. My father follows my gaze and looks up at them, too. I think they'll back away from the window at first, now that we're staring. But they don't. And we don't.

Jasper is the first one to turn away.

I wonder what will be said about us. Maybe he'll get the whole story. Maybe he won't. Maybe it won't matter and he'll only remember what I confessed to him and he'll question how he could ever even begin to trust me again—if he thinks I was worthy of trust in the first place. And he'll know the moment he told me the key to his undoing.

Will it be enough that I never used it?

I hold my dad's arm as we walk to the curb, get in the car service. He stares straight ahead as we drive away. He's heartbroken, but I know it won't be forever. I think of Mimi, wanting me to understand where I came from and what I was born into. How showing me photos and recording clips was enough because a love like that is easy to understand. It's the simplest thing.

"Do we have some time before your flight?" I ask.

"I have an eternity," he says. "You want to have lunch? I'm not very hungry, but it's about that time."

"Yeah," I say. "And I want us to talk."

He deserves his own chance to explain it to me. And I deserve to hear it from him. I know that no matter what we say about it, I won't lose him.

There are some things that are too complicated to understand unless you know the whole of it. The entirety. What came before and what comes after. The broken-down parts, each piece making both the foundation and the destruction. A moment-by-moment recount until the abhorrent conclusion.

I can read my father's face right now—sad and broken, but hopeful, even if slightly weathered. He's thinking that what's been done can never be undone. He's wondering how he'll explain it to himself. He's running through all the possible ways this backfired on him so badly, counting the ways everything's already been ruined.

He comes to the right conclusion, though.

After we cut over toward the other side of Cashmere, start moving straight on toward the water, he wipes his hand over his face, taking extra care in rubbing his eyes. He rotates his shoulders. He looks out the window at the tall trees sliding past him under the skyful of clouds. He clears his throat. And then he turns to me.

"What do you want to talk about, Collins?" he says.

I lean back, resting my head against the seat, finally relaxed.

Some things are very simple.

Four Months Later

He finds me standing on the shore of Lake Mendota, exactly where I'm supposed to be. I'm on the University of Wisconsin-Madison campus, having just finished lunch with Mimi at the Memorial Union.

In the fairy tale version of this story, the boy pines for the girl. He wishes he could've said goodbye to her before he left Rutherford so suddenly.

But, Theo told me, those were the last things on Jasper's mind.

In the fairy tale, when he turns himself in for cheating to win the decathlon, he's rewarded for his honesty. He's not stripped of his medal and kicked out of the prestigious boarding school he was attending months before he was supposed to graduate; Dartmouth doesn't revoke their acceptance.

But when I wave to him, and he comes toward me, he smiles. He doesn't look quite the way I remember him. He's missing the heavy drag in his gait, the concern living in his brow, the guilt of the secrets he kept, the way he let all the wrong things dictate his life.

I hope he notices everything I'm missing, too.

In the fairy tale, we probably waited for each other; we probably talked every day. Supported each other through it all. But there are some battles you have to fight alone, and honesty doesn't always come with the reward you think it will.

"Jasper," I say, pointing to his name tag.

He rubs his hand over it and smiles to himself. "Surprised to see me?" he says.

I nod. It was strange when I heard him call my name. It was a sound so familiar that at first, I wasn't startled at all. But then there he was, crossing the grass to reach me, dressed casually in shorts and a T-shirt, looking out of place in my life, but perfectly in place to his surroundings.

"I'm on a campus tour," he says. "Or—I was." He doesn't say, *until I saw you.* He doesn't have to. And for that moment we are part of the fairy tale.

"Mimi's enrolled in summer courses," I say.

"Amazing," he says. "So how does she like it? Would she recommend it overall?"

"Wait—are you thinking of going here?"

"To be honest, I'd be lucky to get in. But they're looking at me for the lacrosse team, and if that comes with a scholarship, then I'll be here in a heartbeat."

Next, we talk about mundane things. The beauty of the campus. How it's not supposed to be as crowded in the summer, but we've never seen it in the fall, so we have no comparison.

I admit that I've kept up on what he's been doing because of Theo, and he admits the same thing. But there's still plenty to catch up on.

We walk as we chat, through the campus, through the downtown streets, around the capital building. We walk as the sun beats down on us and the sky stays clear.

For him, last year was a gift, even though it was full of turmoil; it was a fall from grace. But he's better off now, happier than before. For me, last year was an experiment, and the results were that you can let people get close to you; you can trust them with the fragile parts of your being.

I wish most that one day Rosie tallies these results herself, that she believes them. That she'll be brave enough to reap the rewards. Jasper wishes that his parents will learn how to endure the financial loss, that they'll find jobs they can enjoy, even through the rough parts, even though they're not used to it and it's not what they thought they wanted.

"In the fairy tale, we get exactly what we want," I tell him, letting him in on my thoughts.

"But I wanted all the wrong things," he says, and we laugh as I say, "So did I."

"Present company excluded," he says. He blushes, but his stare doesn't waver.

"Me too," I say. And since he's being so brave, I say, "I'm sorry."

He nods and says, "Collins, it's okay," like he knows it's what I need to hear.

"You never told me," I say after a while. "Where's the best view at Rutherford?"

He smiles. "The roof of the auditorium. Someone from the theater department can lend you the keys. Go up around sunset, right before dinner."

I picture myself at Rutherford, racing up the concrete stairs leading from the loading dock of the auditorium to the roof. Pushing open the metal door at the top. The sun starting to lower, the sky growing dim but still putting on a show. The way the forest becomes ten different colors of green, and the ocean sparkles.

I'll be standing there, looking at that view. And where will he be?

Right now, with him next to me, it's like before. He's the part of the story that makes you want to stay up all night reading. The first full breath after a long sprint. The light at the end of the tunnel. The cozy cabin after a long road home.

Is he someone who comes back even after you let them go? Am I?

These thoughts float away, dissolve, and disappear. I'm excited for everything I don't know, for whatever happens next.

I smile at Jasper, and he smiles at me.

Acknowledgments

Thank you to my editor, Melissa Frain; Lucille Rettino, Isa Caban, Anthony Parisi, Saraciea Fennell, Elizabeth Vaziri, Lesley Worrell, and everyone at Tor Teen.

To my agent, Suzie Townsend; Joanna Volpe, Pouya Shahbazian, Mia Roman, Veronica Grijalva, Dani Segelbaum, and the entire team at New Leaf Literary.

Thank you to the community of writers near and far, who kept me company with dinner, retreats, and advice while I worked on this book, especially: Virginia Boecker, Kim Liggett, Kara Thomas, Jessica Taylor, Stephanie Garber, Shannon Dittemore, Adrienne Young, Kristin Dwyer, Demetra Brodsky, Joanna Rowland, Tamara Hayes, Jenny Lundquist, Jennieke Cohen, Jeanmarie Anaya, Shelley Batt, and Tanya Spencer.

And to my family and friends: Bob and Jennie, Tom and Sheri, Sarah and Lucas and Zoella and Ira, Rowdy, Stefanie, Brienne, Crystal, Jen, Val, Leslie, Liz, Andrew, and Ryan. Lea, Karisa, Brittany, and Kelsey for brainstorming with me. Lyndsey, my first writing partner, for lending the main character's first name. And, always, Justin.